THE DAWN OF
YANGCHEN

THE DAWN OF
YANGCHEN

F.C. YEE

AMULET BOOKS · NEW YORK

Special thanks to Mike DiMartino and Bryan Konietzko of Avatar Studios

PUBLISHER'S NOTE: This is a work of fiction. Names, characters, places, and incidents are either the product of the author's imagination or used fictitiously, and any resemblance to actual persons, living or dead, business establishments, events, or locales is entirely coincidental.

Cataloging-in-Publication Data has been applied for and may be obtained from the Library of Congress.

ISBN 978-1-4197-5677-1

ISBN (B&N/Indigo edition) 978-1-4197-6464-6

© 2022 Viacom International Inc. All Rights Reserved. Nickelodeon, Nickelodeon Avatar: The Last Airbender, and all related titles, logos, and characters are trademarks of Viacom International Inc.

Jacket illustrations by JungShan Chang

Book design by Brenda E. Angelilli and Deena Fleming

Published in 2022 by Amulet Books, an imprint of ABRAMS. All rights reserved. No portion of this book may be reproduced, stored in a retrieval system, or transmitted in any form or by any means, mechanical, electronic, photocopying, recording, or otherwise, without written permission from the publisher.

Printed and bound in U.S.A.

10 9 8 7 6 5 4 3 2 1

Amulet Books are available at special discounts when purchased in quantity for premiums and promotions as well as fundraising or educational use. Special editions can also be created to specification. For details, contact specialsales@abramsbooks.com or the address below.

Amulet Books® is a registered trademark of Harry N. Abrams, Inc.

ABRAMS The Art of Books
195 Broadway, New York, NY 10007
abramsbooks.com

FOR MY SISTERS, MELISSA AND BLYTHE

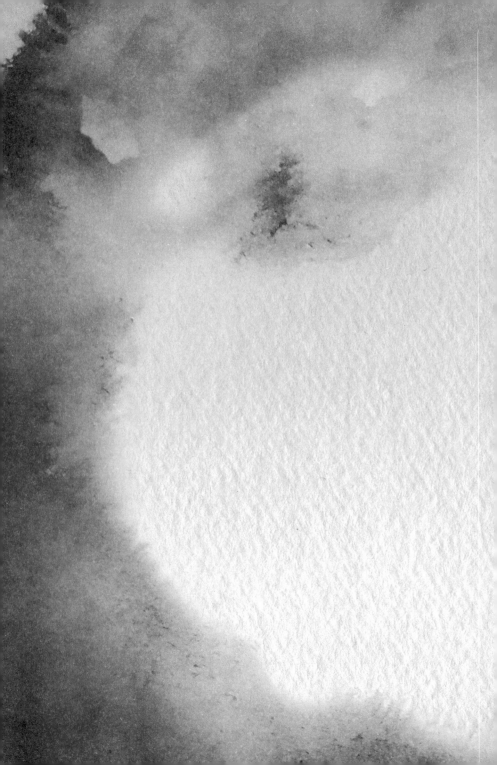

VOICES OF THE PAST

JETSUN PACED down the hallway, trying to stay ahead of the screams.

The high ceilings of the Western Air Temple tended to make echoes of whispers and explosions of dropped teacups. Though the girl was back in the infirmary being watched by the elders, her cries of pain sprang from every surface, bouncing off the hard stone.

Jetsun couldn't take it anymore and broke into a full run. Ignoring decorum, she sped past her sisters, ruffling robes, upsetting inkpots, prematurely ruining colorful sand paintings that were meant to be ruined only once they were finished. No one scolded her or gave her sharp looks in passing. They understood.

When she ran out of floor, she jumped. The upside-down construction of the temple meant that despite its overall size, there was very little space to stand on, nothing connecting the spires but thin air and a three-thousand-foot drop. She didn't have her glider. Eminently dangerous, but she could make the leap without it.

Air at her back and air against her robes gave her enough loft to land on the next tower, the one containing the Great Library. Tsering, chief caretaker of the books, waited in front of the tall shelves. The older woman's kind eyes were edged with worry. "I saw you coming. Is it happening again?"

Jetsun nodded. "Mesose," she said.

Tsering blew out a breath, a silent whistle of frustration. "That could be Mesose, famous scholar of the Ru Ming era. There's a Mesose village in Hu Xin; it might have been named after a founder. Or it could just be someone called Mesose, in which case we're stuck."

Avatars tended to run in exalted circles. Or they elevated the people around them to fame. "It has to be the first one," Jetsun said.

Another wail turned both their heads. The child was suffering. "Help me and it'll go faster," Tsering said. "Northwest corner, start with the poetry shelves, *Ru* with the three drops of water radical."

They split up to search different sections of the ancient vault. Jetsun ran her eyes over labels and titles as fast as she could. Not every book fit on a shelf. Many of the tomes kept at the Western Temple were so old they were written on bamboo slips instead of paper. She passed rolled bales of text wider around than some of the pillars connecting the ceilings to the floors.

Five minutes later she emerged from the library's depths, clutching a treatise on she didn't know exactly what. What mattered was the author's name.

Tsering met her by the door. "I couldn't find any leads. You're holding our best shot."

"Thank you." Jetsun sprinted back in the direction she came, the book tucked under her arm.

"Use your glider next time!" Tsering yelled.

Jetsun burst back into the infirmary. The huddle of elders parted to let her through. The girl's thrashing had settled into dry, cavernous sobs. She pounded her fist on her pillow over and over, not the involuntary shaking of a fever but rather the deliberate motion born of a steady, all-consuming anguish that should have been beyond her eight years.

"We'll leave you two alone," Abbess Dagmola said. She and the rest of the nuns filed out. Too many people sometimes ruined the effect. Jetsun opened the book to a random page and began to read.

"'The level of risk can be determined by elevation, nearness to the source of water, vulnerability to rapid flows, and potential economic damage,'" she said. Confused, she briefly turned the volume to look at the cover. *A Discourse on Floodplain Management.*

Why in the world do we have this book? Jetsun shook her head. It didn't matter. "'Understanding previous measures taken to mitigate the damage from flooding is essential, for they might compile danger instead of reducing it.'"

The girl took a shuddering gasp of air and relaxed. "Half a year and that's as far as you've gotten?" she said, smiling at no one. "You have to stop taking on so many projects at once, Se-Se."

It worked. Thank the spirits, it worked. Jetsun kept reading, plowing through the unfamiliar concepts mechanically. "'On the subject of silt deposits . . .'"

The first time the child went through this, they had no clue as to what was happening. The healers did their best to cool her fever and keep her as comfortable as they could. As the incidents reoccurred, her babbling, incoherent at first, started to coalesce into sentences, names, slices of conversations. The words meant nothing to her caregivers until one day they heard her talking to His Majesty the Earth King Zhoulai. A man she'd never met, who'd died three centuries ago.

Thankfully, the abbess had thought to take notes. She'd written down every intelligible scrap, and in scouring her pages she pieced together a pattern. The names. Angilirq, Praew, Yotogawa. Names from every nation.

Names of past Avatar companions.

Not every phantom the child spoke to had made it into the annals of history, and some that had were never acknowledged as having close ties to an Avatar. Jetsun could only imagine the stories lost to time, filtering through the girl, merest fragments sticking in her throat.

And the conversations were pleasant, frequently enough. She would laugh with her friends in towns that had been renamed, provinces that no longer existed. Jetsun had watched her leap from her bed and bellow at the success of legendary winter hunts, sit on the floor and meditate with someone else's inner peace.

But occasionally she would have waking nightmares. Bouts of sorrow and rage that threatened to tear her apart. She wouldn't mutter names but scream them as if she'd been betrayed by the universe itself.

By accident, they discovered she could sometimes be calmed by figuring out the past figure she was talking to, when it was possible, and speaking back to her from that perspective. The deeper they could dive into the role the better, like parents reading a bedtime story, doing voices and parts. Familiarity was the best balm they had, and they acted their hearts out for her.

The girl nodded off by the time Jetsun reached a chapter on the proper construction of seawalls. Tsering entered the room.

No glider, Jetsun noticed. She probably wanted to see if she could still make the jump too.

"How is she?" the librarian asked.

"Better," Jetsun said. "Who was Mesose?"

"A companion of Avatar Gun," Tsering said, coming over to the bedside. "Skilled poet and engineer, who died in Ha'an when Gun failed to hold back a tsunami."

Jetsun found a sour taste rising in her mouth. "Failed?" Not the choice of words she would have used for someone, Avatar or not, bravely confronting a force of nature. Ha'an still stood today as a port when it sounded like it could have been wiped off the map along with everyone who'd lived there at the time.

"It's what's written. After Mesose drowned, Gun disappeared for quite a while before returning to duty."

You were grieving. If the waters that Gun fought were the same ones that killed Mesose, then both the girl and the past life raging through her might have personally witnessed their friend take their last breath before plunging below the waves. They would have searched for a body in the wreckage.

And worst of all, Jetsun thought, they would have had to struggle with the terrible question of *what if I'd done things differently? What if, what if, what if?* Perhaps Gun was the one who'd demanded the label of failure.

It was simply unjust. To remember the events of a single life was painful enough. Reliving dozens of lives would be . . . well, it would be like getting caught by a tsunami. Swept away by forces beyond your control.

"She's a smart kid," Jetsun said. "If she keeps having these visions, she'll figure out who she is long before she turns sixteen."

Tsering sighed. She reached out and stroked the sleeping girl's hair, now matted with sweat.

"Oh, little Yangchen," she said. "What are we going to do with you?"

THE FIRST STEP

AT THE age of eleven, Yangchen had known who she was for a while on an intellectual level, and treated her Avatarhood with a child's seriousness at the behest of her elders. *This is a very important secret, all right? Like Tsering's custard recipe. Best not to talk about it until we figure a few more things out.*

The involuntary bouts of vivid memories still occurred. The ease with which past Avatars slipped into Yangchen's speech troubled the leaders of the Western Temple. She would eavesdrop on their discussions about her, air spouting herself under windowsills, hiding behind pillars.

"You know, we keep asking that question, *what do we do with her?*" she heard Jetsun say one day, sharper than she usually was with her elders. "The answer is, we'll prevent her from hitting her head on the ground, and when the memories are over, we'll carry on. That's what she needs from us, so that's what we'll give her. Nothing more, nothing less."

As if Yangchen needed another reason to worship her older sister. Jetsun wasn't related to her by blood, or maybe she was in the manner of fourth or fifth cousins, but it definitely didn't matter. The girl who cut up fruit in a stupid way but at least gave you the symmetrical pieces was your sister. The girl who showed you no mercy on the airball court and laughed in your face as she kept you scoreless was your sister. Jetsun was either the person who would listen to Yangchen cry with utmost patience, or the one who'd upset her in the first place.

So it made perfect sense that Jetsun would guide her through her first attempt at meditating into the Spirit World. A guide was an anchor as much as a pathfinder, a calling voice in the darkness. "Don't have so many expectations," Jetsun told a Yangchen buzzing with excitement. "Not everyone has the ability to cross between realms. You won't be less or more of an Avatar, or an Air Nomad, or a person, if it doesn't happen."

"Pfft. If you did it, I can do it." *If you did it, I need to do it. To become more like you.*

The older nun rolled her eyes and flicked Yangchen on the forehead where her arrow point would eventually be.

They went topside to the meadows above the cliffs of the Western Air Temple. There was no need to travel all the way to the Eastern Temple, the jumping-off point for many spiritual journeys, when they could try closer to home first. Besides, Jetsun scoffed, the extra sanctity of the Eastern Temple was more reputation and less proven truth.

In the grass was a meditation circle, a stone slab floor laid level in the earth. Five columns of rock jutted out around the circle, unevenly spaced. They looked like fingers and a thumb, the triple Air Nomad whorls at their tips the prints. Yangchen knew about this place but had always avoided it. "It feels like a giant is about to grab me."

"Or let you go," Jetsun said. "A hand either opens or closes. But it can't do either of those twice in a row."

Yangchen never knew how Jetsun managed to be so blunt and cryptic at the same time. The two of them sat in the giant's palm, facing each other. They weren't alone. Abbess Dagmola and Librarian Tsering had come along and relegated themselves to assistants, setting up incense, a windhorn. The abbess herself was going to ring the meditation bell. There was no hesitance by the two much older women in deferring to Jetsun as guide.

The session began. The smoldering incense was sharp and earthy, like tree resin. Yangchen could feel the overtones of the horn through her stone seat. She lost count of the bell strikes that both marked time and pointed out its meaninglessness.

She suddenly saw a bright glow through her closed eyes, as if she'd been laboring under clouds the whole time. When she opened them, the light was intense but not blinding. Colors were brighter, as if the elements themselves had been ground in a mortar and then repainted on the backing of the world. Red flowers in the meadow glowed like embers, green veins pulsed through canopying leaves the size of house roofs, and the sky was bluer than a cake of solid indigo dye.

Yangchen had performed a feat of Avatarhood. It had not happened to her involuntarily, it had not struck her down like thunder between her temples, it had not racked painfully through her limbs to damage the landscape. She'd done it. *She'd done it.*

Her victory. And best of all, her favorite person in the world was right there beside her to share the moment. "Huh," Jetsun said, in one of her classic understatements. "First try."

Yangchen wanted to laugh and leap a mile into the air. But she would maintain a cool head, just like her guide. "Maybe I only remembered how."

"Humility isn't more important than the truth. I think you pulled this off yourself."

She thought her heart would burst. Over the hills of the Spirit World, a pod of great winged whales, translucent and jellylike, slowly floated through the sky. Nearby, a bouncing mushroom released a cloud of spores, which turned into twinkling fireflies.

She was struck by a question. "What do we do now?"

"That's the beauty of it," Jetsun said. "We don't do anything. There is no *use* to the Spirit World, and therein lies the great lesson. Here, you don't take. You don't anticipate or plan; you don't struggle. You don't worry about value gained and lost. You just exist. Like a spirit."

A pout of disappointment crossed Yangchen's lips. "Do we have to exist in this one spot only? Can we at least explore?"

Jetsun grinned down at her. "Yes. Yes, we can."

Yangchen took her sister's hand and decided there was a chance she might like being the Avatar.

VOICES OF
THE PRESENT

MIDDLERS OFTEN had difficulty understanding how quickly one place's fortunes could rise at the expense of another's. In the continuing wake of the Platinum Affair, many of the new arrivals to Bin-Er seemed caught off guard by the city's explosive growth even though they were part of it themselves, swept along by change.

Kavik, on the other hand, knew vital locations could shift great distances without warning. Herds moved like water. Schools of fish moved like water. People did too, when their livelihoods depended on it.

And the flow wasn't always peaceful. Currents of human beings could rush too fast into a single pool without an escape, smashing chunks of ice and flotsam to bits. If your boat ever got caught in such a vortex, the key to survival was figuring out how long you had until you suffered the same fate.

Kavik wasn't sure how much time Bin-Er had left as a whole. But as for himself, right now, he was thinking there were maybe ten, twenty minutes before things got ugly. Out-of-control ugly. He'd been trying to cross the square in the international district when a large crowd, buzzing with hostility, blocked his way. The heavy winter clothing everyone wore to survive along the northern edge of the Earth Kingdom continent made it difficult to squeeze through the cracks.

Usually Kavik was on top of these kinds of disruptions. "What's going on?" he asked the people nearby.

"We finally pinned Shang Teiin down," a large man said while peering over the top of the crowd. "He had to leave the walls of his estate at some point. Either he listens to us here and now, or he gets to spend the night holed up in Gidu Shrine."

Kavik swallowed his alarm. "And . . . how did you do that exactly? Teiin's normally hard to find, isn't he?"

"We pooled our money together and paid for an errand runner to copy the shrine's schedule of private reservations," the man said, grinning with satisfaction. "Gotta use the enemy's methods against him. And wouldn't you know it? Tonight is the anniversary of Teiin's grandfather's death."

This wasn't going to end well. Teiin was no talk, all stick. The idea that the powerful shang would interrupt his ancestral rituals, appear on the steps of the Gidu Shrine, and benevolently acknowledge his employees' grievances was misguided at best and dangerous at worst.

He needed to get out of here. "Give that old goat-dog the business," Kavik said. He turned to leave.

A heavy hand landed on his shoulder and spun him back around. "Stay with us, brother," said the man, staring at him intently. "If the shangs don't get an earful now and then, they'll pretend we don't exist. Every voice counts."

Newcomers just had to be difficult, didn't they? He was asking Kavik to take a firmer stance. And a boy asking questions could have been in the pocket of Teiin or another shang, a spy sent to monitor the crowd. He gave Kavik a jostle, equal parts fraternal and threatening.

"Sorry, but I have to place an order at the apothecary's," Kavik said. He had his own tasks ahead of him and didn't want to make any new friends.

"At this time of day?" The grip on him tightened.

"I know it's late," Kavik said quickly. "But Uncle Ping takes his time closing and always lets me get a request in before he goes home."

He watched the story work its way through the man's head. Perhaps he'd overdone it with the details. But the delay alone was enough. "There he is! There's Teiin!" came a shout. When the man turned to look, Kavik slipped out of his grasp and into the crowd.

He fought his way through the moving mass, swimming parallel to the riptide, and spared a glance at the shrine. The stone steps of Gidu rose fifteen feet into the air and culminated in a double-roofed hall where the wealthy could pay their respects to their ancestors and leave offerings for the spirits. Shang Teiin, a slight but hale man of sixty, had emerged atop the sacred little island and sneered with distaste down at the people boxing him in.

"Cheat! Fraud!"

"Pay us what you owe us!"

The angry cries seemed to bother Teiin about as much as falling leaves. He took a deep breath through his nose, and Kavik's heart began racing. That wasn't the face of a man ambushed. That was the expression of a man going on the attack.

The shang signaled with his fingers and a squad of men poured out of the shrine behind him. Hired toughs, headkickers, lying in wait. Whether through bribes, betrayals, or hiring spies of his own, Teiin had caught wind of the demonstration and prepared his countermoves in advance.

The paid muscle descended the steps and slammed into the front ranks of the crowd. The screaming started, and Kavik pulled his hood down as low as it could go. He ducked under elbows and spun on the balls of his feet and shoved people from behind when he had to, until he reached the edge of the square.

He tried to avoid looking back. The fighting would only get so bad. Yes, there would be fists thrown, and he assumed Teiin's goons probably had saps and coshes hidden up their sleeves, but that would be the extent of it. Any bending would be just for bruises. No one in Bin-Er, shang or otherwise, wanted to bring Earth Kingdom law into the city by committing a capital offense.

The whole incident had nothing to do with him. Never mind that Kavik was the errand runner who'd broken into Gidu Shrine a week ago to copy the reservation list in the first place. If he hadn't taken the job, it would have gone to someone else.

It'll be all right, he told himself over the chorus of violence behind him.

Only two blocks away from the square, there was peace. No disturbances, no signs of fighting. Just the muffled quiet of the day winding down. In Bin-Er, a short walk could land you in another realm entirely.

Kavik passed men and women filing out of shipping offices into the street. They looked neither to the right nor the left at the empty stands that served only midday meals, the closed shops providing paper and brushes sold by the bale, the auction houses where the prices of cloth and porcelain across the Four Nations were decided. Only straight ahead, to their beds.

They'd learn about the scuffle in the square, and then they'd simply go around it. The same way you'd take a different route to avoid an overturned wagon. An inconvenient ruckus, to be certain. One that happened more frequently these days in Bin-Er, but that was the cost of doing business, no?

Kavik turned off the main street into an alleyway. He hadn't known who the buyer of the shrine information was going to be. That was the whole point of using a broker like Qiu, to keep both sides of a deal anonymous. Kavik had assumed it was simply another shang who wanted an edge over their rival, the way most of the business for errand runners in Bin-Er was generated.

He reached the house he was going to break into.

The Blue Manse sat at the very edge of shang territory. Beyond it was nothing but a vast open field, bisected by the border of the Earth Kingdom proper. He could see the lantern glow of the guard stations in the distance.

The agents of the Earth King were supposedly on high alert across the continent after His Majesty's most recent rampage in Ba Sing Se. Qiu claimed the walls of the Upper Ring were painted with all the highborn traitors and spies purged from court in this latest round. Not with their blood, but the people themselves. They managed to throw enough conspirators up on the walls to get nice, even coverage.

For a broker who needed to deal in quality information, Qiu believed the dumbest stories. But still, Kavik knew it was bad for your health to get embroiled in a national fray. His work lay completely on the shang side, and for that he was grateful.

He took cover behind a landscaping shed that was probably used for one month out of the entire year. When it was clear, he sprinted across the open ground and pressed himself against the correct wall. It gave off a chill he could feel on his exposed face. Unlike its brick-and-board neighbors, the Blue Manse was made entirely of ice.

Kavik wriggled his nose, trying to brush off the itch of many different annoyances at once. The Blue Manse was someone's idea of a grand polar residence, but it failed to mimic

Agna Qel'a's architectural traditions. The fancy guest house was too square, too chunky, built without consideration of the natural movements of melt and snowpack. He knew it required the regular employ of Waterbenders to reshape and refreeze the walls.

Sorry, friends, Kavik thought. *At least I'm giving you more work.*

He shed his parka, folded it neatly, and placed it in a shadow so it would stay dry. Braced by cold and regret, he made a gesture that resembled a swimmer's plunge, melting an alcove into the corner of the building. Kavik stepped inside.

A coffin of ice glittered around him. He was a strange bird squeezed inside a strange eggshell. He couldn't afford to make the chamber any larger or else he'd hatch prematurely into the hallways.

Now came the hard part. With small bending motions, he transformed the ice above his head to water and carefully—carefully—coaxed it to run down the surface in front of him. Before the drip soaked his feet, he pressed himself upward using the walls to the left and right. Once his legs were in an elevated straddle, he froze the pool underneath him into a solid floor again.

Six inches. The complex series of steps that had taken him weeks of practice had elevated him by about six inches. Now he had to do it over and over again until he reached the third floor.

An observer might have wondered why he didn't go faster at the expense of getting wet. An observer could shut their trap and go back to the middle of the world, where it was soft and warm. As it stood, if Kavik remained perfectly dry, he had about thirty minutes before death from the cold set in. If freezing water got on him, he might be incapacitated in less than five.

He painstakingly lifted himself higher through the corner of the building, closing the tunnel behind him. Maybe a better

Waterbender, Kalyaan the Great for example, could have flowed through solid ice unimpeded. Kavik the Lesser had to squiggle his way through and was going to need healing for frostbitten hands once he was done.

The walls of the Blue Manse were intentionally opaque for privacy. But they weren't perfect cover. While the corners offered the thickest ice for hiding in, someone passing close by might notice his presence. He could hear voices congregated toward the center of the ground floor, some kind of large gathering Qiu said would serve as a distraction.

It worked well enough. No one wandered over to his corner, and Kavik ascended through the first story without any problems. He paused for breath, crouching in the thick layer of ice that made up the first ceiling and the second floor, and thinned a portion of the ice to peek at the next stage.

There were people in the outer hallways this time. With the darkness of night behind him, and the light of oil lamps inside, he had a slight vision advantage. He could see about four or five blurs standing completely still, not talking. Were they waiting in line for something?

Suddenly a pair split off, tromping in sync down the hall, neither outpacing the other. Kavik would have banged his head against his tiny chamber had he not been afraid of breaking through it. Those weren't idle guests. Those were patrols.

Qiu, you bleeding hog-monkey. Kavik had been told the job was a light grab from a visiting bureaucrat, and there wouldn't be any formal security. Now he was stuck between sky and earth, freezing his tailbone off, inches away from real soldiers and not goons for pay like Teiin's.

He had to wait until they were gone before he could move. And he had to pick a direction. Up, and take the biggest risk he ever had as a runner. Down, and lose the lead he'd been working on for months.

Kavik was forced to burn more of his body's time limit just sitting there, counting off the guard rotations for a window to move. His teeth began to chatter. Hard. *When the next pair leaves. Not this pair. The next one.*

As soon as their backs turned, he resumed his climb. By his best guess, he now had to move twice as fast as he was prepared to.

Cold trickles ran down the back of his neck. Sweat would have been bad enough, but this was runoff from the ice above. The freezing water made him want to scream. He had no choice but to endure it. The guards would be on their return leg now, and he was only a third of the way up.

He hurried and got wetter for his troubles. To make things worse, the glow of a hand lamp rounded the bend, someone he hadn't accounted for. A servant fetching a drink or a snack.

The thought of being nabbed for such a stupid reason was too much to bear. Kavik scrabbled upward, throwing caution to the wind in the exact manner he promised himself he wouldn't. By the time the lamp holder passed beneath him, he was tucked away inside the ice between the second and third floor, his knees pressed to his chin, drenched.

He might as well have plunged head-first into a turtle-seal's breathing hole. There wasn't enough space to dry himself with full-armed waterbending. In less than a minute, his muscles would stop moving, and then any sort of death would be free to take him. Proper freezing, suffocation. The floor under him could give out and he'd fall three stories.

He needed to get warm and dry immediately, and the nearest place he could was the room he was trying to break into. There was no other choice. If the occupants were still inside, he'd throw himself upon their mercy because the cold didn't give a lick.

With a burst of desperation, Kavik brought his hands up and melted a small portal. He squirmed through and flopped onto the third floor like a landed fish, gasping for breath.

The first thing he did was whip the water off himself like it was a cloud of mosquito-leeches. He spotted a large oil lamp across the room and pushed himself over to it with his heels, hoping he could get close enough before he blacked out. Kavik had no other concern but the heat. At this point, if he got caught, he got caught.

But in the first bit of luck he'd had all night, no one interrupted his crawl for survival. The room was empty. Fate allowed the giant soapstone lamp to do its work, and blood slowly returned to Kavik's extremities. Once he had the strength to raise his head, he looked around.

He was in the poshest quarters of the Blue Manse, that much was obvious. Rich wooden furniture harvested and shaped from continental trees. Walls insulated with foreign wool rugs. Decorative plants that surely would have perished the instant they left the sanctuary of this floor. No furs though, strangely enough. Not a single scrap, when desirable hides and skins were one of the staple commodities of Bin-Er.

A desk topped with a giant slab of polished obsidian drew his eye. It held a messy pile of books and scrolls, stacks of correspondence. That was what Qiu had sent him for. Information. More valuable than gold in Bin-Er, if it came from the right people, and the magnificence of the room indicated the occupant was definitely the right sort of people.

Kavik got up and wobbled over to the desk, planting a hand on it for support. His orders were to make his way into this room and memorize anything that looked important, but his brain was barely working, and there was so much potential treasure here. The right document could be worth a hundred times its neighbors.

Might as well start with the ones being used. A large scroll had been spread out, its corners weighed down by books. A building plan of some sort. He couldn't read the notes so he carefully removed the weights, noting how they lay so he could replace them, and held the paper up to the light.

The door opened. He lowered the scroll. A girl, about sixteen or seventeen like him, walked in with her eyes closed.

She wore several layers of orange and yellow robes and a damp towel hung around her shoulders. She flapped her hand at her face and the motion caused her long black hair to stream behind her, blown by an unseen wind. There was a small cut along her forehead, higher than her hairline would have normally been. The redness stood out on the wide blue arrow tattooed onto her scalp.

Nicked herself shaving, Kavik thought. An Air Nomad. Why would an Air Nomad be staying in the Blue Manse, which was normally reserved for—

Oh no.

Oh no.

The girl opened her eyes. They widened a little when she saw Kavik, but not by much. She stopped drying her hair and looked at the scroll in his hands. "Please don't take that," she said. "I haven't finished studying it."

Kavik swallowed. If he could open his mouth to speak, he might pray to the Moon and Ocean that this wasn't actually happening, and he was imagining it all in his head. But the one human being who could intercede on his behalf with the spirits was the very person he'd burgled. She could swat down his pleas, leaving him a luckless forsaken husk.

He handed the scroll back. He could do nothing else.

"Thank you," Avatar Yangchen said as she took the paper from him. "You might want to cover your ears now. I've been told I can scream pretty loud."

FLIGHT

SPIRITS ABOVE, she wasn't kidding. The Avatar's airbending-powered cry hurt Kavik's ears through his palms and snuffed the oil lamp's wick out. The force of her lungs hit him in waves like the roar of a tiger-dillo.

A pair of guards came running down the hallway and blocked the exit. "Intruder!" they bellowed once they spotted Kavik. "Intruder in the Avatar's room!"

One of them raised his fist. Firebender. Kavik didn't think. On instinct, he grabbed the nearest cover and ducked behind it. To everyone's great shock, including his own, that was the Avatar herself.

"Swine!" The Firebender was hoarse with fury. "How dare you!"

Hey, no one felt worse about it than him. Using the holiest figure in the world like a plank shield was not his proudest moment. He turned her so she faced her guards and stayed low, clinging to her waist like a shipwreck survivor to driftwood.

Through the side of his face pressed to her back, he felt a shake. Was she laughing? "Be careful," she said to her guards. "He's a Waterbender."

That's right, he was a Waterbender. And they were inside a house of ice. One wrong move and he could send deadly shards hurtling into her flesh from all directions. If he were a total monster.

The guards hesitated, and that was enough. The Avatar's warning helped Kavik more than anything. He let go of her and stepped back to create some space, jostling the table behind him. A pile of envelopes scattered like fallen leaves.

"What are the chances we can forget this ever happened?" Kavik said to the room. "Genuinely asking."

Dead silence. "No? All right, then." With a flourish, he leaned back and splashed through the floor.

The plan was to ignore the cold for now and break his fall with a liquefied section of the Blue Manse. Plunge to the ground level, and then run out the front door.

For the halfest of seconds he was a genius. A squad of guards barreling up the stairs to protect the Avatar didn't notice the boy dropping behind them. He reached for the ice that made up the first-floor ceiling and melted it enough to avoid an unpleasant impact, squeezing through the makeshift portal and then—

—he got stuck. The water had solidified around one of his ankles, nearly tearing his hip out of its socket, and now he dangled upside down in a reception area, full of tables laden with fine food.

The party was abandoned, the very important guests having fled when the Avatar screamed, no doubt. The only people who remained were two Water Tribe guards who approached Kavik cautiously, one of them wearing a waterskin over his shoulder so he wouldn't have to ruin the architecture like the intruder had. He must have been the Waterbender who'd trapped Kavik like a side of meat hanging in a smokehouse.

"Brothers?" Kavik tried.

The non-bender hefted a ball club. His partner flicked the cap off his waterskin.

Okay, reasonable. Kavik flung his arms around, freezing the water inside the pouch. The act would buy him an extra moment as the man struggled in confusion to get his element out of its container. Fire was always fire and rocks were rocks, but water-bending had the extra snag of managing the change from solid to liquid and back again.

While the bender was distracted, Kavik pulled himself toward his ankle and freed his leg, just in time to avoid the club and fall on the off-balance man who swung it. He clung tight to the guard's parka, planted his feet in the man's hipbones, and rolled them over to put his opponent on top so he could take the brunt of the water blast the bender finally managed to get out.

The blow was hard enough to knock the man unconscious. These guys were out for blood. Kavik flung the limp guard off him and spun on his back, not bothering to rise, and kicked a strip of water off the wall, connecting his foot to the other bender's. A yank took the second man down.

The closer to the ground they stayed, the more they flopped around, the better. Kavik was only average at the push and pull of traditional elemental combat, but no one had beaten him at wrestling in years. Bending gave him more limbs to work with.

Kavik dodged the water whip that sliced down at his head and froze it to the floor, turning the liquid into ice all the way back up the other bender's arm, pinning him in place. Now was his chance to get away. He scrambled to his feet and leaped out the door.

But before his foot touched down, he was sucked back into the jaws of the Blue Manse by an unseen force tugging on his shirt from behind, slurped up like a noodle in soup. He'd taken too long. The Waterbender must have freed himself faster than expected and reconnected them. Kavik landed in the welcoming embrace of four more guards. It was over.

They dogpiled him, twisting his arms behind his back. Through the muffling of their furs, he heard the Avatar's voice. "Don't hurt the boy," she ordered. "Take him to the basement and make sure he's unharmed. I wish to speak with him in a few minutes."

The full weight of his crimes sunk in as they hauled Kavik away. This wasn't just a bad run. He wasn't just going to the magistrate's cells. This was the *Avatar* he'd crossed. What kind of punishment did you get for that?

FORGIVENESS

IT TURNED out Kavik's punishment was pretty basic. It started with a regular old beating.

"Street scum!" A boot landed square in his stomach as he lay curled up on the basement floor. He wrapped himself tighter around the ball of pain in his gut. "How dare you defile the chambers of the Avatar! Laying your filthy hands on her!"

Kavik noticed the trimming on the guard's clothes as they kicked him. Red, green, blue. At least hurting him was a multinational effort. He tried to explain with the little remaining air he had left. "I didn't mean to—"

"Shut up!" A fist cracked him across the jaw. Blood spilled into his mouth.

Kavik buried his face back into his elbows, but no more blows came. "Stand him up," said the leader. "She's coming."

They hoisted him to his feet while he was still in a daze. He heard footsteps coming down the stairs. A swishing hem, a clatter of beads. Once his vision unblurred, the Avatar stood before him in her full regalia. A bloom of yellow and orange, dappled with wooden medallions. She was startlingly pretty. Against the frosted basement walls, her serene features and deep gray eyes stood out like artwork.

He caught himself and quickly banished the thought from his head. This was the *Avatar*.

She noticed the small trickle of blood leaking from the corner of Kavik's mouth. "Captain Gai," she said to the leader of her guards.

"Yes, Mistress?"

"You're fired."

The bluntness of her statement caused it bounce off Kavik's ears. Gai needed a moment too. "I'm sorry?" he said.

The Avatar turned to him. "You and your men are all fired. I told you not to hurt him and you did. What's not to understand?"

"But . . . but . . ."

"None of you are eligible for employment for security in the Avatar's retinue anymore." Her voice never rose above a conversational level, and yet the men wilted as if she were spouting dragon's breath. "Report to Boma and tell him what you did so he can strike your names from the lists. Now."

Kavik had never seen so many grown men hang their heads like children. They shuffled back up the stairs, leaving him alone with the Avatar. She took a step closer.

He threw himself at her feet, pressing his forehead to the cold floor. "I'm sorry!" he wailed. "I'm so sorry! I didn't know! I didn't *know*!"

"Shh-shh, it's all right." She knelt down and raised his head. Through his tears he saw her bend some clean water from a basin. The pulsing liquid shone when she pressed it to his face.

The swelling subsided, and he could feel the gash on the inside of his mouth seal itself.

"Hands now," she said. "Before they fall off."

She'd noted the early stages of frostbite. Kavik held out his hands. The Avatar layered his fingers between hers, the gesture uncomfortably intimate, and this time the glow was warm. Feeling returned to his skin. Fixing damage from the cold was a lengthy, specific process, and he wondered how she came by the knowledge.

"Are you hurt anywhere else?" she asked. "What about your body?"

He shook his head. His stomach was bruised but his ribs were still intact. "I'm fine."

She looked like she doubted that very much. "You picked the wrong stage in the Avatar cycle to rob. Air Nomads don't have much in the way of possessions."

He owed her the truth. "I didn't know it was the Avatar's room. And I wasn't after valuables. I wanted information I could sell."

"Ah." She raised her eyebrows, her interest piqued. "You must be one of those errand runners Bin-Er is so famous for. I was warned before coming here that I'd be entering a city of spies."

So she'd heard. In the shang territories, information intelligence was by far the most desirable currency. Fortunes traveled on paper. Deals in the making, contracts, meeting notes, even sharply worded letters could herald business opportunities with unlimited potential upside for anyone in the know. Sometimes there was only a verbal agreement tying obscene sums of money together, in which case you needed a person listening in the right place at the right time.

The Avatar sighed and shook her head. *"Everyone you meet in Bin-Er is in someone else's pocket,* or so I've heard the saying go. Which shang do you work for?"

"None," Kavik said. "I'm independent. I'm just trying to survive day to day."

"Supporting a family?"

"No." His voice cracked. "I came to Bin-Er by myself after my parents died. I thought there'd be steady work, but I couldn't find any. I've got nothing to my name."

"You're alone." She stared into the distance, as if she were mulling over a strange scent, before returning to him. "I'm sorry. I've never really been alone, not ever. I can't imagine what it's been like for you."

"It's hard in the city." He sniffed and wiped his nose. "Touts for work crews come to your village and tell stories about how the streets of Bin-Er are paved in gold and anyone who's clever enough can become a great merchant as long as they work hard," he said. "Then you get here and find out the harsh truth. You're not worth anything until someone else decides you are."

The lamplight flickered, and he thought he saw a flash of anger, approaching hatred, ripple across her face. But he must have imagined it. Her expression of Air Nomad grace was all the stronger for the troubled twist of her lips. "I'm hoping I can change such attitudes before they become permanent. Let a problem last for too long and people begin to believe it's not a problem." She chewed on her cheek. "Maybe I can start with you. You only run errands for the money, right?"

Kavik shrugged. "Why else would anyone get into this line of business?"

"Well, that settles it." She reached into her wide sleeve and pulled out a large purse. "If you had some silver weighing you down, maybe you'd be less keen a burglar."

"Wait." Somewhere along the line they'd skipped a few steps. "I don't understand."

She thought he was confused about why she had money to begin with. "Diplomatic expense budget," she explained.

"That's not it." Why would she be loading his pockets before sending him to face his punishment, unless . . . "You're going to let me go?" Kavik asked.

"What do you want me to do, throw you in Air Temple jail? Trust me; this is a matter of convenience. I don't have to deal with the work you'd create otherwise, and you get to stay off the streets for however long this gift lasts." She loosened the drawstrings.

He couldn't believe it. His eyes and ears deceived him. "Wait!" Kavik sputtered, remembering various bits of spiritual regulations he wasn't even sure were correct. "An Air Avatar shouldn't touch money!"

She rolled her eyes, and for his sake more than hers, widened the mouth of the bag without touching the contents. Holding it like a pitcher, she poured a stream of coins into his hands. He watched the flow of generosity, a miracle in a city as mercenary as Bin-Er.

When she was done, she gestured at the wall behind him. "There's an exit that leads out the side. Get out of here while you have the chance. And don't let anyone see you."

Air Nomads really were different in spirit. Kavik put the coins in his pockets and pushed open the iced-over door. He climbed the cramped stairs, disbelieving each step he took. In defiance of how his night had gone, they led to the street, and freedom.

No one accosted him. It was as if the Avatar's blessing lingered over his skin like armor. He went around the building and picked up his parka. Once he was fully dressed, he joined the remaining stragglers in the international district.

What just happened? he thought, looking up at the starry sky. He would never be able to explain it, not in this era or the next.

Kavik walked for a couple more blocks and then took a sudden right, using a big man as a screen so anyone following him from behind wouldn't see his change in direction until it was too late.

Sprinting down the alley, he opened a door he knew was unlocked and left it slightly ajar to make it look like he'd gone inside when he hadn't. His real path was the brick wall covered in a thick layer of ice from a leaky drainpipe. With a pull of waterbending, he shaped handholds that let him cross to the other side with ease, and then broke the ice. It fell to the ground and shattered, looking like a victim of its own weight.

He took another right, then a left, and a right again. Only when he was sure he hadn't been tailed did he walk around the block to the entrance of a dimly lit hall. He knocked on the door normally, without any pattern.

It swung open. A gray-haired Water Tribe woman peered up at Kavik.

"Well, you look smitten," Mama Ayunerak said. "I haven't seen that dopey grin since Meihua dumped you."

Narrowly getting away with one's life could do that to a man. Kavik looked over her shoulder inside. The shelter was packed tonight, benches and tables full of men and women tucking into bowls of searoot porridge.

Ayunerak ran a kitchen for workers caught without work, mostly newcomers who relied on the free meals she provided. The city might have doubled in size while she'd lived here, but the old woman wasn't going to let the customs of Water Tribe hospitality be forgotten. Food was meant to be shared with anyone who needed it.

"I have something for you," Kavik said. He produced a fistful of coins, the first of several.

Ayunerak's mouth fell open in shock. "Wha— Where did you—"

"Don't ask." He scooped the money out of his pockets into her hands, trying not to drop any. He should have asked the Avatar for the bag itself. She was nice enough to have given it to him.

"It's been a while since you visited your cousins in Port Tuugaq, right?" Kavik said. "Take some of that money and go see them. Do it for all us saps who don't have travel rights." He gave the stunned woman a quick nuzzle on the cheek. "I wasn't here."

Ayunerak was too dumbfounded to shout at him as he ran back around the corner. Near her kitchen's refuse trough, close to the ground and covered by rotting cabbage leaves, was a loose brick. And hidden behind that was a key.

Without further incident, he reached Bin-Er's Water Tribe Quarter. Its dwellings were fitted to the seasons, and right now built with panes of windblown snow. Made of winter to withstand winter. When it got warmer in the summer, the residents would switch over to sod houses and tents as necessary.

Looking at the white domes, Kavik scrunched his upper lip in a burst of fresh irritation at the square ice of the Blue Manse. He could easily imagine it having been built for Middler dignitaries who merely wanted the novelty of sleeping under frozen water.

But what right did he have to criticize? Nearby was one of the largest homes in the neighborhood, a creaky stalwart of old Bin-Er that looked like it belonged in Omashu. He walked up the hard dirt path, shook the snow from his boots, and used his key to unlock the door.

Warm, steamy air bathed his face. "I'm home," he called out.

Inside, a woman looked up from the pot of stew she was stirring. His mother brushed a loop of hair out of her face and gave him a smile. "You're back late. How was your day?"

"Was okay." *Almost died. Met the Avatar. Stole from her.* He wedged his boot off and retrieved the folded envelope he'd managed to grab from her room before he'd plunged through her floor.

Taking items themselves wasn't as good as leaving them undisturbed. The Avatar would realize one of her letters was missing, and then it would be off to an endless cycle of her knowing someone else knew what she knew. The information game often devolved into such never-ending spirals, a spider-snake swallowing its own tail.

But the envelope was still worth something for merely having passed through her hands. He had to decide whether to break the seal; the value could be higher with an aura of mystery around it.

He tucked it under his shirt for later. "Be careful passing through the square tomorrow," he said to the man sitting behind a desk in the corner. "There was trouble earlier."

His father barely looked up from the ledgers he'd brought home from the counting house. A grunt came back in response. More acknowledgment than Kavik got on most nights. He hung his parka up. Without the extra layers he could hear his stomach rumble. Despite the bruise he knew was growing on his stomach, he was hungry.

"What's for dinner?" he asked his family.

UNWINDING

HE THOUGHT the thrill would have lasted longer. But after a big score, you had to go home, he supposed. You had to wash up and put food in your belly—tonight, arctic hen and sea prune stew. Obligations, none of them particularly exciting.

Kavik emerged from his room, his prize stashed away, his hands and face cleaned of his activities. He hadn't spotted any visible wounds on his face, and neither had his parents. The Avatar's healing was flawless.

"Are there any letters?" Kavik asked. He always asked. The answer was always no.

"No," said his mother, who knew how important the question remained. "I checked not long before you returned."

His father finished his tabulations, swiping back and forth in the air on an imagined abacus with his left hand and scratching the results into a book with his right. Once he was done, he put down his sharpened charcoal and got up from the desk.

Kavik's mother brought the cookpot over to the rug and set it on the low table. Three settings lay equally distant from each other. As she ladled broth into their bowls, Kavik thought about what the Avatar had said earlier. *Let things slide for too long and you'd be tricked into thinking they'd always been that way.*

"What put you in the square at this hour?" his father asked.

So much for the moment of quiet contemplation. "I was . . . Old Chan asked me to do a favor and pick up an order for him at the apothecary." Might as well reuse material. Kavik's parents had heard him talk about a string of odd jobs since leaving Nuqingaq's; currently he was sweeping up at a tea shop.

"I stopped by Chan's earlier," his father said. "He claims he hasn't seen you in weeks."

Crud. An unforced error. They'd been doing so well for so long, avoiding conflict over Kavik's activities. But he supposed another round was due. The tides would always come in.

"I was working on the other side of town," Kavik said, truthfully. "I wasn't doing anything dangerous." Less so. "I didn't tell you I left Chan's because you worry about every little change that walks into my life."

"I wish you didn't think us fools," his father said. "At least tell us who your boss is."

In case you disappear too. Too bad he couldn't, even if he wanted to. Kavik might have lied to the Avatar about not having a family, but the part about being an independent runner was accurate. He really wasn't in the pocket of Teiin or any of the merchant leaders. He'd managed to carve out a niche in Bin-Er as the runner who didn't charge much and would take answers to certain questions instead of money.

"Kavik," his mother said when he didn't respond. "You know where this path ends."

"Yes," he said, his tongue loosening before he could stop it. "Right here. With the two of you doing absolutely nothing."

"Kavik," his father said.

It seemed so unfair, the way he had to heap point upon logical point whenever he argued with his parents, but all they had to do was say his name. He could never balance the scale when his feelings and ideas were considered moss against their stone. Months of pent-up frustration poured out. "You told me to wait. What has waiting gotten us? When I am out there, I am looking for him. I am following leads. I am working to get Kalyaan back."

"Kavik, please," his mother begged. "Please, stop."

Stop hurting us, their faces said. *Stop breaking our hearts. We can't lose you too.*

He came to with a blink. When had he raised his hands in the air? How loud had he gotten? He flushed with regret and shame. His mother and father were loving, kind, patient with him beyond reason. Losing control was a failure on his part to act grown.

A knock came at the door. Thank the spirits for that.

At this time of day, it was probably one of his father's colleagues from Nuqingaq's coming by to pick up or drop off more paperwork. Kavik and his parents made sure their expressions were back in order, not wanting to show any signs of strife in front of a caller. They were on thin ice with the rest of the Water Tribe Quarter as it stood.

His mother went to the front entrance and unlatched it. The door swung open and she let out a cry, her stoicism stripped away before it had a chance to settle. *"By the lights!"*

Kavik thought she was screaming because of him. In a way

she was, because a young Air Nomad woman now stood outside his house.

"Hello," the Avatar said. She spotted Kavik over his mother's shoulder, and a gleaming smile spread across her face like a sharp knife slicing open a patch of leather. "My name is Yangchen. May I come inside and talk for a moment?"

THE VISITOR

KAVIK'S MOTHER tried to sink to her knees but Yangchen quickly put a stop to it, propping her up.

"Please, please!" Yangchen said. "I didn't mean to put you out."

"Avatar, we are honored beyond belief!" Kavik's father said. He mopped his brow with his cuff, trying to remember the rules for greeting the greatest spiritual presence in the world. "Of course you may come in! Our home is your home."

Kavik's parents were better at recognizing faces from portraits than he was. Then again, the Avatar did tell them her name right away. Yangchen slipped off her shoes and stepped inside. She was alone.

"You have a lovely house," she said, wielding the compliment like a club against Kavik. "May I?"

She held up her staff, indicating she wanted to lean it next to his parka. His parents nodded so hard their heads threatened to fall off. They shuffled further and further backward the deeper inside the house the Avatar got. Kavik's mother reached up and pushed on the back of her son's neck. His gaze wasn't humbly lowered enough.

"There's no need to be formal," Yangchen said. "Maybe . . . consider this a visit of alms? Would that work?"

For the sake of practicality, she was asking to be treated as regular Air Nomad, touching down on the middle of a journey to seek donations of food and shelter. But Kavik's parents would have pulled out every stop for that too. Many families across the world would, regardless of nation or circumstance. To give hospitality to a monk or a nun was a great fortune. A peace laid upon one's spirit.

But not to Kavik. Not this time, and not with this nun. He was prey caught in a snare. Like a cornered lop-eared rabbit, he had to avoid thrashing his back out in fear.

Easy now, he thought, swallowing hard. *This'll play out however it plays out. I don't have to be the one who makes the first move.*

"We were about to start dinner," his mother said. "We would be blessed to share a meal with you."

She ushered Yangchen over to the rug, but Kavik's father suddenly dove between the Avatar and the pot, as if the steam itself would contaminate her. "Wait!" he shouted. "There's meat in the stew!"

Kavik's mother went pale. She'd nearly corrupted the Avatar with her carelessness. Tears welled in her eyes.

"It's all right!" Yangchen said, trying her best to avoid a scene. "The Western Temple believes we're allowed to consume meat if that's what's available for sharing. Some of us still abstain, but it's a choice. There's no harm done."

His mother didn't look convinced. "I can eat around it?" Yangchen offered.

The compromise was enough to prevent disaster. Kavik's father retrieved the fourth plate and rearranged their settings. North, east, south, and west once more.

Yangchen gracefully tucked her robes under her as she knelt. "Is it just the three of you?" she asked.

There was a slight pause. "Yes," Kavik said. "It's just the three of us." He glanced at his parents. They were unsure but let him deal with the question. "We don't have many guests these days."

"Bin-Er is a busy city, as I've learned," Yangchen said, fixing Kavik with her gaze. "A lot going on."

Family and visitor ate their meals. Kavik's serving of stew had no sea prunes, his portion of the dried fruit given to the Avatar. His appetite had vanished anyway. The cookpot had become a Pai Sho board, the girl across from him his opponent.

"If I may ask, what brought you to our door?" his father asked.

"I'm in the city on Avatar business," Yangchen said. "But to best serve people, I need to talk to them directly, learn about their lives firsthand." She managed to sip her broth *at* Kavik, somehow. "Tell me about yourselves. What does your family do? How is life in the city?"

His parents, unused to talking about themselves, started out slowly, from the beginning. They were originally from the Long Stretch region, west of Agna Qel'a, normally a land rich with access to fishing grounds and roaming herds. But an extended spate of bad hunting seasons and poor catches led them to seek options.

Encouraged by distant relations who had already crossed the straits, they came to Bin-Er to ride out the hard times. The shang system was still in its infancy back then, so the city was smaller, and security wasn't so tight. The family set up in the Water Tribe Quarter, where some of their neighbors were former hunting partners. And they went to work at Nuqingaq and Partners, where most of their colleagues were current neighbors. The little all–Water Tribe shop was one of the many counting houses that triple-checked the figures on the flow of trade goods between shang cities, and it enjoyed a sterling reputation due to his folks' long memories and boundless patience.

"How long ago was that?" Yangchen asked.

"Five years," Kavik said. Saying it out loud was a defeat in itself.

"Have you ever thought about going back to the North?"

"Every stinking day."

The truth could have been more delicately phrased. His parents' disapproval was clear. "We would love to return home," his father said. "But it's impossible to get real exit passes. The control office is so corrupt these days, you can only get clearance if it benefits the shangs somehow. They're able to bring as many workers as they want into Bin-Er. But if you try to leave, suddenly you're a security risk."

"Still, we've been the lucky ones," Kavik's mother said. "The city's changed so much while we've been here. The newer arrivals . . . I don't know. The shangs discard them like scraps, at whim."

"There was a riot in the town center today," Kavik muttered, stirring his bowl with his spoon. "Folks are starting to get fed up."

He looked across the pot to see the Avatar genuinely taken aback. She hadn't been aware of the violence taking place a few blocks away from her quarters. She couldn't really be blamed for not knowing; based on the timing, she would have been meeting with dignitaries in the Blue Manse while the square grew heated.

"I want to change that," Yangchen said, repeating her earlier statement, when she and Kavik had been alone. "I want to change how the vulnerable are treated."

Kavik believed her. But it wasn't like telling him and his parents was going to do much about the situation. She needed to be talking to the people with power in Bin-Er. "It's nice to want things," he said.

He should have kept his mouth shut. Yangchen raised an eyebrow at his sarcastic comment, the motion made prominent by her missing hair, and decided a response was in order. She pushed her bowl aside. "Your son," she said sternly to Kavik's mother and father. "As delightful as this visit has been, *he's* the real reason I'm here. Did he tell you what he did earlier?"

The air went deathly quiet. The night had been one of the most joyous occasions in his parents' lives, and now it threatened to sink into the abyss due to their child's foolishness. A rebuke from the Avatar herself. They'd never survive the shame. "What . . . what did he do?" Kavik's father croaked.

The Avatar turned and looked at Kavik the way an assassin might drink in her victim's dying groans while wrenching the knife back and forth. "He stopped a thief for me."

All eyes turned toward Kavik. Yangchen did not elaborate. She was going to let him find his way out of the forest she'd dropped him in.

He had to pull together a few scattered pieces, backtrack over who in his audience knew what information. "I went to the square late in the day because I heard rumors something was about to go down and I was curious," he said. Seeking out danger would be the crime in his delayed confession to his parents. "So I was walking along the edge of the crowd, and I see this man running away from some guards. He was holding a satchel in his hands, which was weird. Normally you'd sling a bag around your shoulder, right?"

Yangchen tilted her head back, as if she were trying to get a better look at him with the benefit of distance. This was the second time he'd lied in front of her. There was a chance she was impressed.

"I didn't get in his way," Kavik said. "That would have been dangerous. I kind of stepped aside and then slapped the satchel out of his hands as he passed. He kept running. The guards thanked me and took the bag away. Then I left. I didn't know it was related to Avatar business."

There. Perfect. His parents didn't have to imagine him facing down a dangerous criminal and he didn't have to admit to meeting Yangchen in person.

"Your son recovered a crucial piece of political information." she said, picking up where he left off with ease. "Without him, I couldn't tell you what might have happened." A slow shake of her head implied the worst. War, famine, spiritual barrenness spreading across the land.

"How did you know where to find me?" Kavik asked her. Only he and the Avatar recognized the question as a counterpunch. *I went; now it's your turn.* "How did you know where I lived when you didn't see me yourself?"

"Oh, I arrived a little while after and asked the witnesses," she said breezily. "One of them said they recognized you and gave me your address." Yangchen bowed to his parents. "Kavik did the world a service today. Is it all right if I talk to him alone for a bit?"

Not only did they agree, they nearly dismissed themselves from the main chamber. The Avatar asked Kavik to show her to his room. His mother gave him a glare, warning him not to embarrass the family.

By the time Kavik closed the door, Yangchen was already looking around, taking in every detail she could to build a picture of him. Books, lack of books, level of tidiness. Was he a person who kept mementos? Decorations? Weapons?

She finished her sweep. "Really?" she said. "You sleep in a completely bare room with nothing on the walls and no furniture other than a bed? A man with nothing to hide. You'd fit in fine at the temples."

"You followed me." He was so sure he'd been careful.

"I did." She raised a finger. "Most people forget to look up."

Her glider. She'd been flying above him the whole time with a perfect view, probably laughing at his efforts to cover his trail. "Aww, don't look so glum." Yangchen punched him lightly in the arm. "You got moves. Good ones."

How stupid was he to think he had successfully played her? Those little gestures of openness she'd made while she was healing him, the parted lips, the slight nods—she'd been putting him at ease.

Now her expression was full of mocking sorrow. "Pretty low of you to lie to me the way you did, when so many people in this city are living on the edge. From what I can tell, you have a loving family and a roof over your head." She reached out and brushed her fingertips along the wall. "I mean, there's a full second story on this house. You're a rich kid!"

"Not that rich," Kavik muttered, fully conscious that he was using the same defense the merchants used when they turned down Mama Ayunerak's requests for donations.

"But not that poor. I followed you to see which shang you reported to. Imagine my surprise to find you had a separate little base of your own. Your parents don't know the full extent of your activities, do they? Why are you running errands and nearly freezing to death when you could be working alongside friends and neighbors at the bookkeepers, safe and warm?"

Why indeed. There were answers that were given, and there were answers that were earned. The Avatar hadn't earned squat from him. "I value my freedom," he said, managing to say it slowly and curtly at the same time.

Kavik hoped she had enough pieces of the puzzle to leave his room, leave his house, leave him alone. Instead, Yangchen sat down on his bed without asking and made herself comfortable, crossing one knee over the other, holding it in place with her hands.

"Well, that's too bad," she said. *"Everyone you meet in Bin-Er is in someone else's pocket.* From the moment you appeared, I was trying to figure out whose pocket you were in. Now I finally have the answer."

A fresh slash of a grin spread across her face. "Mine," Avatar Yangchen declared. "Now you're in mine."

THE PROPOSITION

KAVIK DID what he forgot to do at the beginning of this conversation and took a quick peek outside to see if his parents were eavesdropping. They were not. Of course they respected the Avatar's privacy more than his own.

He shut the door again and leaned his back against it, forced to the edge of his own room by this invading presence. "If you're going to have me punished, just do it and get it over with."

"I'm not turning you in to anyone," Yangchen said. "This is a recruitment pitch. I want your skills put to use for a nobler cause." She paused, and then clarified. "Me. I'm the nobler cause."

"You . . . want me to run errands for you?" This was a world leader he was talking to, not a low-rent broker like Qiu. "Why?"

"Because I can't run them all myself. To be an effective Avatar, one needs to make informed decisions. Informed decisions require good information. And the information I get fed on a regular basis by my so-called advisors and companions . . . is lacking."

She saw he was confused. "Think about it," she said. "I may be the most watched and scrutinized person in the Four Nations. All of the attendants foisted upon me by the leaders of the world, the ministers, the diplomats, advisors, sages? They're spies, more often than not. Spies reporting back on me to their real masters. In the past I've had my decisions leaked before I've announced them, my moves anticipated before anyone could guess, and been fed falsehoods till bursting."

She hugged her knees again and swung her feet back and forth. "So. While in the open, I adhere to tradition. I attend the meetings. I perform the ceremonies. But when I need to gather information or act in secret, without the trappings of the office weighing me down, I do it out of sight, with the help of a small number of associates who I know aren't compromised. Here is where you come in."

This wasn't the same person Kavik had surprised in her room, the gentle nun who'd healed his face. He could have been talking to a Bin-Er native right now. One of the shrewd youths who thought of everything in terms of transactions. Even the way she strung her words together was more broker than wise woman.

"You could get anyone in the world to work for you," Kavik said. "Why would you pick me? You don't know me. We have no connection."

"That's precisely why I want you," Yangchen said. "Good candidates don't fall into my lap very often. You're from a comfortable family, not beholden to anyone by money or debt. You're too low-level to be worth anyone's attention, but just skilled enough to be useful."

"Wow, thanks."

"I'm not selling you short," Yangchen said. "I completely bought your act about not having a family. It's very rare these days that I can't tell someone is lying to my face. And you really do have moves. You would have gotten away from the guards if I hadn't personally intervened. Twice."

Kavik shut his eyes. Of course. The Avatar was a Waterbender by definition; she'd been the one who'd trapped him by his feet. And the one who'd yanked him back inside the Blue Manse with precise airbending. "Do you have other people working for you?"

"Not as many as I'd like. Normally I have to stick to close friends, those who owe me favors, fanatic devotees to the Avatar. I need more help. Serving the world requires new blood. What do you say?"

He didn't have to think very hard. "No," he said. "Thank you for the offer, but no. I appreciate your consideration. No."

"Oh, I'm sorry," Yangchen said, undaunted. "I didn't mean to imply you were *that* special of a case. You fit neatly into the category of *owes me*. I did save you from punishment for your very serious crimes. Not every Avatar in history took attempted theft of intelligence as lightly as I did."

"You're going to blackmail me?!"

She didn't seem terribly insulted by the accusation. "I wouldn't put it that way. I'm giving you the chance to do some real good and hoping you take it. The shang cities—Bin-Er, Jonduri, Taku, Port Tuugaq—are wellsprings of corruption and suffering. Some of them are just more obvious than others. I need someone like you who knows this kind of environment to help me fix their problems. Think of it as doing exactly the type of work you've been doing, only with me as your broker."

She drummed her fingers on the edge of his bed. "But you're right. It's not fair for me to threaten you with the inside of a jail cell. And you catch more ant-flies with honey than vinegar."

Yangchen popped up and waved her fingers at Kavik. A gust of wind from a point of origin that should have been too close to exist pushed him out of the way. She left his room without waiting for him.

"Hey!" Kavik said, trailing after her. "What are you—"

The Avatar reentered the main chamber. Kavik's parents looked up from where they sat waiting.

"I have an announcement," Yangchen said to them, as proud as a sifu graduating her student. "In recognition of his good heart and bravery, I have offered your son the chance to become one of my official companions, to stand by my side and help me keep the world in balance."

Kavik's mother shrieked in joy. His father tried to say something but had to turn his face to hide the tears of pride gushing from his eyes. Companions of the Avatar went down in the annals of history. Their truant son was going to make greatness of himself. Their suffering hadn't been in vain. Truly, utterly, they'd been blessed tonight.

Kavik watched his parents bawl into each other's shoulders with happiness. "You're free to refuse, of course," Yangchen whispered out of the corner of her mouth. "My offer of companionship is legitimate. You can say no."

Like he could and still live here. She'd as good as pushed him off a cliff.

With each ecstatic sob from his mother and father, another chunk of Kavik's spirit left his body.

"I hate you," he muttered.

"I'll let you sleep on it," the Avatar replied.

THE PARADE

YANGCHEN OPENED her eyes and stared up at the ceiling. Clay. Not ice. Still Bin-Er, though. Still Yangchen.

She was pretty sure of it.

She lay in bed and went through the exercises Abbess Dagmola had developed for her when she was younger. She thought about the previous night's events, linked them to her tasks for the day to come, and purposely skipped over the wild clash that had gone on inside her head in between, forging a mindful connection to herself.

The idea was to create a sturdy bridge between the banks of her memories. Only sometimes it was afloat with a fraying rope tied to it, hurled a bit short.

Today was especially confusing due to the change in sleeping accommodations. After the intrusion, Masters Sidao and Boma both had insisted on relocating. Yangchen rejected all of Sidao's suggestions for new guesthouses. Those were likely spots he'd scouted in advance, with plenty of listening nooks and hidden doors only he knew about.

She'd chosen a new place to sleep at random. Semi-random. Her instincts may have led her to point at the map and land on a small, ancient inn that mercifully turned out to have heated floors. She wasn't as good at ignoring temperatures as her sisters and brothers, found the warming Breath of Fire technique draining on her energy reserves, and the Bin-Er winter was a hostile beast, full of intent and malice.

The out-of-the-way location served a purpose besides comfort. She had to take the precaution that Kavik wasn't the first part of a double beat, a ruse designed to give her a worthless victory while the real theft happened in the aftermath once everyone's vigilance subsided.

The boy's name was Kavik. A smile played across her lips. She was jealous, in a way. Last night's follies would be a lighthouse in his memories. He was never going to forget the day he ran into the Avatar twice.

Master Boma knocked on the door. "Avatar," came the gruff, grandfatherly voice. "Breakfast is ready. Master Sidao said that if we want to keep our schedule with the shangs, you should eat soon."

The Avatar doesn't answer to the shangs, Yangchen thought. *Thousands of years do not give way to a decade.* "I'll be down momentarily," she said.

The interruption knocked Yangchen out of her flow. She found resuming the mental exercises where she left off too daunting, starting over again an impossibility. So she didn't. Herein was the danger. Not that Abbess Dagmola's wisdom wasn't effective, but that Yangchen, with increasing frequency, didn't follow it.

She got up slowly out of habit. Sometimes she could forget

her joints were still young, only seventeen years of use on them. She propped herself up against the wall, hoping the cloudiness would drain out of her head, and lifted her arms for Pik and Pak to land on them.

They didn't come. Right. She'd left her winged lemurs in the care of the Northern Air Temple. Maybe she should have finished building the bridge after all.

To avoid thinking about it, she turned her attention to the mound of clutter in her room. Her documents had been moved here from the Blue Manse in a hurry. Her notes were out of order, her speech drafts were scattered everywhere, and worst of all, relocating her quarters had given unvetted people a chance to examine her research and correspondence. The double beat could have happened during the transfer.

Yangchen moved to the edge of her bed and plucked a roll of paper off the pile, the one Kavik had tried to steal. She spread the architectural plan of the old Bin-Er gathering hall across her lap. The building had been torn down and reconstructed so many times that several different people thought they held the original designs. But *this* was the true oldest version, its provenance guaranteed by one of Yangchen's trusted sources.

She examined the layout of the structure from corner to corner. A good general studied the terrain whether a battle was on the horizon or not. A sailor watched the skies even when they were clear. And Yangchen had been both of those at some point. If she couldn't make any progress in her formal meeting today, she'd have to resort to unconventional methods.

She spotted an interesting detail in the plans. The gray fuzz between her ears began to clear.

Well, what do you know? she thought. *Heated floors.*

One of the few joys she could pursue in public these days was messing with Sidao. The Minister of Special Territory Relations was an ever-growing presence in her retinue, and he often acted more like a tutor of etiquette. She wasn't supposed to plummet in from the sky on Nujian when meeting dignitaries to conduct formal business. Nor was she supposed to glide. She was the Avatar, not a screeching bird of prey.

Riding on the ground to her destination projected the correct aura of dignity. It also let her publicly send signals and declare favor through her choice of companion. For example, the special territory minister's importance might be demonstrated to all by giving him a seat close to hers during processions.

In compliance, Yangchen had taught Nujian to perform an exaggerated trot whenever they had to satisfy Sidao's definition of procedure, mimicking the high-stepping bounce of beasts with fewer legs. It looked ridiculous and made children laugh. And Sidao suddenly no longer wanted to accompany her on the way to her conferences. Victories all around.

Today, in the glistening cold, she rode through Bin-Er on Nujian's withers while Boma sat behind her in the saddle. He was used to any sort of ride, bumpy or smooth or through the sky in a storm. The residents of Bin-Er lined the main street for a chance to see the Avatar. If it made them happy, she would show her face.

Sidao shivered in the open-topped carriage ahead of her. He hailed from Nanyan, near Foggy Swamp, and the cold disagreed with him worse than it did Yangchen. "Mistress Avatar," he said, turning around in his seat to face her. The tonic he used in the foot-long beard that hung off his chin must have been water-based, because it was starting to turn into an icicle. "May I remind you that she who commands all four elements still cannot bend time? Our delays compound."

"'Ah, the falling grain of sand, the merciless hound at our heels, the spoke of the season's wheel,'" Yangchen quoted.

Whenever Sidao got cranky about the schedule, she liked to pluck adages from ages past to remind him what time really meant in the grand scheme of things. "Ten tons of bison running hard along the ground will feel like an earthquake and damage property. You may go on ahead to inform the shangs we're running behind."

Her permission to leave gave Sidao pause. *I know you're on their payroll,* she thought. *Show me who your true masters are, whom you're really afraid of displeasing.*

With a frown, Sidao told his driver to speed up and round the bend. There it was. Leaving the Avatar in the dust was rude for someone so concerned with etiquette, but duty called.

It was just her and Boma on Nujian now. Yangchen looked around. She'd thrown her hood back, and the crowd had reciprocated the gesture by uncovering their heads as well. Their gazes shining, rapt. So many of them had their hands clasped in front of their chests in a universal symbol. *Please.*

I'm trying, she thought.

This might be the only glimpse of her they got in their lives. She would have liked to stop and talk with a few of them, like she had with Kavik's parents last night, but she really didn't have the time today. The Avatar's personal blessing was much sought after, but it scaled horribly as a good.

Bin-Er needed more than a wave and a smile anyway. The shangs had done their best to scrub the streets for her visit. The parade route took her through the prosperous neighborhoods, past the pointed houses of commerce and the frozen fountains, showed off the carved, gabled architecture of an older version of the city that hadn't been relevant for decades.

But it wasn't enough to fool the eyes of an Air Nomad, sharpened by gazing across mountain peaks. Not five minutes into her procession, Yangchen had spotted an overlooked alleyway full of abandoned blankets and mats, their owners probably told to vacate or suffer the consequences.

This couldn't stand. You couldn't put all your grain on one corner of the saddle and expect to remain in balance.

"Perhaps we could hurry a bit more," Boma said in the back, jarring her back into place.

"Worried about the shangs' patience too?"

"No. It's the crowd. They're a little close for my liking."

Boma usually wasn't so curt when it came to the throngs of the devout. As if to agree with him, Nujian grumbled and snorted, breaking his stride. Yangchen looked around.

The captivated front lines had pushed forward a bit, but that wasn't a problem. Not compared with the figures lurking behind them who'd kept their hoods on. Three men trying to keep pace with her.

All right. It came with the territory. She'd come here because people were unhappy; it would be unfair for her to be bothered by the presence of unhappy people.

She knew she was dealing with troublemakers, not assassins. She'd seen this very incident play out through the eyes of her predecessors and felt little danger. Landing a shot on her by surprise would be difficult enough. While cold was a foe beyond her, she was excellent at feeling and reacting to airflows.

The rotten fruit that came flying at her head might as well have been moving at a snail-sloth's pace. Yangchen formed a small cyclone with a flick of her wrist and used the funnel of air to guide the missile into her hand.

Papaya, she noted with some amusement. They must have scavenged refuse from a household rich enough to import—

"Aagh!"

The sound of shattering clay turned her head. Boma held his face while blood dripped down his fingers. The fragments of an empty jug lay scattered over the saddle.

A red rage swelled through Yangchen's veins. They couldn't hit her, so they'd aimed at an old man. Her friend.

She rose higher on her bison's neck. *"I am here to* help *you!"* she shouted.

Nujian reacted to her runaway emotions and slammed the gigantic paddle of his tail down. A gust of wind rushed outward, flattening the crowd. Any screams of fear were blown far away.

Amid the half ring of stunned people, Yangchen saw the person who'd thrown the jug. It wasn't a young miscreant. It was a man who was the same age as Boma, if not older. She could read the fear and bitterness in his eyes like a scroll. *What help? You up there, and us down here, what help?*

It didn't matter that as an Air Nomad she owned fewer possessions than anyone here. She had freedom. She had status—the most status, in fact. More status than anyone else in the world.

But as soon as she followed Sidao's path, rounded the corner, and disappeared from sight, these onlookers would return to their lives no better off than before. Unless she could do something for them, even the most fervent believers in the Avatar would realize she was a brief breeze on a scorched day, pleasant for a moment but ultimately meaningless. Some would turn to sorrow, others anger. The man who'd struck Boma was simply further along the journey than most.

In a fit of frustration, she hurled the brown, oozing fruit in her hand at the wall high above his head. The skin burst, sending seeds and foul pulp raining down. Someone yelped in terror.

She knew she'd regret the act tomorrow, if not minutes from now. Such outbursts poked a hole in the painting of her and let the real light through.

Yangchen shook her head and spurred Nujian onward.

THEATER

"AHH, DON'T worry about it," Boma said as Yangchen tended to his scalp with fresh water. "Injuries above the neck always bleed worse than they really are."

"It's my fault," Yangchen said. "If I hadn't fired Captain Gai, security would have been tighter." She finished healing him and tossed the pink-tinged water to the side. It stained the snow on the lawn, a dot of diluted ink on a sheet of white. The attack had made certain they'd be late.

Today's meeting was going to take place in the Bin-Er gathering hall, a disjointed complex consisting of a magistrate's courthouse, an assembly wing, and a small barracks. She had been told only the courthouse saw any regular use. Town councils were a thing of the past, and the shangs weren't allowed to maintain a fighting force under the very terms that gave them their positions.

She left Nujian at the gate and walked across the lawn, Boma trailing behind. Where the snow would have dampened the hems of her robes, she pushed it away, broadening the path between the banks around her as she walked. They entered the assembly wing, a drafty silo built in optimistic denial of the dominant weather.

Inside the large room were arcs of benches, and very few of them were full. This was no meeting of the masses. The shangs were a small group of merchants from across the Earth Kingdom, Fire Nation, and Water Tribe who'd made residence in Bin-Er as part of the agreements granting them sole permission to move goods internationally.

Sidao, standing by the door, breathed a sigh of relief as she came in. He twiddled the jeweled badge around his neck that marked his office and announced her while Boma took her cloak. "May I present Avatar Yangchen of the Western Air Temple, master of the elements and bridge between humans and spirits," Sidao said.

The shangs got up slowly from the puddles of fine furs and wools keeping them warm. Some of them not at all. The disjointed sequence, their reluctance to remove their hoods, could have been a natural reaction to Yangchen's lateness. It also could have been intentional.

Boma tolerated many things, but never disrespect to his charge from those who should have known better. "In the Four Nations, you *rise* in the presence of the Avatar!" he snarled.

Her guardian occupied a strange, undefined role in her retinue, and Yangchen never cared to formalize it to others. He was Boma, just Boma, and his presence beside her was not to be questioned. He didn't look the part of a dignitary, not with his weathered face and plain way of speaking, and nobles sometimes rankled at his presence. He had no problem rankling back.

The laggards among the shangs finished their bows and engaged Boma in a staring competition. She put a hand on her friend's arm. They were not off to a good start for her mission.

"Apologies, Avatar Yangchen," said a man in the center of the room. "The cold makes us all a little slower. I am Henshe, Zongdu of Bin-Er. We are blessed by your visit."

Henshe was a deeply handsome man in his mid-twenties. The youngest person ever to hold his position, if Yangchen's research was correct. She returned his bow. "Thank you, Master Henshe. You have a . . . lovely city." The first part of the compliment slipped out by reflex and the latter out of obligation.

He motioned at a large, raised chair that had been reserved for her. "You don't have your famous lemurs with you? A shame, I've been told they're adorable."

They were. But it was hard to be taken seriously at times with Pik and Pak chasing each other around her shoulders. She took her seat and wondered if it was intentionally too big, with a slippery bottom that threatened to dump her on the floor if she leaned back.

Tea was poured for everyone. Yangchen noticed the cups were lined with silver, the metal twirled into the porcelain with outrageously expensive craftsmanship. A single piece of the service alone could have fetched ten times as much money as she'd poured into Kavik's hands last night. "I understand this is your first visit to a shang territory," Henshe said. "If I could be allowed to give you an overview of our wonderful system and how it was formed?"

She already knew how the current version of Bin-Er came to be. And Taku, and Jonduri closer to the Fire Nation, and Port Tuugaq near the Southern Water Tribe. The system wasn't ancient, and there wasn't much history to learn. She was about to say so but Sidao, who had taken up a position next to the zongdu, looked at the ceiling and flared his nostrils, as if the refusal halfway out her mouth was giving off a smell.

Fine. If she didn't follow protocol and listen now, someone was going to accuse her of ignorance later. She reached for the armrests, found them too far away, and settled with folding her hands in her lap.

Henshe cleared his throat. "When I was but a young boy living in the outskirts of the Middle Ring, I dreamed of a place where opportunity could be reaped by anyone with the will to sow. As I grew older, I often spent my days down at the supply gates, watching the carts full of trade goods flow in and out, in and out, like lifeblood through a beating heart . . ."

Yangchen fought her groan a little too hard and ended up making a strained noise like she was earthbending a rock too big for her to lift. Henshe didn't notice and carried on without a hitch. His summary of the situation, once the glaze of his own life story had been scraped away, was generally accurate. The harsh truth was that Bin-Er and the shang cities owed their privileged status to the worst blunder of international politics in generations. The Platinum Affair.

In the long annals of the Earth Kingdom, rulers came and went. And so did the various military leaders, ministers, and family members who tried to depose them. Time's unceasing passage made the exercise of determining who would control the largest of the Four Nations seem dry. The occasional tussle that sprang up now and again.

Living through such strife wasn't so academic. Eight years ago, the world watched with bated breath as the loyalist forces of Earth King Feishan and the rebel legions of General Nong danced around each other, avoiding a pitched battle. Neither side wanted to throw away their chances for success in a single moment.

The Fire Lord and the Chief of the Water Tribe lost patience and conspired in secret to back Nong. While keeping up the pretense of friendliness toward both sides, they loaned funds to the Earth King in the form of paper bank notes, and sent Nong ingots of platinum, superior to gold in purity and portability.

The idea was to influence the war in favor of the renegade general by supplying him with more valuable money. Given only written promises, the loyalist soldiers on the other side would lose confidence in their king's ability to pay them and eventually refuse to fight.

What no one accounted for was the Earth King's hidden boldness and surprising battlefield acumen. He found the moment he'd been waiting so long for, fell upon General Nong at Llamapaca's Crossing, and wiped his enemy off the face of the map.

The Earth King knew what his fellow heads of state had done. In retribution, he closed his nation's ports, cut off diplomatic communication, and expelled ambassadors from his land. And he'd kept the captured platinum, melting it down and using it to plate the giant badger-mole statue behind his throne. Relations would return to normal when the entire surface fully tarnished and appeared as stone, he declared. Which was to say not for a century or more.

The Water Tribes and Fire Nation struck back by announcing similar states of isolation and for a little while there was quiet, silent panic behind closed doors. Three out of four nations were now blind to each other's actions, and that made them paranoid. Very few people other than Air Nomads were allowed to travel as they did before.

But despite the climate of political hostility, Earth King Feishan and his court still liked Fire Nation pepper and Water Tribe lamp oil. There was still money to be made exporting fine Omashu silk. So, in a face-saving handshake between king, chief, and lord, a few cities were chosen to handle controlled amounts of international trade under the strict purview of selected noble and merchant families. Those people became known as shangs.

"Each shang city has an elected officer called a zongdu who is responsible for solving problems and collecting customs revenue on behalf of our respective nations," Henshe said, once he was done explaining the state of world affairs. "A zongdu serves for a few years at most, before we step down and are replaced by another."

"In a way, they are Avatars," Sidao said.

Yangchen snapped to attention. "They're *what* now?"

"A zongdu is like a modern-day Avatar," Sidao said. "They serve others in their time, in an endlessly repeating cycle. They hold one of the few important positions in this world granted by means other than bloodline. They negotiate between international parties and need not be born of the country they work in. Zongdu Dooshim was Henshe's forebear, as Avatar Szeto was yours."

Clever analogy. And another slight to her and her past lives. Yangchen raised her palm to quell the fury she knew was running through Boma and glanced at the zongdu himself. Henshe clutched his notes and gave her a wide-eyed little shake of his head. *I didn't tell him to say that.*

"The shang cities are stable, balanced, and self-sufficient," Sidao went on, as proudly as if he'd invented them himself. "Avatar Szeto would surely have approved of our great system."

An unusual Avatar, Szeto had also managed to hold the position of Grand Advisor to the Fire Lord during his era. Many people weren't shy about telling Yangchen the young Air Nomad what her venerable predecessor would have thought, would have done. She waited for others to cut in after Sidao, but no one did. They were keeping things simple for her.

Good. An opening. "Thank you for the enlightening glimpse into recent history," she said. "Bin-Er and its sister cities are quite the marvel of human accord. A testament to the great feats that can be accomplished when the powers of the Four Nations are aligned in a single purpose."

A few nods from the shangs. Everyone liked compliments. "But no system is perfect," Yangchen said.

Sidao's head turned so sharply that his beard generated its own breeze.

"A mountain is more than its peak," Yangchen said. "We cannot declare true prosperity from looking at only a handful of accounts. No tower can stand on a mire of suffering."

What is she doing? Yangchen was accustomed to the question flying around in her presence, usually silently, on occasion out loud. Glances darted across the room like volleys of arrows in a heated battle.

"There is a great deal of misery in this city that goes overlooked," she said. "I would ask the people here, who have benefited so much from the arrangements made in the wake of the Platinum Affair, to listen harder to the spirit of generosity that I know lives in each and every one of your hearts."

Henshe cleared his throat. "Are you asking my masters for alms, Avatar?"

She was glad for the direct question; it meant she could stop flowering her language. "No. I am asking you to help me create a place where alms aren't necessary."

A forest of frowns had sprouted. She had an example prepared thanks to Kavik, who was already providing value as an informant. "There was a riot in the square last night, was there not?" Yangchen asked.

Henshe's grimace gave him away. Sweeping the incident under the rug would have fallen on him. "There was an incident, yes, but it was quickly resolved."

You mean hidden from me. Based on Kavik's description, Yangchen spotted an old man dressed in a strategic blend of muted colors sitting in the middle of the pack. That was the funny thing about the shangs. Unlike some glad-handing nobles and ministers who rushed her during meetings, hoping to impress their name in her memory, most of these merchants preferred to remain part of an indistinguishable mass.

Well, no longer. They would be named. "It was you, Master Teiin, who shortchanged your workers to the point of starting a riot, was it not?" Yangchen said, singling the man out with her finger. "It seems you canceled a construction project of your own volition before it was finished and then decided you didn't have to pay for any of the work at all."

A murmur went through the room. Not at Teiin's sharp practice but at the fact that the Avatar knew about it. Teiin shifted in his seat and answered her with a watery hiss that she could barely hear. "Last night I was waylaid by violent ruffians whom I didn't recognize. As for my dealings, they are entirely my own and no one else's."

You need at least two sides for a deal, Master. "My point is, we can ease the troubles of Bin-Er by treating its occupants with respect *before* they grow as desperate as they did last night," Yangchen said. "That means paying them fairly, instead of abusing their lack of options due to the restrictions forced upon them by the Platinum Affair."

She wrinkled her nose. "And despite what I said earlier, more alms are always good. The situation is dire enough that supplicants are sneaking out of the city without clearance and seeking refuge at the Northern Air Temple. Abbot Sonam has his hands full trying to take care of them. There is a direct chain of events between excessive desires in the present and widespread pain in the future." She was trying so hard not to use the word *greed* to avoid offending her audience. *Why?* she wondered. Why was the obligation on her to dance?

"Avatar," Sidao pleaded. "There are no such formalities in place for what you're asking."

"Then we can draft them," Yangchen said. "I'm willing to hold the brush. My friends, every day the chance to make the Four Nations a better place pays us a visit. Every day, rain or shine or snow, the opportunity comes calling. Let us not turn away such an important guest."

She paused and swallowed. It was a good speech. She thought it was a good speech. Perhaps not Szeto-worthy, but enough to make her point clear. Wasn't it?

She wasn't going to get an answer from her audience. The shangs were as unresponsive as corpses. She tried to fill the void. "I have plans, based off successful policies from the archives of Omashu, that I'd be more than happy to share. The cost would not be onerous to any of you in the least—"

"Avatar." The woman who interrupted her was draped in pearls from shoulder to shoulder. "Is there a spirit in the room with us?"

Yangchen blinked. "I don't understand the question, Mistress . . ."

"Noehi." The name was delivered with a quick, practiced smile, eyes included in the squeeze. "Many of us have heard of your great prowess in spiritual matters. How you quelled the afflictions of the Saowon clan in the Fire Nation. The lives you saved in Tienhaishi from the great spirit." She tilted her head. "Though I have heard from some it was actually a typhoon that leveled the city."

Yangchen remained quiet, as she often did when it came to her battle with Old Iron.

Noehi took notice and smirked. "I asked because, well, unless we're being haunted right now by a glowing presence demanding the silver from our purses, I don't see the merit of your demands," she said. "Bin-Er is a city of reason and commerce. We're not superstitious bumpkins who rely on oracles like the court of Tienhaishi, nor are we petty Fire Nation lords cowering in our castles, praying for better harvests."

This obviously wasn't the first time the woman had delivered a gentle letting-down in a delicate social situation. *Poor dear, best to be direct.* "The fact of the matter is you don't have any right to tell us what to do."

Opening her mouth to retort would have only made Yangchen look foolish. Because there was nothing she could say in response. She thought she'd come to Bin-Er armed with the truth. But so had her opponents. And their weapons were sharper.

Noehi drove the point of the spear home. "You don't have any power here, Avatar," she said. "You simply don't."

KEEPING SCORE

YANGCHEN BLINKED and looked around, even though she knew to search for help would be a flaring signal of her defeat. Boma couldn't meet her eyes. He'd been privy to all her business so far as the Avatar, but her guardian was out of his depth here. They both were. What Noehi said wasn't a slight to her office; it was a simple fact.

Sidao probably should have said something to preserve the dignity of Avatarhood itself. Yangchen was nominally his employer, after all. But he was caught between his money and his duty.

It was Henshe the peacekeeper, her supposed counterpart, who took pity on her. "Avatar, your wisdom is much appreciated," he said with the grace of a diplomat. One who was on the winning side. "We will meditate upon your advice and seek to incorporate it into our lives."

Advice. Was there ever such a useless gift? Advice was like fanning the sky and claiming responsibility for the weather.

Sitting in her grand chair, Yangchen saw the future as clearly as she saw the past. She would leave Bin-Er, to carry out the next of her never-ending list of duties. And the shangs would turn to each other and say, *Well, wasn't that interesting?*

"Surely . . . surely you can see a long-term . . . long-run . . ." Yangchen took a deep breath. She needed to offer them something, but what? "Surely you can see the long-term benefit of investing in the people of this city. The spirits smile upon those who take care of their neighbors."

The shangs in the room, not just Noehi, fought to hide emboldened smiles of their own. *We're trading blows with the Avatar and coming out ahead. What else can we do? Fly?*

"If the spirits have a problem with Bin-Er, they haven't shown it yet," Noehi said. "Unless . . ." She made a droll performance of looking around her shoulders, above her head for the phantom she mentioned earlier.

Chuckles. They were laughing at the Avatar. That was fine. Yangchen would let them mock her, give them anything she could, equal status at whatever imaginary table they wanted. "Please," she said, debasing the one asset she had left to give. "Whoever unites with me in this effort would be marked by history. I urge you, join me in companionhood and duty."

Status as an Avatar's companion was going cheap these days. But she could find no takers. "Our duty is to manage the flow of trade between the Four Nations," Teiin said. "Not to throw bones at every barking animal in the street. As long as Earth King Feishan gets his portion of the revenues, he doesn't care how we manage our business."

Teiin sniffed and drew his thick cloak around him. How dare she waste his time. "Henshe put it sufficiently," said the man who thought it cheaper to beat people than give them their due. "Your advice has been heard. I think we're done here."

Yangchen's fingers dug into the armrests like claws. The only person who sensed the danger was Boma.

It would have been easy to blame another life, to pretend a bad memory of being scorned pushed her over the edge. But it was Avatar Yangchen alone who decided that she was no longer giving advice. And that they weren't done.

She stood up before Teiin could. "The Earth King cares about being cheated," she said. "He cares about treason."

The silence that fell upon the room rolled back and forth, flattening the occupants under its belly, squeezing the air out of them. Yangchen's words sucked the blood from faces, tugged jaws downward, turned the members of her audience to stone.

"What— Why would you say that?" Sidao asked, total shock stripping the high flourishes from his words.

Henshe wiped his mouth with his palm. "Avatar, you know as well as we do the ramifications of using such indelicate language in matters concerning His Majesty the Earth King. Can you explain yourself?"

She could. "According to your latest charters, the shangs of this city are allowed to move cargo with twenty-eight specific authorized grand junks. But I can personally attest to the fact that forty-four distinct ships docked last month."

The lack of response told her the numbers were accurate enough. "They're easier to count from above," Yangchen explained, pointing upward. "I've been surveilling the city for weeks."

Revealing to the shangs that her official arrival date had been false, and she'd been watching them in secret, tipped her hand a great deal. She told herself this was a strategic provocation. Not an attempt to assert herself in a group of older men and women who had shown her contempt.

Jump off a cliff and you might as well flap your arms. "Bribing enough harbormasters to run hidden traffic must be expensive," Yangchen said. "Which means the returns must be significant. Could it be that Bin-Er is generating a large amount of revenue that the Earth King doesn't know about? When we all know how sensitive His Majesty is about not getting his due, thanks to Zongdu Henshe's wonderful lesson?"

Sensitive was an understatement. The man had carved bloody grooves into the world over money. "Even worse," Yangchen continued. "Any ships unaccounted for could be holding spies and other security risks to His Majesty's rule."

No one was chuckling anymore, not even in defense. "If there *is* an excess of money in this city, perhaps it's only a rounding error and can be reconciled by directing the funds to more charitable efforts," she said. "Sometime before I next speak to the Earth King."

Boma cleared his throat. "Avatar, I believe you are scheduled for an audience with His Majesty three months from now."

"Is that so?" Yangchen said. "Well then."

The shangs said nothing. Henshe looked to the side and made a face Yangchen couldn't see. Another brawl he had to clean up. "Thank you, Avatar," he said in a weary rasp, his voice already overused. "I'm sure a reconciliation can be achieved."

FALLBACK PLANS

THE REST of the meeting . . . went. Tongues formed words, words came out of mouths, but nothing of import was said. The Avatar's challenge was an iron pillar in the middle of the road. Every piece of conversation had to go around it.

Toward the end, Yangchen realized how big of a mistake she'd made. She cursed herself over and over again. Strategic provocation, nothing. It was a reckless bet, spurred on by her wounded pride.

The session concluded with a second round of refreshments. Never before had tea been drunk so fast. Yangchen announced she would be returning to her lodgings for the rest of the day, pretending she was hiding a sore throat.

"Avatar, I beg your permission to stay behind a bit," Sidao said. "The hall contains some minor historical artifacts of interest to me."

The request came easily, and his excuse had already been prepared. Sidao collected many times his official salary in

F. C. YEE

kickbacks from the women and men in this room, and he most
certainly had to smooth an entire nest of ruffled feathers. She
gave him her leave.

Henshe offered to see her out and she accepted. Yangchen
walked down the long corridor side by side with the Zongdu
of Bin-Er, Boma trailing behind like a chaperone to a couple
weighing a political marriage.

"Avatar, I . . . ah . . ." Henshe tried to find his footing. "I wish
you had brought the matter of the ships to me first, in private. I
would have been in a better position to help you."

She had been thinking the same thing. The zongdu could
have negotiated with the shangs for better conditions behind
closed doors. She and Henshe together could have let the merchants say no at first, and then chipped away at their stubborn-
ness gradually until a new shape of the future was ready to be
unveiled. They could have pretended it wasn't blackmail.

"I regret the delivery," Yangchen said. "But not the contents.
Your masters are men and women so enamored with themselves
that they justify squeezing commonfolk and cheating kings."

Henshe sighed, as if that were rebuttal enough. *You just
don't know how the world works.* "It's their right to look out for
themselves and their families."

Yangchen *did* know how the world worked; that was why she
acted like she did. "Family isn't an excuse to trample upon others, Master Henshe."

"Well put. I will do what I can to convince them of your wisdom." Henshe bowed slowly, deeply, the full gesture of respect
for an Avatar.

His wince on the way down brought forth a surge of pity
in Yangchen. She could believe in this moment Sidao's claim
of equivalence between an Avatar and a zongdu. "I'm sorry for
causing you trouble."

Henshe shrugged and smiled. "Problem-solving. It's our job."

70

Yangchen waited until he was gone before beckoning Boma closer. "I need you to do something for me." She whispered instructions in his ear.

She had to salvage something useful from the pieces of the deadlock she'd so clumsily broken. The shangs would react. Confer with each other. If they were going to blow wind, she needed to know the direction.

Boma's whiskers twitched as she explained her plan. "*Please* reconsider."

"It's just listening. Is that not my job as the Avatar? To listen?"

He had to offer a token amount of resistance to her ploys to soothe his conscience. He'd sworn an oath to the Western elders to keep her safe. Luckily, she wasn't planning anything as dangerous as fighting a giant armored spirit right now. "Tell me when," Boma said.

"I will. Keep walking."

The two of them strolled down the vaulted corridor of the hall. Searing brightness came through the windows, the higher sun reflecting off the snow. They reached the door Yangchen had memorized from the building plans Kavik nearly stole before she had the chance to. She took a quick glance around once they were shielded from view by a little foyer. "Now," she said.

Yangchen twirled off her heavy hooded cloak and draped it over Boma's shoulders. As he stepped out into the snow, he tried to get a little bit more height by straightening his back and rising on the balls of his feet. Anyone watching from the second floor would see the Avatar heading back to her bison.

The effect was . . . not good. Boma's impersonation of her looked tipsy, and she'd failed to consider the obvious. Two people leaving were now one.

She didn't have time to bemoan the shortcomings of her plan. She earthbent a section off the plastered-over wall next to her, keeping the bricks together as a single panel, to reveal a cramped nook. She stepped inside and pulled the brickwork shut behind her as tightly she could.

This maintenance tunnel was her access point to the underground flues running below the original gathering hall. In days long past, hot air and smoke from an ancient furnace flowed underneath the leaders of Bin-Er to keep them warm. Yangchen didn't know why the system had been abandoned when the hall was rebuilt through successive generations. Maybe a cost problem. She flicked her hand open to hold a candle's worth of flame and looked around.

She frowned once her eyes adjusted to the darkness. The dusty gap before her was between knee and waist high. The plans had been a top-down view only and made no mention of this axis.

No matter. She lowered herself, wadding up her robes and her body as much as she could, and shoved her legs into the crevice. With a series of grunts, she managed to get her whole body underneath the floor.

She had just enough space to roll onto her belly and start crawling. The heat chamber hadn't been cleaned before it was abandoned for good, and she had to make her way across a layer of soot.

Her head bumped into one of the squat stone columns that supported the layer above her. These, at least, had been on the map. From the entry point, she wanted to go five columns north, twenty columns east.

Twenty. She had to hurry.

Ghostly cobwebs brushed across her face and flecks of ash wandered up her nose, forcing her to snort them out like an ostrich-horse. Boma and Sidao alike would have withered in shame at the indignity she was subjecting herself to.

For a good cause. And I remember doing more embarrassing things than this, many times over.

Theoretically, her ploy would work. Vital intelligence had been gathered over the centuries by eavesdropping behind secret hollows of the Fire Temple and opaque screens in the Northern Water Tribe palace. She could already hear an attendant pass above her, muttering to himself about the poor mood his master would be in later this evening. But she needed to make it back to the assembly room, and quick, if she wanted to gain any product of relevance.

Her bulky, dragging robes snagged on a crumbling column. Yangchen swore under her breath using words she'd overheard down at the docks. She rolled onto her side and tugged hard on her caught hem. There was a *chak!* where she expected to hear a tear.

The sturdy wool had pulled an entire section of mortar loose. Her eyes widened as a crack traveled up the column and across the upper surface of the chamber. Heavy stone tiles began to drop.

Her light went out as she traded firebending with one hand for earthbending with two, catching the masonry before a crash gave her away. She managed to stay the tiles farthest away, like a servant in a stage comedy floundering for spilled teacups, but the last chunk came down right over her and broke its fall on her ribs.

Yangchen gasped in the dark. The tile that had made it through the defenses she'd been so vain about earlier hadn't traveled far, but it was heavy and sharp. Worse, the pain was excruciatingly familiar to someone who wasn't her.

The right kind of hurt delivered at the right time could knock her off-kilter no matter how many of Abbess Dagmola's exercises she'd performed in the morning. In the void of the chamber, there was no sight or sound of the present for her to latch on to. The chalky air scraped her throat raw. Her heart slammed against the walls of her chest, trying to break free.

"Not you," she dared to whisper, the need for silence pushed aside. "Not you. Not you."

She didn't know whose terror had paralyzed her, whose memories had boxed her in, but it didn't matter. It was pure math. Out of a thousand lives, at least a few Avatars would have been debilitatingly afraid of confined spaces.

It was *their* fingernails raking across the soot, seeking purchase. *Their* voices closing shut in a chorus of suffocation. She fought to maintain control. *Avatar Yangchen isn't afraid of being buried alive. You're not going to die here. You're not going to die.*

But she had perished so many times, hadn't she? The downside of being endlessly reborn, the endless ends. Her body and mind remembered how to take a final breath. Yangchen clamped her arms around her stomach and curled in on herself, trying to compact into a featureless lump before the closing walls did it themselves.

WAKE UP.

A voice from her own memories. Not a previous Avatar's. Jetsun's voice.

WAKE UP.

Her own memories. Hadn't the Water Tribe boy who'd tried to crawl through the walls of her room gotten stuck like this? He had survived. His name was Kavik, and he'd survived his ordeal. She was fairly certain.

She blinked slowly. No one else in the cycle had met the audacious burglar named Kavik. The boy's name was Kavik, and he had nice teeth, and she'd held his frozen hands until they warmed. Yangchen had done that. Her name was Yangchen, and she wasn't afraid of cramped spaces any more than she was of soaring heights.

She took a deep breath and gagged on dust. Right. She was in the middle of embarrassing herself for the sake of duty. Who *but* Yangchen could she be?

The bout of someone else's fear had cost her time. Seconds, hours, she couldn't be sure. She'd find out once she got to where she was going. Reaching out to judge the space, she aligned herself in the direction she hoped east was. She'd done this trick once before, through the pillars of an airball field, and Jetsun had been furious at her for a week.

Let it be said that the Avatar who followed Szeto was more foolhardy than fearful. Yangchen grabbed the crumbling columns to the left and right of her and launched herself forward, spinning like an arrow with offset fletching.

Her robes wound around her body while she bent a spray of air that kept her from colliding with floor or ceiling. She landed on her back and skidded to a stop. Amazed she hadn't dashed her brains out, she snapped her fingers for a flicker of light and counted the columns. Twenty-two. Overshot by a bit, but close enough.

Voices above her, the creak of benches, told her she was back under the assembly room where she could listen to the shangs' response to the fire she'd set to their seats.

There were people above her, but little conversation. In a massive stroke of luck, it seemed like she hadn't missed much. The shangs were waiting, probably for Henshe, whose voice she hadn't registered yet.

She would have to be patient as well. Yangchen made herself as comfortable as she could and settled in for her opponent's turn.

OUTSIDE OPTIONS

HENSHE SPLASHED water from the basin across his face. It was cold enough to blue his lips if he dunked his head in it for more than a minute. He was a "Middler," as the Water Tribe youths of Bin-Er liked to call people from the Earth Kingdom and Fire Nation, but he never really minded the frigid climate. It was and always had been the least of his concerns.

He squeezed his eyes shut, letting the liquid drip down his nose. Then he grasped the small wooden tub with both hands and hurled it against the far wall of the empty barracks. The water spilled across the floor. The basin made a hollow *thunk* and bounced instead of breaking, as if to make light of his rage.

This is what he'd been reduced to. Hiding in the washroom, weeping. He wanted to scream at the injustice of it all.

Henshe took his time drying his face with his sleeve. Ablutions were one of the few moments of the day when he wasn't at the beck and call of the shangs. They'd harangue him in his dreams if they could. He walked past the empty wooden beds, the weap-onless racks. Bin-Er, like its sister cities in the other nations, was allowed nothing to protect itself against the sovereign land around it.

In the hallway, he beckoned the leader of his watchers over, a young woman named Miki. He had placed attendants around the windows and corners and told them to stay on the lookout for anything suspicious. "Where's the Avatar?" he asked.

"She left. I saw her take off on her bison."

"And her companion?"

Miki's eyes widened. "I don't know."

Henshe stared at her. "You lost track of a slow-moving old man?"

The woman couldn't answer. She was a non-bender with a younger brother at home, Henshe remembered. Not the healthiest scamp, always sick with some kind of cough or another.

"I'll tell you what, Miki." He gestured at a bamboo scaffolding reaching all the way up to the highest window of the hall, long forgotten from an interior repainting job abandoned halfway. "Why don't you go check that he's not on the roof, spying on us this very moment?"

"The—the roof, sir?"

"I know it's steep and a little icy, but it's where I need you the most right now." Henshe placed his hand on her shoulder. "We've been put at a disadvantage because we didn't consider anyone watching us from an elevated position. Let's not make the same mistake twice."

Henshe paid all his watchers out of his own coffer, and he'd specifically chosen people with few alternative means of making a living. Without his continued blessing, they'd be on the streets. Miki's lip trembled, but she went to the scaffolding and, with difficulty, hauled herself up to the first level.

The joints of the structure were loose from neglect. The bamboo wobbled and creaked under her weight, months-old dust raining down. She looked back over her shoulder before attempting to climb any higher. Henshe smiled encouragingly at her.

"You're doing great, Miki," he said. "Keep up the good work."

A few deep breaths were necessary before he parted the doors to the assembly room. The men and women inside were already standing. Had they been mirrors in the sun, he would have been cooked alive.

Henshe maintained his grin. "What a meeting, huh?"

Teiin, famous among the Bin-Er commonfolk for never saying a word in public, was the first to lose it. "I don't like being pointed at, Henshe!" he screamed. *"I don't like being pointed at!* You said you would handle the Avatar! That wasn't handling it!"

Teiin whipped around so he could tear into Sidao, who was supposed to be their spy on the inside of the Avatar's retinue. "And you! What do we pay you for, you idiot? You let her scout the docks for nearly a month? How hard is it to keep track of a single girl?"

"She's unpredictable!" Sidao wailed. "None of this would have happened if you all had kept the flow of traffic within limits!"

Wrong response. The people who paid you were never at fault. Henshe watched as the merchants swarmed upon Sidao, a school of fish devouring a floating corpse. Something about this city stripped away decorum from its people and exposed the raw skeletons underneath. A high-ranking Fire National would never throw a tantrum in a formal setting. An Earth Kingdom citizen forgetting to maintain face? A Water Tribe trader withholding their legendary generosity? Unheard of. Unless they were shangs.

An Air Nomad having us by the throat, Henshe mused. Only in Bin-Er.

As fun as it was to watch Sidao suffer instead of himself for a change, Henshe did need to do his job. He walked up to the raised dais where the Avatar had sat and stamped his foot like bailiffs of years gone by. "My friends," he said. "Please remain calm."

Mistress Noehi, who had so enjoyed provoking the Avatar earlier, chewed on her knuckle like a soup bone. "Calm?! The Earth King is going to raze us to the ground, Henshe! *You* try staying calm!"

He was. He was trying. Unlike the rest of them, he couldn't afford public panic. Henshe continued to beat a jig on the platform until everyone was paying attention to him. "My *esteemed* friends! As hard as it is to believe, we should be grateful to the young Avatar."

There was no way Henshe could get away with saying that if he hadn't a solution in store. So the shangs gave him the benefit of the doubt and let him continue. "She's reminded us of the fatal flaw in our system," he said. "We exist purely at the whim of a petulant Earth King. Nor are we any less vulnerable to the Fire Lord, or the Chief of the Water Tribe, should they decide to back out of their trade agreements. Any head of state could end us if they wanted to."

Noehi snorted. "Are you saying you have a way to fix that flaw?"

"I do. You've heard me talk about it before. Unanimity."

A few of the younger shangs, those who had more recently come into their positions, didn't recognize the code name. "I thought the Unanimity project was a goose-monkey chase," said the old stalwart Teiin. "A theoretical obsession of your predecessor. He never shared with us the details, only the possibilities."

"I assure you it's completely real, and it's finished," Henshe said. "Dooshim was working on it with Zongdu Chaisee of Jonduri, just in case a scenario like this one ever occurred."

The shangs were nervous despite the project representing the very answer they were looking for. Henshe found their indecisiveness abhorrent. At least the Avatar had the courage to escalate.

"We have been caught out in a bad position," Henshe said. "Unanimity is how we recover our footing. We never had a solid position to fall back on when it came to negotiating with the Earth King, but we do now."

He paced along the dais, around the grand chair and the small table where the Avatar's tea setting remained. "If we bring it into play, neither the Avatar nor the Earth King will have power over us. We'll have complete impunity. The Earth King will sign any charter you want him to sign. We'll be able to rewrite the laws in Omashu if we feel like. And the Avatar will be forced to keep her nose out of other people's business."

This was where the nun had erred. To reach agreement on something, you overpromised first and worried about the delivery later. You sold the moon for a silver piece and handed over a ladder. "Now," Henshe said, "I will do what I always do and solve this problem for you. Any objections?"

None, for once. Henshe picked up the half-full cup the Avatar had left behind and raised it in the air. Toasting himself since no one else would, using his opponent's words. "To our future." He drained the rest of her tea.

One of the stupidest parts about being the zongdu was how you were judged on a day-to-day, moment-to-moment basis. Have one bad conversation in the morning and you were a failure forever. Make a convincing speech in the afternoon and you were solid. A reliable presence.

Today Henshe was so-so at his job. He'd brought a sliver of hope to a disaster with nothing but sheer confidence. As the shangs left, Mistress Noehi gave him parting words. "What's mine is mine, Henshe," she said. "I'm not giving up what I've earned. You'd better see to that."

"Of course." Henshe hid his scoff with his bow. Noehi acted like she'd clawed her riches from the sea with her bare hands, when she probably had never seen a spiraled oyster that hadn't already been shucked. Her father had been granted the pearl monopoly simply because he'd had the same calligraphy tutor as the Earth King, and then he died of a heart clutch, leaving the entire business to his daughter.

Earned. That was the thing about these merchants. They feigned enterprise and risk-taking when all they were doing was drinking from a river no one else was allowed to approach.

After they left, Henshe almost didn't realize Minister Sidao was still in the room. Once it was just the two of them, the Avatar's advisor sat down on the dais itself and hugged his knees, as if Henshe cared about his troubles and was going to offer a shoulder to cry on.

"I'm as good as burned," Sidao moaned. "There's no way Teiin or anyone else will keep me on after today."

You're old enough to be my father, you pathetic sea slug. "Don't worry about it," Henshe said, staring at the man's back. "You're not burned until she signs your dismissal. In fact, you have the most important role to play here. I need you to personally deliver the message to Zongdu Chaisee in Jonduri that we're moving forward with Unanimity. She needs to quit dawdling and make sure the shipments get to Bin-Er as soon as possible."

Sidao stroked his beard, latching on to the glimmer of hope that his pockets would remain as heavy as always. "You're not going to send her a messenger hawk?"

"Chaisee doesn't do important business by hawk; she doesn't think they're secure enough." One of Henshe's many annoyances with her. "This is going to require an in-person visit."

"What exactly is Unanimity?"

Like I'd share that information with a gob like you. "A means of making a very convincing argument. Chaisee will explain everything after you deliver the message."

"My traveling rights are linked to the Avatar's official business," Sidao said. "I'll have to trick her into declaring Jonduri as her next official stop."

Henshe was struck by the peculiarity of two grown men plotting their hearts out against a young girl, an Air Nomad no less. *We've declared war on the Avatar,* he thought. *She just doesn't know it yet.* "That shouldn't be hard. She'll want to try her message again with a different audience; I'll bet she's already planning to visit Jonduri as the next stop on her tour. Make sure you give her the impression that she'll get what she wants there."

The Master of Elements was still a person with needs, and he knew people and their needs. "The Avatar should have what she desires most," Henshe said. "A pretty little place in history. A few paper victories and a nicely burnished image. She'll be able to show the Four Nations she *cared*."

He stared at the empty chair on the dais. "Do you know what former Zongdu Dooshim did after he left the job?"

"No," Sidao said, despite being the one to bring up the man's name earlier. "Why?"

Case in point. "I'll tell you. Dooshim took his mountains of gold and bought an inn near Su Oku. Spent his days soaking in oils and perfume over a rushing waterfall. And then he died! Peacefully in his sleep. He got in and got out."

Henshe sighed. "No one really keeps track of my predecessors. No one cares to remember them. They all got what they wanted, and then disappeared one way or another."

A faint scream came from outside, and then a plummeting *thud* like a clump of snow sliding off the roof.

"How lucky they were, no?" Henshe said.

Yangchen reentered the inn where she was staying through the window. Boma was waiting in her room, nodding off in a chair. When he saw her, covered in soot and robes torn, he yelped in fright.

"WHAT—" He quickly caught himself and lowered his voice. *"What happened?"*

"Not now. Just . . . not now."

Boma had seen her in every state and every mood, hurt and healthy. He knew when she needed space. He nodded and left. Yangchen sat on her bed without bothering to change and laid her face on her hands. She rolled her cheeks against her palms, up and down.

The zongdu's viciousness, his complete lack of hesitation, had shaken her. His initial performance as the beleaguered administrator had been so convincing. Was she losing her touch? First Kavik had nearly tricked her with his poor little pious thief act, and now this.

The dirt pilled between her skin. Her escape had been a matter of waiting until Sidao and Henshe left, and then slowly, painstakingly earthbending herself a passage that led a safe distance away from the building. She'd emerged from the ground, covered the hole, and made a leap onto a nearby roof without anyone noticing her. Functionally, a clean getaway.

But then she'd spotted a disturbance back at the hall, the kind of crowd that formed around misery. She laid low and waited until the slow-moving hubbub passed underneath her.

Peering over the edge, she saw an unconscious woman being carried away on a stretcher, her body limp and arm twisted.

It must have happened while Yangchen was still under the surface of the ground. She wanted more than anything to drop down and provide healing right then and there. But had she reappeared so quickly, Henshe would figure out she'd never left the gathering hall. A few leaps of logic and he might realize she'd listened in on his plans.

So she waited, her nails chiseling crescents into her palms, until the stretcher passed. Whoever the injured woman was, her pain was on Yangchen now. The Avatar who didn't help.

She had to make amends. Both to the woman she'd ignored, and the people of this city as a whole. She would never be able to make things right if her opponents possessed a trick up their sleeves that made them untouchable.

Unanimity. What kind of project or asset or weapon could give Henshe and the shangs such confidence against the Earth King? Yes, Yangchen had brought the mercurial, rage-prone ruler into play in a clumsy manner. But His Majesty should have represented the boundary where the Avatar and the shangs, recognizing a mutual danger, agreed to back away and stay within certain limits.

Henshe had assured his masters that soon they would have no limits. "Unanimity" would make them answerable to no one. She couldn't have that. She didn't think the world could handle that. It fell upon her to deny the shangs their prize.

Sometimes Yangchen wondered if she was justified in racing out to meet problems instead of reacting. But she had dozens upon dozens of times observed passive Avatars, lived their overwhelming regret and shame. She would remember Tienhaishi in her own life and think about how differently things might have worked out had she been able to talk to Old Iron earlier, before he donned his armor and reached land.

Nowhere in any great library of the world did it say one had to let a mighty injustice occur before getting out of your chair. Better to parry the sword than heal the wound it made in the flesh.

Yangchen stood and flicked the rolled-up dirt from her hands. *If you want a fight, I'll give you one.* She called Boma back in and gave him instructions to search every doctor near the gathering hall for an injured woman matching a certain description and pay for her treatment with the rest of the Bin-Er budget.

Once he returned, he could help her pack. "If you're leaving the city, this may be a good chance to ditch Sidao," Boma said. "Corrupt little elbow leech couldn't even hide which side he was playing for very well."

"No, not yet." She'd play as dumb as she could about the minister's loyalties. Henshe's message to his fellow zongdu in Jonduri had to be delivered by a trusted courier, after all. "Sidao and I have travel plans to discuss."

And she, alone, had a recruiting pitch to complete. One that had suddenly leaped in importance.

THE TRADE

NEW RULE, Kavik thought. No more traveling through the square itself, no matter how big of a detour he had to make.

It was simply too risky. Since Teiin's forceful exit from the Gidu Shrine, the square had become a regular meeting place for the people of Bin-Er to air their grievances. More men and women flocked to the crowd every day, and their chants against the shangs could be heard from blocks away, carried on the wind.

The ice was building. The waters were foaming. A time would come when the center of Bin-Er collapsed in on itself, and since Kavik didn't know when that was, he would simply never be there, ever. To avoid the whirlpool, you avoided the boat.

He still managed to get to the teahouse on time. The Golden Cloudberry, unfamiliar to him. The interior was dark and full of corners created by partial walls and screens. The proprietor was busy in the back, judging by the sounds of clanking pots. Kavik kept his hood on and waited.

Qiu arrived, and to Kavik's annoyance, chose to sit down in the booth behind him so they were back-to-back. He supposed the older boy wanted to mask their conversation, but the act didn't help when they were the only two customers in the shop.

Whatever. After his disaster with the Avatar, Kavik no longer had any grounds to complain about someone else's skill at legwork. "You cabbage slug," Kavik muttered. "You knew whose room you were sending me into, didn't you?"

"You were safer than you've ever been," Qiu said. Replying to the empty air in front of him wasn't suspicious at all, no. "What's an Air Nomad going to do, kill you? Listen to you bellyache. You got in and out without a hitch."

Kavik mulled over the blatantly false statement. So word on the street hadn't linked him to the Avatar. Dinner with his folks had remained a secret, and whether it was out of lingering loyalty or a hefty exit payment, the fired guards hadn't spread the news in Bin-Er about an intruder in the Blue Manse.

Which meant the market value of the letter he'd stolen from Yangchen was still perfect, as high as it got. "It wasn't a perfect run. I was able to grab an envelope and that's it."

He heard the rustle of Qiu straightening up in excitement and then the slump of him trying to play it cool. "Could be nothing. You didn't damage the seal, did you?"

"See for yourself." He held the envelope out, low and behind him. Qiu groped around blindly until his fingers landed on the paper and snatched it away like a starving snowgull fighting over a dropped bun.

Kavik let his broker take his time examining the outside of the letter. Sad as it was, Qiu was the closest thing he had left to a friend these days. Once the residents of the Water Tribe Quarter stopped talking to him, his social circle had withered down to just his fellow miscreants in errand running. Mama Ayunerak didn't count.

"Enough playing around," Kavik said. "I just picked you over the Avatar, and she's a lot prettier. Tell me what I want to know." He ran the pad of his thumb over his fingers. He didn't want to add up the price of this answer, not really. The going rate for an errand runner was easy enough to tally, but the discord with his parents wasn't.

"All right, so my contact in the pass control office was able to get some time alone with the records. She doesn't find Kalyaan's name in the approved section, but she finds a description. *Water Tribe man with eight fingers applying for exit out of Bin-Er. Destination to be decided,* which is really rare. That's got to be him, right? She says the pass was granted around the last time you or I or anyone else heard from him."

Qiu shifted in his seat. "It's like you suspected. Your brother's gone."

Kavik, twelve years old, had been nervous about stepping onto the soil of the continent. Though the gray climate was little different on this side of the strait, the journey across the water had boiled his fears into a heavy lump.

"We'll make the leap together," Kalyaan said to him. "If we do, the spirits will keep us safe no matter what."

At his instruction, the entire family shed their mittens and made a chain. Kavik grasped his brother's hand, his fist fitting neatly into the space left behind by Kalyaan's missing ring and pinkie fingers. While Kalyaan counted down from ten, their parents playfully teased their younger son for being silly, and their eldest for humoring him with such a bad idea. The wind stung and chapped their exposed skin.

Kalyaan stayed on focus and winked at Kavik. ". . . three . . . two . . . *one!*"

The four of them stepped off their umiak in perfect unison and cheered, swinging their still-connected arms high in the air. The other families making their landings rolled their eyes and shook their heads, but Kavik felt more relief than he could describe. He hadn't fallen through the gravel or been skewered with arrows. The charm of unity had protected them.

The great docks of Bin-Er lay off to the side where the water was deeper. Workers swarmed the fat-bellied cargo ships made of overlaid wood planks and broke down their contents with iron hooks and shovels. Barrels rolled down improvised ramps, sometimes falling into the water with a splash, but no pause was spared to recover them. A certain amount of lost goods were acceptable casualties.

The activity reminded Kavik of a polar bear–dog feeding on a carcass, scraps of wasted meat flying across the snow, and he shuddered. But his convoy from the North had made the trip without fuss in their own vessels, the shallow drafts allowing them to beach safely. Just like any other move between camps.

Maybe this new land wouldn't be so bad, he thought as man in a heavy green uniform walked up to greet them.

Early on in his duties as a junior clerk at Nuqingaq's, Kavik had marveled at how *steady* the wages were. You knew exactly how much coin you were going to make every week. And while you couldn't chance upon a bounty on the level of a whale-walrus or a net bursting with a whole school of cuttle-perch, you'd never go wanting for too long either.

How lucky he was, he used to think as he rubbed his bleary eyes at his table. Many of his benchmates had come to Bin-Er on their own, leaving wives and husbands and parents and children behind, but Kavik was and always would be with the people he loved most under one roof.

Kalyaan stayed with Nuqingaq's for less than six moons.

He hadn't shown any signs of dissatisfaction. He just failed to show up for his shift one morning, and then again the next. There was no third time because he was fired and barred from ever setting foot on the shop floor again.

The silent ruckus that followed Kalyaan leaving his job and the way the family became pariahs inside their own place of employment taught Kavik a lot about how things really worked in Bin-Er. Through eavesdropping on upset exchanges between his coworkers, he learned the true asset of Nuqingaq and Partners wasn't its low error rate but its highly limited involvement in the greater swirl of forces in the city.

Because its employees kept to themselves and had such little contact with anyone from the Fire Nation and Earth Kingdom, because the business wasn't in the pocket of a particular shang, in principle they would be left alone. And it would be easier for them to get exit passes to leave Bin-Er when they wished. But Kalyaan suddenly going off by himself to whereabouts unknown threatened that privilege—assuming it had ever really existed.

For the incautious, Bin-Er was a fishing weir that drew them in and didn't let them go. No one at the bookkeepers, Kavik included, wanted to live in the city forever. Putting the group at risk because of your own foolhardiness simply wasn't done in the poles. You looked out for your own.

Kalyaan still came home in the evenings, though he deflected any questions about what he was doing. He had found different work, he told Kavik. Everything was fine.

Whatever new job he had, it paid better than bookkeeping by orders of magnitude. At Nuqingaq's, Kavik heard the whispers about his brother, and they used words like *runner. Lackey. Spy.*

Kalyaan started coming home less and less often. That was fine too. Young men and women moved out of their parents' houses; that was to be expected. Sure, it usually coincided with a marriage, but Kalyaan was as tight-lipped about his social life as he was his working hours.

He also gifted them an entire new house. Not forcibly but forcefully. It was better to live closer to the international district, he said. Sure, the wooden structure was harder to keep clean and warm, but it was *better*. Why? Kavik didn't know, and neither did his parents. They listened to Kalyaan and moved their oil lamp and the rest of their belongings. He sounded very confident. The change in residence did not go unnoticed by their neighbors.

Then one morning, it happened. All the bookkeepers, clerks, and assistants were called to the shop floor. Someone with intimate knowledge of the client list and the timing of their contract renewals had poached their most critical customers, the boss explained. Many of the people gathered here were going to lose their jobs.

Kavik watched as his neighbors were culled. His first real lesson in how an agreement, a numerical projection, arcane words floating without a trace through the physical world, could lead to a person losing their livelihood. He and his father survived untouched. There didn't seem to be any logic behind the decision.

The Water Tribe Quarter rallied around their members who weren't as lucky. It was their way to support each other. But there was no doubt who was to blame for the incident, because Kalyaan never came home again after that.

Kavik and his parents waited for him while suffering their due. In the poles, those who committed unforgivable offenses against the community might wake up one day to find the camp had moved on without them. There was nowhere to move to in

Bin-Er, except around corners when Kavik approached, away when he sat down at the workbench, off to the side when he tried to speak.

Was there a breaking point? A specific moment when he'd swallowed too much of Bin-Er, and his body reacted to purge itself? He couldn't remember. Kavik *could* remember how brightly the obvious solution to his problems burned in his mind as he put on his parka and became the second person ever to voluntarily walk out of Nuqingaq's.

Most kinds of quarry rewarded patience, but there were some exceptions. You didn't wander off in a random direction when stalking a herd of finned caribou; nor did you sit down and freeze, waiting for them to return. You followed their tracks as closely as you could. To find his brother, he would have to walk in his brother's footsteps.

Kavik would run errands just like Kalyaan had. He would play the game and hunt down leads until he caught up to the former golden child of Long Stretch. And then he would drag him back home, kicking and screaming if necessary, so their family could leave this spirits-forsaken city the same way they arrived.

Together.

The start of his quest. The hard knocks of learning the information game had been shiny and charming for a while, as much as picking through stolen meeting minutes and absorbing back-alley drubbings could be.

But that vow had taken place a long time ago. His self-imposed mission was dead now, Qiu its less-than-likely pallbearer. He didn't know what to do.

Assuming Qiu was telling the truth, the timing lined up. It would explain why Kavik was having so much trouble finding a man in a city most people weren't allowed to leave. And it would mean that his older brother, without so much as a word or a letter, had walked out on his family and left them behind for good.

Kavik felt very small and alone, sitting across from no one. He cleared his throat. He cleared his throat again.

"Hey," Qiu said in a rare moment of sympathy. "I'm sorry. I know Water Tribe families are close."

"Yeah, I . . ." He wanted to talk about something else. "What are you going to do with the letter?"

"Same as Kalyaan. Ditch this place." Qiu wasn't so sorry or so sensitive as to avoid treading on the fresh wound. He smacked the paper. "I know where I can get in touch with agents representing overseas buyers. They'll bring me to them. I'm aiming for Taku. Getting out of the cold for good."

Qiu didn't have anyone to take with him. Kavik pushed the shapeless feeling inside him away, before it had the chance to become pity or envy.

Qiu got up and rearranged his heavy coat as he left. He paused by the door, giving Kavik a view of the undisguised glee on his round, pockmarked face. He was free. "Give Kalyaan my best if you ever see him again," he said, and disappeared into the street.

And with that, Kavik's chances of reuniting his family melted away. He slumped in his seat and pressed his skull against the booth wall until it hurt.

READING LEAVES

"ORDER SOMETHING or get out."

Kavik opened his eyes to see a gruff old man shaped like a barrel standing over him. He thumped the bamboo platter he'd been drying for emphasis, displeased that a potential customer had dipped in and out without spending anything.

They engaged in a stare down. Kavik was going to comply, but in the slowest, most annoying way possible. He was in a mood.

"Sorry, sorry," said a voice on the cusp of familiarity. "He was waiting for me."

A figure slid into the seat across from him. She wore plain Earth Kingdom winter clothing of quilted cotton, probably to avoid the furs of the Water Tribe or Fire Nation. Her hair, though, was carefully styled in a pair of upper-class buns. Thick, impenetrable bangs reached down over her forehead to her eyebrows.

This was the second time he'd shared a table with the Avatar and still he was nearly fooled.

"The square is completely blocked," she explained to Kavik, her breath short. "I had to go all the way around. I hope you're not upset with me."

"Of course he isn't, dear," said the owner, suddenly all smiles. "Please, take your time. The menu's on the slate board."

Kavik frowned at the old man. *Really?* He got nothing but a warning sneer back, as if his new company were too good for him.

Spiritually speaking, she was. "That's some wig," Kavik said to Yangchen once they were alone.

"Do you like it?" She mockingly primped the sides with her gloved hands. "I hear the style's all the rage in the Fire Nation. Unfortunately my clothes don't match, but it was the best disguise I could put together on short notice."

She looked more fetching than he cared to admit. "It's only slightly less subtle than giant blue tattoos."

"Yeah, well, I don't have much of a choice. This city has given me its official welcome. I've got so many watchers posted on me now that Avatar Yangchen can't say hello to anyone in the street without the shangs knowing."

Hmph. If anything, Kavik's attempted burglary was her introduction to how things worked in Bin-Er. "Did you get a good enough look at my broker?"

"I did. You weren't lying about being independent. That guy's the opposite of a power player. Sloppiest handoff I've ever seen."

Before leaving his house the other night, Yangchen, in one last jab to his professional pride, told Kavik he hadn't been as quick-fingered as he'd thought. She'd seen him pilfer the envelope from her room and stuff it into his boot. But instead of demanding it back, she instructed him to deliver it to Qiu as promised. "What was in it?" he asked.

"Garbage. I make fake versions of my correspondence from time to time, each copy different in one tiny but critical way, and let them get intercepted. Based on how my opponents react, I can trace the chains of leaks. I also wanted to protect you in case someone along the way got upset you came back empty-handed. This way, everything's fine."

Wow. If Kavik worked for the Avatar, he'd have a much smarter, more diligent boss than Qiu. But they weren't quite there yet, were they? "I thought about your offer," he said. "I need more specifics. It's only fair to tell me what I might be getting into."

She took her time answering. Kavik had intentionally put her in a difficult spot, and fairness had nothing to do with it. She could reveal more and risk him fleeing with knowledge of her intentions or lose her potential new recruit. The choice was hers.

After some thought she made her decision, and Kavik could see the determination flow through her posture like water through a pump. The girl did not hesitate once she settled on a course of action.

"I have reason to believe the shangs of Bin-Er and Jonduri are planning to get their hands on an asset that would give them unlimited leverage over the people inside their cities and the Four Nations as a whole," Yangchen said. "I need someone to help me intercept it and make sure it never sees the light of day."

Interesting. "What is this asset?"

"I don't know yet. Logic would dictate it's some kind of weapon, but I'm having trouble imagining what could give a bunch of merchants enough power and confidence to think they can turn their noses up at the leaders of the world combined. It fits in shipping crates and can be packed on a boat."

"Maybe it's lots of weapons?" Kavik suggested. "Enough swords to arm a force of their own?"

"It could be, but the shangs would be foolish to think they could put together more steel than a single division of the Earth King's army. I've run through so many possibilities. Poison, or an apothecarial drug. A secret, maybe, blackmail on a head of state. A small, compact treasure of immense value? I know High Chieftain Oyaluk is obsessed with recovering his family's lost dynastic amulet and would give nearly anything to get it back."

Yangchen rubbed her eyes. It looked like the questions had cost her sleep. "They call it Unanimity," she said. "That's all I have."

Very, very interesting. "I assume there's not enough evidence to get the rulers of the Four Nations involved."

"I don't *want* any of them involved," she said. "If Unanimity is as powerful as the shangs believe, then it could tilt the world in favor of whoever possesses it. I would like to find out what the asset is, and then make it go away. Quietly."

A surge of yelling outside turned their heads. A group of people on their way to the square, raising their voices early. The spell of curiosity she'd cast over Kavik broke. "This is bizarre," he said, shaking his head. "You're the Avatar, and you're plotting schemes in a dark teahouse. Why aren't you out there, keeping the peace?"

"Keeping the peace?" There was a vibration in the air. "What do you believe that entails, *keeping the peace*? Are you of the opinion that I should fly above the square and tell the hungry and poor of Bin-Er they should shut up and go home?"

"I didn't mean it like that."

"You did until I pushed you." She slumped in her bench, sullen, looking like her age for once, the same as Kavik's. "I tried talking to the people who could have made a real difference, and they spat in my face. The shangs are going to continue to run roughshod over the people of this city unless I can deny them the power of Unanimity. I presume you've heard of the waterbending saying, 'A feather's weight moves a wagon's load'?"

He had. A classical teaching to focus on redirecting force instead of relying on brute opposition. Subtle moves for maximum effect. "This scheme, as you put it, is where I apply the feather," Yangchen said. "If I can even manage that."

She scoured her eyes again, and when her fingertips came away, they were damp. "I'm tired." A normal thing to say, but she made it come across like a grave confession of an unforgivable crime. "I'm very tired of fighting this battle over and over."

The proprietor came out from the back, carrying a steaming kettle. He plunked it down on the table, followed by two large cups filled with pearls of dried tea, even though they hadn't ordered anything yet. "Here, darling," he said to the disguised Yangchen. "Our best, on the house. You look like you need it."

Kavik sputtered over the principle of the thing. No shopkeeper in Bin-Er gave stuff away to normal customers. The old man didn't know she was the Avatar. She wasn't even in her Air Nomad clothes.

"Thank you, uncle," Yangchen said. She reached for the pot and poured.

As the tea steeped, she found a hidden reserve of energy to chat with the owner about Bin-Er and how it must have changed over the years in his eyes. Talking face-to-face seemed to be her style with people regardless of whether they knew she was the Avatar. The man eagerly shared his opinions with an attentive listener. By the time he was done, Yangchen was all but his legal heir.

"You," the owner said to Kavik. "You treat a nice girl like her right, you hear?" He let loose a final warning glare and went to tend the stove.

Kavik watched the leaves unfurl in his cup. "Is this job going to be dangerous?" he asked. He knew the answer, but there were rituals. Meaningless statements passed off as due diligence.

"What do you think?" She didn't hold back her snort. "It's going to make powerful people very angry. Funny how we're talking about it, no? We have ourselves to blame if anything bad happens, not them."

At least she was being honest. "I have a price," Kavik said.

"I suppose you do. Name it."

The request came so easy, as if it were a retaliation against his vanished brother. After Qiu's revelation, there was nothing left holding him and his parents to Bin-Er. "I want passes out of the city for me and my family. Real ones. I want them so clean you could eat off them." She didn't respond. "As the Avatar you can get those, can you not?"

"I can. It's just . . ." She bit her lip. "Your parents said it themselves. The Bin-Er control office is one of the most corrupt, leaky institutions on the continent. If I put your names through the process, it'll be a signal pyre to the shangs that you're working for me, and you'd become useless as a spy. I wouldn't be able to procure the passes until you complete the mission."

He could guess why she was uncomfortable. "You don't like how that makes you feel," Kavik said. "You would like to show an act of generosity first and then have me serve you out of a sense of obligation. The goodness of my heart."

The emotions behind gifts were tricky, Kavik knew well. "But if we go in this order, you're withholding payment until I finish rendering services. It makes it more obvious that you're simply using me to get what you want."

The Middler expression he'd heard used was "sky-pointing needle," referring to a scale that had been balanced down to the motes of dust. A perfectly reciprocal transaction. Once a foreign, abhorrent idea to a Water Tribe child who'd been raised to share without counting, to give everyone he met what they needed without keeping score.

"Welcome to Bin-Er," Kavik muttered. "Do you have any other options?"

Yangchen sighed. "I do not. I need an agent in Jonduri immediately."

The delicate jasmine had finished steeping. Kavik picked up his cup and took a moment to consider the amber liquid. Tea poured by the Avatar herself. Nobles could go their whole lives without ever being granted such an honor. "Then I guess you'll just have to trust me."

Before he could drink, an iron grip clamped around his wrist. Droplets of tea spattered the table. Yangchen leaned forward, a sprung wire. "Before we make this official, tell me. The money I gave you. Who did you hand it off to? I saw you transfer the coins to someone while I was tailing you from above, but I couldn't make them out."

He had an idea what she was doing. "I gave it to—"

Yangchen loomed her face dangerously close to his until they were breathing the same air. "Look me in the eye while you answer," she said. "Don't blink."

Kavik stared into irises as gray as storm clouds before a vicious downpour. "I gave the money to a woman named Ayunerak who's lived here since before the Platinum Affair. She runs a kitchen to feed the hungry. She'll put the coin to good use."

The Avatar tilted her head back and forth, trying to see him in subtly different angles. "All right. All right. Points in your favor. Now tell me. Are you working for a shang? Are you a plant?"

"How would I possibly be a plant—ow!"

Her fingers tightened. She was stronger than she appeared. "You're my age," Yangchen said. "Quite nice to look at, if you don't mind me saying. You're certainly not another minister or dignitary trying to order me around. When I ask around the Water Tribe Quarter, no one has a bad thing to say about you."

More like they refused to say anything at all about him. His countrymen tended to keep business, good or bad, to themselves. "We met under very unlikely circumstances where you managed to demonstrate a number of useful skills to me," Yangchen said. "One of which is being an adept liar. I made the choice to bring you on. Do you know how the best cons work?"

Kavik did know. "By making the target feel like they're in control. You think there's a chance this was one big ploy to gain your trust."

"There's a Pai Sho saying: 'A good move for you is a good move for your opponent.' Now answer the question. Are you working for a shang? Are you working for Zongdu Henshe?"

"No," Kavik said, and he couldn't stop himself from smirking. Bluntness was the goal here, in both her question and his response. She was measuring his physical reactions. "I'm not working for a shang or the zongdu or any of the powers that be in Bin-Er. I hate this city with every fiber of my being, and I want nothing more than to leave both it *and* you behind."

He let his declaration soak in. "Now if you're done measuring my pulse and checking if my pupils are changing width, my tea is getting cold," he said.

She let go of his wrist. He and his parents had done the right thing by not bringing up Kalyaan. There was no way the Avatar would have given him this opportunity if she knew his brother had been a runner for the very people she was trying to bring down.

Yangchen studied him for a bit longer, sitting so perfectly still she resembled a statue. Then she grudgingly picked up her teacup and held it to Kavik's. "I suppose that'll have to do for now," she said. "To a successful partnership."

They both drank slowly. Watching each other the whole time.

THE NORTHERN
AIR TEMPLE

IF YOU asked around the Water Tribe Quarter, Ujurak and Tapeesa's wayward boy was sick with the wet cough. A moderately serious illness that required a couple of weeks of bed rest. Sometimes longer if you were unlucky. He'd probably caught it in the international district during one shady outing or another, but no one was going to give that opinion to a Middler or anyone remotely connected to the Earth King's law. If he had any shame left, he'd lay low for a while after he recovered.

Kavik the newly inducted Avatar's companion was undergoing intense study and meditation under Yangchen's wing and wouldn't be showing his face for a very long time. Kavik's parents understood how important the training process was and had sworn themselves to secrecy. Becoming a celebrity was a frequent and undesirable side effect of working with the Avatar. The mind had to be strengthened first without outside interference so one could better serve the spiritual needs of the world.

"Jingli," the nobody who possessed a shockingly high level of clearance, was sitting in the back of a wagon safeguarding a load of pottery. No one in the supply caravan bothered him about why he had such an unusual name for a Waterbender. Sections of Bin-Er were cosmopolitan enough that it wasn't too out of the ordinary.

The idea of using someone else's real identity made Kavik deeply uncomfortable. It was one thing to make up a fleeting background when necessary, but stepping into an existing life and taking it for your own was the sort of theft Kavik wanted to avoid. When Yangchen gave him the wooden tag, similar to his own internal city pass but with a different grain pattern, she assured him Jingli was the most expensive and hard to obtain kind of cover—completely fabricated. An empty set of clothes looking for a body to fill them, only good for trips between Bin-Er and the Northern Air Temple, nowhere else.

The wagon train he rode in was part of an alms mission. A small number of shop owners in Bin-Er looked to soothe their own spirits and keep the winds of fortune blowing in their favor by donating unsold goods in bulk to their local Air Nomads. The crew of volunteers Kavik rode with had been making the journey into the mountains for decades and had been given exceptions to the rules set in place by the Platinum Affair. They were a dour, uninterested bunch, and Kavik wondered if they cared that many people in the city would have paid small fortunes to have the same level of travel clearance.

The outskirts of Bin-Er were a bleak scrubland of month-old snowdrifts and reeds crispy with ice. The little guardhouses marking the line between the shang territory and the Earth Kingdom looked pitifully inadequate to cover such a large tract, but that only meant the men inside were committed to pursuing you across the open ground, nothing blocking their sight lines, until you were caught.

When the wagons pulled up to the guard station and halted, Kavik's stomach became the same cauldron from when he first set foot onto the continent, the overheated roil warning him to turn back and go no farther. The Earth Kingdom soldiers frightened him worse now that he was older. Instead of being faceless, stoic green giants, they were human beings, unpredictable and dangerous. He could smell the scallions on their breath and tell which ones hated their captain. The plan might fall apart if one of them simply happened to be in a foul mood.

He held his breath while the soldiers pulled back tarps and inspected jars of vinegar dregs, bundled scraps of rags, tubs of broken grain. They asked for his pass, and he handed it over, trying not to scream as the protective token left his possession. There was a high chance of getting caught right here.

They let him through without a hitch. Him and the entire caravan.

He couldn't believe it. The thing he'd wanted to do, this whole time, had been done. He'd left Bin-Er. The Avatar had made the impossible happen. Such was her blessing.

His awe faded as he remembered his grand escape was merely a component of a larger plan. His parents were still stuck in the city behind him. *The Avatar's blessing,* he groused once his heart stopped pounding in his chest.

They reached the mountains. From there it was a miserable four days in the back of the leading wagon, using slips of water to keep the fragile goods from cracking against each other over the rocky trails. The driver, whose name was Choi, spoke little to him as they went down and up the slopes, winding through treacherous passes. Nights passed in silence around the campfire.

On the fifth day, as the caravan rounded a bend, a cry went out. Kavik looked up, his neck popping, and saw the spires rising out of the mist.

He and a few other members of the crew who hadn't made the trip before stood up and pulled their hoods back to stare in reverence. It was impossible not to. From a distance, the Northern Air Temple seemed a jeweler's piece, carved from the peak itself with tools of needlelike precision. The green caps of its towers as fragile and delicate as the heads of mushrooms. A palace floating in the sky.

"You can quit gawkin'," Choi said. "We ain't goin' there."

The man was technically right; there was no way for a wagon to reach the temple proper. Instead of rising higher, the procession dipped down into the valley below, where there were several fallow barley fields. And to Kavik's surprise, a small village. When asked the name of it, Choi shrugged.

They pulled into the main road next to a storehouse and unloaded the wares, simple storage jars for grain and vinegar and vegetable oil. Bog-standard labor by the side of the street. And yet Kavik was as dumbstruck by the town as he was the temple. At least a third of the people out and about were Air Nomads.

He had never seen so many members of the wandering nation gathered in one place before, conducting their business—if it could ever be called business for them. Monks of all ages were just . . . walking around. With their feet touching the ground.

Orange-shawled children chased each other past the knees of their elders and received words that could be interpreted as stern when they bumped into people. The adults casually conversed with the layfolk, sharing complaints about the weather, truculent animals, the availability of eggs over the last month. These Air Nomads made faces when they stepped in mud and groaned in dismay when they realized they'd forgotten their gliders on the other end of town.

Unbelievable. Kavik watched the regular villagers, wondering how many would froth with spiritual joy before his very eyes.

The answer was none. The ordinary men and women stepped out of the way of the Air Nomads but didn't grovel. At the beginning and end of a conversation with a monk they'd make small covered-hand bows, but as proper punctuation, not as a declaration of unworthiness.

"Where are these people from?" Kavik asked as he lowered another small pallet of jars to the ground with a column of bent water.

"Places," Choi said. "They ain't Airbenders or nothin'. They just live here, farm what crops will grow in the mountains. There're settlements like this one around the other Air Temples where the monks and nuns can pick up what they need."

Kavik unloaded the last of the cargo. Choi grunted in appreciation for the soft touch of a Waterbender. "We finished early so you can go explore the village if you want. Mind yourself though. You're still close to a holy place."

Like he could forget, surrounded by so many shorn heads. Kavik leaped down from the wagon. He made it no farther than a few steps away when a little boy in yellow robes accosted him.

"Fruit pie?" the young Air Nomad said in a piping lilt, holding a tray of baked goods above his disturbingly lumpy head.

"Sure?" Kavik wasn't hungry, but he didn't want to be rude. He picked up a round saucer-sized pastry topped with a purple curlicue and bit into it. The filling was good, sweet yam, but it spilled over his fingers, making a mess.

"Ahem." The boy held out a bowl with a few coins in it and jangled them, expecting an addition.

Oh. So the snack wasn't a gift of hospitality to new arrivals. Kavik had to do a dance of embarrassment, fishing in his pockets with his free hand while keeping his half-eaten pie away from his clothes.

The smallest he had was a silver. "No change," the young monk intoned, fixing him with dark, abyss-like eyes. "Proceeds go to funding the hospital." He gestured at a large building farther up the side of the valley. "The Avatar awaits you there. Hasten now, traveler."

Whatever you say, unsettling child. Kavik dropped his money into the bowl and walked uphill to meet his new boss.

Kavik's specialty as an errand runner was that he could count accurately and fast. By his estimate, the hospital was twice as big as it should have been, given the number of residents he put the town at. He paused by the door of the stone building, looking for a trap that might swallow him whole, and went inside.

Rows of beds spanned the open floor. Air Nomad attendants traveled through the furrows, trying to see to the sick and injured, but there were too many to treat at once. Everywhere he looked, Kavik saw cases of frostbite, malnutrition, foot rot, snowblindness. Bandaged limbs and sunken cheeks. The results of going into conditions that would kill you quickly if you weren't prepared.

Dry herbal incense burned in the corners, and there was a monk whose sole duty was to keep a breeze circulating through the windows, but the stench of decay was unmistakable. Kavik had been breathing pure mountain air for the past couple of days, and the shift was hard to bear. *Bin-Er smells like this. You just got used to it and forgot.*

The Avatar was easy to spot. She moved down the aisles, flanked by a contingent of older monks and nuns who worried loops of wooden beads through their fingers while she healed the bedridden. While Yangchen worked, she talked quietly with one elder in particular, a mustached old man who was so naturally bald that the remnants of his white hair formed a tiny, sideways-pointing skirt around his smooth head.

He looked up at Kavik. The wrinkles around his eyes read like a multitude of different texts written on top of the same paper, either expressing the friendliest welcome or the most vehement disdain. Then he leaned back to Yangchen's ear, no doubt resuming a conversation of great spiritual importance.

"*Seriously?*" Head Abbot Sonam said, managing to make the faint whisper sound like a wail of protest.

Yangchen kept her eyes on her task. "Yes."

Most Air Nomads were very good at talking out of the corner of their mouths. They'd all been young once, even ancient fixtures like Sonam, and a great portion of their childhoods were spent sitting in neat rows, facing the same direction, while an elder gave incredibly long lectures. Muttering under your breath to your neighbor was second nature to her people.

"Avatar, we talked about this." Sonam's mustache gave him the advantage of an extra shield. "You cannot bring your spies into the temple."

Yangchen hovered over a woman whose stubborn fever just would not break. She tossed aside the water she'd been using into a waste bucket and drew a fresh batch from an attendant's basin. The blob of liquid glowed cool and blue between her hands. She gently applied it to the woman's forehead, the same way she might a damp towel.

"First off, we're not in the temple proper right now," she said. "Second, he hasn't started spying for me yet, so as far as anyone's concerned, he's only my guest. Third, look around us. We're drowning. This is *one city* out of balance, never mind the world. I need him."

"Bringing the business of the other nations to our doorstep is not going to simplify matters. You have no idea how the leaders of the world would react if they knew you were launching operations from the temples."

Yangchen refreshed her water, spilling a little on the floor, and started over again. "She may not wake easily," Sonam said. "Perhaps you should move on for now."

No. "Not when she's so close. She's so close to making a turn for the better." *Come on,* she whispered in her mind to her patient, who was burning up on the inside. *Fight. Help me fight.*

The woman's arms and legs started to jerk. Yangchen swore through her teeth, and Sonam stepped back to give her space. "Fetch a big tub!" she shouted over her shoulder. "I need to get her into more water!"

"They're all full!" said an attendant. "We don't have any more!"

Her patient's shaking grew violent. Swelling in the head. Yangchen couldn't move her hands for fear of losing the woman entirely. She let loose a string of whispered curses that, had anyone heard, could have damaged her image as the Avatar more than any public mishap.

"Make room!" she heard Kavik shout.

He must have run outside to get snowmelt, the only explanation for the sheer amount of water he carried in the air above his head. He struggled to Yangchen's side, needing a lot of effort to keep the mass of liquid contained, but she wasn't going to complain. "Surround her body and keep it flowing!" Yangchen ordered.

Kavik encased the woman in the fresh water from neck to toe, weaving his arms with full-shouldered motions. He gently pressed her twitching limbs back in place with his element, stabilizing her so Yangchen could work.

When she applied her control alongside his and made their shared water glow, he gasped out loud. A common training exercise for groups of Waterbenders was to weave a current between them, guiding each other's form, shaping each other's flow. Water was the most communal element, according to many bending sifus.

But partnered healing went far beyond the push-pull of sparring. She imagined the elation Kavik must be feeling right now, the potential for a miracle at his fingertips, the intense connection between him, Yangchen, and the patient. The bonds of life itself.

After a few minutes she managed to get the swelling under control. "Up, so I can reach her spine."

He tightened the circles of his arms. Yangchen got her hands underneath, the two of them working together to cradle the woman in midair. Sweat beaded on Kavik's brow, but Abbot Sonam himself dabbed it away with a cloth, the leader of the Northern Air Temple giving the outsider boy an approving nod.

The woman's fever broke, a subtle shift in temperature that rippled through the water like a wave spilling against the shore. "Down," Yangchen said, letting out a long breath. "She's out of danger."

Kavik lowered the patient back to her bed and split the coffin of water into a series of small buckets the monks had carefully placed around them. When the last one had been filled, he gasped and fell forward onto the empty corner of the bed. "My arms are jelly," he croaked.

Yangchen waited until he regained enough strength to lift his head. His eyes were shining with excitement, his skin flushed, his grin nearly manic. "I've never helped revive anyone like that before."

"You did well." She let Kavik's happiness wash over her, like bathing in the sun. Saving a life could be a powerful rush.

Their patient stirred. "Where . . ."

"You're near the Northern Air Temple," Yangchen said, clasping her hand. "We found you in the mountains. You were very sick, but you'll be okay. You made it. You're safe now."

The woman couldn't believe her eyes. "You're the . . . You're the . . ."

"Yes, I am," Yangchen said. "Rest."

The woman lowered her head, tears streaming along the grooves of her ears. "Thank you, Avatar. Bless you. The spirits bless you." She shuddered in relief. "Where is my son?"

"Your son?" There were no children in the beds nearby. Yangchen turned to Abbot Sonam.

His face was pale. "The patrols found her yesterday, collapsed along one of the trails," Sonam said. "She was by herself."

"That's not possible," the woman said. She struggled to a sitting position. "My son was with me. We escaped Bin-Er together. Where's my son?"

Yangchen couldn't provide an answer. "Did you see signs of anyone on the wagon route?" she asked Kavik.

He shook his head, wide-eyed and ashen. His joy had turned to dust in his mouth. Kavik was from a place where the land could be hostile. He knew very well the odds of survival in this terrain, this weather, overnight and alone.

The woman grabbed Yangchen's robes, latching on to her in a burst of frantic strength. "Avatar, where's my son?" she cried. "Where is he? *Where is my son?*"

MAKING READY

KAVIK WAITED for her behind the hospital in the circle of trampled grass. "Were all of those people from Bin-Er?" he asked Yangchen once she emerged.

He sounded calm in the way one had to force. "Most of them are," Yangchen said. "Sneaking out of the city without clearance usually means forgoing enough provisions or the right knowledge to make it safely to the Air Temple. We have to patrol the surrounding areas on our bison to pick up the lost and stranded. You get turned around in these mountains and, well . . ."

"What's going to happen?" he asked, pointing his chin back inside.

"Abbot Sonam will send another team to search for her child." There might turn out to be more to that statement. One could only hope. She took in Kavik's taut, uneasy stance, the weight he kept on the balls of his feet, as if there were an opponent he could fight in hand-to-hand combat for the fate of the missing boy. If only it were so easy.

"You can't let it get to you," she said instead. Rote. Words she'd heard throughout more than one lifetime. "You saved someone's life. You have to hold on to the victories and let go of the defeats, or else you'll never sleep again."

He stared at his feet, as if better wisdom were buried in the dirt. "Come," she said, chucking him in the arm. "I was going to show you around the Air Temple. You need a few stories to tell your parents."

"I thought I was staying down here. I'm allowed on sacred ground?"

"You're the Avatar's guest. You're allowed in a lot of places. Step back a bit."

Yangchen distanced herself before curling her tongue, pursing her lips, and letting out an ear-piercing whistle that started low and went higher and higher, to the point where a human could no longer hear it. A gigantic shadow grew around Kavik's feet. He warily leaped out of the way in case the noise had dislodged a chunk of snowpack or a boulder above them.

No landslide came. Instead, Yangchen's sky bison slammed to the ground, trembling the earth beneath its six feet. Nujian tossed his curly mane back and basked in the golden light of the falling sun, one front paw raised.

"Quit preening," Yangchen said to her animal companion. Nujian lived for entrances, admiration, absolutely reveled in being the Avatar's bison among bison. Sometimes it was unbecoming.

"*Uaq.*" Kavik stopped himself, his hands already reaching out to touch the fluffy fur. "Can I?"

Yangchen nodded. He stroked the bison's gleaming white topcoat and got an appreciative rumble in response. "Nujian thinks you're all right," she said. "That's a good sign."

"You named your bison 'Arrow'? A little unimaginative, don't you think?"

"I was eight! Shut up about it!" In a huff, she used a small tornado to lift herself onto her bison's withers, landing with a plop as her robes settled around her. "Are you getting on or what?"

Reluctantly, Kavik stopped petting and hauled himself onto the saddle behind her. The broad platform had no designated place to sit. He gripped the railing and peered over the edge at the spots where the bison's fur was braided into the saddle's frame. "How does he know when to take off instead of walk? Do you have to do something with the reins or say a particula*aaagh!*"

Nujian shot into the air as fast his namesake. Yangchen had learned to communicate with her companion through her heels, a glance, a change in tone. Kavik fell backward, steadied himself, started to shout at the jerk sitting in the driver's position. But giddiness caught up with him too fast.

Yangchen had wanted to startle him out of his funk. It worked. The wind in their faces was sharp and cold. The noise that came out of his throat was made of pure exhilaration.

They were *flying*.

Yangchen couldn't help her grin, watching Kavik whoop with such unfiltered glee. As silly as it was, she hadn't been kidding earlier. Passing the Nujian test carried weight. Her bison companion instinctively disliked many of the members of her crew who turned out to be plants, Sidao in particular. But this boy had a heart made for the skies.

"Do a loop!" he shouted.

Perhaps too well made. "If you're going to travel with me, you'll have to learn to guide Nujian yourself. And that means knowing what you can and can't do in the air. Bisons fly without support; humans don't. Even if they're Airbenders."

Her greater message was lost. "I get to take the reins?!"

Yangchen rolled her eyes and pulled her bison into a banking turn over the ribboned walls of the Northern Air Temple. Hardly any natural level ground existed within the confines of swirling stairs and ramps, and the stark relief of its towers against the sky made its feeling of isolation stronger. The Southern Temple had karsts for neighbors, and the East and West were built like connected islands. But the North stood on its lonesome.

She let Kavik gawk from above at the training court with its circle-walking pattern, the open-air cloisters, even flew straight through the hammered goalposts for bison polo. Nujian landed on the terrace right in the middle of the large blue center stripe.

"That was amazing!" Kavik bellowed, his voice still trying to compensate for the rushing wind. "Sorry. That was amazing. Is flying this much fun every time?"

He'd been such a glum boy in Bin-Er, but now, his happiness was downright infectious. Yangchen felt warmer, as if struck by a sunbeam. She liked things that made her feel warm. "I haven't gotten bored of it yet."

Kavik dismounted first and reached up to help her down. She jumped over his head and landed behind him. "Right," he muttered. "Airbender."

"Points for gallantry though." Nujian left with a parting rush of wind to go forage lower in the tree line. Yangchen led Kavik to the temple, warning him not to step on the mittened hermit crabs littering the path.

There were no doors blocking the passageway to the great hall. One could walk straight in, staring the whole time at the fearsome bison relief carved into the far back wall. Yangchen thought it looked more snorting dragon than bison, but perhaps when it was created thousands of years ago, her people's animal companions were less companionable.

She preferred the artwork on the walls, paintings of monks against the clouds done in colors meant to fade over time to teach the lesson of impermanence. Maintaining them required passing on skills from generation to generation, constant effort through the centuries. The exercise was ultimately futile against the power of time but still worth pursuing. Like most things in life.

Kavik twirled as he trailed her, attempting to take in the statues of great elders in the alcoves. "So many," he said. "Will they ever put one of you up?"

"After I'm dead, the temples are obligated to by Avatar tradition." Yangchen winced. "Hopefully mine'll be smaller than those. I don't need everyone staring at my giant head for eternity."

They entered the ringed cloisters. A group of young nuns visiting from the Eastern Temple going in the opposite direction bowed solemnly to Yangchen while she gave a gesture of benediction. A few of them raised eyebrows at Kavik but said nothing. It was well understood the Avatar had to conduct worldly affairs with the help of people from other nations.

The insult came only after they passed each other. *"Which way do Westerners go?"* shouted the lead nun. Yangchen spun around to see her making a three-fingered gesture toward the ground. The rest of the girls responded in unison. *"DOWN DOWN DOWN!"*

By laws as ironclad as any among her folk, Yangchen was obligated to answer back. She cupped her hands around her mouth. "You're seven and ten in my era! *East side, least side!"*

"Gap's closing fast, Avatar!" The Eastern nuns backed away with grins and arms spread tauntingly wide, only returning to a proper form when they crossed the boundary into the great hall.

Kavik looked dumbfounded. "Airball rivalry," Yangchen explained.

She led him up the stairs toward one of the turrets. They overtook a line of younger monks finishing their chores, carrying buckets of sudsy water, knocking their knees against the wooden tubs. Kavik looked around the rock formations. Perhaps he felt the faint tug of his element within them; Yangchen certainly could. "You know," he said. "If you drilled a few holes and knocked down some of those older walls, you could get a flow going at a higher elevation."

That must have been the city in him talking. Yangchen shook her head. "People should know the weight of water. The purpose of life isn't convenience." All the same, she turned around and bent the loads of water out of the buckets, raising the blobs into the air. The young boys cheered as they followed her and Kavik higher, temporarily freed of their burden.

"One time only!" she told them. "Don't squeal to the abbot!"

After reaching the top of the stairs, they left their little parade behind and entered a turret. Yet another series of steps waited for them inside, spiraling higher and higher along the wall. For the sake of his pride, she didn't push the pace. The air was thin in the mountains, and not many people were used to the concept of "Airbender flat." Up a long way, down a long way, end up back at the elevation you started. No big deal.

The top of the tower was a small meditation floor, open on all sides. To the west, the fall of the sun dyed the blanket of mountain mists a soft violet. The cliffs surrounding the Northern Air Temple fell away so sharply that the view from its windows tricked you into thinking you were floating atop nothing at all, treading along the sky itself.

"Gorgeous," Kavik said with a sigh.

Yangchen stepped around him so she wasn't blocking any of the light. "I have to catch at least one sunset every time I visit the Northern Temple. This was the favorite spot of my . . ." She forced herself to say it. There was no point in hiding from Jetsun's memory. "My sister. She first showed it to me."

"You have a sister," Kavik repeated, still entranced by the orange glow in the distance.

Yangchen puckered her lips. "Is that so odd?"

"No. Sorry. That's the normal part." He turned, the sun cutting across his fine cheekbones. "There's such a big difference between . . . I mean . . ."

He waved his hands to clear the slate and start anew. "Up-Here-You is exactly like how I imagined the Avatar to be. Heroic. Inspiring. Down-There-You is something else entirely. I can't wrap my head around it."

Ah. Right. The old question. *Why are you like this?* A different context than usual. In the past it came out of the elder's mouths while they were teary and frightened for her. "Have you heard of a place called Tienhaishi?" she asked. "It used to be a city of great art and culture. The grandest in the world, from certain perspectives."

"Where you fought the great spirit," Kavik said. "I know the basic story. It's hard to believe I'm looking at the same person who took on a giant from the sea." He paused. "But over time I heard more often it was a typhoon that made landfall. Don't get me wrong; I'd be just as impressed if you managed to stop a storm in its tracks."

Yangchen found it exhausting that no matter what happened, no matter how many witnesses saw something happen, somebody would stamp their foot and declare events had gone a different way. Making petty little attempts to seize authority over a story that wasn't theirs. "For what it's worth, it was a spirit," she said. "You should have seen the battle. I was Up-Here-Me. Powerful. Magnificent."

She made a fist in front of her face, palm in, and then opened her hand outward, the most succinct way she could summarize the Avatar State. Kavik probably didn't know exactly what she meant by the gesture, but he seemed to follow well enough.

"I struck a deal with the titan," she said. "He would lay aside his aggression, and human settlers would leave that section of the coast alone. My people currently take care of the land where Tienhaishi used to be and maintain the proper rituals as part of the agreement. So far, it's working. If there's one thing the Four Nations respect, it's the sacred sites of the Air Nomads."

Kavik nodded. A job well done by the Avatar. And it was, it really was. The problem was the aftermath, the trailing eddies, the smoke after the fire.

"The fight left the city a ruin," Yangchen continued. "Homes destroyed. The residents had nowhere to go. I stayed with them, searching for new places for them to live. I didn't think it would be easy, but I thought there would be progress. 'Have faith,' I told the people of Tienhaishi."

The sun became a sliver. "We went from town to town, doors slamming in our faces, until I couldn't even get them to open for me anymore. I would find mayor's men waiting, armed, telling us to keep walking. We slept in fields, lived on alms. I had my fellow nuns and monks making supply runs for us, begging far and wide." She remembered sending Nujian away out of fear he would eat too much of the locally foraged food. Gleaned seeds, edible tree bark, and the like.

"Once we started losing people to illness, I made a promise," Yangchen said. "I would cajole, wheedle, whine, use any tactic at my disposal to do what had to be done. Everything became easier once I started playing the game properly, applying leverage in the right situation."

She didn't have to give him details, but they poured out of her like water. "In one case I was able to place most of Tienhaishi's craftsmen by lying to two competing nobles about how badly the other wanted to be the patron of so many skilled workers," she said. "Had to forge a couple of letters. That was fun. Another time I scared the spiritually inclined husband of a governor so badly that he threatened to run away from her if she didn't show more kindness and open their territories."

She waited to see if Kavik was disgusted, if she'd ruined the image of the Avatar for him. Then she remembered she'd already done that back in Bin-Er. "Eventually the people of Tienhaishi were absorbed by the continent," she said. "We found arable land for some of them to work; others reached family in Ba Sing Se. I'm sure a few of them are in the shang cities right now, needing more help. Can you imagine? The Avatar failing you miserably, twice in one lifetime."

Yangchen made faces into the growing shadows of the tower until she was sure she wasn't going to lose her composure. The light over the mountains was cool and dim. An appropriate stage for the origins of Down-There-Her. "I learned I can't force people to do the right thing. But I can . . . maneuver them. I can deliver tailored, expedient truths that help them see from a more enlightened perspective. The Airbender term is 'shaped teachings.' "

She was butchering the definition to make herself feel better. Picking up the techniques of spycraft and trickery and false-hoods was never the obstacle. Avatars were often prodigious to some degree, fast learners when properly motivated. Yangchen had access to so many lives lived to healthy ages. Which of them *wouldn't* be a practiced deceiver by the time of their deaths? August Szeto alone was a library of intrigue.

There was silence. *He's judging me,* Yangchen thought.

"What does your sister think about it?" Kavik asked.

She was caught off guard by the question. "What?"

"What does your older sister think about how you do things as the Avatar?" He scratched his head. "I assume she's older, for some reason."

"I . . . I don't know how she'd react to what I'm doing now." To Yangchen, her life before and after Jetsun were pieces that never meshed, no joinery possible. "She died a while ago, before I really started my work. I looked up to her more than anyone in the world."

An Avatar Yangchen with Jetsun by her side could have been a very different leader. "I'm sure she'd tell me to slow down. Be less rash. Stay focused on the long-term. How did you know she was older?"

Kavik crossed his arms tight. He could have been trying to stop his answer or force it out. "I had someone in my life like that once," he said. "Another errand runner I tried to emulate. Older. Smarter. It's as if I keep looking over my shoulder each time I make a decision. Waiting to see if they're watching."

So they had a weakness in common. "It's because they would never let us make the wrong choice," Yangchen said. Without the nods, without the headshakes, without their weight and presence, you were off-balance. Forever doubtful of your next step. "This friend of yours is gone?"

"Very gone," Kavik said. "He didn't really have anything keeping him around Bin-Er, so he hopped out of the city as soon as he got clearance for himself."

The two of them must have been close for such bitterness to leak around the edges of his mask. Kavik rubbed his chest with his arms still folded, like he was trying to settle the contents of a bottle. "I suppose you and I are stuck having to decide for ourselves, aren't we?" he said. "No one to tell us which path to follow."

"That's right." Yangchen was glad she had chanced upon someone who understood. It was ungrateful of her to think so, but all of the wisdom stored away in her past lives couldn't add up to Jetsun's steady hand holding onto hers, gently nudging in the right direction. "Are you having second thoughts about your choice to join me?"

"No. Not if we're going to prevent more situations like the one back at the hospital."

His fierceness surprised her. "If Bin-Er took better care of its people, that woman wouldn't have risked trekking through the mountains," Kavik said, running his tongue over his teeth, a tell of genuine frustration. "She wouldn't have been separated from her child."

And we'd have had our victory. Yangchen could tell her new agent saw the chain of events leading from greed to negligence to suffering. More importantly, he was *willing* to see it. And his reaction was one of deep discontent.

Good. "You know what?" she said.

"What?"

"I think I trust you a little more each time we talk."

Outside, the fireflies began their twilight dance. The temple grounds became a pinpricked lampshade. The sun went down early this time of year, which shrank the number of hours the rescue teams could safely roam the mountains to search.

A crazed flapping noise filled the air, summoned by the tower lantern, now one of the bright sources of light in the sky. Kavik heard it and went on high alert, but he couldn't tell which direction it was coming from.

"What's that noise?" he said, right before a fuzzy white mass collided with his face. Another struck him in the back of the head.

Chaos broke loose. Yangchen couldn't tell who was screeching louder, the boy or the winged lemurs. "Pik! Pak!" she shouted. "Stop it!"

Kavik flailed his arms while Pik hung on tenaciously to his hair. "Get them off me!"

"Stop panicking; they're my friends! I just left them alone for too long and they're upset! Calm down and they'll calm down!"

Her advice went unheeded. She had to unhook Pak's claws one by one from Kavik's ears. Kavik managed to get Pik at arm's length, threw the struggling animal out the window, and doubled over, spitting and wiping his tongue with his fingers. "*Peh!* I've got fur in my mouth! *Pehk!*"

He'd discovered firsthand the origin of Pik and Pak's names. They often latched on to strangers who got too close to her, and they also shed profusely. She couldn't eat a meal around her lemurs without her food getting hair all over it.

"If they act up around you again, just do what you did," she said. "Get them into the air and they'll glide away." To demonstrate, she let Pak run up the length of her arm and sail back into the darkness.

"Those things can fly?!"

She squinted at Kavik. "You dropped my lemur out the tower without knowing it could survive the fall?"

"I defended myself from a horrible little rat beast that attacked me, if that's what you mean!"

And to think they had almost shared a moment. "It's getting cold," Yangchen said. "I'll show you the rest of the temple. Hopefully you won't wet your pants at the kitten-moths."

"I hate you."

"So I've heard."

Kavik had trouble sleeping. The thin air kept him from fully relaxing inside his quilt-lined guest room. And during the evening tour, a greater irritation had nagged him throughout.

He felt the itch in his gut when he saw monks, done with their studies and meditation, conversing by candlelight or sitting on the terrace steps without a care in the world. And again, when he was invited to partake in the evening meal and shown by his neighbors how to mix butter into his barley gruel.

The feeling named itself by the end of dinner. Jealousy.

Kavik was jealous of the Airbenders, so at home in their great temple. He supposed anywhere was home for them, being nomads, but surrounded by people content in their element, his longing for the North became overwhelming. He made the mistake of teaching the younger monks the stick pull game and had to turn in early for the night lest he burst into tears watching them.

A gust came through the small window in his room. He got up and rested his elbows on the sill, gazing out over the mountains. The temple peak was so steep he couldn't see the land underneath. If he wasn't careful, he might roll off the edge of the world.

His eyes landed on a solitary figure standing on the tallest column of what he'd been told was the airball field. Even at a distance he knew it was the Avatar. She was lightly dressed and rose on her toes to meet the wind.

Maybe she'd taken the Easterners' taunts a little too seriously and was getting in extra practice. Kavik watched as she trailed her fingers in an invisible stream and fell forward off the pillar. It only sunk in that she lacked a glider or a bison after she dipped out of his vision. *"Hey!"* he shouted, even though his voice wouldn't have reached her. *"Don't!"*

He needn't have panicked. Yangchen shot into the air, pitching and yawing like a dried leaf, directionless. She reached the peak of her ascent and whipped her hands at the ground.

From the force of her own airbending, Yangchen tumbled higher. Her path veered randomly this way, and this way again, before going back that way. Not flight, but the disordered twirl of surrender to the wind. The Avatar had given up control. She danced on emptiness.

No, Kavik thought. It wasn't a dance.

Had he been a random observer, focusing solely on the beauty of her movements, he would have assumed she was dancing. Entertaining herself. But Kavik had met more than one Yangchen. This version pummeled the ground with blasts of air, lashing out with so much pressure she was blown into the sky as a result.

He could feel her anger all the way across the temple, tempered by distance into a gentle breeze. Her element would leave no trace of her frustrations in the morning. *You have to let go of the defeats.* Kavik knew Yangchen had not taken her own advice and moved on from the missing child in the mountains. She had not let go of anything at all.

The Avatar's skill and power aside, the dangers of being suspended in the air without aid were still very real. Kavik waited until she thrashed herself weary and returned safely to the ground. He watched her go back inside the cloisters for the night and made sure she stayed before seeking his own bed once more.

Sleep came to him much easier afterward.

BREAKING IN

TRUE TO her word, Yangchen let Kavik fly Nujian. But only in a straight path, low to the water, for a short time. He barely got to hold the reins before she took them back. "We can't risk veering off course," she'd explained. "You'll get more chances in the future."

They skimmed along the low waves of the Baizhi Sea. The warm, wet air made Kavik's skin clammy. He was down to his kuspuk. Heavy winter clothing was a relic of the past, unnecessary where they were going.

"We're crossing into Jonduri waters," Yangchen said, examining the sky and the horizon, reading winds and currents Kavik could only guess told her their position. He wasn't an experienced open ocean wayfinder. The Avatar's lemurs perched on the saddle horn, their polished greenstone eyes fixed on him in case he made any sudden moves.

He could admit in daylight, when they weren't screaming and trying to steal his teeth, they were very cute. Pik, the one with the torn ear, had eaten some seeds out of his hand and accepted a few scratches under the chin.

There were no other humans present. They'd departed on Nujian in a caravan of Air Nomads and bison, the residents of the town below the temple cheering as they flew overhead. Toward the end of their trip, Yangchen diverted off on a separate path. The other Airbenders pretended like they didn't just see their spiritual leader leave them without saying where she was going.

"The pickup boat knows to come to a specific location should I ever announce a visit to Jonduri," Yangchen had explained earlier. "I will hand you off there, and then return to the caravan since it's part of my official cover."

She had no reservations about referring to her fellow Air Nomads as such. "My minister left before us on a ship, while we were still at the Air Temple, and made public arrangements for me to plead my case. The Avatar still hopes for better conditions in the shang cities, and she's willing to go to each one in turn. Like a proper beggar."

"This minister is the one from Nanyan who's selling you out?"

"Yes." Yangchen puckered her lips. "My actions are believable because of how badly I fumbled my first try in Bin-Er. I'm sure by now he's let every shang on the island know I was refused."

"And when I get to the safe house?"

"You sit tight until I return from groveling in front of Zongdu Chaisee. It won't take long because she'll refuse me too. She's the one who currently has control of Unanimity, after all. My contacts have experience and local knowledge, so we'll want to consult with them on a plan to find out which shipment the assets will be traveling on."

"If your loyalists in Jonduri know what they're doing, why don't you have them try to get closer to Chaisee instead of me?"

"They're too old," Yangchen said curtly.

Kavik tilted his head at her. "What I mean is, they've lived in Jonduri for a while and people know them," she explained. "You, however, will be a completely fresh face once you're on the island. We barely even need a cover for you. You came from the North because you were promised work. No family or friends in town."

"The same story I used on you."

His one victory over her, no matter how short-lived. She took the reminder well. "If it works, it works."

After a few more minutes, Nujian came to a stop, hovering above the water. Yangchen hopped over to the saddle and rummaged through their supplies until she found a large empty bladder. With the might of airbending, she inflated it in one breath and tied the seal tight.

"What is that thing, some kind of signal?" Kavik said. "And if we're at the handoff point, where's the boat?"

She tossed the bladder over the side, where it bobbed gently, a makeshift buoy. "The boat won't be here for another hour. Nujian and I can't be spotted anywhere near it. And the float is for you to hold on to. I know I said it was a handoff, but it's really more of a dead drop."

Yangchen made a scooping motion with her arms and Kavik was sucked bodily into the air, the same way he'd been caught when they first met. He flew backward over the edge of the saddle and into the water. Popping his head above the surface, he grabbed the float. His eyes burned with salt and indignation.

"This was always the plan," Yangchen said. "Consider it payback for trying to kill my lemur."

The sea was warm. Kavik was a Waterbender, a good swimmer to boot, and in no danger of drowning or freezing. But that was beside the point. "Pik forgave me!"

Yangchen callously nudged him in the forehead with the end of her staff, sending him drifting away. "Pak did not."

Kavik rode the serene ripples of the water up and down and cursed the Avatar's name with each one. She'd flown away without so much as a glance back.

He wasted some time dreaming of an appropriate prank as revenge before remembering he had no plans to remain in Yangchen's company any longer than necessary. The point was to get out of Bin-Er, not live up to his parents' hopes and dreams for companionhood glory.

The pickup boat arrived sooner than she'd promised. The small fishing vessel approached with sails furled, pushed along by the man standing in the stern. His motions of waterbending were different from the form Kavik practiced, prone to sudden fast movements among the slow, his hands winding around each other as if he were reeling bolts of silken thread.

The boat came to a stop beside Kavik. The man reached down and they clasped each other by the forearm. The sensation of being helped out of the water by a strong, reliable presence made Kavik think for a moment that Kalyaan, wearing a different face, had come to pick him up.

His rescuer looked nothing like his brother though. The wiry Waterbender was twice as old, in his forties. He had a longer face and a chin like a stone plinth. After pulling Kavik on board, he broke out into a large smile. "Hey!" he said. "You're kin!"

He was. Kavik dried himself off with a flick of waterbending, stepped back, and bowed. "Kavik, of Long Stretch, named after my mother's grandfather. My parents are Ujurak and Tapeesa."

"Tayagum," the man responded. "Of the Orca Islands, after my cousin. My parents are Angtan and Taganak." He tossed Kavik a heavy pile of rigging. "I need you to help me get out of these doldrums, Kavik of Long Stretch."

Together, they turned the boat around and waterbent swells to ride out of the patch of windless sea. Acting as the sole force moving a vessel was tiring work, and Kavik was glad when the breeze picked up. Once they unfurled the sails, they could take a breather. "It's nice to meet another Waterbender," he said as they worked on the rigging.

Tayagum seemed amused by his new passenger. "Don't they have those in Bin-Er?"

Kavik shrugged. "It's nice to be out of Bin-Er."

"Mm. I spent some time there once. Of course this was before the Platinum Affair. Take in the jib a little bit, would you?"

Kavik hunched over the cleat and shortened the lines. "Little more," Tayagum said. "Is Mama Ayunerak still doing her thing over by the Inner Corridor?"

Kavik wasn't surprised he knew Ayunerak. The woman was a landmark, weathered by the changes in the city but still recognizable by visitors far and wide. "It's the international district now," he said. "Her place is still standing though. Is this enough?"

"Perfect! And they say city kids can't sail."

Kavik scoffed as he got up. "I'm not a city kid. We only moved to the continent when I was—"

A rope looped around his neck. *Garrote,* his mind screamed. Kavik barely got one hand up through the slack before it tightened, smashing his own forearm into the side of his head.

The boom of the mainsail dropped. Kavik was hauled into the air by the connected line, his feet dangling and kicking. With his free hand he launched a water whip at Tayagum, but the man diverted the blast with a flick of his wrist.

Tayagum looked up at his catch, who was struggling and twisting in the wind. "La's fins, what do we have here," he said in an unwavering rhythm, no hint of a question. "It's a good thing I found you. What happened to your boat?"

Kavik grabbed the line above his head and pulled on it to relieve the pressure. "A rogue wave knocked me overboard," he said between gulps of air. "I should never have been sailing alone. I'm lucky you came along."

"I was following a school of silverskim. I guess I was meant to bring home a different haul today."

That was as far as the prepared exchange went. Finally satisfied, Tayagum took the bottom of the rope suspending Kavik and gave it a deft flick. The line unwound and Kavik dropped back to the deck on all fours.

"Okay, look," Tayagum said. "I don't know what kind of raggedy kid's games you play in Bin-Er. But in Jonduri, you better keep your head on straight or you'll lose it. The pickup could have been compromised. You should have been ready to gut me and steal the boat the instant you laid eyes on me."

Kavik wanted to tell him off, but he was right. The shame hurt worse than the rope burns. He was Qiu to this guy. That really stung.

"Would I have been able to?" he asked, deflecting the conversation away from his own sloppiness. "Overpower you and steal the boat?"

Tayagum snorted. "No. Don't forget your passphrases next time."

Jonduri grew swiftly on the horizon, an undulating rocky wave between the layers of blue. Kavik had heard stories about the sweltering island from contacts with international privileges. The place had a reputation for thin walls and hard checkpoints.

"Most of the island is surrounded by cliffs and dangerous shoals," Tayagum explained. "So we can't get you in through beaching the boat."

"How dangerous are we talking about?"

"Nearly every section of the coast has a name like Tigerdillo's Roar or Limpet's Teeth. Neither of us are good enough Waterbenders to survive an attempt to lay ashore. There is only one usable port in all of Jonduri."

"Which I assume is guarded to the gills," Kavik said.

"You assume correct. This boat is authorized to leave and enter the harbor with only two people, me and my assistant."

Tayagum tossed a copper plate to Kavik. It was green with corrosion from the salt air. "Here's his pass. He's hiding out for today and you're taking his place on the return home. The harbor agents know our faces. But one of them is brand-new and so far, not spectacular at his job. If everything went off perfectly last night, he should be too hungover to notice the switch. You're the same height and build as my usual guy, so keep the sun at your back and the inspector won't even look you in the eye."

Kavik couldn't believe what he was hearing. After Tayagum's warning to be on top of his game, he'd expected a secret entranceway buried under the water, or a hefty bribe to secure their entry. This was walking straight in through the front door and hoping no one noticed. "Are you kidding me? I've seen shell games run by twelve-year-olds less flimsy than this plan!"

"This was the plan we had time for, so therefore it's the plan. Simple beats complex, most of the time."

This distinctly felt like one of those other times. "At least tell me what this person sounds like, talks like. Is there anything noticeable about his gait?"

"*Asu!* I'm not asking you to perform *Love amongst the Dragons* here. Just keep your mouth shut and do what the agent tells you."

Sweat beaded on Kavik's brow as they got closer, humidity and fear working together against him. He could see the city of Jonduri now, the towering bamboo constructions inlaid into the steep hillside, the green riot of vine-covered cliffs. A gentler slope was painted in stripes—terraced tea fields.

Grand junks with battened sails dominated most of the harbor, behemoths at a trough, needing to be fed. Their sheer lines swooped fore and aft high above the water, wooden walls as thick as castles, as if to let anyone walking their decks sneer down at the surface dwellers below.

Smaller docks handled the boats the size of Tayagum's. In the distance, Kavik saw a man already limping down the long pier, presumably to greet them. "Blast," Tayagum muttered. "Blast, blast, *blast*. That's not Ping waiting for us. That's Ping's boss."

The boat rocked under Kavik's feet. "What does that mean for the plan?"

"He's seen my assistant before. Not as often as the junior agents, but he's definitely met him at least once."

Kavik took it to mean they were up a creek and steadily losing their grip on the paddle. "Do you think he'll remember?"

"Shut up and let me think."

"You don't have much time to think!"

Tayagum ran around to the stern and pushed hard with waterbending to slow their approach. Kavik started to help him but was waved off. "No! If we stop too soon it'll look suspicious!"

Arriving to their doom at the correct speed seemed like the wrong priority. Kavik could come up with only one idea, and it stunk. "You said I was the same height and build as your normal assistant. Do we have the same hair?"

The other Waterbender was too busy with the boat to look up. "What?"

"Do we have the same hair?"

"Yes, for Tui's sake! You're both lanky brats with wolf tails! Why?"

Kavik waited for the boat to rock in case the man on the dock was already watching. On the next upswell, he snagged the toe of one foot on the heel of the other, fell face-first into the railing, and landed on his nose with a crunch.

Stars of pain blinked in the darkness. Kavik caught the blood pouring from his nose and smeared it all around his face. The motion shifted his broken cartilage, and he screamed through clenched teeth.

Tayagum came running. "What did you—oh! *Oh.* This might work."

It had better. Kavik kept his eyes shut as the boat pulled in and Tayagum lashed them to a piling. He was helped onto the planks of the dock.

"Harbormaster Lee," Tayagum said. "Where's, uh, where's Ping?"

"Ping was terminated for incompetence," said a voice like scraped sinews. "What happened here?"

"Got his foot caught on a coil and bashed his face in," Tayagum said. Kavik groaned. He tented his hands over his face, droplets of blood pattering down from his elbows.

"Let me see how bad it is," said Lee.

Kavik peeked through his fingers. The blurry shape of a weathered, ancient Fire Nation man came into view. Lee's wrinkled frown was stone cold, but Kavik detected a hint of grandfatherly concern in his dingy gold eyes. Of all the ways he thought he might get nabbed in Jonduri, the kindness of a security agent wasn't high on the list.

Kavik suddenly doubled over and retched pink slime near Lee's mirror-shined boots. He wasn't completely faking. Too much blood had trickled down his throat.

Lee hissed and jumped back, quick for his age. "You idiot," the harbormaster snapped. "You've been at this job for how long and you still don't have your sea legs?"

"Apologies," Tayagum said. "I'll get him fixed up." He grabbed Kavik by the collar. "You keep your head down and forward, you hear?" he said. "Else you'll choke."

"Guh-huh," Kavik moaned. Tayagum led him down the pier, his face lowered out of courtesy. People got out of their way.

He was in. And he'd bled for the Avatar. His parents would be so proud.

A PLACE TO LAY ONE'S HEAD

THEY HUSTLED down the streets of Jonduri, Tayagum leading the way. Kavik's eyes were too blurry to make anything out, but he could hear the shouts of the famed city hawkers offering morsels of food cooked to order right there in the open stalls, the clamor of dry goods pitchmen demonstrating the durability of their iron wares by bashing the metal together.

When they passed a square full of indistinct hollering, he thought they'd stumbled across a riot of the Bin-Er sort. But Tayagum said it was the clearing exchange, where merchants shouted orders at each other in a great crowd, using eye contact and hand gestures to move sums equal to pounds of gold at a time. Kavik was missing the sights, but he didn't much care. He wasn't in Jonduri to play tourist.

They moved up bouncing bamboo steps into a house on stilts. Tayagum gave him a place to sit and drip to his heart's content.

When the flow from his nose stanched to the point where he could see again, he discovered he was in the common room of an inn.

A Water Tribe–owned inn. There was a large soapstone qulliq in the middle of the floor providing smokeless light. While the room was too big to be completely lined with pelts, there were a few fine examples around the walls and floor. His house in Bin-Er looked like this. An effort to bring home outside the poles.

"I'll leave you in Akuudan's care for now," said Tayagum. "I have to smooth things over at the dock. I'll be back."

He left before Kavik could ask who Akuudan was. Presumably it was the giant who came plodding down the stairs. Kavik was surprised the second floor could hold him.

"What the— *Tayagum!*" the huge southern man roared. "Get back here!"

"He's gone," Kavik said. "You're Akuudan?"

"I am." Akuudan sighed. "And you are a mess. I can bone set. Sit tight."

Akuudan went behind a counter. As he picked through his shelves, Kavik saw he had only one arm, but it was bigger around than some people's legs.

He brought over a leather roll and undid the knot with his teeth, unfurling a series of pouches, each with a different smooth, polished wooden instrument poking out. He selected a wishbone-shaped splint and two rods the size of brush handles. "Hold this curved one against your cheekbones," he said to Kavik. "This is going to hurt."

Without further warning Akuudan jammed the rods deep into Kavik's nostrils to realign his breathing passages.

Ah, blinding pain. His old friend. "It's been a long morning," Kavik said, seeking the floor to lie down on while the setting implements remained attached to his face. "Do you mind if I close my eyes? Just for a minute."

"Go wild. Take two."

When Kavik woke up from his nap, he found pelts underneath him and a protective mask strapped to his head, shielding his nose from further injury. And Tayagum was back. He chatted quietly with Akuudan by the lamp, the two older Water Tribesmen occasionally glancing over at their guest.

Kavik struggled to his elbows. The swelling had gone down in his face, which was now clean and a little cold. Tayagum must have washed him off and applied ice with waterbending while he was passed out. Maybe some basic field healing too, but nothing on the level of the Avatar's miraculous touch. He could breathe well enough to smell something delicious.

"Blood soup," Akuudan said to Kavik. "To replace what you've lost. I also cooked seaweed noodles, and Tayagum picked up a chunk of turtle-seal. Still fresh. Taken properly, thanked by the hunter, and given a drink."

Kavik swallowed his saliva. "How do you have fresh seal meat this far away from the poles?"

"Jonduri likes two things above all else," Tayagum said. "Order and food. A lot of the exchange traders are Tribe who are willing to pay for a taste of home."

The one thing about the shang territories was they were cosmopolitan. Kavik found the soup as hearty as any he'd had back home. The noodles as good as his mother's, he was loath to admit. The meat was cut from the backbone, a prime morsel usually chosen quickly following a successful hunt.

Because of how delicious the meal was, it took Kavik a while to notice they'd been eating in complete silence. "Business seems a little slow," he said. A joke. The inn was empty, even though the street outside had sounded busy. "This assistant I replaced on the way in. He doesn't live here?"

They grunted but didn't respond beyond that. Tayagum's initial friendliness from the boat had vanished. The standoffishness hurt Kavik more than he wanted to let on. These were the first Water Tribe folk he'd met since he'd moved to Bin-Er who weren't upset with him over his brother's dealings.

He took a minute to observe his hosts. A series of small blue discs hung from a band around Akuudan's arm. Tayagum had a similar piece of fabric wrapped around his bicep but with only one carved amulet hanging from it.

"So are you two former Northern Guard?" Kavik asked. "Thin Claws maybe, to be so far from home?" He was referring to the elite warrior retainers of Agna Qel'a, granted the status of brethren to the chief himself. When they weren't stationed in the poles, they served as scouts and rangers who patrolled farther away from the Water Tribe homelands.

Tayagum snorted.

"What?" Kavik said. "You both look like you can scrap. At least one of you has been to the continent a long time ago." His pickup man may have been justified in giving Kavik grief over security, but he'd let slip facts about himself as well.

Akuudan shook his head. "Don't do that," he said.

What, pry? Learn? What do you think my job is? "I'm just speculating," Kavik said, turning his attention to the big man. "For instance. Unless you lost your limb in an accident, I'm thinking you might be related to royalty. An offshoot branch of the clan, maybe." The Northern Chief's lineage had at least one notable ancestor born with one arm, a legendary whaler, in fact.

"You're annoying, is what you are," Tayagum said. "And unvetted. Neither of us enjoy having to support walking liabilities."

So it was going to be like that. Kavik hadn't even briefed them on the mission yet. "I'm the person the Avatar chose."

"I know," Akuudan said. "And I'm saying she may have made a mistake. She looks for the good in people first. She wants to find it in them with all of her heart. She's too trusting."

Kavik shook his head in disbelief. "Are we talking about the same Avatar here? Yangchen? Spies on people? Owns disguises and is really comfortable using them? The most un–Air Nomad Air Nomad to ever exist?"

Tayagum's nostrils flared, and Akuudan's lips pressed into thin lines. Clearly they didn't like Kavik speaking about their boss in anything less than a reverent tone. "Look, she and I struck a deal," he said. "I need her to come through on her end, and she needs me in return. I don't see why the two of you get to look down on me for it."

Akuudan examined Kavik like a jeweler determined to reject a stone. "Do kids these days know about the Platinum Affair?" he asked after a lengthy consideration.

Do I know about the circumstances that trapped my family in a city I hate, led to losing my brother, and brought me halfway across the world? "I know some."

"Tayagum and I were expedition quartermasters during that time," Akuudan said. "We were escorting the Water Tribe's payment to General Nong under diplomatic pretenses. The Earth King's forces at Llama-paca's Crossing ran us down along with the platinum we were guarding. The Water Tribe ambassadors couldn't get us released right away. Eventually they stopped trying."

"We were disavowed by Oyaluk," Tayagum said bitterly. "Maybe as punishment for failing to protect the money, maybe to save face, but either way, we were thrown into an Earth Kingdom prison to rot. We would still be there if the Avatar hadn't negotiated amnesty for us. No one asked her to. She took it upon herself."

"So we don't follow her out of a *deal*," Akuudan said. "Nor because she's the bridge between humans and spirits. We follow her because she's a person who will help others without question."

"Ah." Kavik nodded. They were true believers. Or maybe they were just indebted. "Did she attend your wedding as well, or were you already together before the Platinum Affair?"

Both men peered at him. "You're wearing what I assume are betrothal armbands," Kavik said. If he was correct, they'd modified the traditional custom of giving a hand-carved necklace to your promised. "The only thing I don't get is why Akuudan's has so many stones on it."

Akuudan broke out into a grin, the first real and warm expression he'd shown in front of Kavik. "We met before. Dumb-dumb here kept messing up the stone he was going to use. But I made him fish all of his failed attempts out of the rubbish. You can see a little progression of him getting better each time."

Tayagum leaned over and pressed his nose against his husband's cheek. "The one you made looked great on the first try."

They finished their meal and cleared the dishes. Over herb tea, Kavik briefed his hosts on Yangchen's plan for him in Jonduri. Despite the loyalty to the Avatar they'd professed earlier, they were far from enthusiastic.

"All right, she definitely made a mistake," Akuudan said, rubbing his temples with his thumb and little finger. "This is madness. You're going to get yourself killed."

"I've been caught snooping around warehouses and docks before," Kavik said. Most often, one shang would want to spy on another's assets before entering a deal—or breaking one. More information meant more leverage. "Usually I get the snot kicked out of me and sent on my way."

"Huh," Tayagum said. "Never heard someone boast about losing fights."

There were few other ways for the son of accountants to learn the trade. The standard cost against benefit calculations applied to any physical confrontation in Bin-Er. Teiin had paid a squad of headkickers because he could get away with it as long as no one died.

"Bin-Er is not Jonduri," Akuudan said. "And while they both hold the title of zongdu, Henshe is to Chaisee what a moose-lion cub is to its full-grown version. If the Avatar trifles with her, comes at her with the wrong tools, it's going to be a disaster."

"Why is Chaisee such bad news?"

"Her grip over the shangs in Jonduri is absolute," Tayagum explained. "They do business exactly as she tells them, she keeps the Fire Lord out of their hair, and everyone reaps massive profits. She's the most effective leader they've had since the system began."

"She also controls the flow of intelligence on the island," Akuudan said. "Every errand runner in Jonduri works for her as a member of a single association. They monitor the residents who might be a threat to her smooth operations. Merchants, workers, anyone who doesn't like the way she runs things. There is no class of independent agent like you, who could be persuaded to turn against her interests."

The two formidable-looking men, who had definitely seen their share of trouble, were talking about Chaisee like a spirit that brought bad luck. The kind that taboos were put in place around, for one's own protection. "The Avatar's meeting with her face-to-face," Kavik said.

They hitched with worry. "If it's entirely aboveground, about legitimate business, then she should be okay," Tayagum said. "Is the Avatar going to come here afterward, before you march off to your doom?"

That was the plan. Kavik nodded. "Good," Akuudan said. "We'll have a chance to talk her out of this."

Maybe she'll talk you into it. While the men obviously revered Yangchen, Kavik could see why she might have been hesitant to act through them. They were focused on the cost, not the benefit.

"Don't give us that look," Tayagum said. "We've been playing the game far longer than you. Professionals know when the risk is too great."

If Kavik wanted to play it safe, then he wouldn't be here right now. "Oh yeah? Then tell me which of you very serious professionals will break your assistant's nose tomorrow."

They were confused. Kavik pointed at his own face. "To match me. If Lee sees your man show up at the docks in pristine condition, he'll know it was someone else who came back on the boat today."

There was a long moment of silence before the three of them cracked up laughing.

Kavik couldn't stop. His sides hurt more than his nose. The idea of some poor sap getting walloped for something he wasn't a part of was completely unfair. Which was probably why it was so funny.

Suddenly Akuudan went quiet. "I'll do it," he growled, slamming a fist the size of a brick on the table, upsetting the tea.

A MEETING
OF MINDS

AFTER YANGCHEN dropped Kavik off in the water—his squeal of shock worth the trip alone—she rejoined the procession of Air Nomads on its way to Jonduri. Because her visit to the island city was part of her public agenda, the residents knew she was coming and greeted her in full force. The landing area, a small plateau in the lower hills, was surrounded by a large crowd cheering and waving ribbons of yellow and orange in coordinated patterns. Yangchen could see directors among them exhorting their sections. *More! More enthusiasm for the Avatar!*

She and her fellow Airbenders landed and were immediately showered with flower petals tossed high into the air. Smiling children, no doubt selected for the honor, bade her bow low so they could drape garlands made from more flowers around her neck.

Despite the grand welcome that Sidao had organized for her in advance, her minister was nowhere to be found. A demure, well-dressed man with a scar over his eyebrow was the only person who dared speak to her directly. He was the representative for Zongdu Chaisee, and he was happy to bring the Avatar to her while the rest of the traveling group were provided hospitality. His name? Oh, it didn't matter.

Yangchen shared a glance with Samten, the Northern elder who was in charge of organizing this trip. He wasn't part of the mission. Samten and the other monks were traveling like normal Airbenders, and Yangchen's presence was the aberration that had brought on this over-the-top welcome. He mouthed *we'll be fine,* right before the blast of several horns startled him off his feet.

She left her animal companions with Samten. Chaisee's representative led her up a path that took them away from the main city and past the shang compounds nestled deep in the greenery so only their entrances were visible. Eventually they came to a perfectly level walkway leading to a small square house jutting out of the hillside.

The zongdu's residence was extremely plain compared with some of the gilded gates Yangchen saw on their way up. If she hadn't known who waited inside, she would have thought it was the home of a country doctor, or a Ba Sing Se University professor's research station. It was probably the highest walkable point on the island.

The elevation gave a perfect view of the city below, letting anyone inside watch the ships come to harbor and the throngs of traders filling the exchange floor. Kavik would be down there by now, if everything had gone according to plan. She avoided staring too intently at the general area of the safe house and went inside.

Chaisee's hall was crafted from exposed bare wood treated to stay straight in the humidity. There were two chairs and a small table in front of a desk but no adornments to cover the walls, no freestanding ceramic pieces to fill the empty space. It was as if her office were once a training floor for barehanded fighters and needed to be ready for its original purpose at a moment's notice.

The one potential indicator of her host's personality was the massive bookshelf behind the desk. Yangchen focused on the spines within reach of the chair.

There was no organization by subject. *The Pearls of Laghima.* She knew those essays by heart, one of the many attempts over the generations to interpret the teachings of her people's most legendary guru. Huiliu's *Ten Chapters on Celestial Circles and Other Artful Mathematics.* She'd read those too—though had it been her or another Avatar? The treatise explained how to calculate the unending ratio between a circle's outside and its width by using ever-narrowing straight-sided shapes.

The Flame in the Mind: Oscillations and Harmonies, an old, popular layman's compilation of techniques to assist in meditation from across the Four Nations. It described the incense and singing bowls of the Air Nomads, the flickering focus candles of the Fire Sages, the beat of the Water Tribe's drums, the wire brushes used in the Earth Kingdom to lightly strike the limbs and unlock *chi* paths. There was a common interest across the world in losing oneself with the help of light and sound and the senses.

Yangchen didn't recognize the thin slip of a volume lying flat and crooked by itself, as well-worn as a reference manual. *The Complete Works of Shoken.* Whoever this Shoken person was, they hadn't had a very long career. Or perhaps they were just very concise.

Her curiosity was interrupted by Chaisee entering through the far door and shuffling slowly into the room. The Zongdu of Jonduri was only a little older than Henshe, somewhere around thirty. A short woman who kept her hair and clothes plain.

To Yangchen's surprise, Chaisee was about seven months pregnant. None of the reports she'd read about her in the last year mentioned the detail.

"Zongdu Chaisee," Yangchen said, standing up to greet her. "Congratulations. I didn't know you were expecting."

She went over to help the older woman into one of the chairs, but Chaisee waved her away. "Please, Avatar, sit. You are my guest, and I am honored by your presence." The zongdu turned to her attendant who had been loitering behind Yangchen. "Fetch some tea, would you?" The man bowed and left.

There was a momentary silence as Yangchen waited for the inevitable request. Soon-to-be parents were some of the most ardent seekers of blessings from Air Nomads, a service she was happy to provide. But Chaisee didn't ask. She was content to sit calmly and let her visitor speak first.

Yangchen coughed. A false start to the conversation. Her fault for assuming.

She reminded herself of the plan. Act like a visiting Avatar. And get out. The real work was going to come after she linked back up with Kavik at the safe house. Right now, she only needed to justify her presence.

"I was admiring your books," she said to ease into things. "We have similar tastes, it seems. Though I haven't read any Shoken yet."

"Oh, but you must." Chaisee had a smooth voice free of excess touches, much like her furnishings. "He posits human beings are but surfaces, points of contact that don't exist unless we interact with others and the world around us. The only space in which a road and a wheel become relevant is the infinitely thin, ever-changing stripe where they touch. Together, the cart rolls."

"Negation of the self," Yangchen said. "A very Air Nomad concept."

Chaisee nodded. "He was a contemporary to your Great Laghima. Though he can be a little more drama-prone in his phrasing. 'To possess a mind, destroy it first.' Sounds like a harsher version of *Empty, and become wind,* no?"

"It does. What nation is he from?"

"Shoken? Unknown, like me. Which is probably why I'm partial to him."

Yangchen frowned as politely as she could. "I thought the Zongdu of Jonduri would certainly be drawn from the Fire Lord's subjects."

"Yes, but that's a matter of maps more than blood," Chaisee said. "I'm not really Fire Nation, not traceably so. I grew up on a small island in the south Mo Ce, the daughter of shellfish divers. No benders of any sort in the family, no clan traditions to uphold. My own ancestry remains a mystery to me, which is sad, I suppose, but common enough for those of us who come from in-between places."

She proffered a direct look into her eyes. They were hazel.

"You've risen to great heights," Yangchen said. "I know Chief Oyaluk and Earth King Feishan envy Jonduri as the jewel of the shang system."

The attempt at flattery only got a shrug out of the zongdu. "If there's one thing I can be proud of, it's that I've turned this city into a place that doesn't care where you were born. Opportunities are available for people from around the world. Hidebound traditions can be cast aside."

"In favor of business," Yangchen said, allowing an involuntary note of sharpness into the word.

"Yes. In favor of business."

Yangchen let the pause soak while she considered how to play the conversation. Besides relaying the request to deliver Unanimity, Sidao would have informed Chaisee about the disastrous ultimatum in Bin-Er. Between then and now, would the Avatar have decided to keep threatening the shangs by using the nearest head of state as her weapon, or would she have seen the error in her approach?

Best to fit her image. She was a young Air Nomad, and despite all evidence to the contrary, not a complete idiot. She would have been mortified with herself after Bin-Er. She *was* mortified with herself.

"Zongdu Chaisee, the truth is . . . I have grave concerns about the nature of the shang system itself. I don't mean to denigrate your accomplishments, but they lie atop an inherently imbalanced foundation. A small number of people reaping disproportionately to what they've sown, while more and more commonfolk—"

"Stop, I beg you," Chaisee said gently. "You needn't go into every detail. I know what happened in Bin-Er."

Yangchen wrung her robes, pretending to be caught out before the older, more experienced leader. "Minister Sidao must have explained matters to you already. Why is he not here?"

The question served the purpose of making her look like a child searching for the steady hand of her older advisor, but she also needed to know. "He decided to return to Bin-Er after helping me prepare for your arrival," Chaisee said. "Despite his short stay, I understand very well what you want. You've come here to try your message again in Jonduri. Do I have that right?"

More or less. "It is as you perceive," Yangchen said.

"Getting a shang to part with their gold is like watering a desert. Difficult. Foolish." The zongdu wiggled her head from side to side. "But it can be done."

"I'm sorry?"

"It can be done. We can make the city a fairer, more balanced place."

"I'm sorry," Yangchen repeated, a flush rising in her neck. "Are you talking about Jonduri or Bin-Er?"

"Both. Port Tuugaq and Taku as well, provided we're patient. The shangs of this island will do as I say. But I don't have as much influence overseas, and old curmudgeons like Teiin have to be talked to in a certain manner. I heard from Sidao you made mention of historical reforms in Omashu as a template. I'm familiar with them, which would speed things up."

Yangchen couldn't believe it. The Zongdu of Jonduri was not only giving in to the Avatar's requests but was offering to help. She'd thrown her weight at a door and found it wasn't latched.

Hope squirmed captive in her chest. She had to poke her cheek with her tongue to keep from grinning like a fool. "Your counterpart in Bin-Er wasn't quite so decisive."

"Henshe's an empty set of robes who only got his position because he looks good in front of a crowd," Chaisee said, punctuating her assessment with a sniff. "Now that the two of us have met and fallen in league, we can focus on action. The road and the wheel, together."

Yangchen had had it wrong the whole time. There wasn't going to be a need for skulduggery. It had simply been a matter of talking to the right person. The surface layer, the fruitful one that really mattered, was as deep as they would go. She wouldn't have to visit Earth King Feishan and feed him the unpleasant truths of the shangs malfeasance—

Oh.

She was getting everything she wanted, wasn't she?

Yangchen had a brief sense of falling, the ground curving away from her feet. She almost said the *oh* again out loud, so jarring was the impact of landing.

How did parents deal with truculent children? How did you say no without saying no? By saying *yes,* and simply doing nothing afterward. Chaisee had dangled compliance in front of Yangchen and she'd snapped it up like bait on a hook, even though she was speaking to the very woman whom Henshe was relying on to deliver an asset that would grant them complete impunity. The Avatar wasn't being helped. She was being handled.

A squeak of the floorboards announced the attendant's return. He placed a steaming cup of tea in front of Yangchen and served Chaisee plain hot water. Yangchen picked up her drink but couldn't summon the energy to bring it to her lips. She held the cup, the heat deadening her fingers.

"Is something not to your liking?" Chaisee asked.

"No," Yangchen said. "It's just . . . how long do you think such reforms might take?"

"As long as they need to."

Good answer. If one were being pat. "Would not such a large effort, executed smoothly, take many years?" Yangchen shook the aftermath of Tienhaishi from her head. A single night's battle. So long to see it through to the end. "I might end up having to work with one of your successors, and I don't know if they'd be as capable or committed. Might there be a plan or a loophole to keep you in your role as zongdu past your term limits?"

Chaisee's eyes flickered in the direction of her servant, who was waiting to be dismissed. Her hand drifted to her stomach. "No," she said quickly. "That is one of the unbreakable rules of my position. We have to do as much as we can with the time we are given."

Yangchen couldn't agree more.

"Avatar, would you mind joining me for a short walk in the garden?" Chaisee said. "The tea would benefit from a longer steeping."

There was barely a distinction between the lush overgrowth of the surrounding jungle and the curated plants belonging to the property. The sweet fragrance of climbing orchids lay heavy on the nose.

"Are you sure this isn't too much exertion?" Yangchen asked as they picked their way through the gravel path. She moved aside the draping vines and hanging branches for them both. Under a tree she noticed a pile of broken eggshells that must have come from a sizable bird, and when she looked up, she saw a platform made of planks, holding a nest. Raven-eagles, judging by the loose feathers.

"It's good for my swelling feet. Avatar, I have to give you a bit of advice. Be careful what you say around people you haven't vetted. To wit, my servant is a spy for the Fire Lord."

Yangchen turned her head in surprise and was swatted across the temple by dewy leaves. She had kept Sidao on the roster, yes, but she'd never let anyone she suspected get so close to the places where she lived and ate. Her off-duty moments, her homes in the Air Temples and especially the Western one, were inviolable to her. "You're sure?"

"I'm sure." Chaisee adjusted the shoulder of her linen robe. "Fire Lord Gonryu enjoys the revenue I bring him, but he has no desire to see any particular zongdu linger. If he believed I meant to stay in power longer than my allotted term, there would be a great deal of trouble."

"I'm sorry," Yangchen said. "I—I can't imagine what it would be like. To live your life being *spied* upon."

"I could teach you a great many things about the experience. For now, the man is a useful instrument to make sure Fire Lord Gonryu hears what I want him to hear. Once that's no longer true I'll dispose of him."

Yangchen halted. "What do you mean by that?"

"I mean, I will make him go away so completely that his own masters will wonder if he ever existed in the first place. People will take as many liberties with you as you let them, Avatar. I could teach you how to deal with such offenses appropriately."

Chaisee was still in the mindset of dealing out advice. Philosophy. She saw nothing wrong with what she was saying, and she overtook Yangchen along the path as if lost in thought.

"For instance, I know ruffians tried to pelt you with stones in Bin-Er," she said. "Assaulting the Avatar in the street? Such a thing would never happen in Jonduri. Disgraceful, the way Henshe did nothing to find the perpetrators. If it were me, I'd have nailed their hands to their skulls so they could beg your forgiveness in the proper pose. And with the appropriate level of enthusiasm. One can easily survive such a punishment."

Chaisee took a few more steps before noticing Yangchen wasn't following her and turned around slowly. The Avatar stared the zongdu down, the two of them hedged in by green bamboo. The vegetation seemed to press them closer like gamblers urging on a pair of fighting cricket-snails.

"You will refrain from making awful jests in my presence," Yangchen said. Reveling in violence in front of her face? No. There had to be a line, where the games stopped and the masks were put aside. "And you will cease any misguided beliefs you might hold that I would ever be party to such heinous deeds."

Chaisee inhaled deeply through her nose. "I have offended you. I thought a leader in your position might be receptive to discussing various strategies. Of course, my words were all hypothetical."

She bowed slightly, limited in her range of motion. "I apologize. Perhaps we should end our visit for now."

At Chaisee's plea, Yangchen waited by the walkway while the zongdu went back inside to fetch something. She emerged from her house holding a slim book, bound with string.

The works of Shoken. Chaisee pressed it into Yangchen's hands. "In my childhood village, it was our custom to give honored visitors a gift of personal value upon their departure. The practice ensures a link between the host's past and the guest's future. I see you as a great Avatar in the making, and I wish to be of one mind with you."

She values unanimity, Yangchen thought, *in the truest sense.* The tight smiles of selected residents. Manipulating image and information. An underlying threat of violence. The order of Jonduri was dependent upon control.

Henshe with unchecked power was a callow menace. But Chaisee, unfettered . . . Yangchen couldn't predict her eventual form, the marble waiting to be freed from the block, and that scared her. She had to get into the town below, under cover, and confirm Kavik made it in safely. From there, they could figure out how to locate the critical shipments before—

"One more thing," Chaisee said. "I have a message for you that came to me by mistake." She produced a small scroll, bent and torn.

Yangchen took it, frowning at the unlikelihood. "How did you get this?" There was a scratch on the back, and a brown dot that might have been a speck of dried blood.

"I chanced upon an injured messenger hawk on the hillside. Jonduri lies underneath several flight paths, and occasionally the animals end up here when they shouldn't. They're convenient, fast, but they're not infallible. No substitute for a trusted human courier."

Yangchen unfurled the paper and read. The message was indeed addressed to her. A few words in and her fingers began to tremble.

"From Duke Zolian of the Saowon clan," Chaisee said. "I'm sorry to have read your correspondence, but I didn't know it was for the Avatar's eyes only. It sounds like things have taken a turn for the worse in Ma'inka since your last visit. I've never heard the duke use such desperate language before."

Yangchen wadded the scroll in her fist. She squeezed it until it burst into flames, the hot ash turning to dust against her skin. Despite her earlier rebuke of Chaisee, she had never been so close to wanting to commit premeditated violence herself.

"Those poor children," Chaisee said. "You can imagine how my heart goes out to them."

The Zongdu of Jonduri stared out to sea. From her house she could see the harbor, every ship entering and leaving her domain. "I assume you will want to make haste for Ma'inka immediately," she said to Yangchen. "Each passing moment spent here could mean another life lost."

Chaisee smiled faintly into the breeze. "And that is the one thing we cannot abide now, isn't it?"

THE GAMBLE

THE AVATAR was supposed to check in at the safe house as soon as she could after dropping Kavik off. He waited by puttering around the customer-less inn, helping Akuudan with inside chores while Tayagum went out to fish. He scouted the streets as much as he could without drawing suspicion, observing Jonduri residents. The ones who'd lived on the island since birth spoke sentences that burst up and down like noisemakers. They doubled up words for emphasis and slung the term *sifu* around as a casual greeting, a shocking use of an honorific so esteemed in the wider Four Nations. *Hey, Sifu! Get your broke-broke behind out the way of my cart!*

By the middle of the third day, though, Yangchen still hadn't shown up. "Something's wrong," Kavik said to his older teammates.

"So astute of you to notice," Akuudan snapped, as testy as a father whose child had paddled out to sea in the middle of a storm.

Tayagum, as Kavik had learned, was in the habit of freezing and melting and refreezing water into different strand patterns between his fingers when he was worried. The string game, but for Waterbenders. "Most likely she's being watched and can't shake her tails yet," he said, reassuring himself as much as anyone else. A crystalline net as delicate as silk glittered in his palms. "No one in their right mind would harm the Avatar."

"I don't know about that." Kavik was no historian, but he could name at least a couple of famous examples off the top of his head who'd fallen in battle.

Tayagum shot him a dirty look. "You're thinking of wartime champions who went out in blazes of glory. Avatars don't get knifed in the middle of busy cities." He distractedly dropped a loop of water, ruining one side of the bridge of frost. "To my knowledge," he muttered.

"And she hasn't sent any word by hawk?" Kavik asked.

Akuudan shook his head. "Aerial messages tend to vanish without a trace in Jonduri; we've never been able to rely on them for communication going to and from the island."

So they were stuck. Yangchen was supposed to be their decision maker. The person with the final call on what moves to make.

"We found a good lead on how you can get in with Chaisee's association, but the problem is the window closes tonight," Akuudan said. "The dock loaders are unhappy with their working conditions, and the flow of traffic is slowing. At some point, Chaisee is going to have to send her people in to resolve the conflict. This is biggest bout of unrest since her term began, so she's been hiring fresh blood in preparation. You would try to join her recruitment drive."

The same story, reincarnated across the waters. "I thought there was no unrest in Jonduri," Kavik said.

"You think that because Chaisee always sends her people in to 'resolve the conflict,'" Tayagum said. "This is a chance to get right up close to the assets we're looking for."

After Kavik's briefing, they'd all agreed the docks were their best bet at intercepting the Unanimity shipment. "What do you think it is?" Kavik asked, curious about their take on the matter. "Weapons? Alchemical ingredients?"

Tayagum and Akuudan listened to Kavik rattling off the list of possibilities he and Yangchen had come up with on the flight over. In unison, they shook their heads.

"For my mind, there's only one thing it could be," Tayagum said. "Money. Stamped coins, raw bullion, stacks of contracts worth huge amounts, maybe. But I'll guarantee you it's money, in one form or another."

Kavik was going to say that was an unimaginative guess, but the more he thought about it, the more it made sense. The Platinum Affair had thrown the world off balance, and these two men had been right there to see it happen. Enough money could buy an army or force a city to its knees. It could be moved on a boat and stored until its eventual release, an arrow loosed from a bow.

"I suppose the only way we find out is if I go get recruited tonight," Kavik said. "We'd just have to act without the Avatar's blessing." *Without her protection.*

Back at the Northern Air Temple, he'd confided in Yangchen about the emptiness over his shoulder. The uncomfortable freedom that came when no one was watching out for you. For Kavik, it tilted the ground underneath him, pushed him along uncertain paths, lent him speed. He was used to it by now, after Kalyaan had been gone for so long. You could run faster downhill, provided your feet kept up.

The two older men looked unconvinced. "She would go for it," Kavik said. He'd recognized a kindred spirit in the Avatar, right before her lemurs ruined the moment. "Granted, I don't know her as well as you do, but it feels like she would take the risk herself if she could."

Akuudan grunted in resignation. "Then you know her perfectly well," he said.

Jonduri at night was a red glow of lanterns, a fume of spilled drinks, a raucous, too-loud conversation over spicy food. The temperatures after dark wouldn't kill you like they would in Bin-Er; in fact, the heat became almost tolerable. The residents of the city took full advantage and packed the streets, flowing from one night market to another.

The meeting point for prospective recruits of the zongdu was set in a creaking hall innocuously named Kee-Hop Merchant's Association.

Kavik wondered why it lay over a rotting dock, as if the occupants had to keep an arbitrary separation from the dry land of Jonduri. The answer was clear once the burly enforcer let him through. Inside was a gambling den.

The interior didn't have a floor so much as a series of planks laid haphazardly over bamboo struts, and the lapping water underneath the building was visible through holes big enough to fish in. Gaming tables bounced and swayed as players pounded on their tops. Now and then, a grateful winner or a loser needing a change in luck would flip a coin into one of the holes, resulting in a small splash. The place was built on wishes.

Akuudan and Tayagum had told him there might be some kind of trial. He was going to have to think on his toes in order to get accepted into Chaisee's confederation of runners, spies, and headkickers.

A table manager glanced at him and then at the far end of the hall, where tightly placed paper screens formed a corner office.

There was someone inside, and a small slat of loose weave would let the occupant peer out onto the floor while remaining hidden.

The manager's glance turning into a full-blown stare gave Kavik a decent guess as to what a first test might be. His potential employers wanted to watch him gamble. Was he an all-or-nothing type of player, a small-talker, a bluffer?

He spent a few minutes assessing his surroundings. A small group of motley individuals, old men all, was playing street-style Pai Sho in the corner. But most of the floor space was dedicated to a four-person game played with elemental solitaire tiles. Kavik had never liked solitaire—despite perfect play, sometimes you just couldn't win due to the way the pieces were stacked—and he decided not to go anywhere near this competitive version. The speed and dexterity with which the gamblers clacked their tiles said he would be eaten alive.

He had some money with him, but not much, and he was pretty sure going bankrupt before the signal would mean getting tossed out from both the building and the selection process. Kavik thought about it a bit more and went over to the Pai Sho section. He asked for a standard rules game from one of the hustling geezers and was denied until he promised to give his opponent four times the stakes if he won.

But the bet would never come to completion. Unlike the fast-paced chance versions, regular Pai Sho could be stalled out near indefinitely. Kavik sat on a stool and played like a stone wall. Ba Sing Se had nothing on his defense. He was never going to win, but neither was he going to lose, and if the candidates were selected by the last purse standing, he could sit here and let chance ruin them.

He stroked his chin and contemplated the board state sagely for what seemed like an hour until a hall-wide raffle was announced. A large wire birdcage filled with dice was brought out, and the gamblers paused their play at the tables to check slips of paper with characters written on them.

Kavik looked up to see the floor manager standing over him. "Boss-boss says go to the back."

Kavik left the Pai Sho table over the protests of his elderly foe. A small door near the screens was open. He kept his eyes lowered, not wanting to offend the boss-boss as he approached. He held his breath as the shadow inside shifted, and only let it out once he was through the door. He might have just passed within inches of the infamous Zongdu Chaisee.

Outside was a dock barely big enough to hold Kavik and the other four candidates. A boatman pulled closer in a rowed skiff.

"You two get in," he said, using the oar to point at Kavik and another boy about his age with a notch in his ear, like Yangchen's lemur Pik. Or was it Pak? "You other three go back inside."

So over half of them weeded out already. The winners boarded the boat and the losers started to protest, but the boat-man pushed off against the dock pile regardless. The vessel floated away into the night, leaving those who didn't make the cut at a loss for what to do.

"How did you fare?" asked the other passenger. Kavik had noticed him playing the elemental tile game like an expert. He tossed up a heavy purse and swiped it sideways. "That bad, huh? I probably should have stayed back there if the Sparrowbones tables can be cracked this easy. I doubled up at least three times."

Maybe the boss-boss liked extreme differences in strategy. Maybe Master Lucky over here was going to be his new partner in the association. Kavik had very little to go on but decided he would dread the thought anyway.

The reflected moon guided them around the edge of the shore into a steep inlet that would have been hard to see in broad daylight. A large flat-sided building waited for them, comically crowded behind a tiny slip of beach, lamplight peeking out of a row of windows.

They disembarked and stopped in front of the door where a reedy fellow who looked more like a clerk than a guard took note of them and scribbled on a chalk slate. Being recorded took Kavik on a swift, unpleasant journey back to the first day he stepped on the Earth Kingdom continent.

"Your little test was clever," said the other boy. He tossed the bag of coins onto the slate, nearly making its holder drop them both. "But I think I'm a bit more profitable than our Water Tribe friend here."

The man seemed confused by the money. "What? What test?"

"You were watching us gamble over the evening. Seeing which of us made the most money." The boy jostled Kavik with his elbow. "You must have noticed it too. Tell him."

Kavik composed his features into a blank, dull stare. The boy's grin, which had started out wide as the crescent moon overhead, was now waning steadily. "Come on," he said to Kavik, like they were in this together. "Why else would they leave us there for so long before the signal? And take only you and me if they weren't doing an evaluation?"

"We were *late*," said the boatman. "And I told the others to stay behind because the skiff's not safe when it's overloaded."

The clerk had had enough. "All right, you know what, kid? Get out of here. You can have a ride back, and then we never want to see you again." He pointed at Kavik with his chalk. "You. Stay."

"But—but—" The boatman pressed his unwilling passenger away using the oar.

"Rude," the clerk muttered. He fished an intricately carved wooden key out of his robes and pushed it into the door lock.

Before turning it, he paused. "We *were* watching," he said quietly to Kavik. "And we like runners who can play dumb and avoid being noticed." The mechanism clunked into place and the door swung open. "Welcome to the association."

Kavik was hit by a wave of sweat and fish and decaying kelp. The building had to have been a fish-drying operation at some point to explain the smell wafting from the floorboards, but now it seemed a cross between a training ground and a social club. Over by an expanse of straw mats that badly needed airing, there were sets of satchel-shaped weights, loaded exercise maces. In a different section, tables and tiles for the exact same game being played back in the gambling den had been set up, alongside rows of cots. A stove next to a woodpile.

Association members could relax here, keep their muscles warm, nap. Kavik was puzzled by the setup until he remembered his job, and the job he was pretending to seek.

This place was a safe house. He'd been momentarily confused by the scale. Chaisee had a huge private building for her runners as opposed to Akuudan's tiny inn. Numerous operatives to Yangchen's one runner. Kavik felt puny, and a little indignant on the Avatar's behalf.

Right now, none of the equipment was being used. Everyone inside was gathered near a wall, two dozen people jeering and shouting and laughing in rapt attention. There would be an odd noise, *thunk!* and then a reaction from the crowd. *Gaah, come on!*

"You can call me Tael," the man who'd let him in said.

"Kavik." Like Yangchen said, in Jonduri he was completely clean. It was simpler not to make something up.

"We pay per job, Kavik. We give you something to do, you do it, and you don't ask questions. You're lucky to be here, you understand? Boss-boss had a good feeling about you. There's a lot of dock action going on these days, and I want a Waterbender on hand."

It *had* been easy. But if he was in demand, he was in demand. "So you know I'm a Waterbender," Kavik said. He avoided phrasing it as a question.

Tael smirked, proud of his own observation skills. "Your reactions to the sea, the moon. You look at the water more often. It's hard to ignore a big presence of your element. Earthbenders are always glancing down more than they think, you know?" Huh. Kavik supposed that was true. "Boss-boss likes to put people to work right away," said Tael. "At sunrise we got a job for you and whoever wins this contest we're having right now."

Tael bade Kavik come see what was happening by the wall. The two of them circled the crowd until they found a gap to watch through.

Thunk. The sound of metal hitting home in wood. A knife-throwing competition.

The two participants must have been at it for a long time because the target, a stump turned on its side, had been gouged into a bowl. Most of the association members were rooting for the dashing, well-dressed youth who almost looked like a son of a shang, trawling the bottom of the city for adventure. Money had certainly been placed on him.

His opponent, a stocky kid in ratty sleeves who looked tense and furious even when he was waiting for his turn, had far fewer backers. A broad, wrinkled stripe of a scar ran down the middle of his forehead to his nose, as if he'd accidentally smeared acid on a sunburn instead of ointment.

A hush fell over the crowd as the well-dressed boy toed the line. He held two daggers in the same hand by their points in an upside-down *eight* character. He wiped the sweat from his brow and ignored a heckler who claimed he was doomed to failure. With a carefully considered heave, he sent the weapons tumbling through the air.

The first dagger landed home in the center of the target, followed instantly by the tip of the second burying itself in the wooden pommel of the first. An arrow split, but with knives. And on the same toss, no less.

The onlookers burst into cheers. A once-in-a-lifetime sight. But the noise died down as soon as the scarred boy stormed up to the line, gripping his knives the exact same way, presumably to match the feat. He didn't seem to think it was a big deal. A waste of a throw, really.

"Come on, Jujinta!" someone shouted. "Just forfeit the match! Some of us have places to be!"

Jujinta spotted Tael and called out to him in a nasal, squeaky voice. "You said if I lose, Shigoro here gets my spot on the next job, right?"

"That's what I said," Tael replied.

Jujinta cracked his neck and gave his next move some thought. Without warning, he stabbed the meat of his opponent's throwing shoulder with one of his daggers, leaving the blade stuck there.

Shigoro screamed and dropped to the floor. "I lose," Jujinta said to Tael over the shock of the crowd and the cries of pain filling the hall. "But I don't think he's going to be employable for a while."

"Can't argue with that logic." Tael turned to Kavik and slapped him on the back. "Meet your new partner. I'm sure the two of you will make a great team."

LEGITIMATE BUSINESS

FROM ABOVE, Ma'inka always looked like a fish's head to Yangchen. Open-mouthed, goggling. Bisected from the rest of the body. She could relate.

One of the eastern islands in the volcanic chain making up the Fire Nation, Ma'inka belonged to the Saowon clan. An old, proud Fire Nation lineage dating back to pre-unification history. Her immediate predecessor, Avatar Szeto, had skillfully managed the Saowon and their rival noble houses during a time of deep crisis in his homeland, and tempered ancient feuds into a lasting peace.

Yangchen *thought* she had lived up to Szeto's legacy with a victory of her own the last time she was in Ma'inka. The message to her that Chaisee had intercepted had proven otherwise.

She circled the carved spires of Duke Zolian's stone manor and landed between moss-draped walls and a reflecting pool that was developing a green skin on top. Her greeting by the servants was somber. They told her that while the duke had been informed of the Avatar's arrival the instant they spotted her bison in the air, he was still finishing some business with the clan elders. She would have to wait.

For a brief moment, Yangchen wondered how future generations would look upon an Air Avatar challenging a Fire Nation noble to an Agni Kai. She'd win too; she was pretty certain of it.

After calming down, Yangchen left Nujian with the stable hands and was led inside the ancestral seat of the Saowon. In Zolian's private study, Yangchen sat by herself, drank smoked tea, and swallowed her misgivings.

She'd made the gamble to drop everything and come here instead of meeting with Kavik like she'd promised. Trying to make contact at the safe house before traveling to Ma'inka was an option, yes. But Chaisee's vantage point from the peak of Jonduri, plus the watchers she surely put on Yangchen after their conversation, meant sneaking back into the city would have been a long and laborious process. Time was of the essence here. She had to hope Kavik possessed enough sense to lie low with Akuudan and Tayagum until she returned to Jonduri.

The door opened and Duke Zolian entered. He'd lost weight since their last meeting, and his beard was grayer. Behind him was his heir and much younger cousin, Lohi, who held a large carved box in his arms.

A gift. She was going receive a gift to make it all better. The two men bowed deeply. "Avatar," Zolian said, his voice cracking with relief. "You got our message. Thank the spirits, you got our—"

"Shut up," Yangchen snapped. She'd shown all the tact in the world on her first visit, but circumstances were different now. "Shut up. Shut up. Shut. Up."

Her command hung in the air. *Until further notice.* They waited dutifully, heads hung. Their shame a testament to how badly they'd erred, and how desperately they still needed her.

She must have seemed like she was drawing the moment out to exert her power, but really Yangchen couldn't find any words. She tripped over every sentence in her head.

"You . . . you only had to do one thing," Yangchen said, eloquence nowhere to be found. "It was working. It was working and you— All you had to do was uphold your end of the bargain! You only had to do one thing *and you mucked it up!*"

Control over her loudness, also gone. She wondered why they weren't talking until she remembered she'd specifically ordered it. "Speak."

"Avatar." Lohi shifted the weight of the box that Yangchen still refused to acknowledge. "I understand you must be disappointed, but please let us explain."

"What is there to explain?! No human was to set foot within three li of the cavern edges! Did we not set up boundary warnings? Did we not communicate the terms to the assembled family heads before I left? There's nothing to explain!"

This should have been the one of the most straightforward of matters for an Avatar. One of her most basic duties. An easy victory, even. The Saowon had asked her for help dealing with unseen forces causing damage along the edges of their villages. And she'd given it.

After interpreting the will of the spirits, she informed their human neighbors that in order to end the troubles, they'd have to keep their distance from the cenotes dotting the island and leave what looked like perfectly good, arable land untouched. Settlements were pulled back, the destruction of the sinkholes ceased, and balance had crept into Ma'inka. Delicate but real.

Those efforts had been wasted. Duke Zolian's chin trembled. It didn't matter that he couldn't bring himself to speak; there were only so many answers to choose from. *We didn't think the rule applied to* everyone. *We broke the rule by accident and nothing bad happened immediately, so we figured it was fine. We didn't think you were serious. We thought the problem had eventually gone away by itself. We realized, in retrospect, that we just didn't care about anything other than what we wanted in the moment.*

Yangchen had heard so many variations on the underlying melody, but it was all the same song. "You have hamstrung my ability to help you again. Give me a reason why I shouldn't leave right now and let you face the spirits on your own this time."

The threat surprised her as it slipped out. She wouldn't abandon people in need. So then why did she say it? Why did it feel good to imagine flying away, leaving them behind to plead with the sky?

Here, Zolian was ready with an answer. "Our children," he said. "It is as we wrote to you. The phoenix-eel spirits have— They've done something to our children. A curse. Across the island, Saowon youth are not waking up from their slumber. They will waste away if we do nothing."

"Every healer we've consulted says the sickness is borne of the spirit, not the body," Lohi said. "I know you may not believe us, but we could take you to a hospital, show you the effects—"

"*NO!*"

They were confused by her violent refusal. Avatar Yangchen was known for healing the sick with her own two hands; it was arguably the image of her the Four Nations liked best. It was true she had treated many gruesome injuries and illnesses, seen the worst kind of physical damage.

But to look upon a wasting dream, the peaceful form of a body damaged in spirit . . . No. She couldn't subject herself to that, not after what happened to Jetsun. "I believe you," Yangchen said. "There is nothing to prove."

Zolian knelt and touched his head to the floor. "I beg you not to let them suffer for our misdeeds. Please, Avatar. Negotiate with the spirits on our behalf once more. We will honor the outcome, honor you, for an eternity."

Lohi stepped forward with the box. "We have collected a penance from our clan, to show our sincerity." He opened the lid and showed her the contents.

When Yangchen realized what the dark lumps inside were, she had to avert her eyes. Piled in the box, like the organs of a slaughtered animal, were bundles of human hair. Judging from the jeweled and gilded pins intentionally left in them, the top ranks of the Saowon clan had all undertaken the ritual of dishonor.

The meaning, the weight of that harvest, heaped upon Yangchen's neck, making her dizzy and nauseous. They'd wanted to move her. They couldn't have imagined how successful they'd be.

She had *been* Fire Nation scores of times over, held her honor in the highest esteem, and lost it on a few occasions. The fact applied here as much as it did underneath the floorboards of the Bin-Er gathering hall.

Yangchen staggered backward and caught herself on her chair. "Get that away from me," she said. "Close the lid." With everything weighing on her, she could not afford to lose control in front of the leaders of a major Fire Nation clan. She fought back the heaves running through her gut. She swallowed and swallowed until the danger passed.

The act of willpower was not a moment to be proud of. Brute suppression had a cost. Her body and mind were sure to pay the price later, with interest.

Zolian and Lohi took her shudders as acceptance of the gesture. Of course the benevolent and loving Air Nomad would be moved. "There are only two more additions to be made," Lohi said. He put the box aside, drew a blade from his waist, and knelt beside his elder.

Yangchen and Lohi left Zolian recovering in a chair with the help of his servants, a damp cloth draped over his eyes. The display of shame had worked, the Avatar had acquiesced, but the mental strain of losing his topknot had rendered the duke incapable of further discussion.

The younger Saowon had needed only a minute to collect himself before offering to show Yangchen out. They walked through a hallway exposed to an open courtyard on one side, patches of moisture seeping through joints in the stonework overhead. The manor had a temple-like construction, its ancient architect no doubt influenced by the strong link between the Saowon clan and the Fire Sages.

Lohi's hand drifted upward toward his shorn patch only once—to check in disbelief that his hair wasn't still sitting on his head—before he snatched it back down and kept his fist balled at his side. "My clan would have me beg your forgiveness," he said. "We needed as much land as we could plant. In lean times, every acre counts."

Lohi had proven to be sensible the last time Yangchen was in Ma'inka, someone she could work with. He surely recognized how weak the excuses coming out of his mouth sounded. "We did try other measures before contacting you again." Lohi gestured toward an empty alcove as they walked by. "The family treasures. Some of them were sacrificed on pyres to no avail; the rest had to be liquidated to feed our retainers. Straits are dire, Avatar."

"They didn't have to be." That was the most frustrating part. Neither Yangchen nor the spirits had demanded a complete beggaring of the Saowon.

"Indeed. Your initial message was delivered impeccably. It was our stubborn ears that refused to open."

Yangchen remembered the original council among the family heads when she'd explained the demands of the spirits. The elders had hemmed and hawed instead of nodding, and when Zolian announced they would comply, several pairs of eyes had glanced at each other instead of their clan leader.

"My duke was unable to keep some of the branch houses from defying the contract," Lohi said. "He is a good man, but occasionally soft when it comes to his family. When it is my turn to lead the Saowon, I promise you I will enforce unanimity within my clan."

A mere coincidence in his choice of words. And yet Yangchen had to struggle not to scream.

A servant brought her staff. She was going to have to fly fast. "Tell me something," she said once she and Lohi were alone again. "The family heads who broke the agreement. Would they have listened the first time if I'd told them the treaty was the word of Avatar Szeto himself, and not mine? If I'd told them I'd communed with his spirit beforehand, and the terms were simply what he commanded me to put down on paper?"

She'd thought of the tactic after her flop in Bin-Er, too late to help her there and long after her first attempt to assist the Saowon. Speaking with the voice of her past life, the respected elder statesman could have helped her cause in front of Teiin and Noehi. It certainly wouldn't have hurt.

But in the Fire Nation, Szeto's name was a sledgehammer. Had she trotted it out, her decree to stay away from the sacred cenotes would have landed upon the Saowon with the force of a mother, a father, a sifu, the Fire Lord, all rolled into one. She could have leveraged her predecessor's credibility, provided she was willing to acknowledge she had none herself.

Lohi's pause was all the answer she needed. ". . . Did you?" he asked. "Did you talk to Szeto?"

Yangchen frowned, snapped the wings of her glider open, and took off.

THE DISPUTE

SHE WASN'T going to take Nujian to the largest cenote. Her companion could get jittery around spirits these days and had every right to be after the Old Iron incident. Yangchen flew over the humid jungles of Ma'inka on her glider, pushing the winds as hard as she could.

She spotted a clearing in the trees and landed on a woven floor of roots. It was necessary to proceed on foot for the last part of the journey, let herself be vulnerable, or else she risked flying back and forth over her destination wondering why she wasn't seeing anything out of the ordinary.

Sunbeams combed through the tree trunks. She could hear chittering insects and screaming birds. The smell of life was also the smell of decay, overwhelming rot and fertility attacking through her nose.

Yangchen stepped from stone to stone and fallen branch to fallen branch. There was no such thing as a straight path under the canopy. She avoided using her staff for balance; the end would sink into the damp soil and ruin the tail fins.

Her disturbances sent squirrel-toads hopping in circles. Several of them decided to follow along and keep pace. Leaves fell from overhead. She looked up to see monkey-marmots trailing her through the trees.

"Shoo," she said. The furry creatures, reminiscent of lemurs, blinked and waggled their head tufts. Yangchen sighed.

Animals were often drawn to her for no discernible reason. It was how she'd ended up with Pik and Pak. People envied her for it, but there were drawbacks. The other children had cried on Bonding Day when most of the bison calves flocked to Yangchen instead of distributing themselves equitably. She had to flee with Nujian before she ended up with a whole herd of companions instead of just one.

After a half hour of walking, she encountered the problem. The true reason why she was here.

A large plot of land had been cleared by slashing and burning. Inside the swidden was an encampment constructed on top of bamboo piles, giving it the thin-legged appearance of Jonduri in miniature. A network of sluice chutes sprouted outward from the village center. They led to nowhere, no vessels for containment, and had the slurry inside not dried up since the camp's evacuation it would have spilled in waves over the jungle floor.

By following the chutes, she found the last piece of evidence, a derrick topped by a pulley, the setup for a drop drill. A blunt-force mechanism to smash away at the earth with an iron bit until substances that should have been deep and buried could be sucked to the surface. Either the rig had to be abandoned too quickly to hide, or the owners hadn't bothered at all, thinking she wouldn't know what it was if she discovered it. Air Nomads had no use for such devices, after all.

Somewhere along the chain of communication, from the disobedient branch families, to Zolian and Lohi, to her, the truth had been twisted. This wasn't a farming plot. This was an excavation zone.

The affronted phoenix-eels had made their displeasure clear. The longhouses and bamboo scaffolds had been crushed in several places, narrow stripes of destruction that looked like they could have been caused by falling trees. But there was nothing in the wreckage except for great splashes of acidic discoloration, extending from the broken buildings to the vegetation around them. Channels of dead vines and unnaturally yellowed shrubs led deeper into the forest.

Yangchen shuddered. The village was a scar crossed out by another scar.

She exited the clearing on the other side, in more ways than one. Her animal followers did not come along, one of the first signs the encampment marked a boundary, the start of a new country where the common laws of reality binding the Four Nations loosened their grip. At her presence, the sour wind through the branches made a low moan, the kind that began in a throat.

Her eyes burned with unchecked sweat running down her shaven head. The forest no longer spoke with animalistic chirps and howls, but in the fluttering of tongues and whispers of nonsense much too close to language for comfort. Yangchen knew at this point, turning around and heading straight back would not take her to the camp or to the Saowon manor or to any human land at all.

Tendrils of unknown plants drifted around her knees as if she were walking along the floor of the ocean. She ignored their slimy touch, the way they sometimes closed tight, just missing ensnaring her legs as she walked. Off to her left stalked a presence, a shadow out of the corner of her eye, long-limbed and muscled like a puma-goat. It was at least twenty feet tall. She dared not look at it directly, and slowed down to let it cross her path. Once it had gone, she saw giant handprints left behind, shaped like a human's down to the palm lines.

After more walking she came to the edge of a hole a mile wide, the center so dark and deep it tugged on her throat and made the level ground under her feet feel like a slope, down, down into the emptiness. A great fall waited without the relief of an impact.

Little egg.

With her weight on her heels so she wouldn't topple forward, Yangchen called out. "I am here. We must talk."

Spirals of water rose out of the hole, winding higher like ivy. The liquid took on color and definition, grew a beard of beaks underneath a face full of glowing red eyes. The phoenix-eels. A braid of competing heads and thoughts, only unified when wronged. And they were unified before Yangchen.

The first time she visited these spirits on behalf of the Saowon, they had not darkened to such an extent. They resembled animals from the physical world, glowing with energy, sunbeams full of dust. Back then the phoenix-eels had snapped the piles of encroaching settlements, flooded portions of fields, carried off heads of livestock. Their sole intent was to warn humans off portions of Ma'inka, their actions almost mischievous. Negotiating with them was still possible.

Under the terms the Avatar brokered, the spirits got what they wanted. To a degree. The humans got to expand. A little. No side was fully happy, an outcome Yangchen could live with.

But evidently, some members of Zolian's family could not. Now the phoenix-eels had only punishment in their hearts. Yangchen felt the anger and hatred emanating from their forms, hot as coals, stoked by betrayal.

Spirits were not humans who could watch an act of bad faith and figure they would get theirs back in the future. They were sharpened rails, signs before the cliff drop, harsh tutors who swatted your hand the moment your brushstroke swayed. Parents always forgot the lessons they told their own children. *Don't touch that flower or you'll be pricked by the thorns. That's just what happens; if you don't like it, don't touch it. Stay away from those woods or the spirits will take you. That's just what will happen.*

The phoenix-eels undulated and coiled, dripping water down shimmering scales. Snakes curled before they struck too. *Hollow shell. Little egg, with no yolk inside. We know why you are here.*

"If you know why I am here, then release the children from their sickness."

She dares. Against her own word, she dares.

A monstrous beak came rushing at Yangchen, snapping shut in front of her face. It was too large, filled too much of her vision for her to react with the proper fright. But had she been standing a foot closer she would have lost her nose.

She blinked slowly, one of the few shows she was allowed, while her heart bounced up and down. The price they exacted for losing control could vary beyond comprehension.

The phoenix-eels understood why she was being silent. *You come with nothing. You stand on nothing.*

True. This was an escape attempt by the Saowon, a go at the most human of follies—trying to avoid consequences. "The people who broke their promise have displayed a willingness to atone. They have shown their dishonor."

No penance, what can be forgotten with time. We will feast on their eternal regret. They will watch their line come to ruin.

The statement was a statement. The facts, not a ploy to get more from Yangchen. The spirits began to descend, slithering back into the abyss.

Out of desperation she dredged up her first success, if the destruction of a city could be called that. "Old Iron listened!" she shouted. "And in return he received perpetual obeisance!"

WE ARE NOT OLD IRON! came the scream. *WE DO NOT LOVE. WE DO NOT RELENT.* The slithering coils stopped their descent. Rage kept them from leaving the table. They would hurt Yangchen now, for offending them. But at least they hadn't disappeared.

A wall of red eyes lowered before hers. The phoenix-eels still had features conceivable in the human realm, which meant there was a remnant of light in them yet. She could detect the flickering shadow of the fully darkened form it might take, a spherical cluster of beaks and fins, unable to choose a direction to exist in.

For now, though, there was still hope, as long as she was willing to suffer their punishment. Yangchen steadied herself. A wispy tendril of the spirit, smoke made life, touched her on the forehead where the arrow point was.

The pain did not take the form she expected. Instead of suffering, she saw.

She saw wandering shadows, threaded in a weft of agony. Human beings staggering in base, groaning lowness. Wounds, all of them self-inflicted, spilling from lips and ravaging lungs like burning, choking chyme.

They cried out to the mist. And there was no answer. No substance for an echo to bounce off.

Everything was malleable in the Spirit World, including point of view. Yangchen had seen through so many eyes before. She'd been jarred from place and time into her past lives, locked into shackles made of moments long gone.

This was different. With the help of powerful spirits, she had been granted a different person's perspective for once. Jetsun's.

The tendril withdrew back into the phoenix-eels. Yangchen was on all fours, as prostrate before them as Zolian before her.

"Le—" She slammed the bottom of her fist repeatedly against the stone ground, as if pounding a heartbeat back into her own chest. "Let her go. *Let her go!*"

We do not have her. Nothing has her. Nothingness has her. Do you like your gift? It is what she sees and will see, forever.

It was an illusion. It had to be. Jetsun was dead. Yangchen had been there when her heart stopped beating.

The wall of scales before her began to move in opposing directions. The phoenix-eels were uncoiling to depart. Yangchen could barely think straight, let alone remember why she had come here. Her ragged mind leaped between every plea, every prayer.

"Wait!" she cried. "The children of the Saowon! They're— they're not punishment enough!"

The spirits came to a stop, intrigued.

"What you want is a truer humiliation, isn't it?" Yangchen said. "Let the children sleep to death and their parents' grief will burn out in a lifetime. There are other, better ways to exact a toll. A *lasting* toll."

This was no longer a negotiation but the doctor fetching a hot iron to burn a spurting artery closed. She was going to have to harm the Saowon in order to save them.

Let us talk about inflicting pain, little egg, the phoenix-eels said. *Together.*

When it was done, Yangchen found herself standing by the edge of a stone cavern in the ground, large but not mind-bogglingly vast. Healthy green vines dangled down the sides, pointing at blue water clear enough to see through. The bottom of the cenote was jagged with rock formations, but otherwise empty.

The physical world had become predominant once more. It might stay that way, depending on the Saowon's reaction to the news she bore. Her glider lay on a flat-topped boulder, placed like an offering. Spirits could be as cheeky as humans sometimes.

Yangchen opened the wings to inspect them for water damage. She found none and took off immediately for the manor.

Lohi had the decency to wait for her return himself. He was the lone figure in the manor's courtyard, by the edge of a waterless fountain. The sun was fading, but that meant little for determining how much time had passed.

"How long was I gone?" Yangchen asked him. She examined his face for signs of aging, a precaution less ridiculous than it sounded. "What day is it?"

When Lohi gave her the answer, Yangchen swore under her breath. If she left Ma'inka now, she'd be more than three days late for her check-in with Kavik by the time she reached Jonduri. Still, she'd gotten as lucky as she could. There hadn't been a leap of weeks or months as reported by some unfortunate storytellers who'd wandered between worlds. "The children will be released from their illness," she said. "Provided more conditions are met."

Lohi shuddered in relief. "I'm glad the spirits accepted our sacrifice. This was a devastating blow to our clan's honor, but with time we may put this unpleasantness—"

"You may not regrow your hair for fifty years."

"—behind us . . . I'm sorry, did you say *fifty years*?"

"Five hundred moons, to be exact. That is how long the spirits of your island declared you must hold your dishonor. You do not get to reset the scales after a single act of penance. And there's more."

While Lohi was still caught up in his initial shock, Yangchen listed the taboos the Saowon would have to observe in order to appease the phoenix-eels. Some of them inconveniences. Others, serious hits to their coffers, or quirks of behavior that would most certainly exclude them from the rituals and celebrations of power in the Fire Nation.

Lohi reeled as if she were kicking him in the stomach with each decree. "We'll be humiliated for a generation!" he cried in sheer disbelief. "We'll never be able to contend at court! Our rivals will dance on our heads! You were supposed to *fix* this!"

Forgotten were the children. Lohi's hands curled into shapes that once fully formed, could lead to regret. "You can't do this to us!" He took a step forward he didn't need to take.

There it was. The calm young man who would likely describe himself as the most rational member of his clan had turned into a slighted bundle of raw nerves. Yangchen sliced downward with her hand, and the weight of the sky dropped on his back, forcing him to halt and stoop.

She leaned down and spoke directly into his ear, so he could hear her over the rushing wind. "*I* have done nothing to you. We arrived here through your clan's actions. You were in control the whole time. And you can undo the bargain in an instant. Simply violate the boundary again. Let me know what form a twice-betrayed spirit takes."

Yangchen let up the torrent. While his face was still lowered, Lohi took a deep gulp of still air and composed himself. He rose, wearing an apologetic mask. "Forgive me, Avatar. It's just . . . unbearable to think about. The Saowon will be much diminished."

"But the next generation will live. With enough time, they might flourish. Is that not worth it?" Yangchen would have to swallow a dose of humility herself. "You have lost the melon," she said, pulling out a proverb. "Hang on to the sesame, no?"

The spark of recognition flickered in Lohi's eyes. It was an obscure saying of Avatar Szeto's, not often heard outside the Fire Nation. Sugaring the choice with her predecessor's wisdom would make it more palatable.

"I will talk to the other clan leaders," Lohi said. "It will be the most difficult task of my life, but I will talk to them."

Difficult. She wanted to laugh. Would he fault the members of his family who thought they had impunity, went against their word, and angered the spirits? Or would he lay the blame at Yangchen's feet? She knew which option was more convenient, and convenience ruled kings and peasants alike.

Yangchen asked to be shown to her bison. She had to get out of here and check on Kavik. The more she thought about it, the less likely it was that a boy who would wriggle through a block of sheer ice and follow a strange girl to the other side of the world would be the type to sit quietly and not get into any trouble.

Nujian waited for her in an outdoor pen, surrounded by stable hands. Yangchen dismissed Lohi and the attendants, neither she nor the young nobleman in the mood for a formal farewell. It occurred to her that he'd waited for her alone not out of any sense of personal duty, but so he could control her message to his clan.

She leaped onto Nujian's withers and heard a crinkle. Patting underneath her, she found a piece of paper, folded into an envelope but without a seal. She frowned and looked around before opening it.

Greetings, Avatar. Chaisee here.

Yangchen sprang to her feet on top of the saddle. She spun on her toes, searching the grassy field again for watchers. She had been gone long enough for a hawk to travel from Jonduri to Ma'inka, and long enough that anyone could have planted the letter, even Lohi himself. The zongdu who did not trust birds had no qualms about violating her own rules.

She wanted to crumple and toss the paper out of spite, to veer away from what was undoubtedly another carefully planned manipulation by Chaisee, but that would have accomplished nothing. She read further.

Given our new partnership in charity, I'm hoping we can be less formal with each other. By now you will either have solved the Saowon's spiritual problems or let them drink fully of the bitterness they concocted for themselves. If you're wondering how I know the full story, well, it's amazing what you can learn about someone if you hold their debts.

I would wager you found a perfect solution, Avatar, because I believe in you. And I am not alone in that faith. Why, the other day I met a boy from Bin-Er, seeking employment from me. He believed in you a great deal as well, right up to the very end of our conversation.

The bottom dropped out of Yangchen's stomach. Kavik.

I told you once that I could teach you how to deal with spies. The first step is catching them. Do you know the best way to catch a spy, Avatar?

The first half of a koan. But all koans were taunts to some extent, the enlightened mocking the uninitiated. Chaisee's faint smile of victory was stamped all over the answer to this one.

You open your door and invite them in.

LOOSE ENDS

AFTER TAKING their wounded compatriot away for medical attention, the association members drifted in and out of the building, mostly out, until very few were left. The ones who remained refused to talk to Jujinta, and by extension, Jujinta's brand-new partner.

Kavik didn't mind. Thanks to Kalyaan, he knew what an inherited shunning felt like.

What he was less comfortable with was having to watch Jujinta's post-victory ritual, which started with deep, fervent prayer to some unknown spirit. The knife thrower scratched a series of marks into the wall, triangles upon cross marks upon straight lines, until an intricate geometric pattern emerged that somewhat resembled a bird spreading its wings. Kneeling in front of it, he whispered to himself, eyes closed, his mutters sounding like angry condemnations of some past unforgivable crime, far worse than the light stabbing he'd given Shigoro.

Well, that's not creepy at all, Kavik thought.

When Jujinta was finished, he came over and sat down on the same bench Kavik was on. Even the way the guy rested was disturbing. He sat as if the back wall would contaminate him by touch and stared straight ahead the whole time, barely blinking. It would have been perfect meditation posture had it not looked like his muscles were fighting each other in a vicious stalemate.

After a while, the silence became too much. "You a bender?" Kavik asked him.

It wasn't idle conversation. If things went Shigoro-shaped between them, Kavik wanted to know if he would need to deal with surprise fire. Hiding your ability was a common enough ploy in the errand-running business, useful for temporary advantages—*ha-ha, secret bender out of nowhere!*—and Jujinta's impeccable blade skills would have been the perfect distraction. People could be good at two things.

Jujinta frowned, having understood the logic behind the question. And he didn't like it at all, being pried into. Not one bit. "No," he snarled without turning his head.

He could have been lying, but Kavik felt his body language told true. He thought the matter settled until after a whole minute, the Fire National retorted. "You anything *but?*"

Kavik squinted at his benchmate. *Well, nuts to you too, buddy.*

Tael came over to interrupt the slow-moving exchange. "It's time."

"There's been enough light for an hour already," Kavik said. His knees were stiff from sitting so long.

"Yeah, but we need the currents going the right way too. Or else you'll be ground up by the Limpet's Teeth and spat back onto the beaches. Come on."

The older man led Jujinta and Kavik toward the back of the

hall. A sweet, meaty stink, even more powerful than the default fishiness, crept through this end of the building. A washed-up land animal, rotting overnight? There was an intestinal rankness not born of the sea lying somewhere underneath. Tael pushed open a wide set of doors, letting the new daylight in over a small gravel beach. "Here's your first job," he said. "Disposal duty."

Kavik shielded his eyes from the sun at first, but quickly switched his hands, clamping his mouth shut. Hot bile leaked past his fingers. Laid on a bed of seaweed, next to silvery fish too ugly and oily to sell, were a pair of dead bodies, beginning to bloat.

One of them was Qiu.

Kavik's mad scramble only lasted a few paces before he emptied his stomach over the surf-polished pebbles. He had the distinct sensation of people other than Tael parting way for him to be sick. A few of them chuckled.

"First time with a raw corpse, huh?" someone said, not unkindly. "It'll getcha, for sure."

Kavik clutched his midsection and spat and spat and spun around. Seeing the bottoms of Qiu's swelling purple feet made him retch again. Why was he—his body here? Why wasn't he in Taku?

"Everyone here has just seen the persons named Kavik and Jujinta get on a boat with a fellow dressed like a high official from the Earth Kingdom and a youth with pockmarked skin wearing the latest fashion from Bin-Er and go on a voyage," Tael announced. "Only Jujinta and Kavik came back. There must have been foul play. We'll testify as such, should authorities from outside Jonduri come asking."

Tael rubbed an itchy eye. "New guy. This is how we keep you loyal. Guilt by association. Be glad we respect the law in these parts. I've heard the real unsavory criminal-type groups in the Earth Kingdom force their new members to foul the play themselves."

"What did these two do to get so unlucky?" Jujinta asked, unperturbed.

"They're spies. And if there's one thing the boss-boss does not like, it's spies."

Tael went in for a closer look at the Earth Kingdom official. Kavik couldn't comprehend how he managed not to gag. He lifted the man's drooping, foot-long beard and let it fall again. "He's the real deal, a sage. This other one"—he nudged Qiu's body with his foot and Kavik felt the toe in his own ribs—"is a broker come bearing gifts way too big for his worth. That's the surest way to tell someone's a plant attempt."

The envelope. The envelope he'd stolen from the Avatar's room. Kavik had put the cause of Qiu's death into his own hands.

"Come on, get them into the boat before you miss your window," Tael said. "You want to be rowing with the tides, not against them."

Kavik had to be prodded toward Qiu's head. Jujinta squatted down and grabbed the body by the ankles, rolling up the salt-eaten trousers to get a better grip on the clammy gray flesh underneath. "Lift with your knees," he grunted.

Far, far away, over the horizon. That was where Kavik had to send his mind, in order not to begin shrieking uncontrollably when he took Qiu by the wrists and his former broker's dead fingers flopped in reciprocation around his own. He barely looked away in time to avoid Qiu's head lolling backward to accuse him of murder with slack, open jaws.

He dipped in and out of coherence. He was vaguely aware of two thuds hitting the bottom of a skiff, and then he and Jujinta were out to sea, each of them rowing an oar.

"So what you're going to do is encase the corpses in a block of sea ice," he heard Jujinta say. "We push the ice and let it float away. By the time it melts, the current will have taken it to a shark-squid feeding ground, and there won't be any remains left to identify."

Kavik hadn't remembered Tael giving them instructions. They must have gone over them while he was wrapped in blankness. Or maybe his partner already knew how to dispose of murder victims.

It was easier to freeze water around Qiu and the other man, new best friends in burial, once he got some momentum going. He could pretend he was layering ice upon ice. The foot sticking out, he quickly covered. There was no kernel to the mass if he couldn't see it.

As the little icebergs drifted away, Jujinta prayed, again.

The rest of the job passed like the sun behind clouds. Rowing back to shore. Tael telling them they did good, and they should report for more work next week. Jujinta's stare drilling into Kavik's back as he navigated from one end of the gambling parlor to the other—that's where this fever dream had begun, right? A gambling parlor? Kavik was no longer sure.

He staggered home in broad daylight, past the wet market. The sound of cleavers thwacking into their bloody blocks made him want to throw up again. On the boat, Jujinta had offered to do some knifework—*to make the pieces smaller, that's why Tael had sent them both*—but Kavik at least had the wherewithal to refuse any more indignities upon the deceased.

No, not home exactly, the safe house. Muscle memory developed in Bin-Er kept him from breaking cover and taking the most direct route. He remembered to pause every so often and sweep for tails. When he burst through the inn doors, surprising Akuudan and Tayagum, he could say with confidence he hadn't been followed. Once he regained the ability to string a sentence together.

The Avatar was waiting for him. By the looks of it, she'd just beat him there, maybe by minutes. Her disguise lay in a pile, a cloak and a wide hat, a simpler getup than the one in Bin-Er, put together in haste. She sprang to her feet when she saw him.

"You're alive," she said, looking utterly relieved.

The fact that she had reason to believe otherwise only made him angrier. They'd talked about the dangers of this mission. Kavik had agreed to them. But right now, a flood of blame was dammed behind his throat.

Unable to speak, he leveled a trembling, accusing finger at Yangchen, and discovered there was an object in his hand.

A small coin purse he didn't have before. His payment for dumping Qiu into the water.

REMEMBERANCE

KAVIK, EIGHT years old, had cursed the hunt. He was sure of it. He'd forgotten one of his amulets, or committed a taboo before heading out, or had made the right gestures to the spirits but without the proper respect in his heart. And now he and Kalyaan were separated from the others, turned around in the vicious blizzard that had swept down upon them like a predator.

It was his fault. He wept, his tears freezing on his nose. His sorrow earned him a *plap!* of a mitten over his face.

"No," Kalyaan said, looming overhead. "We'll be all right."

This was prior to Kavik's growth spurt, and his older brother was still a giant who could block out the harsh skies themselves. The two of them trudged in the direction they believed was home, until the snowdrifts became overwhelming. Kalyaan built them a quick shelter, and they spent the first of many nights shivering and hungry.

The storm only abated in spurts. And during the brief lulls they could travel in, the land was a paper sheet, offering blankness instead of signs to orient by. Kavik couldn't tell how long they'd spent lost. They might have been wandering in a spiritual pocket, a floating space where the realms bled into each other. Kalyaan cut strips off his own mitten and chewed the pieces of hide to make them soft enough for his little brother to swallow. A desperation tactic so Kavik would have the energy to keep walking in the cold.

Even then, they returned to camp with Kavik drooped across Kalyaan's shoulders, barely conscious. They'd been gone for a month, nearly mourned as dead. His older brother had saved his life and carried him back to their parents. There was simply nothing Kalyaan couldn't accomplish to keep his family safe.

He'd lost two fingers to frostbite, though. The spot where he'd opened his mitten. "Don't worry about it," he told a fretting Kavik. "Middlers think eight's a lucky number." He wiggled the stumps on his hand for emphasis.

Kavik did worry about it. He had been a burden, and the signs of his weakness were now permanently etched upon the person he looked up to most. And he was still convinced the expedition had turned unlucky because of him in the first place. The original, unknown offense had not been accounted for.

Since then, Kavik often wondered if he was supposed to have paid a greater price and left a part of himself behind on the ice like Kalyaan had. Maybe he'd cheated the spirits by surviving intact.

Because looking back on it, right around that time was the beginning of the turn. When hunts started souring across the region, slowly at first, but then inevitably, failed season after failed season forcing more people to cross the straits in search of work in the Earth Kingdom and the newfangled shang towns sprouting up.

His family leaving the North Pole, drifting apart, Kalyaan abandoning them, the misery of Bin-Er—the footprints may have been different, but they could have all come from the same shape-changing beast, walking in an unbroken line from the past to the present.

If so, Kavik only had himself to blame.

The Avatar was the one who caught him. Her airbending pushed Kavik back to his feet, a second set of hands reaching across the room, and the rush of wind against his face roused him like a slap.

"You've got to stop passing out in my inn," Akuudan said.

Kavik was not in the mood for teasing anymore. His ribs were bellows, trying to squeeze too much air through too small a hole. Yangchen, recognizing something in his agony, put her hand up for silence from the other two. "Breathe," she said to Kavik. "Breathe first. Don't try to talk until you're ready." Her posture was that of an animal expert, ready to rush to his side if he collapsed but not wanting to spook him yet by coming closer.

It took Kavik five full minutes before he could explain to everyone the initiation process for Chaisee's errand runners in Jonduri. And how the first body taking a ride out to sea courtesy of his efforts was Qiu, the same Qiu Yangchen and Kavik had planted information on in the Bin-Er teahouse. They'd killed him. Together.

Yangchen blanched. "How could this have happened? You didn't say your broker was coming to Jonduri!"

"He obviously changed his mind after I talked to him!" Kavik said. Qiu could have caught wind of Chaisee's recruiting drive, same as they did, and spotted an opportunity for a higher price for the information than he could have gotten in Taku. Except

Chaisee had smelled a plot and responded in the most extreme manner possible. "What do we do?"

Yangchen's gaze was slack, her cheeks red. "What do we do?" Kavik asked her again.

"Avatar," Tayagum said. "This is your call."

"I don't know." Her lips parted and closed, half-formed words failing to take shape. If she had solutions, she was letting them die on her tongue.

This was the wrong version of Yangchen. Kavik needed the schemer who'd had him over a barrel the whole time in Bin-Er. The one who was always a step ahead. This frozen, befuddled girl, he didn't recognize.

"You can't *not* know!" Kavik said to her. "We've been following your orders and now two people are dead! What is the plan here?!"

"*I said I don't know!*" Yangchen's response sent the papers in the room fluttering. "If you could just shut up for a moment! There's too many of you! There's always too many of you, and none of you ever stop! You never stop!"

She picked up the hat and cloak and stormed out the inn.

"*Avat—*" Akuudan cut himself off so he didn't address her by her true identity while the door swung open. With surprising agility, he vaulted over the counter with his one hand.

Kavik followed him outside, Tayagum close behind. The inn shared frontage with a row of produce stands, which Jonduri's many little restaurants kept busy. Customers toted away baskets of bitter gourd and cabbage, shooting starfruit and papaya. Kavik's eyes flitted from head to head. He and the others were only moments behind Yangchen, he knew what her cover outfit looked like, and still the Avatar was gone. They'd already been thrown.

"We're never going to find her," Akuudan muttered.

Kavik thought about the last time he'd seen her anywhere near this upset. It was at the Northern Air Temple, when she'd thrashed her way through a sleepless night, rising and falling through a forest of pillars. Besides the noise from her bending, she hadn't uttered a sound. And that had to be difficult.

He had a hunch. "Where's the loudest beach around here?" he asked.

The crash of surf below the cliffs of Tiger-dillo's Roar was deafening. White water coming in met the brown, sandy backflow going out, in a line of battle that undulated along the coast. The rocks weren't the tallest, nor the steepest or the most jagged, but they were slick with spray.

Kavik spotted a toe of undisturbed beach peeking out from behind an outcrop and suddenly wished his hunch were a lot stronger. Descending the cliffs would be difficult; getting back up nearly impossible for anyone who wasn't an Airbender.

Well, this would be an act of faith, he supposed. Kavik took off his boots and sat down on his rear. He edged forward, and as soon as he felt himself slipping, he frosted the rock under his hands and feet, making his skin stick and halting his slide. Through the cracks in the stone, he wiggled his way down. He scraped his calves and elbows a couple of times, hissing when the salt crept into the cuts.

He dropped the last few feet to the sand. The numbness in his fingers and toes would go away; Jonduri was simply too warm for him to be in the same danger from the cold as he was in Bin-Er. Above, the cliff formed a slab roof, shading the small stretch of calm beach, half a tunnel over his head.

On the other end was Yangchen. Her disguise lay in a damp pile along with her heavier outer Air Nomad robes. She walked a small circle in lighter garments, her arms at her sides, and in the center of her ring a small whirlwind spun, made visible by a column of dust.

Kavik stood back, not wanting to interrupt a meditative practice. But he needn't have worried about being the spoiler. The little cyclone lost its edges, and Yangchen staggered out of the circle's path.

The exercise had failed her. She faced the ocean, and she screamed. Clenched-fist, eyes-shut, doubled-over screams of frustrations so great as to rack the form of the Avatar herself.

The waves drowned her out completely. No human could make themselves heard against the unyielding elements. Yangchen screamed again, a meaningless contortion of her lungs, and flung a slice of wind out to sea, tearing a channel in the waves that quickly closed up like a stitched wound. She did it over and over, and despite the unimaginable power she was exerting, opening the sea like the center of a book, the waters sealed to leave no trace of her acts behind.

She exhausted herself and dropped to her knees in the sand, panting. Then she looked up, her long hair whipped into strands across her face, wild and uncomposed. She saw Kavik.

She didn't seem surprised he'd found her, nor ashamed that he'd witnessed her outburst. She stood up, and while her sides twitched with exertion and her eyes were red, his presence had turned her back to business. Yangchen beckoned him deeper into the stone recess under the cliff.

Kavik followed her. There was room enough for them to stand. She made him come closer and closer, and then when they were at arm's length, she slammed her feet into a low, powerful earthbending stance.

The movement of her lower body alone caused sand to shoot up, forming walls and baffles around them that muted the roar of the waves. Kavik was awed. The sheer amount of earth moved, the sophistication of the idea, the quickness of the act. It was easy to forget the girl standing before him was the most powerful bender in the world.

She opened her hand and held a flame for light. "You said there was another body, besides your friend's," she said. He could hear her now.

"An Earth Kingdom sage with a long Nanyan-style beard," Kavik said. He snapped his fingers as it dawned on him. "That was the guy who turned on you. Sidao?"

"Sidao." Yangchen wiped one side of her face, and then the other. "That means I got him killed too. I have two deaths on my hands."

If she screamed in here, she'd deafen them both. "Do you know what makes an Air Nomad?" she asked.

Was she giving him a koan? Kavik had always assumed it was the freedom to go anywhere in the world. He shook his head.

"It's the ability to sit down quietly, wherever you are, be it dark room or empty field, and just . . . sit," Yangchen said. The firelight danced in her eyes. "To sit with yourself, without causing problems or hurting anyone else. That's it. That's all it is. The airbending pales in comparison."

He knew she was exaggerating, but not by much. Human desires were responsible for the position they were in. "I'm sorry," Yangchen said. Her lips wavered. "I'm sorry about your friend. What happened to him was my fault."

A few minutes ago, Kavik might have agreed wholeheartedly, pointed out that he was guilty as well, the stain covering them both. But the salt air had cleared the stench of panic and rotting flesh from his nose, after he'd been so certain he'd never smell anything else again. Someone had made the conscious decision to end Qiu's life. Treating his killers like a feature of the landscape took the blame away from people who deserved to hold it longer.

"We're pulling out," Yangchen said. "I can't keep you in harm's way. We'll get you back to your parents and I'll find you exit passes. You held up your end of the deal as much as you could."

"No."

The flame wavered. To their mutual surprise, Kavik had taken hold of her wrist, like she'd done to him in Bin-Er to gauge his honesty. He wasn't gripping her anywhere near as tightly, but he could still feel her pulse, fluttering and warm.

How could he explain it? There had to be a point beyond the deal, he wanted to say. The world needed the strength of people like Yangchen, who gave without counting. And the deeper he became entrenched with her, the more it felt like he was finding the bits and pieces of himself he'd thought had been scraped off since leaving the North.

"This is an opportunity," he said instead. "They think they've caught the Avatar's spies. They'll let their guards down. We have to keep going."

She shook her head. "You heard Tayagum. The chance you've been made is too high."

"If they wanted to do me in, they would have already." This morning had been the perfect opportunity to get rid of Kavik were there any suspicions hanging over him. They'd had the setup right there. Jujinta with his knives, the two of them on a boat by themselves. "I think I'm in the clear."

"You're talking about a double beat that cost two lives to set up," she said. "Our path forward would be laid over the backs of the dead. I can't even seek justice for Sidao and Qiu while you're undercover because they only way I could have found out about them was through you."

Yangchen took a deep breath, and the makeshift candle in the makeshift cave rose and fell with her exhalation. "I don't think I could handle it if something happened to you. I— I can't lose any more friends."

Kavik didn't know how to respond. He waited until the perfect answer came to him. "Let's sleep on it."

Dropping the sand barriers and stepping back out onto the beach meant they had to shout in each other's ears to be heard. "We have to get out of here before the waters rise," Yangchen said, her heavier clothes in a bundle over her shoulder. "Unless you want to get flung out to sea or into the cliff, I need you to maintain your balance like you're treading water. You want to stay vertical, not flop on your stomach or back. Now hold your arms up."

Kavik did as he was told. Yangchen swung her free hand and air began to rush around his midsection. His clothes puffed up like fried dough. His heels left the ground, then his toes.

She had formed an air spout under him. He knew the technique since it was a common way to depict Avatars in paintings, symbolically elevated in power, but he had never heard of an Airbender wrapping a controlled cyclone around someone else. "This, uh, feels dangerous."

"Only if you get scared." Yangchen twirled to form a vortex of her own. The two of them rose into the air, wobbling in the eyes of the miniature storms. Her instability looked like the motion of a bough in the breeze, his, the thrashing of a hooked fish.

They reached the height where a fall would break his legs. He made the mistake of looking down and got caught on the inner wall of wind. Kavik circled around and around like a ship in a whirlpool. "I messed up!" he shouted. "I'm scared!"

Yangchen grabbed his hand and merged their spouts. The air pressed them together and she hugged him around the waist. With only one mass for her to worry about, they rose faster, shooting upward and over the edge of the cliff.

The landing was gentler. All their feet touched down at the same time. Kavik's heart pounded in his chest. "You can let go of me now," Yangchen said.

When Kavik realized he was embracing the Avatar tightly he flushed with heat and jerked backward. She made no effort to tease him and put her outer robes back on, adjusting the high collar and smoothing the orange sleeves as if she needed to look presentable.

She didn't follow immediately with the plain cloak that had served as her disguise. "Guard me," she said, before Kavik could point out the danger of someone identifying her. "Look out for anyone coming."

Avatar Yangchen stood on the cliff, out in the open, and began to perform her duties. Chanting in remembrance of the dead.

Kavik kept watch as she spoke to the sea. The Water Tribe had their own spiritual customs for the deceased, but he'd seen an Air Nomad lead a funeral procession through the streets of Bin-Er once before. He recognized the way her single voice split into many, nose accompanying throat harmonizing with tongue to say the rites. After a few repetitions, she made a marked shift into lilting, high-pitched notes, a beautiful, wordless song he didn't know.

Yangchen's rich voice gave the melody a powerful foundation, until she let it trail away into the wind. "A Nanyan mourning lament at the end, for Sidao," she explained. "The best I could do for Sidao. Where was Qiu from?"

"I don't know." Kavik blinked and found there were tears in his eyes. "Someplace warm. He didn't want to be cold anymore; that's why he left Bin-Er."

His sniffling became a shudder. "I didn't even know him that well. He was just . . . he was just some guy, right? No one important. But he had to have had parents. Maybe brothers and sisters. And I made him disappear."

He felt a steadying hand on his shoulder. "I saw him with you," Yangchen said gently. "And that means he hasn't disappeared. If he's part of my memories, then as strange as it is to think, there's a slim chance an Avatar of future generations will understand who Qiu was, through me."

Kavik was comforted by the fact that the lowly could at least have this one place in history beside the exalted. "I don't know why I'm acting like this." He wiped his face with the back of his wrist. "We weren't that close."

"You don't have to be close to someone to know they deserve better," Yangchen said. "That's what being the Avatar is about. That's what being a companion of the Avatar is about. We fight for people we've never met and never will."

The weight of her words was a comfort where it could have been a burden. "Am I one of your companions?" Kavik said. He knew what they'd told his parents, but it wasn't the same thing. "I mean, am I really?"

Yangchen smiled. "Most of the world thinks I dictate who serves me and who doesn't, when nothing could be further from the truth. You're asking me if you're my companion? The choice is yours, Kavik. And it always has been."

It had taken a while, but Kavik finally understood. "I know what I choose," he said to the Avatar.

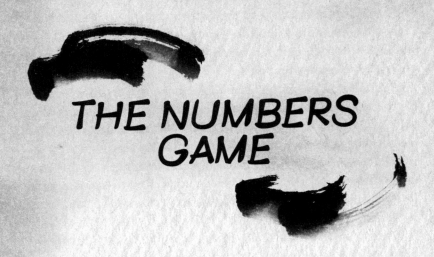

THE NUMBERS GAME

IN KAVIK'S opinion, having to drink tea with someone you didn't like was one of life's sharpest little unpleasantries. The rituals, the waiting, the pouring for your partner, all hinged around patterns of polite conversation or meditative, cooperative silence. When you didn't want the company, it got awkward.

He and Jujinta sat at a table laid out in front of a tea stall that faced the main warehouse row of Jonduri. In the last vestiges of daylight, the outlines of the city were black on a pink sky. They'd ordered the cheapest tea and the largest jug of hot water, so they weren't close to finishing yet.

Pppppphpphp.

To add to Kavik's suffering, Jujinta was the type of monster who drank with pursed lips, sucking in air along with the liquid, making noises like a clogged straw. Kavik tried following each sip of Jujinta's with one of his own in the hopes that the

Fire National would have an epiphany and realize you didn't need to be loud when drinking, but it was futile.

Phpphpppppphppp.

They'd managed not to talk to each other the whole time until now, but Kavik broke and decided words were a lesser evil than the slurping. "What's your deal?" he asked.

Jujinta finally put his cup down, thank the spirits. "What do you mean?"

Why do you work for the association? Why don't you have a topknot? What's up with the rituals you perform at the safe house? "Just making conversation."

"I don't have much of a story," Jujinta said, staring across the street. His manner of speaking was the opposite of a Jonduri intonation: slow, flat, evenly paced where it might have been more natural to change tempo. "After committing a crime, I left my family behind to go seek forgiveness from the spirits. Jonduri is where I ended up. The association keeps me fed, but that's it. I have no great love for our employers, or our compatriots."

That much was obvious. "What did you do that was so bad?"

Jujinta raised his teacup back to his lips. "I murdered my brother."

Kavik couldn't find anything to say after that.

The sun finished setting behind the mountains. There wasn't time for him to decide how he felt about partnering with a kinslayer, if Jujinta was indeed telling the truth. Over by the vendor selling grilled meats, four men, association members all, tossed aside their bamboo skewers and got up from their bench. Another three men walking around the corner merged with them to form a single group. Jujinta plunked down a few coins for the tea and got up to follow them.

He'd overpaid, but that was okay, because Kavik needed to steal the jug. He plucked the large clay vessel off the table and tucked it under his arm. It turned out the rules in Jonduri didn't let people walk around with massive quantities of water without a good reason, which Kavik found blatantly unfair when Firebenders could produce their element and Earthbenders were nearly always walking on it.

Then again, constantly lugging around enough liquid for combat got tiring quickly. Better Waterbenders could make do with less, a single drinking skin's worth maybe, but if Kavik knew he was heading toward trouble, he liked to have as much as he could carry.

People should know the weight of water, the Avatar had said. Kavik was intimately familiar with it, thank you very much. He cooled the pitcher down to lukewarm—he wasn't a monster, after all—and fell in at the rear of the group. The raid had begun.

"I don't like this," Kavik said. "I'm not a headkicker."

A few days before, he and Jujinta had gotten their next job from Tael. A simple task. They were to go inside a certain warehouse near the docks at a certain time with a few other association members and "emphatically vacate" anyone they found inside. If folks got roughed up in the process, all the better.

That was about as much detail as low-level runners tended to get. But Kavik had followed the older members around the association safe house, learned how to play Sparrowbones and intentionally lost to them the money that Akuudan and Tayagum reluctantly provided, wheedled out of them the details of their own tasks for that night. The information he brought back to Yangchen formed a much more complete picture when combined with her knowledge.

"You're going to have to do it," Yangchen said. "Based on what we know, your group is hitting the primary storage facility for goods going from Jonduri to Bin-Er. Unanimity is most likely inside that very warehouse."

"Do you remember what we said about the city's loading crews being unhappy?" Akuudan said, leaning over a rough map of the city he'd drawn himself. "Matters have come to a head. They've staged lockdowns of the warehouses used for sorting and rearranging shipments coming in and out of the harbor. The queues inside are growing and growing, the cargo just sitting there. Shipments that should have gone out days ago, shipments that aren't scheduled to go out for weeks. All there."

"Outbound shipments are inspected by harbormasters before they're allowed to leave port, and harbormasters report to their local head of state," Yangchen said. "To get past the checks, goods must come from their appointed storage spaces and go through their scheduled docks to get loaded onto certain ships. Sometimes they even have to be escorted by specific crew members during the voyage, named in advance. Chaisee follows the post–Platinum Affair security agreements down to the brushstroke and does not let anyone play around with side shipments."

Kavik stared at her. She caught him doing it and blushed. "What?"

"I don't understand how an Air Nomad is this familiar with the rules of commerce."

Yangchen shrugged. "I was an accountant in a past life."

Funny, Kavik had been one too. The Avatar went on with the plan. "Once you're inside, your goal is going to be the logbook," she said. "It contains all of the warehouse information I just mentioned: ship names, handler names, cargo contents, provenance, weights, buyer names, destinations. With that level of information in our possession, we'll be able to identify Unanimity and intercept it in transit. Without the book, we won't have any way to tell what's inside those crates, barring a guided tour from Chaisee herself."

"I wish we had some clue, any clue, to help us narrow the possibilities down," Kavik grumbled. Unanimity remained a frustrating blank, a complete void in their knowledge.

Yangchen looked like she'd been saving her retort since dinner with his parents. *"It's nice to want things,"* she said, batting her eyelashes at him, fanning pure sarcasm in his direction.

He deserved that.

"You'll want to move fast," Tayagum added. "If a fight breaks out, everyone's going to be trying to secure that logbook. Since the goods can't move without the records, whoever's holding them at the end of the night will have all the negotiating power."

Yangchen pressed a small wooden cylinder with a lanyard into Kavik's hand. "To keep you safe."

"Is this a spiritual token?" Kavik asked as he looped it around his neck.

"It's a bison whistle," Yangchen said. "Keyed to Nujian. Blow on it if you get into trouble and he'll hear it; the range should be effective for most of the island. He and I will come to your exact location."

"But if I do that, it's mission over," Kavik said. "Not just for the raid tonight, but the whole thing. Jonduri. Unanimity." The Avatar flying in to rescue him on her bison would be the most spectacular way to blow his cover in the world, but it would still be blown cover.

"I'm not sending you in without an extraction plan. What did I tell you about losing friends?"

Right. But as touched as he was, his safety wasn't the issue. "I know I have to do this," he said. "But it still feels wrong. I'd be going in there to scrap with a work crew. We're talking about ordinary folks who just want a better deal. These are—"

"These are the exact people I should be helping," Yangchen said bitterly. "I know. And I can't. If I make contact with them,

Chaisee will suspect we're circling around that warehouse, and she'll take extra precautions. And I'm also supposed to be reeling from having my two 'spies' taken away from me. For this double beat to work, Chaisee has to believe the Avatar's been beaten."

This was costing her, Kavik thought as she hung her head over the planning table they'd set up in the inn. When they'd first met, he thought she rather enjoyed deception. But now that he knew her better, he could see the daylight widening through her seams.

"Jujinta's probably going to love this mission," Kavik muttered.

"Yes. Tell us more about this partner of yours," Yangchen said.

Kavik explained everything he'd observed about the knife thrower, including his obsessive spirituality. In the association safe house, he'd seen Jujinta whisper to himself or kneel in a corner so many times that Kavik was able to draw for Yangchen a passable recreation of the symbol he worshipped.

"Interesting," she said. "Do you think the boy is going to be trouble?"

Kavik remembered Shigoro rolling around the floor, bleeding from his arm. He vaguely remembered Jujinta guiding him through the body disposal process. It was too late to do anything about his partner now but cope.

"Nothing I can't handle," Kavik said.

"What's the count inside?" Jujinta asked as they crossed the street.

"Should be five right now, give or take," said their leader, a gaunt Earth Kingdom transplant named Pang who was missing his bottom front teeth, knocked out in some long-ago fight. "They've had people coming in and out over the course of the past couple days. Tael said they won't be at full strength tonight."

The association had nine people in their group, including Jujinta and Kavik. Two to one. Kavik did not like how a sense of satisfaction threatened to creep up his spine, being a member of a large pack about to overpower a smaller one. At least the stacked odds meant the association wouldn't need Kavik to subdue the people inside. He could split off from the group and search for the logbook.

They came to the warehouse front. Pang raised his foot and kicked open the workers' entrance, snapping the latch. He ducked inside, the rest of them following close behind. Kavik briefly wondered why the door hadn't been barricaded, but if the workers had to leave in shifts for food and rest, it made sense that they wouldn't block their own passage.

The bigger question was why there were no guards posted. The interior lamps, placed high along the walls at regular intervals to shorten the shadows, had all been lit. Stacks of wooden crates, some of them so large they could only have been dragged with winches, formed towers reaching twice as tall as a person, the smallest boxes neatly placed edge to edge on top, creating sheer faces down the sides. A moat of empty space surrounded each little castle.

He craned his head to the ceiling almost involuntarily, the way Tael had smugly observed. There was water above him, rainwater contained in a giant thin-walled metal tank. At first, he thought it would surely be too foul to drink, but then realized it was probably meant to be used for putting out fires inside the warehouse. With so much of his element nearby he felt a little bit like a sap for bringing his own.

The workers were nowhere to be seen. Pang made a sucking noise through the gap in his teeth. "They must have got spooked and hid between the crates. Gonna be a blasted kid's game, chasing them around an orchard."

"Nah, Sifu," came a voice from the other end of the building. "We're right here. And I think we'll do the chasing." A man stepped out from behind the boxes. And then another. And another. The line of workers kept growing.

"Their group is, uh, bigger than ours," Kavik said.

Not only did they have more people, but each member of the warehouse crew was huge, nearly the size of Akuudan, with thick necks and knotted forearms. *Ah, right,* Kavik thought. These guys lifted heavy cargo for a living.

One of the association members angrily jostled Pang in the elbow. "You said there were five!"

"Tael said there were five!"

"This is *five* fives!"

Indeed. Two dozen very large, very angry workers stood across from them. A better example of why one needed to pay up for a good errand runner could not have been devised. Intelligence mattered. In all his Bin-Er jobs, Kavik had taken care to get his numbers right.

The warehouse crew, many of whom bore a family resemblance to each other, stepped forward and bellowed, sticking out their tongues and showing the whites of their eyes.

"We're not leaving," Pang said to his own men. "You want to explain to the boss-boss that you turned tail and ran, go ahead, but if you think for one second that— Hey!"

There was no one standing behind him. Two of the association members were already trying the door, but it had been closed and barred again, this time from the outside. Kavik slipped out of the way between the nearest crates, giving him a perfect framed view of Pang getting absolutely demolished by a running shoulder tackle from a man twice his weight.

He zigzagged through the alleys of the warehouse, trying to get to the back. Both to see if there was another exit and to get closer to the area where the logbook would be stored. If the office had interior locks, he wasn't above bolting himself inside to wait out the worker's ire.

A bright flash lit up the rafters, and he heard the telltale *foom* of air split by flame. Firebending had broken out; he wasn't sure by which side. Distracted by the noise and light, he nearly ran into the waiting arms of the man blocking his path.

"Where you going, Sifu?" said the hulking worker.

The other way. But when Kavik turned to look, he saw another man had stepped into the lane behind him.

"You carrying drinks for the party?" said the second guy, motioning at the vessel Kavik was still clinging onto. "Cause I'm already thirsty."

Both of the workers laughed, but the first one cut his chuckle short when he realized why someone would be awkwardly hauling a container of liquid around. "Wait."

Kavik flung the entire jug without emptying it at the guy in front of him. A whirl of his arms accelerated the water inside, and the heavy missile slammed into his target's gut hard enough to shatter the clay. The man gasped and collapsed to the ground, clutching his stomach.

Sorry. With a pull to match the push, Kavik yanked on the water, leaving the clay shards behind—because again, he wasn't a monster—and whipped a speeding blob back the other way.

The second guy hunched over and held his forearms crossed in front of his face, hoping his toughness and bulk would protect him. But brawlers went high. Wrestlers went low. Kavik lowered the angle of his flying water and knocked the man's feet out from under him. The poor worker took a hard landing on the hard floor and didn't get up, only groaned and reached for a helping hand that wasn't there. *Sorry.*

Kavik brought the water close to himself and cradled it into a sphere, Grasping the Bird's Tail. Tayagum had laughed at him earlier for admitting to losing fights. But he didn't lose *every* fight.

The logbook. The important documents would be in the back. Every building in Jonduri had its corner office, he reasoned. Kavik crept through the intersections, slowly weaving his element around himself, keeping it in motion, so he could strike with it at a moment's notice.

The sound of snapping lumber made him pause. He peeked around the corner and almost got an eye taken out by a flying splinter.

Four men had trapped Jujinta by wielding long wooden planks, swinging them back and forth like torches against a jungle predator. Kavik's partner fended them off with nothing but a dagger in hand, raised high. The first person to come near him would get plugged.

The problem was that the instant Jujinta picked a target and threw his weapon, he'd get rushed by the others. *He'll be fine,* Kavik thought. He was doing great, holding up a bunch by himself.

Other priorities were at stake. Kavik moved sideways to skirt the fight, fully intending to just sprint the rest of the way to the back office. But some reflex, some twinge, made him pause and look one more time around the corner again.

From this angle he got spotted. Not by the workers but by Jujinta. The two partners made eye contact. The distraction was enough for a plank to come crashing down onto Jujinta's shoulders. He toppled to the ground, and his opponents pounced, laying into him with vicious kicks and stomps.

Kavik swore up and down. At this rate someone else was going to beat him to the logbook. An association man wanting to salvage some small victory, or a worker trying to secure the most valuable asset they knew was inside the warehouse.

He glanced one last time in the direction he was supposed to be going and then stepped out into the open. "Hey, Sifus!"

They stopped kicking the living spirits out of Jujinta. So at least that goal had been accomplished. The rest was up in the air.

The four men still standing looked at Kavik and then each other before chuckling. "Look at this guy," said the worker closest to Jujinta. "I don't think he can count."

Instead of splitting his water between the tentacles of Octopus form, which would have rendered them too thin to do much damage, Kavik wrapped all the liquid he had around his right arm, turning it into a massive limb big enough to wield a bundle of planks as a single giant club.

"One," Kavik said. "That enough?"

Jujinta woke with a start, his face dripping. "What the— Where are we?"

"Shh," Kavik said. "We're still inside the warehouse."

They were on top of a crate tower, to be exact. The fight as a whole had not gone well for the association, and getting to an elevated position was the only thing that Kavik could think to do while Jujinta regained consciousness. The problem was that now they were treed like pygmy-pumas.

"You defeated those men," Jujinta said. "And then you healed me with waterbending."

"Sure. That's what happened." It would be more accurate to say Kavik had scared them off by flailing about wildly. And he still didn't know how to heal. He'd splashed Jujinta over and over again until he woke up. It was the only thing he could do with the little water he had left, and now it was gone.

They crawled to the edge of their stack and peeked over. Below, by the main walkways of the loading area, the other association members had been rounded up and forced to sit on the floor. The invaders looked woozy and beaten, but they were alive. Even Pang, who should have been flatter than a scallion bing after the hit he took.

"You there up on the boxes; you're still outnumbered," shouted the opposing leader, who was not the oldest or most battle-scarred member of their group, but a young man with long wavy hair cascading in abundance around his shoulders.

Jujinta hurled a blade over the side, barely looking, the way a child might throw a snowball from the cover of their fort. Kavik saw the spinning metal tumble point-first into the foot of a worker standing next to the leader. "Less so now," Jujinta called out, as his victim shrieked and fell over, pinned to the ground.

Rather than get angry, the leader of the workers grimaced and rubbed his eyes. Kavik felt the same way. The longer this stalemate played out, the more dignity everyone lost.

"Please stop knifing people for the moment," Kavik said to Jujinta as calmly as he could. He needed time to think.

Jujinta nodded. "Because I've only got two left. Good call."

Pang started to laugh. Kavik thought it might have been from a head swell, but the association man was as lucid as could be. "You and your friends are history, you know that?" he said to the young man holding him captive. "Thanks to our boys up there distracting you, we got the logbook out. You've got no leverage now."

In a panic, Kavik counted the captured men next to Pang. One missing. He flipped onto his back and slammed his elbows into the crate below him in frustration. If he hadn't stopped to save Jujinta's sorry carcass, he might have been able to complete his mission.

"You see, this is what I don't get about you association peo-ple," said the leader of the warehouse crew, his voice wavering. "What has Chaisee given you to deserve your loyalty, huh? Other than the chance to step on us? You'd suffer to keep her in power when she wouldn't spare you one of her sandals to eat."

The man ran a hand through his long hair, gathering the strands. His face was covered in sweat. "Negotiating with her was never an option, was it?" he murmured.

He walked over to the base of the tower Kavik and Jujinta were on, then took a Low Horse stance and inhaled deeply.

"No, no, no!" Kavik shouted in horror. "Don't do that! We can talk!"

The crew leader punched forth a stream of flame at the wooden crates. The highly flammable wooden crates.

"What are you doing?" Pang screamed. "This whole place'll go up before you know it!"

"You ever stand on a jetty and watch a really big wave come in?" the man said as he spread the fire back and forth. "Not knowing whether it'll die down before it reaches you, or keep gaining strength until it smashes you in the face?"

His flames petered out and he flopped down next to Pang, resigned, his elbows on his knees. A campfire outing after a bad day. "We're on the rocks together now, Sifu," he said, staring at the blaze he'd created. "I think we'll all sit here together until enough damage has been done."

His crew seemed to agree. A couple of them took brooms and rolled up sheaves of paper, touching them to the fire. They started going down the crate stacks with their improvised torches. The air began to fill with smoke.

"What are the two of you up there going to do?" the crew leader called out. "Burn for Chaisee's sake?"

Kavik looked at his partner.

"This is the worst job I've ever been on," Jujinta said, sounding as matter-of-fact as he had outside at the tea stand. The crackling of flames grew louder. "Have you ever considered you've been cursed by the spirits?"

Many times. The obvious solution was the water reservoir, nearly at eye level now that they were so high up. But still distant. He wound his arms and tried to pull his element to him. Nothing. The tank was too far away, and the seals were too tight. "I need an opening," he muttered.

Jujinta got to his knees but was wobbly from the hits he'd taken. "Stand back." He took one of his two remaining knives, sighted down the handle, and hurled it hard across the distance, sticking the point in the metal.

Nothing happened. The weapon wasn't heavy enough. "I have to hammer it deeper," Jujinta said. He hefted his last knife in his hand, as if he were making adjustments in his head for miniscule variations in weight and balance.

"You miss and we're both out of weapons," Kavik said.

Jujinta paused. He whispered to himself so softly Kavik almost didn't hear him. *"A Yuyan does not miss."* The words sounded painful for him to say, barbs lodged in his throat.

Whatever the notion meant to Jujinta, he shook it off and made his second throw, duplicating his previous movements so exactly that Kavik was convinced he'd inhaled too much smoke and witnessed the same moment in time twice. The last knife went flying through the air and landed in the pommel of the first, driving the blade further into the tank. A spray leaked around the knives, and then they were ejected by the pressure. Water poured out of the hole.

"That's actually harder than what Shigoro did," Jujinta said, before he slumped over and lay down again, resting his arm over his eyes.

Kavik didn't know what a Yuyan was, and he had a feeling his mysterious partner would be less than forthcoming if they ever talked about it. But that wasn't important right now. Jujinta's precision had opened a breach.

The walls of the tank were no longer an obstacle. Kavik

widened the stream, tearing a bigger hole, unleashing a huge amount of stored-up pressure. *The weight of water.* He couldn't stop this much if he wanted to. He redirected the torrent coming out of the tank and splashed it along the flames, dousing everyone and everything inside the warehouse.

As the men below shrieked beneath the indoor waves, Kavik realized he was in control right now. The only Waterbender present. A king atop his mountain.

And right now, the king had a mission to complete for the Avatar.

THE RECKONING

"**YOU DID** not think this through," Tael said as he led Kavik through the wreckage in the warehouse.

True. It had been a spur of the moment thing. And like most impulses, split between regrettable and victorious.

Some of the crates Kavik had sliced open with blades of water, shearing the faces off whole stacks where they were neatly aligned; others he'd burst open with internal pressure, ripping nails and pegs free from their holes. Everyone inside except for him and Jujinta had gotten knocked off their feet by a flood of slimy rainwater full of debris.

As the last man standing in the aftermath, Kavik had sifted through the wreckage before reinforcements from the association arrived. And to his deepening dread, he'd found nothing out of the ordinary. Nothing that could have spurred a power grab. No money, no weapons, no hidden locked containers inside the crates.

The most likely explanation was that he'd just missed something. But it turned out Tael was the type of jerk who would rub a pet's nose in the spot they'd made to teach the poor animal a lesson.

"Komodo-rhino hides, scraped, five pallets," Tael said, peeking his head inside. "Derelict."

"Komodo-rhino hides, scraped, five pallets," Kavik repeated. He winced as he put a mark next to the entry in the very logbook he'd came here for. "Derelict."

"Chop seal blanks, ten dozen. Fine, surprisingly."

About half the shipments were declared ruined after he and Tael poked through them. "Chop seal blanks, fine." Kavik was getting every bit of information he could have possibly hoped for, in great detail, with an extra eyewitness confirmation. A spy's dream. The only problem was that the logbook he was holding contained a tally of how much money he had personally cost the Zongdu of Jonduri tonight, and it grew in giant steps with each shipment declared unsalvageable.

It was like forcing the prisoner to build his own gallows. "Spotted sea prunes, dried, twenty barrels, derelict," Tael said. "*Striped* sea prunes, dried, twenty barrels, derelict. Mink-snake fur, collars and ruffs, full crate, derelict. Camel-yak wool, second grade, five hundred skeins, derelict."

He turned to Kavik. "And we're done. You kind of ended on a losing streak there."

The value of the wrecked goods was of a size where the numbers didn't matter anymore, as far as Kavik's own life was concerned. "They were going to burn everything," he said. "I didn't destroy this stuff. I saved half of it."

"Bold claim. We'll see if the boss-boss agrees after you explain what happened. Come. I've got a ride waiting outside."

Kavik snapped the tip of his charcoal pencil. The boss-boss? He was going to meet Chaisee? Of course. The larger the mistake, the higher you had to raise the flag of your shame. He followed Tael to the door, his arms and legs suddenly heavy.

Jujinta and the rest of the undersized association squad that had gone in with Kavik waited by the exit. Pang, their nominal leader, sneered at Kavik and nodded as Tael led him out. The new guy would catch the blame, as was tradition.

"Don't look so smug, Pang," Tael said. "You're going to account for this too."

When Pang sputtered, his tongue poked out through the gap on his teeth. "What?! How is this my fault? Do I look like a Waterbender to you?"

Tael was unmoved. "Doesn't matter. You were in charge. Your raid, your loss."

"You sent us in without enough strength and left us hanging! We did the best we could!" Pang was frantic at the prospect of being lumped in with Kavik's coming punishment. "I'll explain to Chaisee myself if I have to! It wasn't my fault!"

Tael halted and grimaced, making the face of a person who stubbed their toe, more annoyed at their own stupidity than anything else. He turned around slowly and then slammed his hand into Pang's stomach.

Pang's eyes goggled out, and he made a single, weak cough. At first Kavik thought Tael had merely punched him, a surprise body blow. No shame in keeling over from one of those. But a dark drip spattered on the floor.

"Chaisee?" Tael said loudly, for the benefit of any and all witnesses. "Who's that? I don't know a Chaisee."

Kavik sprang back from the blood pooling on the ground as if it were a living, skittering insect. He shut his eyes and cowered away, but the image of Tael cradling Pang by the neck with one hand and working the point of his knife upward with the other was going to be etched into his nightmares.

No, he whispered in his head. He crouched down as if getting lower, taking cover, would shield him from another death. *No no no.*

Pang's bloody wheezes became the loudest sounds in the entire warehouse. Then they stopped. "Wrap him in the wool and wet it down before you nail the crate shut, so the whole thing rots," Kavik heard Tael say. "It'll hide the smell until we can throw the goods out."

Kavik opened his blurry eyes a crack to see two men dragging Pang's body away. They were much smoother than he had been with Qiu. Practice must have made perfect.

"Get up, Sifu Waterbender," Tael said to Kavik as he wiped the blade of the murder weapon with a cloth. "The boss-boss doesn't have time to wait for you to grow a spine."

Jujinta stepped between them. He'd recovered his wits from the fight and was back to his usual, imperturbable self. Pang's death had not affected him in the slightest, and neither did Tael. "That's my partner," he said.

Tael threw his head back and sighed. "Juji, I only put the two of you together because I thought it would be good for a laugh. And if you don't back down right now, well, there's plenty more crates that need to be disposed of."

Kavik could only think of how Jujinta was out of knives. Tael still had the one. He rose to his full height and put a shaking hand on Jujinta's shoulder. "It'll be okay," he said, trying to keep his voice steady.

He still had one more out, looped around his neck. "I'll be fine." He tried a reassuring shake. It took three before Jujinta was convinced enough to step aside.

Kavik followed Tael into the street and got into the carriage that was waiting for them. Together they rode off to see where the evening would end.

The night was still young by Jonduri standards. Tael's carriage was enclosed, so the passing sounds of revelry were muffled. A sudden burst of laughter from a drunken party made Kavik clutch the logbook tighter. The fact that he'd been told to hang on to it was probably meant to be demeaning at this point. A weight around his neck.

One of the wheels took a hard dip into a pothole. Kavik's ears perked for a splash, water he might have used to protect himself with. But there was none.

"Something on your mind?" Tael said.

A great deal. "Pang was your man, through and through. He fought for the association and that's how you repay him?"

"Where Pang chose to place his faith is none of my business. He had a problem keeping his mouth shut, and he botched the raid. People who become more trouble than they're worth in Jonduri tend to vanish."

Bile rose in Kavik's throat. Any claim this city was better than Bin-Er was load of crock. It was just more organized. "What's going to happen to the workers?"

"Well, they have families, so we can't make them disappear easily. And it's going to be hard for us to pin blame for the cargo losses on them because none of them were Waterbenders. For now, they'll sit in a harbormaster's brig, safe and sound." Tael thumped the wall of the carriage with his knuckles. "If I remember correctly, *you* don't have family in the city. Do you?"

Kavik shrunk in his seat. He was a fresh face, just like he and Yangchen had discussed. Completely clean. The association didn't have to worry about anyone coming to look for him.

He avoided touching the bison whistle under his kuspuk. *Not yet.* His mind was in as many pieces as the inventory. Despite the fact that he'd come up blank on two different inspections of the warehouse, there was something in the logbook that felt like the missing piece to his mission. He just couldn't put his finger on it yet. If he survived the night and made contact with the others, he could try recreating its contents from memory. If.

The carriage came to a stop. Kavik heard the driver outside jump down and open the door. Tael motioned for him to get out first.

Kavik stepped onto a pathway leading to a luxurious, two-story cottage. The windows, real glass windows, were bright. The chirping of cicada-crickets over the lawn and the gentle clucking of the ostrich-horses made him think of a farm. Animals got slaughtered in farms.

"In there," Tael said. "And keep the book with you."

They walked up to the entrance, which Tael opened for him like a guest of honor. Kavik paused to consider whether the bison whistle could be heard from inside a building. He weighed the option of jumping on the other man right now and fighting for his life. His first step into the house would be an opportune time to slide a knife between his ribs. "Are you not coming?" he asked.

"I was ordered to stay behind," Tael said. "I'm just your humble courier. The boss-boss says you're to go find a seat and wait."

It was now or never. Kavik took a deep breath and crossed the threshold. The door slammed shut behind him.

He found himself in a narrow maze of luxury. Boxed in by a sweet-smelling wooden hallway, his feet sinking into carpet as lush as a bog, an expensive glowing crystal cut with dozens of facets hanging overhead. "Hello?" he tried. No answer.

He moved slowly, as if each piece of furniture he encountered might be a trap. A trunk would open its jaws and swallow him whole, or he'd fall through the squeaking floorboards into a spiked pit. There was only one door open, and it led to a small study.

He took one of the chairs in the corner and waited as he was told. His pulse became the thrum of a dragonfly-hummingbird's wings. His one solace was that this was far too nice a place to kill him. His corpse would make too much of a mess.

The sound of footsteps, coming from the ceiling. The master of the house descended the stairs above the study. Kavik's spine straightened. His lips parted. He froze in a tilted, halfway state, poised to get up but unable to leave his chair.

Between his wooden home and his old workbench on the lowest floor of Nuqingaq's, Kavik had learned it was possible, extremely possible when you were familiar with the person, to tell who was going up and down a flight of stairs just by the sound. His father was a slow *thud-thud-thud,* always catching and settling his weight fully before the next step. His mother's telltale noise was a sliding *swishhh,* since she always held onto a banister if available. If not, she ran her hand along the wall.

And the trail of light thumps that slalomed from one side of the stairs to the other, as if the maker of the noise were slowing their descent down a mountain by following a path of switchbacks, belonged to a single person in Kavik's life. The door to the study opened, and in walked the boss-boss of the association.

"Hi, Kavik," said his older brother, Kalyaan.

CLOSING THE DEAL

NO.

That was all Chaisee had cared to say to Henshe about delivering Unanimity to Bin-Er. Through a hawk, not a human messenger. Sidao hadn't returned. It didn't take a genius to figure out why.

Sitting in his office in Bin-Er, Henshe crumpled the tiny scroll with its one-word response and hurled it at the hawk that had brought it, scaring the bird into flying off before a return message could be stuffed into the tube on its leg. He hated Chaisee's blatant hypocrisy about the animals, the way she sent outbound letters when it suited her but still demanded in-person visits.

He was going to have to play by her rules one more time. Immediately he packed his bags. He reassured the panicking shangs that everything was fine, and he'd be back soon with the solution to all their problems.

Fine? had been their reaction. *Fine?!* Did he not see the barricades going up? Whole sections of town blocked off? Traffic had been cut in half! There were rumors the Earth King was getting ready to step in!

This was exactly why they needed Unanimity, Henshe told the shangs. To blow out the fires they insisted on setting underneath their own chairs. The anger in the streets wasn't the Avatar's doing. Neither was the Earth King's growing suspicion. This was a harvest sown of greed and idiocy. Now, if they could let him do his job, please.

It was the most he'd ever told his bosses off. Which was fine. Either he was going to come back from Jonduri a dead man walking, or with more power in his hands than he knew what to do with.

A perk of his position was that he was allowed unrestricted personal travel between shang cities. He was one of the few people who could enjoy a passenger's status without questioning by harbormasters. Once he was on board, he spent most of the trip lying in his bunk, staring at the ceiling of his solitary quarters, pondering the irony.

Who would have thought that cutting back on the illicit shipments would be the tipping point for the residents of Bin-Er? After the Avatar left, Henshe and the shangs had attempted to erase all traces of the unreported traffic she'd held over their heads, a move that was just common sense. They'd turned junks away, canceled contracts, dumped the workers who would have processed those goods.

That last bit had set everything over the edge. *Why?* Henshe had to ask. So many other past deals under past zongdus had ended in similar fashion. Why did the city have to lose its mind over *this* one?

He wasn't a man who asked for much. He didn't need the whole world dancing to his tune. All he wished for was fairness.

For the cogs to fit together and turn in the direction they were supposed to.

The title of zongdu offered the holder an opportunity to make astounding amounts of money from kickbacks, budget-skimming, and guiding the flow of deals and contracts. That was how it worked. That was why it cost so much money to bribe the people necessary to get appointed to the role in the first place.

The procedure, standardized by the office holders before Henshe, was to go into massive amounts of debt to scrape the bribes together, make even more massive profits during your term as zongdu, and then pay back the original loans. The difference that could be pocketed was potentially so large you'd need every pair of trousers in the Middle Ring to hold it.

Previous "generations" of zongdus had successfully extracted their rewards and moved on. Dooshim had gotten in and out with his money. That was how the process *worked*.

But apparently *now*, during Henshe's turn, was when the gears had to fall off their pinnings. The Avatar had decided to make a name for herself using *him* as a stepping-stone. Forget a profit. If his term didn't end the way he needed it to, he'd be ruined. Lower-than-Lower Ring ruined.

He just wanted what similar people in his position had received. To get in and out. Was that so much to ask? Couldn't the Avatar have delayed her efforts by a few years, until after he'd left Bin-Er and disappeared from the annals of the Four Nations? He didn't love the fundamental idea behind Unanimity, honestly, didn't have the same grand hopes for it as Chaisee. But it was the only tool at his disposal that had the chance of staving off disaster.

When they arrived in Jonduri and he disembarked from the boat, feeling mugged by the humidity and heat, he found a woman waiting for him on the dock among the coils of rope and barrels of pitch. She was pretty, with a smile wide enough to engulf a mango. He knew she was one of Chaisee's attendants. He asked her name.

It didn't matter, she said. If the Zongdu of Bin-Er would be so kind as to accompany her, her mistress was waiting.

Henshe had been to Chaisee's house before, and he suffered the climb through the damp, insidious jungle. Once he was inside, he saw it was still the same plain little training hall, aspiring to a guru's austerity. Nothing had changed since his last visit except for its owner, sitting in her chair.

"You look ready to pop," he said to Chaisee. "What happened to your old servant? The man with the scar over his eye?"

"What *didn't* happen to him?" she said calmly. "I hired someone else. It was a matter of security."

Henshe waited until the new attendant finished pouring their tea and left. The girl didn't need to know about the grisly fates her employer liked to deal out for disloyalty. "It would be nice if you didn't have the same response every time your paranoia flares up. You literally killed my messenger."

"You chose a poor messenger. Sidao was a member of the Avatar's retinue and could have easily passed on your information to her. Did you ever stop to think he might have been happily collecting payments from you and the shangs of Bin-Er while remaining loyal to her? The best of both worlds."

No, Henshe hadn't considered that Sidao had ever gotten the better of him, but he wasn't going to admit it. "All I'm saying is that you don't have to jump straight to permanent solutions."

"Sidao wasn't the only potential spy I had to deal with," Chaisee went on, ignoring his advice. "There was a boy from Bin-Er, an obvious plant attempt. And then the Avatar herself shows up on my island. You were sloppy, Henshe. Painfully so."

She dropped the words he'd been fearing the whole boat ride. "My answer is still no. Unanimity came to fruition with my research and I have borne its costs. We're not deploying it simply because you've bungled the situation in your own city."

Henshe stood up from his chair. He was a tall man, and he loomed over Chaisee like a shade palm. "Do you know what the difference is between you and me?" he asked. He dropped his gaze. "Unlike you, I'm not interested in building a dynasty."

He had her attention now. Chaisee shifted, folded in her chair an inch. "I know you've got plans," Henshe said. "Grand plans for the future. Your bloodline etched into history. Admirable. Really. But if I don't get to see tomorrow, neither will you. I know too much about you, and your little experiments that you're hoping might keep you in power forever. It wouldn't take much for me to convince the Fire Lord he should put Jonduri in the hands of a less ambitious functionary."

He picked up the steaming teapot, still mostly full. "If you don't help me put out the fire in my house, then I will make sure it spreads to yours," he said to his fellow zongdu. He hurled the vessel at the wall above her shelf. The porcelain burst, sending hot water cascading over her precious books and scrolls.

She made no movement, other than to eye him up and down. He let her. The more spiteful and reckless she thought him, the better. Chaisee was the one with the long-term outlook. She wanted to keep her title forever and for all time. She wanted this little island to become her own clan holding, this city the jewel in her crown. In her eyes, she had generations to lose.

She came to a conclusion. "I relent. You've convinced me that the best place for Unanimity is Bin-Er. But I need more time."

Henshe nodded, rocking his head over and over. *So that's how it is.* He knew Chaisee well enough that when she was done talking to you, truly had no intention of humoring a single word coming out of your mouth, she started feeding you promises, details. She would politely delay until you withered on the vine.

"Of course," Henshe said, getting up to leave. "This is an important decision. It shouldn't be rushed."

He walked out of her house knowing exactly what to do. He was going to call in the one person who could get Unanimity from Jonduri to Bin-Er quickly, right out from under Chaisee's nose. Once the assets left her shores, her reaction wouldn't matter in the least.

Chaisee might have thought him incapable of long-term planning, but that wasn't the case. For all her smugness about catching spies, she'd missed a very deep plant Henshe had successfully put inside her organization, someone who had been in his pocket from the day he first stepped onto Jonduri soil.

He just hoped Kalyaan still remembered the signal for linking up. It had been a while since they last spoke.

FOLLOWING THROUGH

"WELL?" KALYAAN said. "Aren't you going to say anything?"

Kavik screamed and launched himself at his brother.

Kalyaan happened to be the one person who could trounce him at wrestling every time. So when he managed to tackle Kalyaan to the carpet and start throwing punches, some part of him knew this was an apology gift. Kalyaan letting it happen.

That meant he had to get his licks in quickly. "You—" he shouted, trying to get around Kalyaan's forearms. His brother was laughing underneath. Laughing. "YOU—"

There was no finish to the insult, because at this moment Kavik truly did not know what Kalyaan was. Someone he hadn't seen in years. Someone who'd walked away from his family. He managed to grab Kalyaan's hair and give the back of his head a thump against the floor.

"Ow! All right, that's enough!" In a flash, Kalyaan was behind him, snaking an arm around his neck and yanking him backward. Kalyaan squeezed tighter until Kavik's spit rattled in his throat and he smacked at his older brother's elbows, a plea for mercy.

Kalyaan dragged Kavik to his feet. Only once they were both standing did he release the hold. Kavik gasped as his windpipe reformed back into shape. He took a lap around the study to catch his breath, his hands on his kidneys like a stooped elder out for his morning walk.

Kalyaan waited patiently, resting against a bookshelf. Kavik's brother had not lost the perpetual leanness in his face that spoiled the chance of a strong family resemblance. His hair had grown out, and he seemed to have given up on keeping it tied. They'd been about the same height when they'd seen each other last, but Kavik was shocked by the fact anyway.

"So," said Kalyaan. "How are Mother and Father?"

"You don't get to ask that!" Kavik snarled. "You don't get to ask that when you could have visited us! Written us! Let us know you were alive!"

"Kavik, I could have done absolutely none of those things." Kalyaan waved his arms to say *look around you.*

Yes, they were in Jonduri. That was the problem. "You were here the whole time," Kavik muttered. "Working for Zongdu Chaisee."

Kalyaan looked embarrassed. "Technically I'm working for Zongdu Henshe."

Kalyaan explained that early on in his errand-running career, he associated with like-minded, ambitious young people in the International Quarter. It was a good way to meet potential buyers. He became friends with a low-level administrator named

Henshe who had an appetite for risk as big as his. They started working together, securing small advantages and trading them into bigger ones.

The two of them were a successful team. With Kalyaan's help, Henshe got his name out in the ranks of Bin-Er leadership and managed to secure more resources for more ambitious plans. Such as getting Kalyaan overseas.

"The idea was that I'd be even more valuable on the other end of a trade route," Kalyaan said. "A deep plant inside another zongdu's organization? Worth a fortune. Jonduri was the biggest opportunity. I arrived here, made my way into Chaisee's association, and started passing Henshe information. I think it worked better than expected."

"*Better?!*" came Kavik's strangled reply. It was as if Kalyaan were still choking him.

Kalyaan made the *look around* gesture again. "I rose faster and higher in Chaisee's ranks than we could have dreamed. I take care of the projects she doesn't want her name linked to, which means I have a say in matters. For example, that mess you made at the warehouse? Not a problem anymore, because I said so. Everyone, including Chaisee and Tael, will see it as the new guy heroically saving half the goods instead of destroying half, because *I* see it that way."

He was acting like he wanted Kavik to share in this feeling. This exuberance. "Once I got in deep, I couldn't contact the family safely. Not even with a messenger hawk."

"Oh, how thoughtful of you!" Kavik shouted. "You were protecting us!"

"I'm protecting you still, Kavik. I got you through the association door because otherwise you would have blundered straight into Chaisee's arms. Just because I slipped past her guard doesn't mean you're capable of it. Why would you risk your life for the Avatar, of all people? There's no gain there."

"You don't know who I'm working for," Kavik said, trying to force the words to come out evenly. His attempt at evasion was pitiful. It was impossible to hide from someone who had your measure so fully.

"I do, though. Given the resources it took to get me to Jonduri, there's no way you could have made it here recently without abusing Air Nomad travel privileges. And the fact that you showed up at the same time as the world's most famous Air Nomad makes it pretty clear you're after something big. Hand me the logbook, won't you?"

Kavik picked the book up from the floor and flung it at his brother's head. Kalyaan ducked, caught it as it bounced off the wall, and came up laughing again. "I assume you started working for her for the same reason I fell in league with Henshe. You thought it was the right move for the family."

Passes. Kavik had just wanted to get passes out, to leave the mess of the shang cities behind. That's how this had started.

Kalyaan laid the logbook open on the desk, inspecting the recorded damage, the itemized contents. Kavik's handwriting all over the pages. "Well, now I also have to assume you've memorized this. Curse our family's steel-trap minds. I'm going to kill Tael for not doing this work himself."

"Like you killed Qiu? Because he might have recognized you if he got too far inside the association? Like you killed that minister who worked for the Avatar?"

Kalyaan did not raise his eyes from the book. Nor did he answer the questions. "You've put me in a really bad spot," he said. "If the Avatar gets too desperate for answers, too scared on your behalf, she might smash apart the whole trade route regardless of the consequences."

He turned a page, and Kavik could see his brother's swift, furious, restless mind working at speeds he had never been able to fathom in the past and still couldn't now. "I need to give her a victory. A distraction, while I pry Unanimity out of Chaisee's grip and into Henshe's. Once it reaches Bin-Er, this'll all be over."

Vintage. Utterly vintage Kalyaan. Striding through the blizzard, impervious to the weather. "Are you going to tell me what Unanimity is?"

Kalyaan gave him the same smirk from when they were younger, when he came back to camp with bigger fish than anyone else. "Nothing bad. Just leverage Henshe needs to maintain balance in Bin-Er. He wants the same thing as your boss, really. Stability. Peace."

The Avatar Kavik knew had railed against the idea of peace bought with suffering. Bin-Er wasn't balanced if the city bled families into the mountains. "You're afraid to tell me," Kavik said. "You're about to give Henshe an asset that'll let him get away with whatever he wants, and you want me to close my eyes and pretend everything will be okay."

"Because it will. Nothing bad is going to happen if the Avatar doesn't get her way. The sun will rise, business will go on as usual. The world will be tomorrow much as it was yesterday." Another flip of the page. "She just needs to receive the right information from the right source. And then all will be well."

The implication was clear. "You want me to turn on her," Kavik said. "You want me to betray the Avatar."

His brother at least had the decency to look up. To keep his shoulders from shrugging. "You make it sound like you'd be plunging a dagger into the beating heart of the Four Nations. I'll give you some good intelligence to pass on, treasure she'd be delighted to have in any scenario. It'll just be a little out of date."

Kalyaan was already talking about his betrayal like an inevitability. An assumption where his loyalties would lie, but a powerful one. "Why would I *do* that?"

"Because you don't owe her anything!" Kalyaan snapped. "How is that so hard to understand?" He slammed his fist into the book. "Kavik, Henshe has me in a bind. I have to come through for him right here and now, or else he'll reveal me to Chaisee. If she finds out I was a plant the whole time, I wouldn't be dead; I'd be *wishing* I was. Becoming food for shark-squids is better than what Chaisee would do to me."

He continued to press the pages until his knuckles cracked. "We're in a vulnerable position. You, me, those two Water Tribe fellows running your safe house. You're very good at slipping tails, Kavik, but not as good as I am at keeping them." Kalyaan twisted his lips. "Their names are Akuudan and Tayagum, right? They seem to be taking good care of you. What are they, substitutes for our parents while you're in Jonduri?"

"Maybe they're substitutes for you."

His brother looked genuinely hurt. "I was going to come back," Kalyaan said quietly. "Once I was ready and had the means, I was going to come back. You have to believe that."

Kavik didn't respond.

Kalyaan shook his head, and his grimace disappeared. Back to being the one in charge, the one who knew more. "I am asking you to protect me, Kavik. Have you forgotten I'm your family? These people, Henshe, Chaisee, Yangchen; they don't matter in the end. Let them play their games against each other. I can admit that we're both in a little too deep at this point. But only one of us is going to be killed if he fails. If there's a person in this world you owe, it's me, little brother. Not the Avatar."

Somewhere along the line, the language of Middlers had infiltrated their relationship. Kalyaan had saved his life before, and now the debt was being called in. What had happened to them? How had they come to this? You didn't try to square accounts with your own flesh and blood. The notion was madness.

"You know, if you play this right, you can have it both ways," Kalyaan said. "Just make the Avatar believe she needs to go to Port Tuugaq. The assets were tested there. She'll find plenty of clues to linger over. You'll be her hero."

He smiled to himself, liking this plan the more he thought about it. "In the meantime, she'll be delayed long enough to miss the real shipment. You'd have plausible deniability afterward; given the evidence, her failure wouldn't look like your fault. She won't suspect you did anything wrong. You can even remain her companion if you enjoy it so much."

The advantage. The opportunity. Kalyaan saw things Kavik could not, aimed at targets over the horizon and hit them as if they were inches away. "You'd love that," Kavik said. "Because then you'd have someone on the inside of the Avatar's retinue."

"Well, yeah," Kalyaan said. "As long as we're being honest with each other."

That was it. Kavik found his limit. He broke. The act of breaking hurt, physically. A deep, shuddering sob ripped through his chest.

He tried to laugh but only succeeded in making a dry, hollow noise, like a ladle scraping the sides of an empty barrel. It was the sound of capitulation. Weakness.

"Just tell me what story to give her," Kavik said.

As soon as Kavik re-entered the inn, he knew his brother's ruse was going to work.

It was the way Yangchen's eyes lit up when she saw him. The Avatar was simply glad her friend was back, safe and sound. She refused to debrief him until he settled down and got comfortable, bade Akuudan and Tayagum to get him something to drink.

"We were wrong about the warehouse," Kavik said, a steaming cup of tea in his hands. He was wrapped in a blanket despite the Jonduri heat; Yangchen had noticed he was shivering and draped one over his shoulders herself. "Unanimity's not there yet."

He started with the truth. The battle in the warehouse. His last stand with Jujinta, whom he took an aside to describe. The fires set by the workers and how, lacking any other options in the moment, he'd brute-forced the crates open.

It was a great story because it was real. At the time, he'd been acting fully in the Avatar's interests. His audience understood very well the risk he'd taken on behalf of the mission.

"Reckless little twerp," Tayagum muttered. But his smirk held a hint of respect.

There could be no better buildup for what Kavik was about to say next. "They made me catalog the damage. So I got a perfect view of all the goods *and* the logbook. There's nothing suspicious inside the warehouse right now. But there *is* a shipment scheduled to arrive in Jonduri from Port Tuugaq with three slots in the storage queues reserved so they can be transferred quickly from Jonduri to Bin-Er."

The information sunk in quickly. Yangchen snapped her fingers. "Chaisee didn't care about the goods inside the warehouse. She only wanted the space cleared."

A lie that rested on an intelligent victim piecing the falsehood together themselves was the most perfect form of the art. Each word that fell out of Kavik's mouth tipped the scales toward his brother's victory. "We weren't too late in Jonduri," he said. "We were too early. Unanimity is coming here from Port Tuugaq."

"Do you know what ship it's on?" Akuudan asked.

Kavik gulped his tea to fight back his nausea. "The *Sunbeam*. Three-masted junk. I don't know if it's departed yet."

He stopped there. He had a scrap of paper in his pocket that backed up his story. The idea was to claim he'd taken a blank sheet and pressed it against the charcoal markings in the log-book, lifting the "proof" directly from the page.

"It's funny; going after this information was a smart move on the Avatar's part," Kalyaan had said as they were rehearsing the story. "You were so close to getting it right with the logbook contents. So close."

Kavik knew with absolute certainty the extra layer to the ruse, the hard evidence, wasn't going to be necessary. "I have to get to Port Tuugaq," Yangchen said, even quicker than he thought she would.

The Avatar's trust impaled him through his heart. She couldn't show him the mercy of second-guessing his memory, making him repeat events for clarity. His word was all she needed. "I have to leave as soon as possible," she said. "Now. If the *Sunbeam* is due to arrive soon, then I can intercept it in open water by following the shipping lanes in reverse. If I catch it before it leaves harbor, even better."

"That could be a short flight or a very long one," Akuudan said. "What are you going to do once you find the *Sunbeam*?"

"I'll think of something," Yangchen said. "Spiritual intervention. Plague check. The only thing that matters is stopping it."

The Avatar's happiness hurt to look at. She'd discovered she was in a better position than she'd originally thought. Who wouldn't be pleased to have more time?

She looked at the others. "You two," she said to Akuudan and Tayagum. "I need you to keep an ear out for the warehouse workers in case Chaisee tries to retaliate against them. Kavik, stay under your cover with the association. If the shipment slips past me, you're our last shot at keeping it out of the hands of the zongdus."

"You can't go to Port Tuugaq alone," Kavik said. "You won't have anyone to watch your back."

The words slipped out without guile. He'd simply lapsed on which goal he was working toward, was caught between two minds. "It'll be fine," Yangchen reassured him. "Our enemies lack compunction, but I don't think they've worked their way up to murdering the Avatar yet."

She bounded over to Kavik and gave him a crushing hug. "I knew I was right about you," she whispered in his ear, fondness radiating from her embrace.

Yangchen had already been putting on plain clothes every time she visited the inn after the first visit. When she donned her palm leaf hat, her posture and gait turned into that of the most common form of wildlife in Jonduri—the oblivious late-night reveler. She went out the door and vanished into the darkness.

At Kalyaan's orders, Kavik spent the next two days at the association safe house instead of the inn. He told Tayagum and Akuudan sleeping there would help protect his cover.

Really, they were being split up so they could be watched separately. "The association will know if you've warned your friends," Kalyaan had told him. "Don't tell them anything. For their own safety."

Kavik took his advice and said nothing to the men who had risked themselves to shelter and feed him. Told them nothing about the danger they were in.

At the association hall there was little work to be found, so the place was mostly empty. He had no one left to talk to but Jujinta. Another dislodged person with nowhere else to go in the city. After some conversation, Kavik came to a fresher understanding of his partner's intense spiritual concerns, even if Jujinta refused to explain where he came from, the exact terms of his brother's death, or how he was responsible.

"There are crimes one cannot live down," Jujinta said over a Sparrowbones table, where the two of them pushed tiles around into winning patterns, unable to play for real without more members of their group. "Certain acts cannot be forgiven."

"Not even by the right person?"

Jujinta seemed determined to remain unworthy. "The person who could have granted me forgiveness is gone," he said. "I ask the spirits every day and receive no answer. I don't know who else I could turn to for guidance."

It wasn't Kavik, that much was certain. He had his own betrayal to finish carrying out. The next day, at Kalyaan's orders, he left Jujinta behind, left both safe houses behind, and got on a ship bound for Bin-Er, alongside the very boxes containing Unanimity.

DREAMS WITHIN DREAMS

YANGCHEN HAD to be careful along the journey. Southern storms could roll in quickly from the horizon, and when dark weather caught you in the air, it chewed you up and swallowed you into the sea.

It was times like these where Yangchen's difficulties with sleep had an upside. She dozed a little when she could. She trusted Nujian to grumble if he spotted signs of people in the water below, and when he needed to rest, she kept watch while he floated in place. They ate sparingly from the same rations of dried vegetables and drank from clouds she condensed with bending, but she knew her companion was burning his fat reserves without the chance to forage on land.

When they passed through the invisible wall of a cold front, and the mists crawling over the waves sent a shiver up her spine, a part of Yangchen wished she had listened to Kavik and not come alone.

Jetsun's previous visits to the Spirit World had prepared her well to guide Yangchen through her first. The older nun stepped sure-footed across a brook of flowing crystal. Yangchen just had to walk where she walked.

"The Spirit World is different things to different people at different times," Jetsun said. "But it's safe as long as you keep respect in your heart. The more you can ask, listen, and give thanks to your surroundings before your impact is felt, the better. Even holding the intention in your mind is good."

Yangchen looked down at the odd cross between earth and water swirling around their ankles, liquid jewels cool to the touch. "Can we bend here?"

"No. That's because our bodies are back in the physical world; the abbess and Tsering are looking after them. If we feel the need, we can remember where we are, think about waking up, and we will."

Jetsun did not slip the word "simply" into her explanation. She knew Yangchen had problems with waking up, bringing herself to the right moment in time and space. Yangchen glanced down at her hands, the ones that could open or close. They looked like her flesh and blood, down to the calluses. If all of her senses were telling her that her body was here, amid these shining, swirling colors, she would have to defy her own mind to escape.

The thought made her a bit nervous, and the waters around her flickered, threatened to change, but she saw Jetsun standing on the other bank of the brook and knew nothing would go wrong as long as they were together. Yangchen gathered her robes and stepped onto firmer ground. Neither of them realized the warning that Jetsun had spoken aloud. *Different things to different people.*

Oblivious, they walked toward a lonesome forest, the edges visible over the flat land like a cake sitting on a table. Maybe that was the mistake. Air Nomads didn't fear the woods in their bones. Airbenders peered down at the tree lines below them from the tops of their mountains, and no beast with claws or fangs really had the ability to climb a peak.

They'd gone only a little way when Yangchen heard a deep huff. The expulsion of air from a powerful set of lungs, bigger than a human's. She'd grown up around the bellowing of sky bison, but this wasn't the sleepy grumble of a herbivore. This was a swift clearing of the nostrils, to better taste the air for prey.

Yangchen's breath clouded in frost, even though it had been perfectly warm seconds ago. As if the trees were not far away, and were only pieces of dressing for a stage, a creature stepped out from behind them. It looked like a tiger-dillo, clothed in blue. Either it wore a pointed hat on its head, or it possessed a horn that looked exactly like one. Painted red lips curled back to reveal rows of jagged white fangs, curving in random directions, more hedge thorns than teeth.

A second spirit, and a third appeared. "Shishi," Jetsun said, gazing at them. "They look intimidating but they're playful." When she didn't get a response, she turned around.

The Avatar had frozen in place.

"What's wrong?" Jetsun asked. "You're not afraid of beasts. You had the Southern Chieftain's polar bear–dog eating out of your hand when you were eight."

True. Yangchen was not afraid of animals. Animals loved her and she loved them back. But Yangchen wasn't the person whose terror the shishi were smelling.

The nuns of the Western Temple had erred. Dagmola, Tsering, Jetsun, and even Yangchen herself. They all believed a visit to the Spirit World could help her establish a solid identity, bolster her young mind against the ancient anguish. An extra tether she could rely on when the ghosts of the Four Nations became too strong.

But they'd never considered an overwhelming memory occurring *inside* the Spirit World, brought on by a previous Avatar's fear of the realm beyond the physical. The shishi licked their slavering lips. Their eyes, which at first had seemed mere daubs on a flat scroll, gained depth and focus. Their faces wrinkled with humanlike, malevolent contours.

"Yangchen," Jetsun said calmly, firmly. "You don't have to stay. You can wake up."

She tasted flowing blood. She'd bitten a chunk out of the inside of her cheek. Her knees locked up. The pack of spirits fanned out into a hunting formation.

Jetsun grabbed the Avatar, tossed her over her shoulder, and ran.

Because Jetsun was holding her charge so close, she was unable to see the child Yangchen had become. Yangchen's sleeves had turned an undyed color. Her hands had shrunk to a younger, smaller size and she cried out in an unfamiliar pattern. *Aam, aam.* Not *ma* or *mama* or *am-ma.* The spirits were black flames licking along the grass, chasing them, closing in.

The growling and panting grew louder. Was there ever such an oft-repeated story? A woman racing for safety, holding a child, chased by predators. "Wake up," Jetsun murmured into her ear. Yangchen didn't know how she had breath to flee and speak at the same time. "I won't leave you here. Wake up for me first, and then I'll be right behind you."

They came to a halt. The brook had turned into a river, raging, churning. Deliverance might have lain on the other side, but the beaded jewels had been replaced by a syrupy dark tar that hissed when it spattered along the bank.

They would never make it across. Jetsun decided on something. Yangchen could feel her determination pass through their chests, two bodies skewered by the same spear.

In one swift motion, Jetsun ripped her orange shawl from her shoulders and bundled it over Yangchen's head. She didn't want the Avatar to see her fate. She took Yangchen under the arms and shoved her as hard as she could into the air. *"WAKE UP!"* Jetsun screamed.

Yangchen fell and fell but never landed. Not on the riverbank or in the bilious flow. She opened her eyes, back in her own skin. She saw Abbess Dagmola cradling Jetsun's slumped-over body, trying to rouse her. Tsering stared at Yangchen like a musician who'd left the last note of the piece unplayed.

Yangchen would forever remember the moment as the first time she was asked a question beyond her years, begged for an answer she couldn't provide. "Avatar," Tsering whispered. "What— What happened?"

BASIC TRADECRAFT

A BODY empty of its spirit couldn't survive long, not even with the best healing.

Wake up, she'd sobbed at Jetsun's bedside. *Wake up. Please. I'm sorry I was afraid. I'm sorry.*

When it was over, they'd honored her sister as a temple elder and companion of the Avatar who'd laid down her life to protect the bridge between humans and spirits. Future Avatars might look at the name *Jetsun* with awe and respect. Or they'd close the book they'd found it in and go back to their lives.

Yangchen sometimes felt like she still hadn't touched down in the physical world after being thrown into the air by her sister, that she'd been subjected to a twisted version of Guru Laghima's famous feat of weightlessness, cursed to never have a stable footing again. After she'd recovered from the ordeal of Jetsun's funeral, she'd spent two weeks in the library's history wing to understand which of her past lives had been so averse to one side of the bridge—with the goal of what, lambasting the dead for cowardice?—and found nothing.

When she was finally able to get back to the Spirit World, there were no shishi. The location she'd meditated to with Jetsun was neither her entry point nor a place she could find, and she walked many a maddeningly similar dream landscape in search of beastly spirits. No success. She never had the chance to definitively prove that it hadn't been *her* fault, that Yangchen could stand up to the exact same creature her past life could not.

The vision the phoenix-eels had shown her, the view purportedly from Jetsun's eyes—a double impossibility. That howling mist. Yangchen had personally never heard of such a place, and if its secrets lay buried deeper in a musty archive or reincarnated memory, then a painful search lay ahead. Was it possible for a human being's spirit to survive onward, long after the body had perished? There were stories, tales of gurus who had departed from their physical forms peacefully, but of course no firsthand testimonies. Finding the answer would require more time and strength than she could spare right now.

The easiest thing would be to assume the vision was a trick. A lie. Because if it wasn't, then her sister had been trapped, still was trapped, in a place of never-ending torment.

She would find Jetsun if there was a Jetsun to be found, she vowed.

She didn't sleep the rest of the way to Port Tuugaq. She was running out of route and she still hadn't spotted the ship she was looking for.

The only vessels Yangchen had seen going the opposite way were smaller boats that would be subject to the snarls of docking long enough where she was able to make peace with letting them pass. She would likely have to reveal herself to confront the shipment, and she had to make sure she didn't waste the chance checking out lesser possibilities.

Eventually the clouds parted to reveal Port Tuugaq, the southernmost shang city. The Shimsom Islands had always been home to trading posts and temporary fairs nestled along its rivers, but the Platinum Affair had forced the locals to choose a permanent victor. Big Island's deepest harbor won, and a town was quickly raised from logs and stone.

Southern Water Tribe traders avoided the trap of "clearance" by staying away from the newly declared city limits and using small numbers of go-betweens to handle the movement of valuable ivory, hides, and nigh-imperishable dried cod-flounder. They came and left the lands around Port Tuugaq as they pleased, which meant the city was neither as big as Bin-Er nor as unhappy. Its zongdu, Ashoona, was in Agna Qel'a for a constitutional that had lasted the better part of a year, and Yangchen had decided he was unlikely to be a player in the current game. If she ran into trouble here, it would be from the agents of Chaisee and Henshe.

Using the cover of a cloud, Yangchen circled Nujian in the air at a distance from the unimaginative blocks of Port Tuugaq, which were scored into the gravel coast like a baker would divide flour. Her bison's path wobbled. Nujian was weakening and needed to forage after the hard journey. She had already given him her remaining rations to keep him airborne up to this point, and she herself felt like a reed drawn through the fingers until the sides touched.

She couldn't stay here in the air indefinitely to wait for a ship matching the *Sunbeam*'s description to leave. She would approach the docks from inside the city itself, she decided. She just had to figure out an entry strategy.

Port Tuugaq, due to its smaller size, had a stockade wall around it. One end opened to the water, and the other bulged around a massive lumberyard containing stacks of logs as big as houses. She had few options for getting inside, none of them good. She could be spotted by moonlight as easily as the sun, caught approaching from the water just as well as land. The guard stations had excellent fields of view over the lands surrounding the city.

She had the urge to simply leap off Nujian's back, to catch herself with nothing but wind like she'd done so many times on the airball court, and land in the middle of the city. It was a foolish notion, would blow her cover, but she could taste the hours, the minutes she might save, more than the food her body was crying out for. *No,* she reminded herself. *You're so close. You're so close. Play this smart. Play this right.*

Despite the very act being painful, she turned Nujian around to land farther away from the city.

Yangchen crouched behind the reverse slope of a small hill, out of sight from the guard stations posted along the lumberyard end of Port Tuugaq.

She chopped sideways with the edge of her hand, earthbending the frozen ground loose along the breadth of the open field—but not moving it. Not yet. Dust and soil moving on its own was a sure sign of bending at work.

But dust on the wind? Just the weather. Once Yangchen had enough earth prepared, she began drawing air to her.

The breeze blowing against the city turned into a gale. The dirt became flying grit. Handily, there were thick trails of wooden splinters and bark shavings outside the walls, adding to the mix of debris.

Yangchen saw the guards in their stations turn their heads away, shield their faces, pull their hoods tighter. As generous a gift as she would get. Yangchen crested the hill and applied more wind to her back.

She ran, barely touching the ground, her feet acting only as nudges to keep her stable. She crossed the distance to the wall in the blink of an eye and sped through the lumberyard gate.

Yangchen didn't stop running until she reached the cover of a massive log pile. She skidded to a halt, gouging small trenches into the ground with her heels, and checked behind her to see if she'd been made.

The pair guards above the gate rubbed their faces and swore at the sky. One of them cursed the spirits, and the other laughed. Yangchen stared at them for a moment before pulling her hood over her head and skulking away.

Port Tuugaq was built out of unsanded Yesso timbers still bleeding sap. Houses were double-walled with sod for insulation. The streets were paved with little splinters of bark, trampled down by countless footsteps.

From the safety of a corner, Yangchen peered into a large avenue, presumably one of the arteries that fed the international sector. The odd clerk scurried from house to house, their shoulders hunched against the wind, but there weren't as many people about as she'd expected.

She needed to get to a spot where she could see the docks. And ideally rest. Eat. The technique of air-assisted speed used up so much energy. If she acknowledged that she was on the verge of collapse after her journey, she would surely teeter over the edge.

Her clothes, the same heavy quilted coat and skirt she'd worn in Bin-Er, blended in well enough. Keeping her chin tucked, she walked down the main street toward the water. After a minute she snapped her fingers in the air, miming the act of forgetting something important. She glanced over her shoulder, wondering if she should go back for it, then waved the idea away and continued walking.

Yangchen turned at the next corner and pressed her back to the wall, staying in the angle of a shadow. One person strolled by, oblivious to anything but the shallot flatbread he was eating, and Yangchen nearly lost count at one, so distracted was she by the smell. Then a second person passed, and a third. The third person, a woman carrying a bale of empty burlap sacks, noticed Yangchen loitering for no reason and gave her a strange look. But that was of no concern.

The *fourth* person she'd seen behind her walking in the same direction never materialized, even though there were no doors he could have plausibly gone into on her side of the street. Which meant he'd paused after losing sight of her. He was hanging back a safe distance.

I've got a tail, Yangchen thought.

Based on the quick glimpse she had when she'd "forgotten something," combined with the process of elimination, it was the short man with the patch on his parka. Normally she would have been thrilled. Tails were for people who were on the right track.

Yangchen went to the other end of the block and kept heading in the same direction along the parallel avenue. If Patch showed up again then she could be sure he was following her. But to do so would be clumsy of him, and she expected better.

There was a group on the opposite side of the street, huddled around an outdoor fire and a steaming cauldron of hot fermented rice drink. She passed the gathering as closely as she could, enough to scrape coats, which caught them by surprise. Sure enough, she immediately overheard two of the men telling their friends goodbye. In their haste they burned their tongues on their final sips and said the names of the people they wanted to give their regards to a little too loud.

So. A pair behind her and one roaming. She'd been marked as suspicious for sure, by men who were likely in Chaisee's or Henshe's pocket. But did they know who she really was? There was no plausible reason for them to guess she was the Avatar. Regardless, her plans had fallen apart. Any hope of recovery was going to require some quick surgery.

She detoured again, her pattern now a zigzag no reasonable person would take. She caught sight of Patch again, in front of her this time. *Well, that's just sloppy.*

Yangchen stalked toward him, expecting the man to slide out of her way in the hope she hadn't made him yet. But he stood his ground. She frowned under her hood and slowed at an intersection to get her bearings. Only one of the drinks stand patrons was behind her, to the south. The other had swung around to close off the street to the west.

She wasn't being tailed. She was being herded.

Flee east. They wanted her to move east; they probably had a trap waiting. *Flee over the rooftops.* Making her escape with airbending would have been trivial. It would also tip them off that an Air Nomad willing to put on a disguise and sneak around their employer's secret project was here.

She would have to pick one element, not air, and stick with it. Water? None at hand. Fire? It was getting darker fast, and she didn't want to draw more attention. Or even worse, light up her face. It would have to be earth.

She must have given away a tell when she decided, glanced down at the ground without realizing it, because Patch did too, lowering his eyes. He was an Earthbender, and now he assumed she was one as well. He would wait and listen as they approached, probably attempt to counteract any moves she made using the earth between them while his partners attacked from the left and right.

Pack tactics. A glint of metal in one of their hands. The three men closed in. The nearest house was dark, no one inside who might come if she yelled.

The urge to run filled her body; Yangchen's breath turned to mist in the dropping temperature. Maybe the reason she hadn't been able to find shishi during her meditations into the Spirit World beyond the first was because she'd crossed over with self-ishness in her heart, failing at Jetsun's challenge to only exist, and not seek. She'd wanted to prove she was braver than her past lives, and the Spirit World, knowing, had forever denied her that opportunity.

The physical world, however, was content to give her plenty of chances to face her fears.

She stamped hard upon the ground, letting her head drift down and to the left. The Earthbender's gaze followed, thinking the attack would come from that section of the street. But the glance was a fake. Yangchen had sought out different earth.

She chambered her fists and clumps of sod burst out of a bad seal in the log walls belonging to the house behind the three men. Patch and the fellow to his right took the soft but weighty masses of earth and grass to the backs of their heads and were out like candles. The third man, however, managed to twist at the last second, catching the sod in the ribs. He fell to his hands and knees, his knife clattering away, and looked up just in time to catch Yangchen's hood falling off her head from an errant flying pebble.

For a moment they were both very still. Recognition dawned on the man's face, and then sheer confusion took over. If he didn't know she was the Avatar before, he certainly knew now. It occurred to Yangchen that they were arranged like a paint-ing, the bridge between spirits and humans receiving a pros-trating supplicant.

She used the man's hesitation to air spout him up, and then drive him back to the ground hard, knocking him unconscious.

Yangchen looked around at the aftermath of the victory and bit the heel of her hand. Captives. She had captives now. Including one who knew she was the Avatar. Letting them go wasn't an option, but any hidden prison she could bend, underground or in the ice outside the city, would more than likely kill them. They had to be brought inside somewhere, quickly.

She stared at her limp, downed foes as if they might offer up a solution. She herself could think of only one. And she really, really didn't want to use it.

While most of Port Tuugaq had been constructed after the Platinum Affair, it had been the site of Water Tribe trade fairs going back into the ancient past. There were a few great qarmat of turf and stone in the city that had been carefully maintained over the centuries, and they remained important centers to those who knew their significance.

Yangchen knocked on the door of one such lodge. The door opened slightly ajar. Inside, flickering lamps cast warmth and light. A Water Tribesman in his thirties peered at her through the crack.

"I'm looking for a game," she said.

At this distance it was impossible for him not to see her face and tattoos. His eyes widened and he tried to shut the door. Yangchen flicked her foot and earthbent a rock into the hinge, preventing him from locking her out. "I said I want a game. You're not going to humor me and get the board?"

"I'm pretty sure you're not a member," he said.

Not the answer she wanted. *"I see you favor the White Lotus Gambit. Not many still cling to the ancient ways,"* Yangchen said, lowering her voice half in mimicry, half in mockery of this man who was trying to bar the garden gate to she who had eaten the fruit and tasted its mysteries. "Those who do can always find a friend," she replied to herself normally.

The man pulled on the handle with more force, to no avail. Yangchen would continue having both sides of this conversation if need be. "Jasmine one-seven," she said. "Rose two-six, White Lily three-six, Chrysanthemum four-six, White Jade five-six, Rhododendron six-six, Dragon at two-five, start with Knotweed at five-two."

She stopped to take a breath. "Repeat tile sequence but mirror the placement along the zero-zero six-six line, repeat for the remaining three quadrants, following Knotweed with the appropriate tile in the element cycle. *Welcome, sister. The White Lotus opens wide to those who know her secrets.*"

He stared at her, bewildered. She didn't have time for him to parse out that her identifying arrangements were indeed correct. "Look, the deal is right there in the last part of the passphrase," she said. "You can't actually be certain that I'm *not* a member. The hurdle is knowing the secrets, and I know the secrets. You are obligated to open wide."

While he didn't comply with enthusiasm, he at least stuck his head out to check if Yangchen had been followed. "What is it you really want?"

She stepped back to reveal the three unconscious bodies she'd sledged here using earthbending under the cover of darkness. "Some help dealing with this."

The color drained out of the man's face. "I need to ask a higher-ranking Lotus," he said. He pulled the door shut hard enough to snap the bottom hinge and left Yangchen waiting in the freezing night air.

CONVERSATIONS

EVENTUALLY THE door keeper and two more men came around to drag away the tails Yangchen had knocked out. She was let into the qarmaq. The first thing she did was to go over to the qulliq and sit down. Without registering any of the other details inside, and before she could stop herself, she nodded off, helpless against her fatigue.

She woke up shouting a curse, unsure of where she was or whether her ship had set sail.

"Relax," said a woman who was tending to the moss wicks of the oil lamp. "You've only been napping for an hour. The world's not going to end before sunrise."

Easy for her to say. "The ships," Yangchen slurred. She slapped her cheeks with both hands until she was fully awake. "Did any ships leave port around sunset?"

"No vessels left after midday. No departures are scheduled tomorrow either, if that's what you're worried about."

Yangchen had already said more than she wanted to in front of this woman who was already prying. Unanimity was still in Port Tuugaq, which meant she could technically rest easy for a little while. Technically. "What happened to the men I brought?"

"They're being held in a secure place until you decide what to do." The woman had grasped the Air Avatar's need to keep them silenced, but not harmed. She leaned closer to the firelight, letting Yangchen take in her weathered face, her pale blue eyes. "You can call me Mama."

Yangchen knew Mama was checking to see if the Avatar recognized her. And the only reason she'd do that was if they'd crossed paths before. But Yangchen hadn't seen this woman anywhere she could remember, at least not up close.

Advantage to her host. "Thank you, Mama."

They were alone in the room. The woman beckoned at a cooking pot over the fire. A trail of soup streamed into a bowl, which she gave to Yangchen. "Meatless," she said.

Yangchen would certainly have been forgiven by the Western Temple in this case, but she was grateful for the accommodation anyway. She took the bowl and said nothing until she'd finished three servings. It was the first meal she'd eaten in days.

"The paths of the White Lotus and the Avatar normally only intertwine during moments of generational import," Mama said. "Not because someone needs to stash a few bodies. I don't know how one of your past lives got access to our recognition codes, but it was a mistake to let it happen."

"How do you know it wasn't me who got access to them?"

Mama fixed her with her gaze. "Because you're an amateur." She filled a cup with tea and pushed it into Yangchen's hands. "You're the rankest sort of amateur there is. You're too active, you do too many things yourself on the operation, and you expect results too quickly. You've no ability to wait, whatsoever."

This was why she didn't ask favors from the White Lotus. For Mama to say that meant they had watched her struggle after Tienhaishi. Nothing during her travails back then suggested an organization of the world's wisest masters was secretly helping her behind the scenes. The White Lotus, like everyone else, had turned their eyes away from immense suffering and done nothing. She couldn't forgive that.

Perhaps Mama was referring to her actions around Unanimity, and she'd been under observation this whole time like an insect tricked into thinking the stick and leaf in her jar made up the entire world. "You're not the local depot keeper," Yangchen said. "As far as I can tell, you're too high ranking of a Lotus. And you're from the North, not the South. That means you've come all the way down to Port Tuugaq for an important task that couldn't be trusted to anyone else. You're investigating something, aren't you?"

Mama didn't answer.

"We could do an information trade," Yangchen offered. "That's what you professionals do all the time, isn't it? If you think I'm such a fool, let's compare leads and see who got further to their goal."

"Stop," Mama said, looking as exasperated as any Western Temple elder. "Just stop. Stop playing around and for once think about the kind of Avatar you want to be."

You mean what kind of figurehead, Yangchen thought. *How should I pose for my statue? Have the people around me been sufficiently awed by my presence? How long did awe feed a person anyway? How long did it keep them warm?*

Mama could see she wasn't getting through. "You think spying and intelligence and deception is a good use of your power. Such a waste when you, more than any person in known history, could inspire people with the truth instead."

"And what do you mean by that?"

"Practically every Avatar struggles to commune with their

past selves," Mama said. "But you! The wealth of knowledge and wisdom at your fingertips! If you embraced your gift, walked with your predecessors along the courses of their lives to the breadth and depth you alone among the generations seem to be able to do, then there would be no limit to your accomplishments! You could guide the Four Nations to a new gilded era, because you were *there* for the old ones!"

"How do you know about my gift?"

Yangchen's question was sharp and swift enough for the older woman to realize she'd made a mistake. The lights grew dim. The emotions of Firebenders could manifest in surrounding flames and right now the Avatar was ready to burst. "How do you know about my gift?" Yangchen repeated slowly.

Only the Western Temple elders fully understood her relationship with her past lives. They'd kept the secret well, just like they'd promised to each other. For a member of the White Lotus to know . . .

That meant Yangchen had been spied upon since childhood. Since before she'd been revealed to the world as the Avatar.

"You had someone in the Western Air Temple," she murmured. "You had someone in my home, evaluating me like an asset. In *my* home."

"You were the most important child in the world." Mama wouldn't look her in the eye. "And you were unstable. It would have been irresponsible not to monitor you."

The lamplight fractured into crosses, blurred by Yangchen's tears. The sheer hypocrisy of telling her not to be concerned with spies, to then go on and explain she'd been the target of spies since before she could remember. "That was my home, do you understand? *That was my home!*"

She was holding tea for some reason. She put it down and stood up. The motion made her dizzy and her shoulder found a wall to rest on. "That was my home," she said again, as if enough repetitions could force Mama to fully understand the extent of the violation, that Yangchen wasn't talking about a place but a time in her life, her *own* life.

Her childhood in the Western Temple was supposed to be the part of her that was real. The part free of manipulations and ulterior motives. And it was gone now. It had been painted with the same dirty ink as every other operation that had gone on in the history of the Four Nations.

Could it have been Dagmola or Tsering answering to the White Lotus? Was she to suspect Boma forevermore? And Jetsun. If Jetsun had masters outside the temple, had been feigning sisterhood with Yangchen to get an outcome better suited to *their* needs . . .

Then there wasn't a Yangchen. There was no person inside the robes. She'd be as the phoenix-eels said. An empty shell with no yolk inside.

She slid down the wall, the seams of her coat tearing against the rough-hewn stone. "That was my home," she said, choking on the falsehood of it all.

Yangchen folded into the corner. Mama came over and knelt beside her.

"I'm sorry," she said, with a flatness that acknowledged how useless the apology was. She turned Yangchen so she wasn't bending her spine sideways and tucked a rolled-up quilt between her and the wall.

Mama's earlier confession robbed the warmth from the gesture. She wasn't trying to provide Yangchen comfort. She was making sure the Avatar didn't hit her head. The White Lotus's agent inside the temple had told them about the liability. The asset had to be protected.

Better not to know who it was. Better never to ask. "I already tried," Yangchen whispered. Her throat was scraped and raw, as if a common illness had chosen to strike her at her lowest point.

"Tried what?"

"I already tried your suggestion." She shivered and pulled the corners of the quilt around her. "I sought out the Avatars of eras gone by. At some point I figured, why not go on the attack, you know?" The emotional storms brought on by memories of her past lives so vivid she couldn't tell who or where or when she was, didn't preclude trying to commune the more dignified way.

"I only let the elders know about a fraction of my successes," Yangchen said. "I spoke to dozens of previous Avatars. Upon dozens. Upon *dozens*."

She watched Mama frown. *You don't actually like that do you? That I've done exactly as you've proposed.* Telling Yangchen to bury herself in history had probably seemed like wise counsel in the older woman's head, but carried out and made real? It cheapened a sacred component of Avatarhood.

"I saw through their eyes, watched their lives unfurl," Yangchen said. "Time doesn't pass the same way inside a vision as it does in the physical world. At first I was overwhelmed by the noise of it all. As someone who appreciates intelligence, I'm sure you understand. The sheer quantity of information you have to sift through to find something relevant.

"And then I started noticing patterns over the eras I witnessed. Repetition. I sat in front of my predecessors humbly, asked so many questions, listened to so many answers. Do you know what I learned?"

Yangchen clenched her fists around the quilt. "Their lives are full of regret," she said. "Lost chances to make the world a better place. To me, that's what sticks out sharpest in their memories. Their regrets over the times they did nothing."

Why are you like this? The answer, here. "I have felt the shame of Avatars gone by," she said. "Lived through failures not recorded in history. And I can tell you with absolute certainty—not a single one of my past selves that I've connected with wishes they waited longer to solve a problem."

Acting only in moments of generational import. Who decided which moments were important? And how many people suffered in between? There had never been any gilded ages, as far as Yangchen had seen.

Mama picked up an atqun and went over to the qulliq to tend the wick. A few touches of the small stick and the flame was restored along the lip of the soapstone lamp. "I come here from the North on a regular basis, to meet with my fellows," she said. "But this time I'm in town to investigate a possible spiritual disturbance. There have been reports of bright lights and loud noises along the tundra outside the city."

Yangchen was so unimpressed with Mama's reason for being in Port Tuugaq that it took her a while to realize her proposal for an information trade had been accepted. "That's it?" she said. "Lights and noise?" That wasn't much, as far as accounts of spiritual activity were concerned.

"I will admit, it's a more interesting lead now that the Avatar is here." Mama cocked her head as if to *say your turn now*. She obviously anticipated getting the better end of this exchange.

Could Yangchen trust the White Lotus? And more importantly, did she need their help? Three bruised men being held against their will said yes. Her exhaustion, her lack of knowledge about the area, said yes. She couldn't let pride be the reason she failed, not at this juncture.

I hope I don't regret this. "I'm not following up on spiritual business," Yangchen said. She told Mama everything she knew about Unanimity.

TRACES

"THIS IS ... news," Mama said as she tried to absorb the salient points. Yangchen didn't think she was feigning ignorance. The White Lotus had been caught unawares by Henshe and Chaisee's secret project. While Mama could criticize Yangchen's recklessness all she wanted, her organization was several steps behind the Avatar. "What was the name of the ship you were looking for?"

"The *Sunbeam*," Yangchen said.

"Are you sure? I didn't see any records of a *Sunbeam* docking here in the last two months."

Hmph. At some point during her investigation, Mama must have stolen a glimpse of some logbooks. Yangchen felt vindicated that her tactics had merit. But the discrepancy didn't make sense. "My source verified the name. Three-masted junk."

Mama's response was immediate and reflexive. "And you trust this source?"

"Yes. Yes, I do." Yangchen felt more energized now that the food had taken hold. She decided she'd been too dismissive of Mama's information. "Show me the area where the spiritual disturbances were reported."

"I can do that." Mama raised her teacup to her lips but then lowered it before taking a sip. "You mean now? You've barely slept!"

Yangchen threw off the blanket and got to her feet. "The night is clear," she said. "There's enough moon. And I've told you how I feel about waiting."

Whoever Mama was, she had enough influence to walk out of Port Tuugaq late at night with a guest in tow. She'd waved a pair of passes at the gate guards but hadn't even bothered to let Yangchen hold hers.

When they were far enough away, Yangchen whistled for Nujian. She noted Mama's ease around the giant bison. They got on and flew farther inland, over a fresh layer of sugary snow.

"There," Mama said, pointing at a large hill in the distance.

They landed on the highest point, where one side fell away sharply into a cliff. The powder reached their knees when they jumped down from Nujian. Yangchen rubbed her arms as she looked around, first down the white slope of the hill, and then at the field the cliff sat atop. No tracks since the snow had fallen.

"Do you sense any spirits?" Mama asked.

Yangchen did not. This area was simply . . . empty. No living creature born of either world seemed to want it. She wondered what it would be like to live here, by herself. "Nothing."

She was going to be the first to give up and propose going back. But a shadow caught her eye, or rather several of them did. She tilted her head and peered back at the field. "Do you see those depressions?" she asked.

"Hold on, old eyes," Mama said. She squinted and frowned. "You mean those very regularly spaced-out depressions."

"Like tarts on a tray." The snow far to the left and right was completely flat, but here, under the cliff . . .

It was in the way of the landscape she really wanted to see. "Stay behind Nujian," Yangchen said. "The winds are about to pick up." She took a running start and leaped off the edge of the cliff.

She made sure to fall a bit before slowing her descent with airbending, twirling herself into a Full Lotus position. If she entered the Avatar State below the top of the cliff, there'd be less danger to her only bystander. With the stars above and the snows below, Yangchen closed her eyes and let herself become suspended, anchorless. Open and vulnerable to the accumulated power of her past lives.

If future Avatars looked back on this moment, she hoped they wouldn't judge her, using their most incredible ability for a bit of cleaning. She swept the entire field, melting the snow, pushing it aside, riding vortices back and forth until a job that normally took a season's change was finished in a few minutes. Once the gravelly earth underneath was exposed, she touched down and let the swell of energy wash away. After her battle with Old Iron, she found the Avatar State easier to summon. But she couldn't cling to it any more than a swimmer could grasp a wave.

Yangchen walked through the thawed field, an early spring-time of her own making. The ground was spotted with craters. The largest holes were as broad as houses and half as deep. And they were all round.

She took a closer look by sliding down into one of the depressions. It was about as big as a sitting room. Inside the bowl, chunks of gravel had melted and blackened. The clay underneath had been scooped out by some great force. *A meteor?* she thought. A meteor would have fit closely, but there were no lumps of ore nearby, no deep impact bores in the ground. And the normal signs of bending, even when fire and earth clashed, didn't mesh with her surroundings.

Yangchen heard the trails of a shout and she turned around. Her fellow investigator waved her hands from the top of the hill, telling her to come back.

"Staying down there was a waste of time," Mama said once she'd returned. "You can read a better story from up here. Look."

From their high ground, the exposed craters made a series of perfect, semicircular arcs. One close, one far, one right in the middle, dividing the distance. "You see those glittering rocks? The ones that don't look like they belong?"

From this angle and distance, the moonlight sparkled against small piles of stones that must have contained reflective mineral. They were regularly placed, as if to make an imaginary grid, one that narrowed until reaching the hill as its focal point.

"Those are distance markers," Mama said. "Siege engineers in the Fire Nation use them to test slings, crossbows, projectile throwers. Earthbending soldiers practice on fields like this one so they can get sorted by power and accuracy."

"But there's no war machine in the Four Nations that could have made those craters," Yangchen said. "And they don't look like the results of any kind of bending I've ever seen."

"I can't explain everything," Mama said. "I can only tell you what I think. And right now, I think this entire place is a target range."

LAST CHANCES

THE QUEEN OF OMASHU was a ponderous five-masted junk, built for stability over speed. Kalyaan had gotten Kavik on board by passing him off as one of the authorized cargo mates, a member of the crew responsible for the secure transport of an individual shipment. Kavik had trouble reconciling how an identity that could pass a harbormaster's inspection could be thrown together so quickly, even by a "boss-boss," until it dawned on him that Kalyaan had already prepared this cover long ago. For himself. Kavik was using up his brother's means to come home.

"I'm sending you back to Bin-Er on the same ship as Unanimity," Kalyaan had said. "Henshe's leaving earlier on a faster vessel and will be waiting for the drop-off. He has to get it without a hitch, do you understand? I'm not safe until he does. Afterward, I want you to go home and take care of Mother and Father. If the Avatar's team snoops around, I'll leave a trail that makes it plausible you were ordered away by the association."

The lights in his eyes danced faster than ever. "The next few days could be . . . important. And I'd prefer you were around to protect our family in case things don't go according to plan."

Once the voyage had begun in earnest, Kavik nearly broke down in a laughing fit. He still didn't know what Unanimity was; perhaps he never would. He'd remain in the dark forever, wandering unenlightened.

But down belowdecks, it was painfully obvious that three large wooden boxes among the many, each about as tall as his head, contained the assets the Avatar had been searching for this whole time. How could he tell? The muscle sitting in front of them.

Two men and one woman never left the containers' sides. They took their meals by themselves and slept in shifts. They were tall and powerfully built. Based on their golden eyes, Kavik assumed all three were Fire Nation. They might have been benders since they carried no weapons, but then again, he doubted the wisdom of shooting flames inside a wooden ship. Their size alone would have carried them through plenty of fights.

Kavik tried some small talk when the other crew members weren't around, volunteered to be the one who brought them food from the galley—they ate massive quantities, easily double the rations of the other crew members. But they were ferociously tight-lipped. The woman's name was Yingsu, the bearded man was Xiaoyun, and the guy with the long ears was Thapa.

They did not want to play Sparrowbones with Kavik as a fourth.

He watched the shores of Bin-Er approach for the second time in his life. During the first, the harbor had seemed so vast, a wide-open mouth ever feeding.

But now he was coming at the continent from a different angle. A bigger ship. And from the top deck, high above the waterline, Kavik noticed signs of trouble before they got close enough to lower anchor.

Several piers at the far end had burned down to their posts, blackened stumps sticking out of the water. Warehouse doors that normally would have been kept wide open during daylight hours had been chained shut. Men with clubs patrolled the docks, the actual longshoremen eyeing them warily as they passed.

The shangs must have liked Teiin's tactics at Gidu Shrine and hired more headkickers. *They're only catching up to Chaisee's level,* he thought.

The *Queen of Omashu* was secured to her berth by expert hands moving around Kavik, who was merely a stone in the river at this point. Hoists and winches were quickly set up to reach across the deck and pluck cargo from the hold. He shuffled out of the way, focusing his attention past the warehouses. There were standoffs occurring all the way down the avenues leading away from the docks, groups of men and women shouting curses, chains of people with linked arms, broken wares strewn over the ground, as if goods had been ambushed and destroyed on their routes deeper into the city.

What happened while I was gone? he started to ask himself. But then he realized his surprise was unfounded. He knew very well the wounds Bin-Er hid under its bandages, and they'd begun to fester.

A team of harbormasters boarded the boat to check clearances. This arrival had to be as clean as the dishes on the Earth King's table. Kavik's cover, or rather Kalyaan's, worked flawlessly, and the inspectors paid him little mind.

He spotted Zongdu Henshe waiting by the unloading area for his prize. Kavik had seen him at public events around Bin-Er;

the word on the street was that Henshe was basically the shangs' lapdog. But did it matter how fearsome his reputation was when he effectively held Kalyaan hostage? Kavik gritted his teeth and kept out of Henshe's line of sight.

The three huge guards, wrapped in bulky coats, walked down the gangplank so they could watch the assets touch down on dry land. They made a cordon around the unloading area by virtue of existing. Henshe pressed closer but didn't address them.

The elevated framework connecting the ship to the dock was completed. The first Unanimity crate rose from the hold, needing the strength of several men pulling on the hoist ropes, wooden spars groaning as the box levitated underneath them, crossing from ship to shore. Kavik held his breath as the assets made their descent. The final stage of the journey.

And then a small flame shot over his head. Less than a candle's worth. If he didn't know better, he would have believed it came from Yingsu's fingers, while everyone was looking elsewhere. He turned around to see a scorched, glowing wound eating deeper into the line. The hoist juddered with each skein that gave way.

"*Get back!*" he and several people cried out at once. There was enough warning to clear the immediate area, but not to save the cargo. The rope snapped, and Unanimity fell crashing to the ground.

When the dust cleared, Kavik poked his head over the rail. The shang men were in motion, screaming and shoving at the frightened dockworkers, demanding to know where the fire had come from. The crate was destroyed, its contents piled on the docks. Kavik stared in shock at the great secret, exposed for all to see.

Unanimity . . . was a pile of stones. Chop seal blanks, to be precise.

That couldn't—how—

Kavik searched for Henshe in the crowd. The zongdu of Bin-Er was already walking away with the three shipment guards in tow, using the distraction to avoid any further notice from the harbormasters. They rounded the corner of a warehouse and disappeared.

You were so close with the logbook, was what Kalyaan had said.

Shipments have to be escorted by specific crew members during the voyage, named in advance, was what the Avatar had said.

Henshe hadn't cared about the physical goods. He'd only wanted a particular delivery to occur because he needed the people who had been cleared to travel with it from Jonduri to Bin-Er. *They* were the assets. *They* were Unanimity.

Kavik shouted, incoherent, no plan in his head to form words. His voice was lost in the din. He ran down the gangplank and ducked through scuffles escalating into brawls until he reached the point where he'd lost sight of Henshe and the other three.

But he was too late. They were gone.

CLARITY

IN BIN-ER, the vortex was spinning. The crushing ice closed in, threatening to smash, skewer anything caught inside. The fracas at the docks was only the edge of the whirlpool.

Kavik headed deeper into Bin-Er to find that the residents had gone from crowding the square to blocking the streets with barricades, some earthbent or frozen into place, others simply construction debris heaped up high. He learned that night skirmishes had been fought to maintain them against the shang brutes seeking to unclog the flow of traffic and force people back to work.

A few arteries through the city remained open to official business, but everyone expected Earth King Feishan to step in soon. There were reports of troops marching toward Bin-Er. Comeuppance for the shangs was at hand, claimed some, gleefully. Others shook their heads in fear at the prospect of an intervention. Who would the Earth King side with? Did he even understand there were sides, or would he simply level the city and start anew?

It was dangerous to cross town, he was warned over and over again by shop owners through the cracks in the boards they'd nailed over their windows, by mothers pulling their children back through their doors by the men and women manning the barricades against the headkickers. Each time, he gave his thanks and continued on his way over their concerns. Someone had told him once that he had good moves. He could wriggle his way through the dangers.

As far as Kavik was concerned, he'd done what his brother had asked. The Avatar had been sent off to Port Tuugaq, oblivious to his betrayal, and she'd missed the crucial shipment. Henshe had gotten his due and had no further reason to threaten Kalyaan.

What was so special about those people that they were worth so much trouble? At least one of them was a Firebender; likely all three were. Kavik's stomach contracted around a stone of uneasiness. He needed to warn the Avatar of their terrible mistake, that the assets in question were human beings. Unanimity had slipped past them and was in Bin-Er under Henshe's control.

Kalyaan had told him he could play both sides. All was not yet lost. He had to find a messenger hawk, fast.

"It's not your fault," Boma said in the back room of the small inn he was staying at.

Yangchen had introduced Kavik to her grouchy old advisor before they departed from Bin-Er, over a cup of tea that was less a proper introduction and more a chance to memorize each other's faces. Boma's frown hadn't changed, was still the same flat line chiseled into his block-of-stone expression, but his gaze was kind and warm. He'd been surprised to see Kavik come back without the Avatar, but the partial truth sufficed. Kavik had been forced to accompany the Unanimity shipment by the association, and now they needed to make the best of a bad scenario.

Boma believed the Avatar's runner had done a good job under the circumstances. And why wouldn't he? Kavik withheld the facts about his brother and his betrayal. He couldn't risk Boma shutting him down, refusing to believe him. A confession might have made the old man react by apprehending Kavik and sitting tight until further notice from Yangchen. Precious time would be lost.

He blinked away tears. Boma must have thought he was overcome with guilt for not being able to stop the shipment. "We have to contact the Avatar and tell her to come back to Bin-Er as fast as she can," Kavik said. "She might still be chasing the wrong leads in Port Tuugaq."

"I'll get a hawk to send to Port Tuugaq immediately," Boma said. "But what if she's already left? If she went back to Jonduri, we won't be able to get word to her by aerial message; it's why I couldn't tell any of you how bad the situation in Bin-Er was. She could be stuck on the island, waiting for an update that'll never come."

Kavik had an answer for that, just not a good one. "She won't linger in Jonduri. If she goes back there, she'll come straight here after, without delay. I guarantee it."

Boma looked uncertain. "Trust me," Kavik said. "A bird to Port Tuugaq is what we need to cover our options."

The old man nodded and got up. He retrieved a small tube and a miniature scroll from a satchel, along with ink and a fine brush.

"I'll leave you to it while I go arrange for the hawk," he said, handing Kavik the supplies. "Write small."

Boma didn't even check the message Kavik had written before sending the hawk. *Trust me.* He'd kept making the demand, and it kept working.

Kavik stayed at the inn over the next few days, unable to go home and face his parents. Boma did him another kindness and checked up on them; they were okay for now. Safe. Still laboring under the impression that their youngest son was training with the Avatar.

During his time there, he slept fitfully through daylight hours, leaving only to scout the city for Unanimity. He was trying to rid himself of the conclusion that he'd done everything he could. Waiting made him feel helpless. Hadn't that been the origin of his troubles? The source of every decision he'd made? He'd come back to the one place he didn't want to be and now he was waiting for the Avatar, waiting for the city's time to run out, waiting for something to shatter.

When he couldn't take it anymore one night, he tried to reach the last remaining presence in Bin-Er who could have granted him some stability. The person who was bedrock, who had certainly weathered great troubles in decades past. He went to visit Mama Ayunerak.

Only to be told at her door that she wasn't there. She'd left the city.

In a daze, Kavik stumbled around her building to the trash pile where he kept the loose brick with his house key. His feet had carried him out of habit. He began to cry, haltingly and without tears, as if part of him still had to be uncommitted, even in his deepest despair. He whispered a hoarse request to the air above for any kind of relief.

He must have been heard by the spirits. And the skies had judged him harshly, because they answered with a blooming ball of flame and a thunderclap that knocked him to his hands and knees.

A whine in his ears. Scorching air licked the back of his neck. He looked up and a halo of smoke drifted away, its source nowhere to be found.

While the streets weren't as crowded as they used to be, there were still some people about, and they were all as confused and frightened and deafened as Kavik. Slowly, he and the other folks who had been flattened by the sudden burst of heat and force got up, trying to understand what had happened.

Through the ringing in his skull, Kavik heard a faint *pop-pop* sound, the bouncing strike of fingers against a tightened drum. And then another burst erupted further down the block.

He saw it fully this time. An expansion of light with the suddenness of a noisemaker. But instead of a cloud of colorful pinpricks, it was a solid sphere of angry pressure, a ball of fire in the sky. Dust and debris rippled outward along the street and he shielded his eyes before he was blown backward by a wave of air as powerful as any he'd seen the Avatar produce.

When he blinked away the grit, there was again no trace of the power that had forced everyone to the ground. Around him, mouths opened in screams. People crawled away in terror, scrambled to their feet, broke out into a panicked stampede.

Nothing bad will happen if the Avatar doesn't get her way.

Kavik still couldn't hear the cries of the people running through the street, but he could hear Kalyaan's voice telling him before he left Jonduri not to worry, that everything would be fine, Unanimity wasn't so bad. It would stabilize the situation in Bin-Er.

There was a third crack above the rooftops, distant enough that Kavik only suffered the report and not the blast directly. The damage was getting systematically spread over the city.

Don't worry about it, had always been Kalyaan's refrain. It had been the case in Bin-Er, when Kavik confronted him about why he wasn't coming home much. And then again, further back in the past when they were stuck in that fearsome blizzard, Kavik thinking for certain the two of them were going to die.

How many times had he heard it during their march through the blinding white, the stinging snow, the storm that plugged their tracks so quickly that Kavik couldn't be sure if they'd already perished, had left their bodies, and were merely floating atop the drifts? *We'll be fine. I'm your brother. I would never let anything bad happen.*

As good a liar as Kavik was, he would only ever be second best in his family.

His family. He had to reach his parents. He got up and ran around the back of Ayunerak's, toward the Water Tribe Quarter. People were scrambling to get inside, abandoning their positions at barricades, fleeing the streets. He raced alongside a group heading in the same direction, his lungs burning. Some of them he recognized from Nuqingaq's.

Another explosion at their right broke their stride. The members of his little pack skidded on their heels, slipped, fell. Some had already begun to kneel where they were to beseech the spirits for mercy, too scared to take another step forward. Kavik turned his eyes away. He'd put his faith in the wrong party too.

He left them and kept running until he reached the Water Tribe Quarter, his house, and slammed his key repeatedly into the door, all misses from his shaking hands, until he finally got it right, one small thing right, and unlocked it.

Inside his parents huddled as far as they could from the walls, while dust rained around them each time a fresh explosion struck. Their silent relief when they saw his face was too much to bear. Kavik knelt down, threw his arms around his terrified mother and father, and hugged them harder than he ever had in his life.

"Kavik, where is the Avatar?" his mother asked through her tears. "Why isn't she here? Why isn't she with you?"

The one person who could have stood up to the nightmare in the sky, who saw the shangs and the zongdus and Unanimity for the brewing disasters they were, who had been right about everything the whole time except for her choice in friends, was somewhere far away across the sea. And that was Kavik's doing.

"She'll be here soon," he said, rocking his parents in his arms, a mirror of the comfort they had given him as a child. "She'll fix this." *Have faith.*

They stayed in their house as much as possible. A peek through the windows at the empty lanes of the Water Tribe Quarter told them their neighbors had fled indoors too.

The city was completely dark at night. No one put up visible lights in their homes out of fear they'd draw the attention of the angry spirits above. Nor could anyone sleep through the noise, which sometimes arrived in walking barrages that crept closer and lower, descending, stalking, until Kavik was certain the final strikes would come crashing through his roof.

Within a short span, it seemed like the whole of Bin-Er had been beaten into submission. The residents of the city were being punished by forces beyond their comprehension. Henshe had secured his version of stability. Kavik wasn't sure how Firebenders in his employ could be so powerful, what kind of technique allowed them to create explosions from afar, but he was certain the zongdu could no longer be challenged as long as he retained control over Unanimity.

Dazed by a lack of sleep, he lost track of how long it had been since he'd returned to Bin-Er. When the knock came at his door, he jumped, fearing any sound that resembled the faint tapping that could sometimes be heard before the greater concussions.

He kept his parents away from the entrance. Before opening the door, he pressed himself against the wall with water in hand. Gingerly, he unlatched it and peeked through the crack. Once he saw who it was, Kavik let the door swing fully open and stood face-to-face with his visitor.

Jujinta stared at him for a good long minute. He leaned to the side to look past Kavik's shoulder, at his bewildered parents crouched in the corner behind the desk. He took in as much of the house as he could see from the threshold, before finally returning his attention to Kavik.

With great care Jujinta reached into his collar and pulled out the bison whistle Kavik had given to him before leaving Jonduri, along with instructions to use it whenever he meditated alone or made offerings to the spirits at shrines by himself. "You were right," he said, placing it back into Kavik's hands. "The answer came to me."

He was a changed man. Before, whenever they'd spoken, Jujinta's eyes had always been slightly vacant and dull, as if part of him were trapped in another place and time. But now he was fully present. He shone with inner purpose. Meeting the Avatar face-to-face could do that to a person.

The fact that he was at Kavik's door with the whistle said the rest. The message to Yangchen had been successfully passed on. The Avatar was in Bin-Er.

"Come on," Jujinta said, never one to waste words. "Everyone's waiting for you."

THE DISPLAY

HENSHE, WHO was arguably the most powerful man on the continent right now, had been reduced to a glorified porter. The three Firebenders—he had no other label for them that fit—ate voraciously, and they were leaving their stations too frequently for food. Given that he was the only person in the city he trusted with the secret of their existence, he went and fetched their meals himself.

He tromped up the stairs of the empty, dingy lodge to the second floor, carrying trays of buns and dumplings instantly gone cold in the chill air, and nudged himself through a door with his foot. Long-eared Thapa maintained his vigil at the window. Since he had the most raw power of the three, his task was to keep the encroaching forces of the Earth King at bay, and his hiding place overlooked the outskirts of the city. The other benders, Yingsu and Xiaoyun, were posted in separate apartments deeper in, with good views of Bin-Er's major districts.

Henshe had selected their locations well in advance and covered his tracks just in case.

He was about to ask for a status update when Thapa put up his hand. "Hold on," the Firebender said, craning his neck. "Movement." He stepped back from the window to perform his technique. Henshe put the food down to watch. It was fascinating every time.

Thapa began a series of inhalations, each one bigger than the last, until his chest ballooned in and out. When he got to about twenty or thirty massive breaths taken, his eyes widened, and he threw his head forward. His gut caved into his body and a rush of air lifted the debris in the room. There was a *pop-pop*, an arrhythmic double drumbeat.

And then the roar.

Far downfield over the snowy plain a seed of fire flowered into a spherical inferno, boiling snow and hurling soil, sending ripples through the air. Fireworks were an obvious but poor comparison. Henshe had once seen a grain silo explode in the Middle Ring, and that kind of damage was more apt. Thapa's little warning shot could have taken out a small city block.

"Movement's stopped," Thapa said. He rubbed his forehead in a strange way after the act, using the fingers of both hands to press into the skin above his eyebrows and stretch it apart. It was as if he needed to widen an imaginary hole in his head to relieve the pressure.

Such destruction at such range. There was no other bending like it in the world. The Earth Kingdom scout brigade amassed at the opposite end of the plain shrank farther back into the tree line, where Thapa had kept them penned. They wouldn't be marching upon Bin-Er anytime soon. Thapa himself had cleverly suggested that he blow apart the ground on occasion, to make Earthbenders considering a tunnel into the city fearful of cave-ins.

The other two Firebenders, who were more precise, had a different mission. Their role was to cow the populace by aiming explosions over the city itself. They'd complied beautifully, stunning unruly crowds, forcing them back indoors. He'd allowed them to aim at empty barricades, blast craters in the streets, even take out the top floor of the Gidu Shrine, which he always found ugly, a mar upon the skyline. Whole sections of town, strongholds of the agitators, had been made to suffer, slammed repeatedly by violent bursts above them throughout the night.

But the benders who comprised Unanimity weren't to kill anyone. Henshe didn't want to destroy Bin-Er or its residents. At some point he needed business to resume, or else he'd never get his money.

Thapa took a break to eat. He consumed the food joylessly, washing down half-chewed mouthfuls with water so he could finish faster. If there was a downside at all to his technique, it was the energy it drained from him, and the time it took to gather enough strength for the next explosion. Henshe shuddered to think of a bender who didn't have such weaknesses.

"How did you come by this power?" he asked. Henshe knew what to expect from Unanimity, how to deploy the assets properly, but nothing about their origins. Chaisee was the last person in the world who would volunteer such information.

Thapa glanced up from his meal. "Bitter work," he said, as if taking offense to the words *come by*. "Torturous training. I didn't find this ability like a coin in the street, and neither did the others. We three are the product of significant investment."

Henshe found it odd that the Firebender could talk about himself so. Especially given how little he'd spoken until now.

"You look disappointed," Thapa said. "Did you want me to say it was chance? A spiritual blessing? Because it was neither.

I took a big gamble on myself to get to this point." He paused in contemplation before taking his next bite. "I mean, a lot of us who tried to develop this technique drowned."

"Wait, what? *Drowned*?"

Thapa smirked as he chewed, taking his time now, as if speaking with his mouth full would be the rudest thing he could possibly do today. "I don't think I benefit from telling you more," he said. "Let's talk about something else. Like the money you're going to pay me."

"We already discussed your compensation." And it had been painful enough. The most crucial part of getting the assets to Bin-Er was Henshe's promise to pay each of the Firebenders an outrageous sum. His debts had birthed children, an entire clan of their own. He was going to need to profit more than all of his predecessors combined to have a chance of coming out ahead.

I can do it, he'd reassured himself. Only he had the full measure of what was happening in Bin-Er. The shangs were holed up in their manors, heard the noise, saw the lights, but they still didn't know the details of Unanimity. He alone held all the information.

"The situation's changed since we last bargained," Thapa said, puncturing his thoughts. "I can still tell what's happening in the city from this room. I certainly can tell what's going on with the Earth Kingdom troops I've been aiming at. And you, my friend, are in way over your head. You're hanging on by your fingernails."

Henshe didn't like how he was being talked to. He wiped the sudden perspiration from his brow. "We have a deal," he said, his voice coming out shakier than it should have.

"We *had* a deal. Let me guess what you were originally trying to do here. Once you had me and the other two in your possession, you were going to work out an arrangement with the shangs and the Earth Kingdom both, where you claimed a good chunk of the wealth in Bin-Er for yourself. You'd keep us a secret, and if anyone crossed you, *bang!*"

Thapa reached for another bun. "But for you to have a credible enough position, you'd need to show the people who you were bargaining with your power," he said. "The way you've had us blasting away without end—it's all been one big demonstration, hasn't it? You can't threaten someone with a weapon they don't understand the effects of."

"Congratulations," Henshe snapped. "You know the basics of negotiation."

"Yes," Thapa said, grinning widely. "Which means I understand your position is worse now, not better. You've demonstrated that Yingsu, Xiaoyun, and I are the only force keeping the army of the Earth King camped outside the city from marching in here to discover your part in the whole enterprise. You've demonstrated to us that we control whether Bin-Er is open for business, not you or the shangs. Our value has taken a leap skyward, don't you think?"

He tore into the soft bread. "I talked it over with the others before we started this little venture with you, in case we spotted an opportunity. Given what the Earth King would do to you if he knew the whole story, I think paying us our original price twenty-fold is good."

Henshe staggered back a step. "Twe— twenty . . ." His foot hit a chair. "You want *twenty times* what we agreed upon?!"

Dark red bean paste spilled from the bun like entrails. Thapa shrugged. "To start."

More sweat prickled down Henshe's neck and back. Blood rose to his face. He felt a pounding in his ears from within.

He couldn't bear that cost, not even in his most optimistic plans. And it wouldn't stop at twenty. Once the Firebenders realized how desperate he was, it would go to fifty, a hundred-fold.

He was lost. Out of every direction his defeat could have come from, it was his own assets. His leverage turning against him.

Thapa finally finished his food. "I bet you thought you held all the tiles," he said. "Funny thing about that. Once you play your tiles, you no longer hold them."

Henshe thought he might explode himself. He imagined his innards covering the floor. Where had it all gone wrong? What law had been written into the cosmos that declared he should fail, where people just like him had received successes and riches out of their wildest dreams?

"Huh," he said. The sound of his complete shattering. *Huh.*

He looked around the room. Behind him, there was a window that faced the interior of the city. He could think of only one thing large enough to break, to hurl, to smash.

"Agreed," he said to Thapa. "Twenty times. You'll get your money. But I realize we've overlooked one thing."

"Oh?"

"We haven't demonstrated how far we're willing to go." Henshe blinked slowly, calmly. "You were right. For the plan to work, I'd have to admit to some degree the explosions were happening under my direction. But so far, I've told you not to kill anyone. What good a threat is that?"

An outsized shriek for an outsized loss. This city had ruined him. He'd make a mark on it in return. "Without some bodies to count, people will think this was all just a warning from some angry spirits," Henshe said. "Let's draw some blood."

Thapa's interest was piqued. "Now you're talking like a proper man on the brink. What should we take out?"

"Whatever you feel like. Whomever. Leave a toll."

Thapa crossed over to the window facing the rest of Bin-Er and gazed into the distance. "Can't see much from here, except for a lot of Water Tribe homes. A couple of wooden houses next to them. I'll start with those."

Henshe made a grunt of indifference.

The Firebender started breathing in, breathing out, forcing the air in his chest to comply with his will. *Five,* Henshe found himself counting, with a strange sort of giddiness. *Ten. Twenty.*

Thapa hit thirty breaths. This blast was going to be huge. There would barely be a Water Tribe Quarter left.

Forty. Forty? "What's wrong?" Henshe asked, confused. "What are you holding back for?"

"I'm not." The Firebender was sweating as badly as Henshe had been a few moments ago. The technique was taxing, certainly, but it wasn't supposed to fail before the blast. "It's like I can't get enough air," Thapa muttered. "I don't know what's . . . what happening . . ."

He backed away from the window, completely abandoning his buildup. He clutched at his throat. Henshe opened his mouth to comment, but as soon as he did his ears were stricken by a bout of uneven pressure. He jawed up and down, trying to relieve the swell. Thapa was saying something to him, but he couldn't hear clearly.

Dizziness. His head spun. Edges of darkness crept around his vision. What in the name of the spirits was going on? It wasn't just him; Thapa's eyes were rolling back into his head, and his face had turned blue.

Henshe attempted to slump into the chair, landed short, his hips sliding off while he clung to the back for dear life. His breath was gone. His lungs had no strength to open. He fought for consciousness and succeeded long enough to watch Thapa keel over.

He felt more than heard the smack of the large man hitting the floor. Someone else must have detected it too, been waiting for it, because the moment after the Firebender collapsed, feet tromped up the stairs and into the room.

With them came air, sweeter than he could have believed. His ears popped and he could hear again, but he was too weak to do anything but hold on to the furniture, as if he'd drown without it. He looked up to see two Water Tribe men, one with a waterskin at the ready, a bender, and the other a giant even bigger than Thapa. While the Waterbender checked the corners of the room for hidden dangers, the huge man hefted Thapa over his shoulder and carried him away with one arm. He had only the one.

A young woman wearing a heavy cloak walked in. She crouched down and threw her hood back to reveal an orange collar, a blue arrow, and a familiar face. "Zongdu Henshe," said the Avatar. "You've been busy since we last spoke."

Henshe finally gave up his death grip on the chair. It slid away with a wooden screech. He collapsed and rolled over onto his back. "How did you know I was— how did any of this—" He summoned enough strength to hammer the back of his skull against the floor repeatedly. He wished he had the capacity to shout instead of wheezing impotently. "How? *How?!*"

The Avatar slid one hand under his head to protect him. "Trade secrets."

"What did you do to us?" Henshe asked, grasping for anything to make sense of it all. "We just . . . collapsed where we stood. Was that you? Is Thapa dead?"

She made a *hush* gesture with her free hand and beckoned the Waterbender over to grab him under the arms. "Unfortunately, I don't have time to chat," she said as Henshe was dragged away. "You're not the last stop on my list today."

EXPOSURE

IN THE end, it came down to tailing. Simple, basic tailing.

Kavik had already started the hunt for Henshe and his assets before Jujinta knocked on his door, slipping out of his house when he could, doing his best not to worry his parents. Once he pooled information with the Avatar, progress came quickly.

He knew the faces of the Firebenders. Yangchen could narrow down which sections of the city they were most likely in based on the pattern of explosions and their range limits, information she'd discovered in Port Tuugaq. They enlisted help from terrified people hiding in their homes to try and pinpoint the directions the noises were coming from.

One night, acting on the hunch he might find luck in a stretch of street that had a handful of Fire Nation restaurants, Kavik spotted Thapa entering an establishment that was closed but still had smoke coming out of its chimney. He managed to follow the Firebender back to an apartment overlooking the outskirts of the city, where it became clear the man was holding off entire squadrons of the Earth Kingdom army by himself.

Upon returning to Boma's inn, he conferred with Yangchen's hastily gathered group. She'd brought Tayagum, Akuudan, and Jujinta with her from Jonduri to Bin-Er, for their own safety and for the extra help. Despite the continuing bombardment plaguing the city, they decided not to move immediately on Thapa.

Their patience paid off. Henshe himself made the next trip from the restaurant to Thapa's station. From there, Kavik followed the Zongdu of Bin-Er to two other locations across the city. He waited outside one of the buildings, wedged behind debris in an alley, until he heard the *pop-pop* close up and saw with his own eyes, barely, a thin wisp of smoke jetting from a window, followed immediately by an explosion further away.

Confirmed. They'd found the Firebenders who made up Unanimity.

The bigger challenge was trying to take all three down as quickly as possible from start to finish. "I just need to get close to them," Yangchen had said over a map of Bin-Er. She'd refused to explain the reason for her grim confidence. "The rest of you will be on lookout and cleanup duty."

The first raid on Xiaoyun's position had been executed smoothly. Kavik had stationed himself under the Firebender's position to give the signal. Yangchen had gone in alone, and as she promised, dealt with Xiaoyun so efficiently that Akuudan and Tayagum only had to pick up the man's unconscious form.

They repeated the process for Thapa. An even greater success since it netted them Henshe as well. Yangchen still wouldn't allow anyone to witness how she defeated the Firebender without a fight.

Apprehending the third and last member of Unanimity, however, was not going so well.

The ground underneath Kavik shook with the impact of the Firebender's explosion. He compressed himself behind a pile of rubble as dirt and rock rained down upon his head.

"Back!" He heard Yangchen yell from across the distance. "You have to get farther back! You're still within range!"

He knew. The problem was that Yingsu seemed to be able to summon her technique much quicker than the other two, and he didn't have an accurate count of the minimum time between detonations. If he broke cover and ran, he might get picked off in the open.

Yingsu had deduced something had happened her fellow benders by the lack of noise. Tipped off, she'd left her apartment and moved to a fallback secondary location—the Bin-Er gathering hall, a perfect defensive position. Kavik had been forced to follow her in a hurry. He'd been spotted and separated from the others in the ensuing chaos.

At least they didn't have to worry about bystanders. The entire neighborhood had long since fled. But there was a large lawn surrounding the building and Yingsu had blown away any obstacles that would have impeded her lines of sight. She had multiple windows to aim out of, and they couldn't pinpoint her inside, where she could shift around the large structure easily. It was impossible to make an approach.

Kavik watched the Avatar lob a huge chunk of the street at a section of the barracks wing where the last fireball might have come from. He guessed she was trying to provoke Yingsu into blasting it apart midair, which would have given him a chance to run. But the dug-in Firebender didn't take the bait. The rock crashed through the wall and went unanswered. Even if it had been aimed well, she'd probably just moved out of its way and saved her return shot.

Which meant they were at a stalemate.

Kavik didn't dare make a sound in case he gave away his exact location. He was pinned. But strangely enough, he was calm, unafraid, accepting of his circumstances. He didn't need to panic. The Avatar's blessing would protect him.

He's going to die, Yangchen thought. Kavik was going to die just out of her reach, and she was going to watch it happen. She crumpled against the wall of the empty, half-ruined house she was hiding behind, covering her face, her breath loud in the hollow of her hands. His death would be on her shoulders. Her fault.

"It will be all right." She looked up to see Jujinta staring at her.

On her return to Jonduri from Port Tuugaq. Nujian had diverted his flight path and beelined for an isolated meadow where a strange boy, not Kavik, was meditating and blowing on her bison whistle with every exhalation. Yangchen's surprise was immense. So was the boy's.

Nujian came roaring down from the sky into the empty field, thinking the whistle meant someone needed rescuing. The impact of the Avatar appearing during his prayers had resonated deep within Jujinta, who introduced himself as a friend of Kavik's. After he relayed a simple message that Jonduri wasn't safe and Yangchen had to get back to Bin-Er, his stony visage crumbled and he'd fallen to her feet, weeping.

She'd had to improvise quickly, figure out the intentions behind Kavik's ploy. Yangchen played the part of the gentle, compassionate nun and took Jujinta with her, along with her safe house runners.

And now here they were, the oddest pair, their situations reversed. Jujinta comforting her. He took things in stride very well.

"We who serve you will not let you down," Jujinta said. She hadn't been able to refuse his declaration of undying loyalty in Jonduri. "Look. Your men return."

From deeper within the city, Akuudan and Tayagum came running toward them, staying out of sight of the gathering hall, heads ducked low out of an abundance of caution. Tayagum had a long, thin wooden case in one hand and a sealskin bundle in the other. They crouched into position next to Yangchen and Jujinta.

"Did you bring what I asked for?" Jujinta said.

"It wasn't easy on short notice." Tayagum opened the box. He and Akuudan had also been forced to accept Jujinta quickly. With Bin-Er a smoking wreck, no one was going to decline a fresh ally.

Inside the case was an unstrung bow. Jujinta reached for it but hesitated, closing his eyes and flexing his fingers as if the grip would corrode him if he touched it.

"You're violating an oath right now, aren't you?" Yangchen said. "A taboo." From the memories of one of her past lives, she understood the meaning of his scoured nose, his penitent rituals, his self-imposed exile.

"This is more important." Jujinta overcame his reservations and picked up the bow. In his hands the weapon seemed to pour new life, or rather an old one, into the rest of his body like a withered plant receiving water after a drought.

He strung it deftly and drew on the string without releasing several times to test the weight, using his thumb despite not having a ring. "Ironspruce," he muttered to himself. "Water Tribe make, cable-backed, about one and a quarter shi. Original owner taller than me. Give me the arrows."

Tayagum presented the quiver. Jujinta immediately tossed aside most of the arrows for not meeting some unspoken standard. Down to two, he hefted them, rolled them between his fingers while sighting along their shafts, examined the feathered fletching.

"I can make the shot," he declared, notching the winning arrow to the bowstring. "The problem is, there are too many spots she could be in, and I need enough time to acquire her. We have to get her to a window for a few seconds, but without her immediately blowing us to pieces."

Yangchen thought it over. In a moment of clouds parting, she landed on the one act she had not done intentionally this whole time while she'd waged her battle of secrets with the shangs, Henshe, and Chaisee. She knew Akuudan and Tayagum would object if she told them her idea.

So she simply went for it.

Before anyone could react, Yangchen got up, took off her cloak, and walked into the middle of the empty street, revealing herself openly to her foe. She would end the deception. She would be herself.

She spread her arms wide as she walked toward the gathering hall, a bright orange and yellow target in the empty street. Yangchen ignored the screams of Tayagum and Akuudan and Kavik. She focused her lungs and bellowed in Yingsu's direction, her natural loudness never so handy before now.

"YOU STAND BEFORE THE AVATAR!"

Her challenge boomed through the air. What else could a pacifist do but raise their voice and hope for the best?

Each step she took was on borrowed time. She didn't want to enter the Avatar State; there was too great a chance she'd be killed inside it. The cycle of reincarnation would end, leaving the Four Nations without their protector.

Will you take the life of an Air Nomad? she thought. *Would you destroy the bridge between humans and spirits? Do you have a line you won't cross?* In her mind, she was addressing more people than the one Firebender in the gathering hall. She saw Kavik start to rise from his cover and knocked him back down with a gust of air. This danger was hers alone.

"WE WILL TALK!" If anyone outside her team was watching, it would have looked like she was beseeching an angry spirit, hardly different from her dealings with the phoenix-eels or Old Iron. Yangchen was struck by the fact that she was putting almost as much trust in her enemy as she was her own people. "WE WILL COME TO TERMS!"

There was silence following her declaration. Maybe the last member of Unanimity had decided to relent.

And then Yangchen heard a faint *pop-pop.*

She should have known better. In her heart she did know better, because her burst of airbending-powered speed was quick enough to save herself. She sprinted forward, just clear of the blast, the shockwave adding more force to her back than she could handle. Yangchen tumbled along the ground, rolling like a clump of dried weeds in the desert, cradling her own head for protection. Through the din of the explosion, she thought she detected the airflow of an arrow in flight, a single note rising above a chorus, but she could have been imagining it.

Her momentum carried her back to her feet and she finished the run to the gathering hall, ramming an entrance for herself with a chunk of earth instead of bothering with the door. The assembly room looked the same as she remembered from her meeting with the shangs: empty benches, the dais where she'd sat. There was a small balcony higher up. If she'd been right about the arrow, the last Firebender was behind the door.

Yangchen leaped to the balcony, generating wind to twirl her higher, and she landed as quietly as she could. She steeled herself for what she was about to do, and she was glad she was alone. Henshe had the measure of it. She'd neutralized him and the other members of Unanimity by using a vile ability, one she could not let anyone know about.

She put her hands out, and for the third time today, prepared to remove the air from the room behind the door.

Anyone trapped inside the sphere of emptiness she created would become unable to breathe and lose consciousness in little more than ten seconds. Death would follow shortly after if she kept it going. And the most frightening part was they'd never see it happening.

There was only an unreliable sliver of time in which she could maintain the technique and remain true to Air Nomad principles of holding life sacred. One mistake and she'd be matching lethality with lethality. Paying back the destructiveness of Unanimity with bending just as insidious. A perfectly even transaction—

Yangchen paused.

No. She still had a choice. Retaliating with full force would be common sense in this situation, the wise thing to do. But her instincts, the silence from her foe, told her to take a step back. She lowered her hands and opened the door, exposing herself yet again to attack.

The room leading to the balcony was a small lounge with a changing screen and a desk that folded into the wall. Inside, a tall Fire Nation woman matching Kavik's description of Yingsu sat slumped in the corner. Her long braids were gathered tightly back to keep them away from her forehead, her high hairline making her resemble an Air Nomad a little. She clutched the arrow stuck under her collarbone. Dark arterial blood spilled out from around the shaft.

Yingsu stared at her with a face growing paler by the second. Yangchen rushed to the window to gather snow from the sill, melted it between her hands, and then slid next to the Firebender, applying the liquid to her wound. The injury was serious. Had Yangchen taken the air from the room, it would have killed her instantly.

Removing the arrow would be tricky; stabilizing her patient came first. "Don't move," she said to Yingsu. "No one's dying today."

Yingsu's head made small circles, round and round, as if she were contemplating the ridiculousness of being saved by the Avatar, whom she'd tried to vaporize moments ago. A futile exercise in Yangchen's opinion, trying to make sense of the world and the people in it.

The woman gave up and closed her golden eyes. "Thank you," she muttered.

RECONCILING

KAVIK SAT alone in his room and waited.

He shouldn't have been as scared as he was for the Avatar's safety. All three members of Unanimity had been picked up. The only force in the world that could have challenged her power on an individual level had been dealt with.

And yet, when the knock came at his door and Yangchen poked her head inside, he was as relieved as he'd ever been in his life. He was clearly not cut out for the management side of missions, where he had to fret and hope the action had gone cleanly. "Can I come in?" she asked.

He let her sit on the bed again. She was wearing the same outfit as she'd worn at the Golden Cloudberry teahouse. "I asked your parents to leave the house for a bit," she said. "I had to come up with an excuse for why I was dressed like this."

"No wig?" She was relying solely on her hood to hide her tattoos.

"No wig."

Their patter was strained. Until now they'd been able to talk solely about the mission, locating the Firebenders, figuring out how to strike fast, take them down. But not anymore.

They could start with the easier, obvious topic. "Jujinta," Yangchen said.

"Jujinta," Kavik echoed, nodding.

Yangchen rubbed her face. "A risky recruitment," she said. "But a successful one. You saw his potential. You appraised his state of mind, his vulnerabilities, and the probability he could be convinced to act against his previous loyalties."

"I turned him." There was no boast in Kavik's statement. Manipulating Jujinta by taking advantage of his troubles was certainly up there on his list of horrible deeds. But at the time, his partner was the only means he could think of to deliver Yangchen a message without tipping Chaisee's association off. They weren't watching Jujinta and had no reason to suspect him of anything.

"Well, I have a new companion now," Yangchen said. "Whether I wanted one or not."

Jujinta's presence, along with Akuudan and Tayagum, meant that Yangchen had gone back to Jonduri first. There, the only thing she would have been told was to get back to Bin-Er as fast as possible. She would have deduced the Unanimity shipment had slipped past them and Kavik would have looked like he was heroically doing the best he could for the Avatar under dire circumstances. "Where are the others?" he asked. "Where is everyone?"

"They're safe," was all she said.

He sensed the wheel turning to its inexorable final position. "I also sent a message to Port Tuugaq for you. I didn't know which city you'd be in. I had to cover both possibilities."

Yangchen reached into her robes and pulled out a small wooden cylinder. She held it between her thumb and finger, like an apothecary's pill that would spread and bubble if dropped into water. The seal on it had been broken.

"I left Port Tuugaq before it arrived, thinking the two of us were simply wrong about the *Sunbeam*," she said. Her finger tensed over the cylinder, her nail whitening under the strain. "The only reason I know what's in this message right now is because the hawk you sent returned to Bin-Er after I wasn't there to receive it in Port Tuugaq."

"I'm glad it did," Kavik said, a pain in his throat.

The message she held, the one he'd sent with Boma's help, contained the additional information he'd learned after leaving Jonduri. It said Unanimity was three people, Firebenders, and gave their descriptions in case Kavik was unable to make contact again with Yangchen in person.

And it also contained Kavik's admission that he had betrayed her.

He'd burned himself. He'd told Yangchen about his brother. He'd told her everything Kalyaan had told him.

He'd written very small.

"You didn't need to send this message," Yangchen said, her voice cracking. "You could have let the situation play out. I would never have discovered you turned on me, and we still would have taken down Unanimity in Bin-Er, together."

She was wrong about that. More than anything, Kavik had to put his betrayal in writing and make sure he couldn't take it back. He hadn't trusted himself to confess in person. He'd wanted a clean conscience and had grasped at the first available means. "How long ago did you read it?"

"It was waiting for me when I linked up with Boma."

So she'd been pretending everything was fine between them

throughout the hunt for the Firebenders. For the sake of the mission, she'd kept up the act. "What about the others?" His eyes stung. "Did you tell them?"

"Do you want me to?"

"Yes." He found it easy to say. He'd put them all at risk with his lies. They deserved to know the truth.

Yangchen shivered like she was fighting back an explosion of her own. "I need you to understand something. When you sided with your brother over me, gave me the runaround, and threw away our chance to stop Unanimity from reaching Bin-Er, you unleashed the worst sort of information possible. You created a ripple that cannot be smoothed."

It didn't matter that Kavik hadn't known what Unanimity was during the moment he turned on her. He should have taken the Avatar's word instead of Kalyaan's. "A small man like Zongdu Henshe did this to his own city for *money*," Yangchen said. "I suppose I should be grateful that he and Chaisee have no loyalties other than to themselves. If someone like the Earth King got their hands on it . . ."

She shook her head and took a deep breath. "Behind closed doors, the leaders of the Four Nations are still at each other's throats, tensions ready to be inflamed by the slightest spark. If they knew a human being outside of the Avatar could possess such extreme power, they'd do anything to control it. The world itself might combust."

Kavik had put his thumb on the scales. Kalyaan would be proud. "I understand," he said. There wasn't enough gall in the universe to mount an apology.

Yangchen pulled her knees to her chest like she'd done ages ago, in a different era. She rocked herself as if trying to find solace where no one else could give it. "You know what the worst part about this is?"

She trailed off, a long pause to gather her thoughts. Surely, she had difficulty choosing between so many bad parts. "In the moment you decided to come clean, some part of me knows you were uncompelled. My inner voice, mine, is telling me you had no ulterior motive, that you were simply being honest with me for the first time."

She cleared her throat. "And I can't afford to listen to that voice. There's a chance you're manipulating me still. You may have only told me about your brother because you want my help extracting him from Chaisee's organization."

Kavik genuinely hadn't thought of that. She was a step ahead of him, playing both of their turns. There was no way he could refute her accusation, given the facts.

Yangchen was right. Kalyaan had staved off the threat of Henshe, but at the cost of acting against Chaisee's interests. It was only a matter of time before the Zongdu of Jonduri found out what Kalyaan had done, and then his formerly invincible luck would run out. Kavik's brother was in more danger than he'd ever been. Unless the Avatar could save him.

Kavik hadn't seen the hidden spiral of logic, but Yangchen had. And she was forced to give him credit when he didn't want any. "I can't take you at face value anymore," she said. "You've denied me that luxury. I can't even trust your confession, Kavik."

Again, he understood. And yet the questions poured out of his mouth anyway, rapidly, as if he were trying to test a barrel for cracks. "What are you going to do with the Firebenders?"

"I don't think that's for you to know anymore."

"What about Henshe and Chaisee? What's going to happen to them?"

"Not for you to know."

"What are you going to do with me?"

Here she took longer to answer, and by the time she did her eyes were dry. Her voice collected and crisp. "What am I going to do with you? I'm not sure yet. But you don't have to worry. With all the information in your head, and all the ways you're connected, you're more valuable than you ever were before."

The day Kavik first met the Avatar, he'd explained the mantra by which Bin-Er operated. *You're not worth anything until someone else decides you are.* She had gotten truly upset, down to her core. Then later, when they were discussing his payment in exit passes, she'd nearly balked at their deal, simply because she was uncomfortable with the idea of using him.

And now, she spoke as if he were grist for the mill. As if the kindest, fiercest, most giving part of her had broken completely. "I made a mistake in trusting you, Kavik," Yangchen said. "You're not one of my companions."

She stood up from his bed and squared her shoulders. "But you might still be one of my assets."

THE EARTH KING

IT WAS a warm spell in winter for the Middle Ring of Ba Sing Se. The sun glinted off layers of thick wet snow, and every so often a hiss would come from the gabled roofs as a miniature avalanche revealed streaks of green tiles trimmed in gold paint. The waters of the canals flowed freely under crackling-thin sheets of ice. Children plunked holes in the frozen surface, tossing any heavy object they could find until their parents scolded them.

Wide-brimmed hats to protect from the glare were reasonable. Yangchen wore one as part of her disguise as she walked up to the counter of an open-air rice wine shop. There was no one else around, so she ordered a bottle from a particular obscure brewer. By an existing arrangement, it came filled with water so she could drink from it convincingly. She waited and watched the children play.

Earlier that morning, dressed in her full regalia as befitting an Air Avatar visiting an Earth King, she'd landed Nujian down on the meridian of the outer court of the Royal Palace. In between the cloud-winged huabiao, with the tiered staircase the size of some small hillside villages looming overhead, Yangchen had been greeted by an army of servants, courtiers, ministers, and attendants bowing silently in ancient custom.

And then she'd been turned away. The Earth King would not be able to make their appointment, and she'd have to speak with him later. A specific phrase was used to cap the denial of her audience. *His Majesty invites you to enjoy the splendors of his city in the meantime.*

She made sure to look like she was appropriately dejected. *I must decline, for spiritual matters call me elsewhere.*

Now she was here in the Middle Ring, waiting, growing a little concerned about how close some of the children were coming to the canal's edge. A man in rough laborer's clothes pushed a few of them back to safety as he walked toward her. He approached the wine shop and took the spot next to her. As he settled in, he tapped the counter with his middle three fingers. Yangchen did the same in return.

Earth King Feishan was twenty-eight, skinny, with sunken cheeks. He looked neither like a soldier who'd smashed his opposition at Llama-paca's Crossing, nor a politician capable of transforming his wrath into reality following the Platinum Affair. A kerchief around his head was enough to finish the simple but extremely effective disguise. An Earth King was forever crowned; changing his silhouette to match a commoner's made Feishan unrecognizable.

He'd demanded that she commit to this ritual should she ever be turned away at his door with the coded passphrase. It meant he wanted to talk in a safe location far from the spy-infested palace. On rare occasions she could be glad for His Majesty's paranoia and the resulting chances to speak with him privately, but today she was going to have to walk a knife's edge.

Feishan partook of her water and glanced around to make sure no one was in hearing distance. "I'd like to know what happened in Bin-Er," he said in a pleasant, melodic voice. "I have the vague reports of fireballs in the sky from hundreds of terrified soldiers. A more detailed perspective would be appreciated since you were there recently."

A reasonable request. Coming from a man not prone to those. Yangchen cut away her hesitation with a butcher's dispassion. She banished her remorse, her shame, her principles. All that mattered now was her ability to spin the tale.

"Your Majesty, there is a great truth that gurus know," she began. "Human suffering begets turmoil in the Spirit World. Our fears, our greed, our hatreds are mirrored there." She rolled her glass between her fingers. "I have seen it happen with my own two eyes, how a spirit can turn dark in the presence of humanity's weakness."

Feishan was as observant a person as she'd ever met. He would know she was telling a truth born of personal loss. Did it lessen her memories of Jetsun to involve them in a ploy?

It was her own pain, Yangchen decided. She could use it as she wished.

"Bin-Er was a broken place that could not sustain itself," she said. "As the situation deteriorated in the physical city, so too did the light in its local spirits. A land defends itself, Your Majesty. Sometimes with great violence, like in Tienhaishi, sometimes with silent plagues, like in Ma'inka. I encourage you to talk to the leaders of the Saowon clan for their perspective."

The Saowon would spit vitriol about the Avatar's inability to contain spirits, even though it was Yangchen's inability to check humans that had led to the near-disaster with the phoenix-eels. The important thing was that if the Earth King did manage to investigate the matter, he'd hear a truth born of rage and blame.

Spirits. It was the spirits. The bridge between worlds failed. The Avatar failed to fix our problem.

Unlike the shangs, King Feishan was a patient listener when he wanted to be. An embodiment of neutral jing. Stillness before the sword stroke. He let her continue.

"Eventually, Bin-Er fell too far out of balance. There was a great upheaval above the city. Dark entities manifested as flowers of thunder and flame, blooming in the sky. I did what I could to appease them."

"Did you succeed?"

Truth born of her shortcomings. "I—no. Not yet. So great was their anger that I couldn't placate them on my own. I had to enlist help from my brothers at the Northern Air Temple. They are tending to the city with alms and blessings. Their presence seems to have calmed the spirits, but our work is not yet done."

That last statement let Feishan know the young Avatar had resorted to begging aid from her elders. But also that there were large numbers of Airbenders in Bin-Er for the time being. If the Earth King's forces marched straight in, looking for violence, it would be poor form in front of so many members of her nation.

Holding up a shield like it would protect against an avalanche. "I've lost a lot of revenue from the disorder in Bin-Er," Feishan said. "A lot of face as well."

"You didn't have to. This was your own fault."

The Earth King's anger flared in the form of a jaw twitch, a lip curl. An actual strategic provocation on Yangchen's part this time. Extremely risky, but fully intentional. "Your Majesty, out of complacency, you let the shangs mismanage the city until neither human nor spirit could thrive. Under your watch they carelessly reaped without sowing back. You have only yourself to blame."

It was a good thing they were alone. What kind of fool would insult the Earth King to his face? An honest one, Feishan would hopefully assume. "There was and still is a better way,"

Yangchen said. Now that she'd riled him, she had to strike quickly at his desires. "I can develop a plan for you that eases the burden of Bin-Er's residents, while providing you more revenue from the city than ever before. More than any zongdu has ever brought to your coffers."

The Earth King scoffed, which meant he at least heard her, instead of having his ears plugged by fury. "What would an Air Nomad know of administration?"

"Very little," Yangchen said. "But Avatar Szeto, on the other hand, knows a great deal."

The sudden gleam in Feishan's eye meant she'd hooked him. "Are you saying you can run Bin-Er precisely as he would, if he were alive? Have him guide you step-by-step? You could consult him on every decision you'd make?"

She could not. Connecting with her past lives did not work quite like how Feishan was imagining it. She could see previous Avatar's memories, experience their emotions throughout the pivotal moments of their eras. But as far as she could tell, her past lives couldn't form new opinions or fresh predictions or make decisions for her in the present world, no matter how conversational the interaction between ancient memories and current information played out during a session of communing.

Avatar Szeto had never seen a shang city. He had never dealt with a situation exactly like the Platinum Affair or an Earth King exactly like Feishan. He would never develop plans on her behalf or whisper in her ear the perfect choice at each juncture.

"Yes," Yangchen lied. "My predecessor would be the one making the calls. Not me. My involvement would be minimal."

Her boldest, falsest claim yet. There was no world where Avatar Yangchen could split herself entirely away from her past lives. It was impossible to remove her own identity from the scales. But Feishan didn't need to know that right now.

The Earth King mulled over her proposal. The skills of a legendary administrator, enriching his treasury. What leader could resist? "I'd want to see those increases in revenue before too long."

"Of course." Much of her wild promise would have to come from utilizing the city's harbor at the full capacity the shangs had been doing before she arrived. The extra ships. She'd split the money from the previously unreported traffic between Feishan and the people of Bin-Er. The shangs themselves would contribute to both recipients where necessary, given the fact that she was the only person keeping their involvement in Unanimity a secret from the Earth King. "With you backing me, I can work with Zongdu Henshe to get meaningful—"

"The man is supposedly nowhere to be found," Feishan interrupted.

Yangchen furrowed her brow. "What do you mean? Did he go somewhere? I know he was one of the few people in the city with extensive travel rights."

"If I knew where he was, he would be found."

She accepted the retort. "Still. With your backing, I can ease the city's troubles in the physical realm and the spiritual. I can see to the suffering of its residents and your coffers both. Withdraw your troops and let me endeavor to restore balance."

She'd spoken out of both sides of her mouth many times in the past, but never to this extent, to someone as important as the Earth King. It was . . . easy. After everything she'd been through, it was easy. She'd been pushed to the brink and found there was always more brink to discover. If Feishan agreed, then gradually, carefully, she would start feeding in the crucial components of real relief for Bin-Er. An opening of movement for people beyond Air Nomads. Better conditions for those who wanted to stay. A solid foundation for the future.

The Earth King examined her one last time before nodding. "I will lend you my support," he said. "Together we will bring prosperity to Bin-Er again."

She tested her luck one more time. "The reformed city might serve as a model for the Lower Ring. A stable and happy capital is a secure capital, is it not?"

Feishan was actually one of the better Earth Kings when it came to looking after the poorest citizens of Ba Sing Se. Either it appealed to his sense of authority, or he was aware that the Lower Ring essentially formed a siege line around the Middle and Upper Rings. He smirked, knowing she was being greedy in her own way. "We'll see, Avatar. We shall see."

He called the proprietor over and sent him to the back stores for a real bottle. A celebratory toast was imminent, and water wouldn't suffice.

While the shopkeeper rummaged through crates full of hay, the Earth King lowered his voice even further, so that Yangchen had to lean her head in to hear him. "And in the meantime, on the slim chance you are wrong about the cause of the spectacle in the sky being angry spirits, I will continue my investigations into what happened," he said.

Yangchen had to force looseness into her limbs, break the crust of ice suddenly encasing her stomach. "Of course," she repeated. "Do you have reason to believe I'm mistaken?"

"I don't mean to gainsay the Avatar on spiritual matters. It's just that before Zongdu Henshe disappeared, he sent a letter saying he had something to show me, and a new deal to strike in Bin-Er. That was all. Very rude. Very cryptic. Like he thought he was suddenly my equal."

The proprietor came back with a bottle and fresh glasses. Feishan sent him away again and poured wine for the Avatar first, before himself. He wanted to do her the honor even if she wasn't going to drink it.

"Shortly after that letter came the lights and noises," he said. "If the incidents are related, I'll find out. Perhaps at a more leisurely rate, now that you've given me your assurances."

He picked up his wine and swirled it, sniffing the aroma. "I'm relieved you're convinced we're dealing with spirits, Avatar. Because if I discover that it was the work of man that lit up the sky above *my* territory, and that someone has created a threat to *my* rule, then I genuinely fear what I will do to the Four Nations in reprisal, the Earth Kingdom included. It certainly wouldn't be good for my reputation in the history books. Or the echoes of suffering in the Spirit World you're so concerned about."

Yangchen said nothing.

Feishan clinked his glass to hers. "To a brighter tomorrow," the Earth King replied to her silence. "I expect you'll come through on your end of the bargain."

HONORED GUESTS

HER HANDS shook the entire flight back to the Northern Air Temple. She wrung Nujian's reins to steady them, twisting, folding, doubling the lines. He grunted in complaint when she'd used up too much of the slack.

She had hoped to distract the Earth King by using his greed to keep him focused on the wrong prize. She had only partially succeeded.

Now Yangchen finally had a common interest with the Bin-Er shangs. They would have to collude to keep the spirit ruse going in front of the Earth King. The shangs if they wanted to keep their heads, Yangchen if she wanted to prevent the secret of Unanimity from being exposed. If she'd sought leverage over Teiin and Noehi and the rest, well, now she had too much.

Three people forcing a city to its knees. Three people holding off an army. Bending could be pushed to extremes, she knew all too well. But this was an entirely new level. None of her memories contained anything resembling the power she'd seen on display in Bin-Er.

The knowledge that this technique existed could not become widespread. Not now, when tensions across the Four Nations were still as raw as the emotions of a slighted king. Not ever, as long as humans were still human.

Kavik had asked what she would do with his brother and Chaisee. Reporting them to a head of state would cause Unanimity—she had a hard time setting aside the name—to leak into a world willing to fight over any scrap of advantage. She couldn't risk taking drastic action personally either, not when Chaisee might have had more assets than just the three benders she knew about. As Yangchen had learned, an entire city could be held hostage.

The answer, had she been willing to give it to Kavik, was nothing. In her current state she could do nothing about Chaisee and his brother. For now, they were immune. Or at least Chaisee was. She could sit comfortably for the time being and receive the upside Unanimity was originally supposed to provide, with none of the drawbacks Henshe had suffered.

The Zongdu of Jonduri understood Yangchen's hands were tied. Before her journey to see the Earth King, she'd received a message by hawk. The only sentence the tiny scroll contained was a taunt, even shorter than a koan.

Wise move. Yangchen had made no move, could make no move, and Chaisee knew it.

She'd been forced to become Mama's ideal Avatar. Waiting calmly, virtuously, while her opponents smiled at her from across the board. They could chisel a statue of her in this state.

She dropped Nujian's altitude when the lonely peak of the Northern Temple came into view. Pik and Pak would be waiting for her there, angry with her again, but she had to see to other matters first. She flew over the town and its hospital without stopping, and wove her way between the valleys, following trails of gravel between steep slopes of ice and rock.

A thin seam of green opened before her. Around the mountains there were a few completely isolated pockets of flat land that were nearly impossible to discover without an aerial view. Most of them went ignored, but a few had small hamlets that could be sustained as long as crucial supplies arrived regularly.

Yangchen descended upon the level patch. It contained a garden, three small stone hutches, and a natural spring of bubbling water. The view over the impassable terrain was starkly beautiful, curtains of clouds pulled back to reveal a stage that took the elements countless eras to dress.

She jumped down from Nujian. Abbot Sonam, leader of the Northern Temple, was there to meet her. They walked side by side, even though they didn't have much space to stroll. She knew it was because he couldn't bear to look her in the eye.

The disappointment and resentment in Sonam's voice was thick enough to hold up the sky. "You have made *jailers* of us," he said.

Across the patch of land, digging in the garden on his hands and knees, was one of Chaisee's benders. The one named Thapa.

Six Airbenders from the Northern Temple surrounded him at a safe distance. They, and the monks who replaced them in shifts, had been selected from a community of pacifists for their martial prowess. They maintained a vigil over Thapa, like their brothers were doing for Yingsu and Xiaoyun in separate plots of land along the mountains.

Constant alertness throughout the hours of the day, watching mindfully in the moment, came naturally to them. The task was similar to the funerary rites Air Nomads were sometimes asked to perform across the Four Nations. A useful meditation, if she really wanted to stretch the definition of "shaped teachings."

The monks parted to let Yangchen through. They had orders to subdue their charge if he made any aggressive moves, and that included the buildup necessary to perform his special technique. Kavik had managed to observe Xiaoyun through a window during the tail. *Before each explosion they have to do a lot of deep, heavy breathing.*

Thapa looked up at her, wiped his smooth, prominent forehead, and grinned. "Avatar."

She kept as impassive as she could. "You enjoy gardening?"

"I do. Your brethren gave me some mountain flower seeds that do well in winter." His smile widened. "But whether I'll get to see them bloom is another matter. How long are you planning to keep me here?"

"That depends on if you answer my questions." *Where did you learn this technique? Who taught it to you? What was Zongdu Chaisee's involvement?* Yangchen had interrogated each of the Firebenders separately.

And gotten absolutely nothing so far.

"Mmm, I still don't think I'm ready to share yet," Thapa said. "I'm rather enjoying my little vacation. Wealthy people pay large sums of money for this kind of setup, you know? Yesterday I saw the most beautiful sunset of my life." He tapped his blunted trowel on a rock.

Despite Thapa's ease with his surroundings, Yangchen knew she had not converted him to the monastic life. He was stalling. He knew exactly how untenable the situation was for her. All three of her "special guests" did.

At first, she'd wondered if they were fanatics to some cause of Chaisee's, or wayward travelers like Jujinta, searching for a purpose to go along with their immense power. But after spending time with them, she'd come to realize they were something far more dangerous.

They were opportunists. Smart ones.

The Firebenders understood their own value, and that it was better to be in the Avatar's custody instead of an unscrupulous authority who would grind them to dust to extract their secrets. So they kept their lips sealed. Chaisee? They didn't know a Chaisee. The most they'd admit to was being hired by Zongdu Henshe to do exactly as he commanded. Prior to that, they might as well have never existed.

Knowing Yangchen possessed no leverage over them, they seemed content to wait her out until the situation broke their way. The opportunity to escape would present itself. Or someone would find out where they were and come for them. She couldn't keep them as hermits in the mountains forever, and they knew it.

Henshe and Yangchen were both wrong to think of them as merely pieces on the board. They were players in their own right, hungry to improve their position. And they muddied the waters to the point where she could no longer see in front of her own face.

How long before I surrender? Yangchen thought. *How long before I beg the White Lotus to take you?* A last resort. She didn't want a secret society to have their power any more than she was content to let Chaisee keep it.

Information tended to spread. The Earth King would draw closer to these benders by the day. So would the Fire Lord and the High Chieftain, investigating the incident in Bin-Er through informants and rumors. Yangchen was flying through a dark, dangerous gorge, and her room to maneuver was rapidly shrinking around her shoulders.

"Let me know if you change your mind," she said to Thapa. "Else we might put your talents to the summer barley." She turned around and went back to Nujian, Sonam following her for the short return trip.

"You cannot keep them here that long!" the abbot whispered once they were both on the other side of her bison. "What you have done to your brothers is an abomination!"

"I'm sorry but I had no choice. I will apologize to each of them for forcing such an abhorrent task into their hands."

"No, Avatar." Sonam shook his head, sad that she'd missed the point. "The problem is that they might enjoy the job too much."

He glanced over to the monks guarding Thapa. They were young men, strong benders all. "Holding dominion over another human being is a mighty temptation," Sonam said. "If we developed a taste for such power, began to crave it . . ."

"Then we would no longer be Air Nomads," Yangchen said.

Sonam handed her Nujian's reins. "Just go," he said. "Please."

Her next stop was less of a hassle. Zongdu Henshe was nowhere near as difficult to guard.

In fact, they'd given him a room that was part of the Air Temple itself, one of the structures built into the stone farther down the slope, below the gently overhanging cliffs. His accommodations were as good as any honored guest of the Air Nomads.

He'd still raged the whole first day and night, unable to absorb the fact that his alternative was the Earth King's hospitality. It became clear very quickly that he was not the true mastermind behind the scheme. Chaisee had successfully kept him in the dark about most of Unanimity's details.

She still had to check on him though. Yangchen knocked on his door and entered. Henshe looked up from where he sat on the bed. He hadn't availed himself of any of the books they'd given him except to hurl them at the walls. They lay scattered in the corners, spines bent, pages torn.

He seemed to be in a calmer state now, perhaps helped by the small pillow he squeezed his fingers into over and over. "I understand my predicament," he said to Yangchen by way of greeting. "But I understand yours too. How much time do you really think you have before the truth slips through your fingers and is loosed upon the world?"

"I have exactly as much as you do," she said.

Henshe was caught off guard by her ominous but true statement. He shook his head and continued. "I have something to trade."

"What?"

"A name. A person." His lips pressed into lines of smugness. "I have a deep plant in Chaisee's organization, very high up, very trusted by her. If you had his identity, you could threaten to burn him to Chaisee. He'd be forced to turn to your side. You could use him to take her down."

Henshe got up from the bed. "Here's the deal," he said. "You clear me of any wrongdoing, convincingly, and make me whole from my losses. I'll give you this person's name, description, family. What do you say?"

He was trying to sell out Kavik's brother. Kalyaan. The one Yangchen already knew about.

"I don't want it," she said.

"What? But I can—"

"I said I don't want your information." If Kavik had ever given her a gift, it was the look on Henshe's face right now. "Goodbye, Zongdu. Until we next talk."

He at least had the courtesy to wait for the door to close before screaming and throwing the pillow.

The tower stairs never seemed to end. Onward and inward they circled, sending Yangchen into loops upon loops. If she were a spider-snake, she would have swallowed her own tail at least a dozen times. She trudged higher, taking each step slowly.

The handle of the bucket bit into her palms, the contents sloshing over her toes. She needed the water to drink and wash. She would know its weight. The interior of the tower was speared through with warm light coming through its windows. The sunset. She ignored it.

She reached the Avatar's quarters of the Northern Temple. She used them so rarely when she visited, preferring to stay in the visitor's dormitories with her sisters, that she hadn't exercised her right to decorate it yet. The interior remained in the exact same state Avatar Szeto had left it.

She shouldered the door open and put the bucket down. The room was completely empty except for the bed and the desk. The walls were bare. To an outside observer, Szeto would look like a man who clearly had nothing to hide.

What a messy life that *was*. She slumped into her predecessor's austere chair and squeezed her head between her hands. The gray fuzz. Back with a vengeance.

Only one thought was sharp enough to cut through the fog, and it repeated itself over and over. It called to her as deeply as the dark wells of Ma'inka, grew in strength until it was as loud as the roaring waves of Jonduri.

She could stop.

After she dealt with the Firebenders, after she dealt with the Earth King and Bin-Er, after she dealt with Henshe and Chaisee and Kavik and his brother—and why not, Mama and the White Lotus as well—she could stop trying to reshape the world. What had she been doing, throwing herself headlong against suffering where she found it? Where had she not multiplied the peo-ple's miseries instead?

She *should* stop.

'he'd still be the Avatar. The figurehead, the object of ven-
ɔ you turned to well after desperation had latched its
'to your flesh. As Lohi of the Saowon had proven, that

was what people asked for first and valued most. The problem addressed, not prevented. The salve, not the cure.

Her heritage provided the perfect excuse to withdraw. She'd embrace negative jing and retreat far, far away, becoming a mountain peak that humanity could see but never reach. They'd be better off. She wouldn't hurt anyone with her mistakes.

She wouldn't save anyone either.

Yangchen was struck by how little the prospect weighed on her. She didn't feel guilty for considering the future lived over the future earned. She didn't feel much of anything. Her parade through Bin-Er might as well have happened in another life, on the other side of a boundary marked by regret.

The blankness she had to push away every morning could be allowed permanent residence in her body, her heart, and her gut. She could embrace it fully. She didn't owe anyone anything.

I'd have time to find Jetsun.

She heard a *whoosh* and a *thump*, and her head jerked up. Another *whoosh*, another *thump*, and Abbot Sonam was standing outside the door she'd forgotten to close. "Avatar," he said, huffing and puffing. His head had beaded over with sweat.

Had he spin-jumped up the tower? He wouldn't have acted so rashly had it not been important. She stood up quickly in alarm. "What is it? The Firebenders? Henshe?"

"No." The smile on his face outshone the flushed glow of his skin. "I'm so sorry that I forgot to tell you. I mean, it was understandable given the circumstances, with all the goings-on and—"

"Abbot, please."

Sonam caught his breath. "Do you remember that woman in the hospital?" he said. "The one you healed with your Waterbender friend?"

Yangchen needed a moment to recall. The patient whom she would have lost if it hadn't been for Kavik's help. They'd done that together at least. The extra pair of hands had paid off.

But the memory was bittersweet. There was a reason why she hadn't wanted to think about it much. "What about her?"

"We found her son. We found her missing son! The search party found him just in time! He's alive and well!"

Yangchen blinked slowly. Her voice came out a creak. "Oh. Good. That's good."

"Without you and your companion—Kavik, was it? Without the two of you saving his mother, we would never have rescued the boy." Sonam beamed brighter than the sun had over the mountains. "Avatar, you never gave up on her. Don't you remember?"

Did she remember. She always remembered. Her lip trembled and she began to weep. The abbot smiled, thinking happiness, alone and pure, had brought tears to her eyes. He didn't know that he'd dragged her back from the edge in shackles. Sentenced her to another turn of the wheel.

Yangchen could pretend all she wanted but it was no use. She would remain the instrument of her own suffering. She'd keep fighting, keep struggling, just like she'd commanded the unconscious woman to do in the hospital. It was her fate to make the same choice over and over again, as generations of Avatars had done before her. To know the past was to know the future.

"They're still in town," the abbot said. "I can take you to them now."

She saw their ages reversed, Sonam the youth sparkling with energy, she the eroded, weary fixture. "Tomorrow. We'll have plenty of time tomorrow. No need to rush."

The abbot bowed and left. She stood motionless where she was, until the sun finished setting and only darkness filled the window. She decided to turn in early. She still had much to do, and she would need her strength.

High in her tower, Yangchen went to bed. And for once fell into a deep, dreamless, restful sleep.

EPILOGUE

KAVIK HEARD Yangchen's name on people's lips often these days as he moved through the streets of a slowly recovering Bin-Er. It was the young Avatar who'd put a stop to the spirit attacks, they said, just like she'd done in Tienhaishi. Since then she'd been spotted flying in and out of the city regularly, never leaving for too long, and there hadn't been any more ravages through the sky. She'd become humanity's champion when they needed her most.

The residents of Bin-Er also took comfort in the increased presence of Air Nomads from the Northern Temple, who normally didn't linger long but now could be seen in every neighborhood. Monks and visiting nuns distributed food and clothing while the flow of supplies returned to normal. They lent a sense of calm and peace with their presence, while also giving the impression they formed a shield of sorts against further depredations by spirit or man.

All signs pointed to this theory being true. The Earth King had not invaded. The shangs and their headkickers had stayed out of sight, as if rightfully shamed by the increased attention upon Bin-Er. The control offices suddenly found their ink, and people started going home.

Even stranger, folks who'd fled the city came back of their own accord, down from the mountains. Some of them professed to have been healed by the Avatar herself, claimed to be alive only due to her graces. It was among these returnees where belief was strongest. Little shrines of wildflowers popped up overnight on street corners. "Yangchen's steps," they were jokingly named, as if life bloomed wherever the Avatar's feet touched the ground. But some people called them that without irony, and any time one of the arrangements was thrown out or blown away, it was quickly replaced.

Everywhere, Kavik was reminded of the Avatar. Knowing she could see him if she wanted to but didn't was the lightest punishment possible for his transgression. It still hurt. He assumed Jujinta, Akuudan, and Tayagum had learned the truth, as they hadn't visited either.

He wandered the streets as if he still had the responsibility of an Avatar's companion. He knew this was what Jujinta must have been doing in Jonduri, drifting until his purpose came along. Kavik had already squandered two perfectly good ones.

But one night, while he was aimlessly skirting the square, his irrelevance came to a grinding halt.

A Water Tribe man appeared twice in the corner of Kavik's eye. He still had the Northern gait of walking softly so as not to break through ice crusts or overturn gravel, which meant he was new to the city. After Kavik paused to have a meaningless conversation with a shopkeeper he'd never met before, he observed over his shoulder the same Water Tribe man paying special attention to the storefront from afar, in case it was a safe house or a handoff point.

There was no doubt about it. Kavik was being tailed.

Despite his quickening pulse he slowly, calmly went through his list of moves, executing broken paths, double-backs, every maneuver he could think of. Nothing worked. He couldn't shake the man, who must have been a hunter and tracker far beyond Kavik's skill, possibly the equal of Kalyaan. Sometimes you could just walk down your prey, even if it spotted you.

As his options for escape were taken away one by one, Kavik found himself at the alley wall he'd climbed over when he thought he was breaking any link between his actions at the Blue Manse and his home life. He hadn't been able to fool the Avatar. He looked up, just in case. The skies were clear. He bent a ladder of ice like he'd done that night.

It melted underneath his feet while he was halfway up.

His face scraped along the brickwork on the way down, a stinging rash against his skin. He landed in a heap. His follower appeared at the other end of the alley.

Kavik reached around him for water but the man had already drawn the nearby sources to himself, the puddles, the melt from the rooftops, spinning the growing mass between his hands with expertise. Their shared element flew to him alone in droplets and streams, leaving Kavik with nothing.

Kavik was split between pretending to be helpless and ignorant, and fighting back with every ounce of strength he had. The one thing he could be sure of was that he would not talk. Even if it was kill or be killed, he was not going to be part of any more games. He was done.

And then he heard a dull *thud*.

The water the man was bending splashed to the ground. He fell forward onto his knees, and then onto his face, revealing Mama Ayunerak standing several paces behind him.

The elderly woman tucked some unseen weapon under the back of her parka. Kavik had never been so confused in his life. With the spryness of a person half her age, Ayunerak went over to the man she'd knocked unconscious and started digging through his pockets, running her hand down his collar for anything looped around his neck, searching his skin for marks and tattoos.

"What is going on?" Kavik asked, his breath short as if he'd been running. He hadn't seen Ayunerak since giving her the Avatar's money.

"This man is a Thin Claw," Ayunerak said, her focus never wavering from her task. "A scout loyal only to High Chieftain Oyaluk. The fact that he was following you means your involvement in Unanimity and its secrets are uncomfortably close to reaching the light of day."

Hearing the code name on someone else's lips was a shock. It made him forget any kind of discipline, took from him the ability to play dumb. "How did you— How do you know about that?"

"It's my job to know things, Kavik. My friends and I know a great deal." Mama Ayunerak looked up at him with the same cool, assessing eye the Avatar used when she'd recruited him. "And I think it's high time you joined us."

TO BE CONTINUED . . .

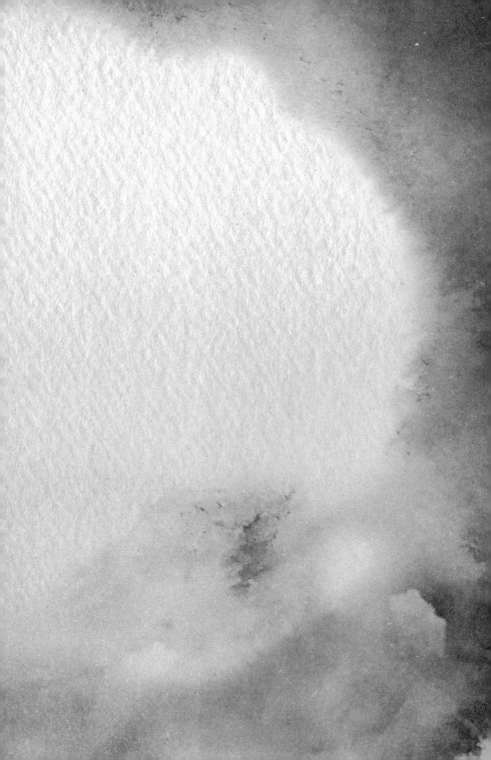

ACKNOWLEDGMENTS

Special thanks to Michael Dante DiMartino, Bryan Konietzko, and the entire Avatar team for making it all possible. Very special thanks to my editor, Anne Heltzel, and agent, Stephen Barr, for guiding me through ups and downs and ups again. And very, very, very special thanks to all the fans of every Avatar. And I almost forgot about Karen.